More Praise for *A Perfect Arrangement*

"Suzanne Berne has many gifts, among them the talent to describe with eloquence and empathy the fault lines of her characters. There's an exotic beauty in Berne's natural world as well. In *A Perfect Arrangement* everyday life outdoors for the Cook-Goldman family is illuminated with the clarity and color of a Maxfield Parrish illustration. Inside the house, Berne's beloved and flawed people struggle to make their way in love and work in the all too modern world."

    —Jane Hamilton, author of *A Map of the World* and *Disobedience*

"Berne uses familiar circumstances to explore the treacheries, big and small, that invade family relationships . . . [She] shows enormous intelligence about expectations, and what people hide from themselves and palm off on each other."   —*The Washington Post*

"Who is 'authorized' to love us, to love our children, our work? Finally, who deserves to share the bounty of our lives? Suzanne Berne examines many kinds of possession—parental, erotic, economic, even environmental—and dramatizes these very challenging questions with dead-on aim and just what *A Crime in the Neighborhood* led us to expect: a scrupulous, unsentimental sympathy beautifully served by the precision of her prose."

    —Rosellen Brown, author of *Half a Heart* and *Before and After*

SUZANNE BERNE's first novel, *A Crime in the Neighborhood,* won Great Britain's Orange Prize and was a *New York Times* Notable Book, as well as a finalist for both the *Los Angeles Times* and the Edgar Allan Poe first fiction awards. A teacher at Harvard University, she has published fiction and essays in numerous magazines and been a frequent contributor to *The New York Times*. She lives with her husband and their two daughters outside of Boston.

Also by Suzanne Berne

A Crime in the Neighborhood

A Perfect Arrangement

A NOVEL BY

SUZANNE BERNE

A PLUME BOOK

PLUME
Published by the Penguin Group
Penguin Putnam Inc., 375 Hudson Street,
New York, New York 10014, U.S.A.
Penguin Books Ltd, 80 Strand
London WC2R 0RL, England
Penguin Books Australia Ltd,
Ringwood, Victoria, Australia
Penguin Books Canada Ltd, 10 Alcorn Avenue,
Toronto, Ontario, Canada M4V 3B2
Penguin Books (N.Z.) Ltd, 182–190 Wairau Road,
Auckland 10, New Zealand

Penguin Books Ltd, Registered Offices:
Harmondsworth, Middlesex, England

Published by Plume, a member of Penguin Putnam Inc.
This is an authorized reprint of a hardcover edition published
by Algonquin Books of Chapel Hill, a division of Workman Publishing.
For information address Algonquin Books of Chapel Hill,
P.O. Box 2225, Chapel Hill, North Carolina 27515-2225.

First Plume Printing, May 2002
10 9 8 7 6 5 4 3

Ⓟ REGISTERED TRADEMARK—MARCA REGISTRADA

The Library of Congress has catalogued the hardcover edition as follows:

Berne, Suzanne.
A perfect arrangement : a novel / by Suzanne Berne.
p.   cm.
"A Shannon Ravenel book"—T.p. verso.
ISBN 1-56512-261-5 (hc.)
ISBN 0-452-28322-1 (pbk.)
1. Dual-career families—Fiction.   2. Women lawyers—Fiction.
3. New England—Fiction.   4. Nannies—Fiction.   I. Title.
PS3552.E73114 P47 2001
813'.54—dc21
00-069451

Printed in the United States of America
Original hardcover design by Anne Winslow

BOOKS ARE AVAILABLE AT QUANTITY DISCOUNTS WHEN USED TO PROMOTE PRODUCTS OR SERVICES. FOR
INFORMATION PLEASE WRITE TO PREMIUM MARKETING DIVISION, PENGUIN PUTNAM INC., 375 HUDSON
STREET, NEW YORK, NEW YORK 10014.

For my parents,

and

in memory of

Constance Kroger Sowell

The world is so full

of a number of things,

I'm sure we should all

be as happy as kings.

—"Happy Thought"
by Robert Louis Stevenson

A Perfect Arrangement

PART I

1

"SHE SOUNDED CHEERY but earnest," Mirella told Howard that morning as she pressed a paper towel into a puddle of milk on Pearl's place mat.

"Cheery," said Howard, angled over the newspaper.

Mirella sat back and dried her fingers on her napkin. "A homey sort of voice." She looked at her watch, then checked the old walnut case clock by the fireplace, which as usual was slow. It was one of those sulfurous New England spring mornings that had been forecast to be mild but felt clammy instead, and as Mirella glanced from the clock to the window she found herself shivering.

"Comforting somehow," she said.

The Cook-Goldmans had been hunting for three weeks for a nanny to replace thick-chinned Grete, their second au pair in two years, who had flown home to Uppsala because she missed her boyfriend, Karl. There had been recent letters, sky-blue aerogrammes covered with Karl's blocky print. A midnight phone call, ending in assertive tears. "Karl needs me," Grete had said, her voice tremulous with complacency.

They were trying a new child-care agency this time, Family

Options Ltd., which specialized in midwestern girls with teaching aspirations. "Could you be comfortable with anything but the best for your family?" queried Family Options' salmon-colored brochure. "Our nannies are dedicated, trained, and sensitive individuals, subject to rigorous screening and psychological evaluation. Guaranteed nationwide FBI criminal fingerprinting and background checks. Drug testing and CPR certification."

So far Mirella had not been impressed by the applicants from Family Options. It took two weeks for the agency to produce anyone for an interview—there was a waiting list of families desperate for a nanny, all the agencies said the same—then when Mirella asked the first applicant, a plump brunette from New Jersey, why she enjoyed working with children, the young woman burst into tears and confessed to having an eating disorder. The second, a former nursery school aide, a thin exhausted-looking person in a black straw hat, tripped over the doorstep when she arrived for her interview, then asked Mirella how much she had paid for her house.

"Always worry about the cheerful ones." Howard scanned the front page of the paper while snapping Jacob into his overalls. Rain predicted, Mirella read, craning sideways to look at the paper, today and tomorrow. The value of the Japanese yen had plummeted. Independent counsel widens presidential investigation. A shooting at an elementary school outside of Spokane. Jacob flapped his arms, his Indian headdress slipping over one eye. "Blud-a-bub," he said. Then he grunted and went limp in Howard's lap.

Mirella found the lid to the jelly jar and screwed it on. "She's been working for a family in Brookline and she used to run some kind of Sunday school program at a church."

"Sit up," Howard told Jacob.

Mirella took a sip of milky coffee, pausing to watch Jacob flutter his eyelashes. Blink, blink, pause. Blink, blink. A white crust of milk glazed his chin; an amber nugget of snot lodged in one nostril. Of course she worried. Only a year since that Boston nanny sat in the news day after day, face blank as a dinner roll, beside all those pictures of the poor little boy. Six months before, a mother at Pearl's preschool came home to find their nanny drunk in the TV room, the one-year-old asleep upstairs on the changing table. People were installing video recorders now. Worry didn't come near it.

Mirella cupped her palms to either side of her face and, for the countless time in the last few weeks, considered what would happen if she forgot about hiring a nanny for Pearl and Jacob, quit work, and stayed home. It could be nice, she thought. Block castles, Play-Doh birthday cakes, afternoons at the park. Immediately a Sahara of days spread across the table, burying the castles and birthday cakes, becoming a quicksand of dirty cups and dishes, hours draining into the laundry basket, trips to the park that took so long to prepare for that by the time everyone was ready, no one wanted to go. Back once more to their own yard— that grainy relief and reluctance as she struggled through the front door and into the hall, loaded like a camel with child, bags, dog leash, stroller. Home again, and again. The cloistered smell of the house becoming her own smell: cold coffee, a diaper left in the wastebasket, the glum reek of last night's fish clinging to the broiling pan left in the sink.

She squinted at the finish on the table, stippled with faint gashes wherever the children had drummed their forks and spoons, then looked at her watch again, calculating that she would have an hour to get downtown after dropping off Pearl at preschool. Five minutes to get from her car to the courthouse. Then two meetings after her hearing, tomorrow's deposition to prepare for, Hayman's restraining order to file, a phone conference at three.

Thank God, she thought.

Jacob had stuck his finger in the butter and was smudging his finger along the table; she reached over and wiped his hand with her napkin, then wiped his nose. "Mmff," he said, twisting his face away.

Because the law, unlike her family, was beautifully reducible. The law was simply a set of rules by which human beings governed themselves. That these rules could be complex, sometimes arcane, and—because they were formed out of language—forever open to reinterpretation, accounted for most of their scope and all of their interest. But what Mirella found moving, what had inspired her to become a lawyer in the first place, was the plain human need behind all lawmaking, the desire for guidance and precedent that went straight to a zone that was humanity itself, that might even, she sometimes suspected, be the deepest of all human passions.

Not that she had a chance to reflect on the essential purpose of law very often. Her clients, mostly women, were afraid of laws, which they regarded as punitive; they became restless and embarrassed, swiveling on their padded red conference chairs, fiddling with their earrings whenever she tried to discuss philosophical aspects of the legal system. And who could blame them? Usually the people who hired her were either terrified or confused, people who had disappointed other people, often without knowing quite how—abandoned wives, assaulted girlfriends, fired employees. They wanted clear satisfactions: money, vindication. Sometimes they wanted revenge, sometimes protection. Mostly they wanted Mirella to give them whatever it was they needed, as quickly as possible.

Jacob stuck his finger again in the butter dish. She reached over and gently pushed the butter dish across the table.

Howard was still reading the paper over the top of Jacob's head. "What's her name?"

Mirella shifted in her chair. "Sandy. We said ten. Apparently she likes doing crafts. And the woman at the agency said she loves to cook—"

"She probably has no legs or something."

Blinking herself now, Mirella let the rest of her sentence vanish into the complicated Italian design on her coffee mug.

"I didn't mean that about the no legs," he said.

Which was only his way, she recognized, a fraction too late, of trying to control what she'd arranged, this interview. Though Howard pretended not to believe in bargaining with fate, he did it all the time. Bargaining, as she well knew, forgiving him already, was what a worried person did to stop worrying. At least for a little while.

"Crafts," said Howard musingly.

Mirella put down her cup and looked at the dining room's wide brick fireplace, which was crammed with stuffed animals and a pair of beach towels. "So do you think you could tidy up a little before she gets here? Just the downstairs. I don't want her to think we're a bunch of cave dwellers."

"Cave dwellers were a civilized culture." Howard fumbled with the last snap on Jacob's overalls. "Why are these things so impossible?"

"And don't forget Jacob has an appointment with Dr. Michaels this afternoon."

"At four."

"Also, the plumber is coming around two about the upstairs sink. And your brother called again to ask if we're staying in Greenwich after Danielle's bas mitzvah. Also Ruth thinks someone from the firm should go to the Women in Law dinner on the twelfth and I said I would."

Howard turned a page of the newspaper, jogging Jacob on his knee. Jacob closed his eyes, letting his head bounce up and down.

Howard jogged faster and Jacob began to sway wildly back and forth. A fixed expression came over his face that seemed unconnected to pleasure, yet had nothing to do with fear.

"Careful," said Mirella.

Howard stopped jogging.

"Okay?" Mirella stood up and laid a hand on the back of his neck, which was warm and slightly prickly. "I'm sorry you're getting stuck with everything today. I forgot I had to be in court at nine." She looked down to discover a postcard under her heel, then bent to pick it up. A postcard from Cornwall sent by Tina, the nanny before Grete; it featured two ruddy children in red woollen sweaters chasing each other along a turfy cliff top. She put her hand back on Howard's neck.

"I've been getting stuck with everything almost every day."

"I know, I'm sorry."

"I've got a lot of work, too, you know."

Mirella gave his neck a squeeze. "I'll try to get home early."

She paused for a moment, not quite expecting a response, but feeling she should wait for one. That morning, she had spent ten minutes washing a pair of Pearl's underpants in the bathroom sink and drying them with the blow-dryer because Pearl had no clean underwear left; she had gotten up before six so that Howard could go for his morning run while she made breakfast; she'd pulled a tick off the dog while reading *The Runaway Bunny* to Jacob. When Howard continued to read the paper, she gave his neck a final squeeze and brushed the back of his head with her lips. "All right?"

But just as she was moving away, he reached behind and caught her hand, then kissed her hard on the palm. "All right," he said into her hand, moving his lips inside her fingers. She leaned against his back, inhaling the smell of Lifebuoy soap, resting her cheek against the top of his head.

"This won't last forever," she said, gently pulling away.

"Pearl? Pearlie," she called. " It's time to get going."

Quickly Mirella gathered the cereal bowls together, the gummy spoons, the juice glasses and both coffee mugs, thinking of the pretrial conference she had scheduled at one-thirty and that phone conference at three, wondering whether to try to move the client she had coming in (Vasshacker? Vassbonner? Vascular something) to four-thirty. This morning's hearing shouldn't go past ten, although Judge Mooney always ran late. Every probate judge ran late; it seemed to be part of their job description. After the hearing, she had meetings until noon, then she'd have about an hour to work on the Boyajian appeal for Friday. She could prepare for tomorrow's deposition tonight.

She piled the breakfast dishes into a precarious arrangement on the hand-painted wooden tea tray she used for clearing, the same tea tray, in fact, her mother had used for clearing the table when Mirella was a child. Colorful stick figures appeared here and there beneath the jumble of bowls and silverware, tiny arms raised as they pursued each other along flaking green stripes meant to represent grass. Last Christmas her mother had presented her with this tray, smiling with confident generosity. "A memento," she said. "Someday you can pass it on to Pearl."

"Kitsch," Howard had said of the tea tray afterward. "Responsible for ninety percent of the world's atrocities."

She carried the tray into the kitchen, then went into the hall to stand at the bottom of the staircase. Where, for an instant, she forgot what it was she was intending to do, which often happened to her in the mornings when everything became a scramble of delays—sunglasses lost, briefcase mislaid, car keys not in the blue enamel bowl by the stairs. In these moments the complexity of what she was leaving behind began to unreel in front of her, as if she were attending a screening of her own absence in the house. Upstairs, clothing exploded from wicker hampers; twisted sheets trailed from the beds; clouds of hair and wadded tissues drifted from wastepaper baskets. Downstairs, dishes congealed in the sink, while old newspapers cascaded off a chair and Magic Markers rolled, uncapped, under the table. Beneath the hallway radiator rested a decaying apple core. The stunning importunacy of so many individual tasks (so much bending and collecting, so much resistance) made her feel incapable of performing any single one of them.

And there was Pearl up in her room, needing her shoes. And Jacob, once more smudging butter on the dining room table, needing his nose wiped again and probably a change.

She pictured herself thinking of them later that day, looking up from writing a memo or talking on the phone to stare out her window at the sealed windows of the glass and granite building opposite. Suddenly there they would be, her children. Wandlike arms, moisture at the folds of their eyelids, apricot wax inside their ears. She was the mother of two children. Such a simple, unremarkable fact—a fact repeated about so many women—and yet the fact of these two children was endlessly complex, endlessly remarkable, from the way their skin stretched across their bones to the hidden helix of each molecular structure to the way they did or did not look up at her when she finally burst through the front door in the evening, arms open to hold them, at the same time calculating when they could be put to bed so that she could finish reading deposition transcripts or drafting a complaint or whatever it was she had left unfinished to get home to them.

Every afternoon, unless she was in a meeting or in court, she called home at three, when Pearl would be back from preschool and Jacob up from his nap, to say hello and to invent a weather report, which Pearl always demanded to hear. "Warm temperatures," Mirella murmured into the phone on freezing days. "Partly sunny," she would say during a rainstorm. "A chance of drizzle." To Jacob she always said: "Are you Mommy's boy? I love you. Do you love Mommy?" To which he gave no response but the steady sound of his breathing.

She glanced again at her watch, for a moment imagining Judge Mooney's turtle eyes shifting about, searching the courtroom, then she turned to peer up the stairs. "Pearlie," she called again. "Please come down here. We really have to go."

"I'm not ready," cried an outraged voice.

"What have you been doing up there all this time?"

"Getting *ready*."

"Well, you should be ready by now. I'll count to three. One. Two."

At the top of the stairs appeared a tear-stained girl of five, clutching a plastic hairbrush. She wore a pink shirt covered with green butterflies, a purple polka-dotted skirt, and orange-and-blue striped socks. Through her long, heavy brown hair she had threaded a piece of yellow yarn, tied on top of her head so that the yarn ends stuck up like short antennae. On each knee, neatly aligned, were three dinosaur Band-Aids.

"Pearl, where are your shoes?"

"I want rain boots."

"It's not raining, sweetheart. You don't need rain boots."

"I need another Band-Aid."

"Sweetie, please—"

"I want another *Band-Aid*."

"Howard," said Mirella. "I have to find my briefcase."

Howard set Jacob on the floor, then stood up and slapped the newspaper off the table. "Why is it like this every morning?"

"It's not *every* morning." Mirella knelt in front of Jacob, who had run into the hallway to clutch at her dress. "Hey baby." She smiled as she straightened his headdress. "Calm down."

"No Daddy," shouted Pearl. "I want Mama."

"Too bad." Howard stepped over Mirella's legs to reach the staircase. "You can't have Mama."

At the bottom of the stairs Mirella straightened up, once again picturing Mooney's little eyes brightening with malice ("How *nice* of you to join us, Ms. Cook"), recollecting also that she should be looking for her briefcase, then leaned down again to kiss the top of Jacob's head, inhaling the damp, cottony fragrance of his skin, mixed with the curdled smell of milk. Briefly he pressed himself against her, but as she stooped to kiss him again he began shuffling away, heading to the dining room to his favorite spot inside the old kitchen fireplace. He fixed nests in there, careful arrangements of stuffed animals, socks, napkins, dish towels. The few times Mirella had pulled apart his nests, Jacob shrieked and ran frantically around the dining room table. Sometimes he tried to hang a blanket from an old iron crane set into the fireplace wall, to make a little tent.

She watched him go, remaining in the same attitude, knees bent, hands splayed on her thighs. Maybe Boston Women in Crisis would change their minds again about meeting today instead of Friday—or maybe Ruth could meet with them—because there was also the bar lunch she'd been hoping to attend; a protegee of Justice Ginsburg's was speaking on civil procedure. Upstairs the toilet flushed. In the kitchen ice rumbled and clunked from the automatic ice maker. She took a deep breath, reminding herself not to stand up too quickly.

Because Mirella had a secret, one that she would soon have to tell Howard, although she had not yet found the right moment: She was, and not by design, except that against her better judgment she'd been hoping for just such a miscalculation, pregnant again. Just how pregnant she wasn't even sure, two months maybe; she'd never been good at keeping track of herself.

"Pearl," she called up the stairs, more firmly this time. "I want you to cooperate with Daddy. I'm going to be late. Pearlie, did you hear me?"

"No," shouted Pearl.

"Five minutes," said Mirella.

Her forehead felt hot. It was always impossible, she thought, gripping the newel post at the bottom of the stairs and forgetting once more what else she should be doing, this business of leaving in the mornings. Somehow it was always accomplished, but every morning she found herself wondering all over again how she would do it. What if they didn't find a nanny this week? Next week? She could take off Thursday. Howard would have to do the rest. There was a chance her mother could come up for a day. She'd call another agency from the office; where was that list? She should be more organized. And as she was thinking about being more organized—and also recalling that she needed to schedule a meeting with the accountant, call for an appointment with Dr. Kaitz, and buy a new shower curtain at Filene's—she suddenly remembered her mother's single piece of advice on her wedding day in Wellfleet, delivered reluctantly although with a certain mournful gaiety. "Try not to ask for too much," her mother had said, hat brim slanted against the sun, "and you won't be disappointed."

A teaspoon fell to the floor in the dining room. Mirella continued to stand at the bottom of the stairs, listening to Howard's low voice, then Pearl beginning to wail. In spite of recalling her mother's advice, or perhaps because of it, she felt a surge of arrogance. This is *my* house, she thought. This is *my* family.

And she thought about how the ocean of obligations always rising to engulf her were hers as well. She had created them, these obligations, required them into requiring her. Husband, house, children, job. Shower curtains, restraining orders, dishes in the sink. That was family life, this unreasonable intricacy, what she'd wanted ever since law school, when she sat inside the Kirkland Street Laundromat brooding over contract law, watching mothers push strollers past the window, envying their tired preoccupation, their stained diaper bags and unbrushed hair. Craving it all with a hunger that gradually lost the piquancy of desire and took on the suffocating absorption of lust. Mostly, she realized now, she had craved that heady, tyrannical power that comes with being wanted by children.

It was a power she pretended to discredit, laughing occasionally with other mothers in the preschool parking lot about the endless, repetitive demands, the incessant asking and requiring. All a good mother needs to be, she'd said at the last Happy Faces' workday, is an excellent waitress. The two women painting chairs with her had laughed, pleased by this breezy understating of their consequence, by the heartlessness of it, which gave them a brief free, lawless feeling, and emphasized how irreplaceable they were; almost instantly they went back to painting and talking about sleep problems and mysterious rashes.

The phone began to ring, accompanied by a crash from the kitchen, then the jaunty sound of an aluminum can bouncing against the floor.

"Oh God," said Mirella, looking up and trying not to laugh. "The dog's in the trash." And suddenly she wished she could stay home, with the trash in the kitchen and the exploding laundry, for the simple gratification of setting things to rights. It seemed so comfortable, the idea of cleaning house on a gray morning, perhaps even baking something—she thought vaguely of muffins, a cup of tea, a fire in the fireplace. She imagined calling up the stairs to describe this scene to Howard, who would tell her not to wish for clichés, although of course most wishes were for exactly that. Instead she glanced down at her blue dress, noticing a greasy thumbprint near the hem.

"I'll get it," said Howard, coming down the stairs.

Abruptly the phone stopped ringing.

"Don't let Jacob play with his trucks too much today," she told Howard, who had paused, once more halfway up the stairs.

"So what do I do if I like her?" he said.

"I'm sorry, what?"

"I want MAMA." On the upstairs landing, Pearl threw her hairbrush onto the floor with such force that Mirella could hear it ricochet into the bathroom and land in the toilet.

"What if I like whoever's coming this morning?"

"Hire her," called Mirella, hurrying away to hunt for her briefcase in the kitchen, heels tick-ticking against the old pine boards.

2

A SITE VISIT TO CANCEL; plans unfinished for the Gourley kitchen; his proposal for the TownCommon co-housing contract due next Friday. Across the back garden, inside the old carriage house he'd converted into a studio, curled rolls of trace paper, his preliminary TownCommon sketches, which, when he looked at them last night at least, were stronger than he'd expected, classical but distinctive, permanent-looking.

Yet as soon as Mirella and Pearl had backed out of the driveway in the Cherokee, red taillights winking as they avoided the Pilkey boy on his purple skateboard, Howard found himself welcoming the almost illicit quiet of a morning alone with Jacob.

And to be truthful, none of his commitments were as urgent as he'd implied to Mirella. To be absolutely truthful, the site visit had been canceled twice already, and the Gourleys owed him fifteen hundred dollars. A bigger firm would probably get the co-housing contract; in the end the development would either be scuttled by the zoning board or by the EPA, which would discover an endangered caterpillar on the property. Or the whole thing would be torpedoed by the governor's second cousin, who didn't want to lose his view of the harbor. This was New Aylesbury, after all, where the town had to approve the color of your house paint.

Up and down the streets of New Aylesbury families were now heading off to work and school, gripping leather briefcases and bright nylon lunch bags, shouting to each other from hallways and brick front steps. Mahesh Gupta, across the road, led his two little girls in pigtails and red plaid kilts toward his white Volvo station wagon, waving to his wife as she headed for her white Acura. His black hair shone, matching the polish on his black shoes and his wife's and daughters' hair. From the living room window, Howard watched the Guptas slip into their cars, then back out of their driveway and drive off in tandem. In honor of the town's upcoming anniversary celebration, several of the houses on Lost Pond Road, including the Guptas', displayed American flags, which hung this morning like damp washcloths from their poles. This summer the town would be 350 years old.

Crows squawked in the maple trees and from the tops of pines. Car doors slammed. Howard loaded the dishwasher. He put away the painted tray. He stuck a postcard that had fallen to the floor onto the refrigerator with a magnet advertising a local realty company.

Then he and Jacob and Martha, the fat golden retriever, went out into the wet garden where, at Howard's instruction, Jacob picked five yellow tulips near the old stone wall for his mother. Howard was annoyed with Mirella, and annoyed with himself for being annoyed, and so, as he often did at these moments, he thought of an affectionate gesture to make toward her, though an indirect one, a gesture that would leave him feeling both generous and unextended. Jacob could pick flowers for Mirella.

For a moment, standing outside in the wan, dripping morning, Jacob holding tulips, the dog snuffling a clump of grape hyacinths, Howard relaxed. Drops of moisture beaded along the branches of the apple tree; as he peered closely he saw that each one contained a minute, convex reversal of the whole garden. There was nothing wrong with this day. He was who he looked like: a man at home with his boy. They would spend the day together, he and his son, building something, a footstool, maybe. They would build it, sand it, paint it, and there it would be—a footstool, their day, not lost but achieved, real and solid, something to prop your feet on. Tomorrow he would get up early to work on those sketches, do some research into colonial fireplaces; the splayed jambs were different in colonials before 1750, as he recalled. The group wanted the houses to feel historical, to blend harmoniously with the rest of the town. They also wanted "green" materials wherever possible, engineered lumber for the four-by-fours, recycled sheathing. Like most clients, they wanted everything.

Howard looked down to find Jacob shivering, his sneakers soaked in the wet grass, clutching the tulips. One tulip head was partly snapped off, hanging from the stem by a green thread. It occurred to Howard, gently lifting Jacob and taking the tulips himself, that he could have made a fuss about taking the day off. Insisted on working on his proposal, forced Mirella to cancel her court appearance, take care of Jacob, and interview the nanny. But the sketches were mostly finished. He could afford to let things go while she could not; also Jacob wasn't much trouble, and it was ridiculous to pretend otherwise.

Although lately he'd noticed that as the day wore on, small sacrifices like this one tended to shrink and harden in his mind until they jingled disconsolately, like loose change.

Howard and Jacob returned to the kitchen to place the yellow tulips in a glass vase, which Howard found in a lower cabinet Mirella reserved for vases. That she had so many vases, eight at least, irritated him all over again; he chose one hastily, without considering whether it was the right shape or size. But once in

their vase the tulips had the mollifying effect of making the cluttered kitchen look neater. He floated the detached tulip head in
a green china bowl of water.

After Howard had written a note to go with the tulips that
said, "To M. from a secret admirer," he and Jacob settled down on
the living room carpet, surrounded by its twisting blue-and-gold
Chinese dragons. The idea of a footstool began to seem too involved—Jacob would mix up the nails in their boxes, and what
if he cut himself. As he had several times in the last weeks,
Howard considered patching the screen on the kitchen door. The
back steps needed repainting. A water stain had recently appeared
on the dining room ceiling from the leaky sink in the upstairs
bathroom. Maybe he would rest on the carpet for a few minutes,
and then they would try the footstool.

He lay flat on the carpet and closed his eyes to allow himself
one of his secret pleasures: picturing the house as it had looked
four years ago on the fall afternoon when he and Mirella first saw
it, reliving his curious shock of recognition, as if he had found not
the house he'd always wanted, but the house he'd always missed.
Holes in the slate roof, a bird's nest above a pilaster by the oak
front door. Ivy had pulled apart bricks on both chimneys. Shad-
owed by two enormous Norway maples, through which sunlight
filtered down in shafts, and surrounded by whaleback rhododendrons, the house had looked almost sunken, as mysterious and
perpetual as a shipwreck.

"It's perfect," he'd told Mirella, in a businesslike voice.

And, in its way, it was perfect. A 1754 white colonial with dark
red shutters the color of hemoglobin, spare yet consequential,
built by a wealthy housewright for himself, still possessing
its original floorboards and a few original windowpanes. Howard
had followed the realtor's blue Swedish boiled-wool jacket into
the house, listening to the uneven floorboards creak, running
his hand along the slightly bulging walls, imagining a table in

candlelight, copper pots by a fire, boot steps on the stairs. Save for an ell that was now the kitchen, the house's exterior was essentially unaltered from the day the housewright drove his last iron nail into the roof.

Mirella, however, found the house incomprehensible. Or rather, she found Howard's interest in it incomprehensible. Carrying Pearl, she trailed gamely after him and the realtor, trying to appreciate all those rusty iron latches instead of doorknobs and the eighteenth-century hand-stenciling still visible on the wainscoting in the dining room. But she stepped back through the front door with an air of reprieve. "This place is falling apart," she noted sensibly on the walkway as the realtor was locking up.

Howard recalled that moment with absolute clarity: the three greenish panes of bull's-eye glass gleaming above the front door; the thick, elephant hide of the old painted clapboards; the crushed soda can on the crumbling circular brick steps. A kind of rapture had flared within him, bringing with it a profound sense of well-being that was almost like exhaustion.

"Howard," Mirella had said, turning to smile at him over Pearl's head. "What happened to our idea of building something new?"

Of course, whenever Howard saw the house through Mirella eyes, he had to disapprove of it, too: because the house, although to his eyes beautiful and meaningful in its age and resilience and in the purity of its simple lines, continued to be a wreck, despite his attempts so far to repair it. The foundation had shifted; half of the windows could not be completely closed. All the ceilings needed replastering, the septic system was out of code, both chimneys smoked. And yet for years he'd dreamed of living on the coast, in the oldest colonial house in the oldest town he could find. He loved colonial houses; he loved them because they were symmetrical and unpretentious and because they seemed designed not only to withstand the elements, but to improve with assault. They had a plain, stringent elegance that he instinctively clung to, for reasons he still did not altogether understand beyond the reflexive ones. His father had loved split-levels; his brother's house in Greenwich was a squat, rococo mix of Frank Lloyd Wright and an Italian villa, with Carrara marble tiles in the foyer, a loggia, and skylights in the bathrooms.

We could have a garden, Howard murmured to Mirella that October afternoon. They were driving back to Boston past glowing maples, which seemed, in their golds and reds, to capture his excitement. He kissed her shoulder twice as she drove and fed her salted nuts, placing each one between her lips. Good schools, sea air. What about my commute? she said warily, shaking her head at another nut. At home he unfolded maps, discovering a Byzantine route criss-crossing Route 128 and involving a drawbridge that would shave ten minutes off the drive if Mirella left before seven in the morning. Eventually she gave in, partly because Howard was so insistent, partly because she was susceptible to arguments involving education or health, and partly, Howard realized, because she never quite trusted her own domestic instincts, deferring to him when it came to matters of taste or style or what she sometimes referred to as "the Living Arts."

Howard spent their first summer in the house working just on the kitchen, a dark, coffin-shaped room littered with mouse droppings and old mop strings. The kitchen was dominated by an enormous Glenwood stove with a single working burner. Howard had saved the stove, but ripped out the dropped ceiling and the fake brick linoleum from an unfortunate fifties renovation. He refinished the pine floor, installed granite countertops and a butcher-block work island, and punched out a bay window to overlook the back garden. He'd done most of the work while Mirella was pregnant with Jacob and while he himself was supposed to be getting Goldman Associates Architects Inc. off the ground, which proved unexpectedly difficult. Or so he had informed Mirella.

Actually, Howard always expected things to be difficult and was rarely surprised by mishaps or obstacles, in a perverse way even relished them, while Mirella had a willful optimism about her own undertakings that left her honestly bewildered when anything went wrong.

He printed up business cards with his logo: Goldman Associates Architects Inc. in an avant-garde font with a Gothic castle riding on a cloud in the card's right-hand corner. He listed himself in the chamber of commerce directory. But for months no one called except insurance companies and a woman who wanted to know if he could design small-scale structures, like birdhouses. So he spackled holes, regrouted tile, reset the oak bannister, and repaired broken stair spindles, afraid to admit how peaceful he was, suspending this time in a reverie of detail.

What beautiful taste you have, people often said to Mirella when they visited the house. It's not me, it's Howard. Howard's the one with the nesting instinct.

Yet it was during this initial remodeling, this enchanted period of reclaiming the house, that Howard, who did not consider himself an untrustworthy person, or callous, or even impulsive, had had an affair. It was the strangest thing he'd ever done—he had an affair with an intern at Quigley & Morrow, a firm in Salem where he worked part time for the design team while waiting for his own clients. A perky-voiced intern named Nadine, whom he'd found only mildly attractive. Why had he done such a thing? He'd asked himself this question again and again and had never found a decent answer. Except that sleeping with Nadine had seemed, at the time, somehow inevitable, and even less complicated than not sleeping with her.

The affair began a few months before Jacob was born. Mirella had just gone into private practice with Ruth, and she was in the middle of her first big trial, representing an ex-stepmother suing for visitation rights. The ex-stepmother claimed she'd spent as much time raising the child as either of the biological parents. Local papers were covering the case; even a national newsmagazine ran a story. SHE'S MINE, TOO, read the headline. Mirella gave interviews; she helped the ex-stepmother give interviews. Howard, Pearl, and the nanny—it was Tina then—ate dinner without her most nights. When she got home, Mirella sometimes fell asleep before she'd finished taking off her clothes.

"This won't last forever," she kept telling Howard.

One morning when Pearl and Tina were out on a walk, Howard had a beer around eleven, then called up Nadine, who often answered the telephones at Quigley & Morrow, and asked her to lunch. A business lunch, he told himself. Both were new in the office, their jobs equally tenuous. They had been working together sketching floor plans for an old icehouse that was being turned into condominiums. Nadine had a pointed little face and a brisk, dismissive way of sticking the end of her tongue between her teeth and smiling at him that he gradually recognized was meant to be provocative. How*erd,* she called him. At lunch that day, Nadine confided to Howard her impatience with Quigley & Morrow. She complained about the new architectural software Quigley & Morrow had acquired—a barbarism, they agreed, a design-by-numbers kit. She said the firm had lost touch with "the art of architecture," and that she wasn't getting enough hands-on experience. *I could give you some hands-on experience,* Howard said, meaning (he did mean) that they could go over drafting techniques. They were sitting on a granite seawall splattered with gull droppings, eating turkey sandwiches and drinking cans of lemonade. *I'll bet you could,* she said, blond hair radiant with watery sun, looking him full in the eyes.

They went to her apartment that afternoon. Afterward he'd felt ashamed and almost frightened, appalled at the easy way he'd unharnessed himself from the rest of his life. And yet he also felt revived by his encounter with Nadine, by the pure energy of it, which he tried to persuade himself was more or less connected to the physical labor he was doing that summer, like the sight of raw wood and the feel of wallpaper glue, and the slick heat of those wide, shimmering, truant days.

But now, lying on the living room carpet, he asked himself again: Had he been angry at Mirella? Bored, restless? He'd certainly missed Mirella and minded her absence, but he understood her absorption at that time in her career. It was a happy summer for him, perhaps the happiest of his life. He used to love waking up each morning and lifting Pearl out of her crib, still drowsy and pink, tucking her into her stroller so that they could take the dog for a walk by the harbor. He'd begun designing his studio by then, something he'd always dreamed of doing. If anyone had asked him, he would have said he was a contented man. He would have said he wasn't the affair type.

And it was hardly an affair; they'd slept together only a few times—once slipping into the house like cat burglars while the nanny was at the beach with Pearl to wedge themselves together on the steel-colored velvet sofa in the living room. He had, he recalled, thought to spread a towel on the sofa.

This small fact caused him slight vertigo as he lay on the carpet: a towel. And not one of their good towels either, but an old frayed green one they used to dry the dog's paws on rainy days.

Nadine. Nadine Fouch. Howard took a deep breath, remembering the brand of sugarless gum she chewed almost constantly, which made her mouth taste like red grapes. Nadine had been twenty-six, small and wiry. Her passion was bicycling; she had once cycled through France. He remembered running his hands up and down her athletic biceps and well-muscled legs, admiring the tanned vitality of her skin. "Just do it," she'd grunted one afternoon, churning on the daisy-patterned sheets in her base-ment sublet.

But that particular afternoon, the last afternoon they spent alone together, he had ended up sitting on the edge of Nadine's hard futon bed, cradling his forehead in his fingertips, a blade of sunlight slicing across his bare feet. Everything had been fine. He remembered pulling off his clothes, the thick excitement of reach-ing for her—and then, in the middle of it all, he'd been repelled to the point of anguish by his own hoarse breathing and by the sight of Nadine's lower lip jutting open in a way that moments before had aroused him, yet now looked sad and practiced. And at that same instant as he was staring into the pink recess of Nadine's jutting lip, at that very second, he saw Mirella, sitting at her desk in her office, ankles crossed, wearing her cream-colored silk maternity blouse and blue jumper, frowning as she gazed into her computer.

Later Nadine had sighed understandingly and in a detached voice that sounded somehow deferred said that it was okay, really it was okay, and that yes, she knew it wasn't her.

And then it was over. The entire affair might as well never have happened. In fact, Howard left Quigley & Morrow a few weeks later when he landed his first contract, designing a summer house in Ipswich for a friend of Mirella's mother. Then Jacob was born, and more contracts followed, although never enough, and Nadine faded away like a label on an old jar.

Until two days ago. When, for the first time in nearly three years, from a pay phone in Vermont, Nadine had called him again. Just to say hello. Just to catch him up. Sometime she'd like to get together to talk—would that be okay?—just to talk. *I've been in therapy,* she said.

It was hardly an affair, Howard repeated to himself. It had hap-pened the way an accident happens. Later you stayed awake won-dering why it had to be you on that street at that moment, and not someone else, what had possessed you to linger over your coffee that morning, or drink it too fast, or forget your briefcase and rush back for it, why today you took a different turn than the one you usually took.

He opened his eyes and abruptly sat up. The dog was gnawing on a rawhide bone near the coffee table, twisting her big golden head sideways, exposing shiny black gums. Jacob had arranged his wooden trucks in a precise line down the carpet. Now he was lying on his stomach, his face pressed close to his line of trucks, humming a little tune composed mostly of tiny gasps, followed by a long sigh. He would lie that way for hours if Howard let him.

"What are you singing?" he asked. Jacob glanced at him, then got to his knees and began crawling away. "Want to stack some blocks?"

Jacob glanced back at him again, either considering this offer or, more likely, registering that he had heard it so that Howard would not ask again. There was a privacy about Jacob that made Mirella frantic, but which Howard found compatible. It was so easy to be with him. Jacob had a kind of innate self-possession (entirely missing in Pearl) that complemented his failure so far to speak comprehensibly, though he would be three at the end of July. His silence was worrisome, and Howard, like Mirella, was worried about him. But it was also restful. Jacob did not whine; he seldom cried, only now and then falling into fits of shrill wailing. His obsessions were unwavering—trucks and trains, the Indian headdress, his fireplace nests—but solitary and easily satisfied. Howard's nickname for Jacob was "Adam Ant." Mirella called him "Mystery Date."

He was small for his age, thin and fine-boned with dusty-looking skin and straight black hair. He reminded Howard of sepia photographs of dark-eyed immigrant children arriving at Ellis Island, their expressions both infantile and unchildlike.

Occasionally Howard wondered if his father had looked something like Jacob the day he filed off the boat, one of those immigrant children himself, small, bony, inscrutable in heavy clothing, a pigeon-toed orphan from Minsk.

On Jacob's forehead, just above his right eyebrow was a birthmark, a raised dime-sized red hematoma that Mirella fretted about and wanted to have surgically removed. It made Jacob look like someone had burned him with a cigarette, she claimed, and in fact people did ask what the mark was, although never, to Howard's mind, suspiciously.

Jacob had been Howard's favorite figure in the Bible, canny and quick, so determined.

A breeze blew in through the living room windows, carrying the fragrance of new grass, low tide and coming rain. Jacob crawled away into the dining room. Howard lay back on the carpet, hands behind his head, his heartbeat slowed to normal, soothed by the grayness of the day and the luxury of not having to go anywhere. Idly, he thought of the sketches lying rolled on the drafting table in his studio; when Jacob took a nap, he might steal out there for an hour. As he was imagining the logistics of this scenario—how he would take the baby monitor with him, make sure both doors in the house were locked—the phone in the kitchen began to ring. After three rings, the machine picked up and he listened to his own disembodied voice announce that neither he nor Mirella were available and to please leave a message.

He held his breath. A woman's voice began speaking: "Hello. This is Alice, Eliot's mother. I'm calling because we need someone to handle publicity for the Happy Faces' summer bazaar—"

In the kitchen, the dishwasher chugged into a rinse cycle. *Minsk, Minsk,* it said.

Howard got up and crossed the hall to find Jacob sitting cross-legged inside the fireplace. He was holding Mirella's sunglasses backward, gazing down into them with penetration. Mirella would be discovering that she'd forgotten her sunglasses right around now, talking to Ruth on her cell phone, one hand digging in her briefcase, speeding down the highway toward her office on Boylston Street and her desk piled with papers and legal binders. Howard pictured the green light pulsing on her telephone console; within the taupe-colored cavern of her computer, e-mail messages hung in electronic darkness, invisibly multiplying.

"You found Mommy's sunglasses," he said.

Jacob dropped the sunglasses. An eggish smell wafted into the air. "Time for a change, buddy."

Without protest, Jacob allowed himself to be lifted out of the fireplace and carried up the stairs to his room, his chin resting on Howard's shoulder. Howard was thinking of the staircase he wanted to design for at least one of the TownCommon houses, with step-end decorations and a newel post that curled into the suggestion of a snail shell.

He laid Jacob on the changing table, then began fumbling with an unopened package of diapers while Jacob lay quietly, gazing at a mobile of paper dolphins that floated overhead. He seemed to be waiting for something. Howard was not sure what gave him this impression, but he noticed a tense, listening quality to Jacob's face this morning, an attention that fixed on the rotating dolphins only because they were available. He extracted a diaper and laid it on the changing table, then pulled open the adhesive tabs of the diaper Jacob was wearing. Careful not to make a face, because Mirella had told him that parental expressions of disgust might make Jacob ashamed of his bodily functions, and further complicate toilet training, but mostly because he felt Jacob deserved his composure, Howard reached for the container of diaper wipes.

"There," he said, after a minute. "All nice and clean."

Jacob continued to stare at the dolphins as if Howard's ministrations did not have anything to do with him.

Howard stuffed the dirty diaper into the diaper pail, thinking that if he got this TownCommon project half his neighbors would never speak to him again. The contract was to design twenty small colonial homes around an oval green—a tiny village of sorts, complete with a playground and one-story meetinghouse. Which sounded unobjectionable, until you added that it was planned for fifteen acres of old dairy farm pastures overlooking the harbor, untended and ignored for decades, the last parcel of open land left in town.

Fortunately, he thought, dusting Jacob's bottom with talcum powder, he and Mirella didn't see much of their neighbors. They waved hello to the thin and overcommitted Pilkeys next door—he real estate, she banking. ("Darn Nice Republicans," Howard called them, or DNR, although they actually were very nice, twice inviting Howard and Mirella over for poolside drinks and oysters wrapped in bacon, then apologizing to Howard, asking if he'd like cheese and crackers instead.) He and Mirella talked perennials and sciatica to the retired Applewhites on the other side, who migrated to Florida in November and didn't return until May. Sometimes they chatted with Mahesh and Vasanti Gupta across the street, both in high tech, from whom Howard once borrowed an aluminum extension ladder and, one morning in wintertime, a stick of butter.

Every time he saw the Guptas, he thought of that morning. Over a foot of snow had fallen overnight and Mirella, excited by confinement, wanted to make pancakes. Outside, the hushed street was a series of white hills. Schools were canceled; roads were still being cleared. He'd surprised the Guptas in their kitchen, coming around to rap on their back door when there was no answer at the front. They were sitting at the table dipping hard-looking biscuits into cups of tea, Mahesh in shirtsleeves; Vasanti was wearing a sort of plush plum-colored robe. The faces they turned to Howard had for an instant retained the pleasure of being alone, quietly marooned together. "Sorry to bother you," he began saying, even before Mahesh sprang up to open the door.

On the changing table, Jacob had begun murmuring in an agitated way, rolling his head from side to side, his headdress knocked askew. Howard bent closer to hear. But it was only something that sounded like "gug gug gug."

He finished fastening the diaper, then resnapped Jacob's overalls. From downstairs came a thunk and then the crepitating sound of disturbed cellophane: the dog was rooting again in the trash.

And at that moment, Jacob suddenly reached up and put his arms around Howard's neck. For a long instant they hung together in a clumsy embrace, Howard angled over the changing table, Jacob reaching up. Outside a car passed by. Howard heard himself make a low, careful, encouraging noise, deep within his chest. Then Jacob let go.

He lay on the changing table, watching gravely.

There would be no footstool today, Howard thought, as he brushed Jacob's hair off his forehead and resettled his headdress, but there had been this, a moment of—what had been this moment? And even as he considered, the moment broke up like smoke and left him.

He lifted Jacob off the changing table. Together they stood at the window, gazing out at the flag in front of the Guptas' house and at the tin-colored sky.

Then the doorbell rang, and their quiet morning was over.

3

"Hi." She hopes the damp moons spreading under her arms won't show. "I'm here about the nanny job?"

Peering at the man in the doorway, she rocks back a little to look up at him. Blue work shirt and khaki pants. Cropped dark hair, gray at the temples, dark eyes, an arching nose. A gold stud glints from one earlobe. He looks like an actor, she thinks, handsome in a stubbly, squinch-eyed way. When he smiles she notes that his eyeteeth are unusually pointed. Save for the earring, and the eyeteeth, he almost exactly resembles a father on a family sitcom; she can't remember which one.

"I'm Randi Gill?" she hears herself say.

"Oh. Yes. Sorry to make you wait." The man rubs the back of his neck as if he's just woken up. "Come in—Randi? I wasn't expecting you this early—did we say ten?

"Sorry," he repeats, extending his hand. "I'm Howard. Goldman. You spoke to my wife on the phone."

He steps back to let her come inside the house, and when she does not move, takes another step back. "Mirella couldn't be here," he continues, following her glance along the honey-colored floorboards of the empty hallway. "She had to be in court. But we're here, right buddy?" he announces to the little boy in a ragged Indian headdress who staggers into view by the staircase. A big golden dog also pads toward them, metal dog tags clinking. Randi is relieved to see the golden dog, which belongs in the picture she has had of this house even before she saw it.

Leaving Randi by the door, Howard reaches out and catches the boy, turns him upside down and tickles his stomach.

It takes her only a moment to recognize that this display is for her benefit, which is why it looks slightly tense and self-conscious for both father and son, as if they are performing a trick on a tightrope. She figures that Howard must want to assure her that he—a grown man at home in the middle of the morning—is harmless, even though his wife is in court. Crossing her arms over her bosom, she smiles and says cautiously, "Nice house."

"Thanks," says Howard. The child in his arms does not laugh, but stares soberly from upside down. His headdress falls off. "This is Jacob." Howard returns the boy to his feet. "His sister, Pearl, is at preschool."

Jacob puts the wooden truck he is holding into his mouth.

"Hi Jake," she says. Howard replaces headdress on the little boy's head and straightens the splayed feathers. One of the feathers is broken, the top half hanging crookedly.

"Hey there," she says, trying again. She holds out her hand, palm forward, stepping closer to him. He's got a mark on his forehead like a raspberry. When he still makes no response, she crouches down to his eye level, her other hand gripping one strap of her knapsack. She taps the end of the truck not in his mouth. "Does that taste good?"

He stares at the floor.

"Yes," she answers for him, straightening up. The dog bumps against her knees, wagging its plumey tail.

For a long moment the three of them and the dog linger in the hallway. Howard touches Jacob's hair again. Jacob sucks on his truck.

Randi watches them both, then looks past them into a long, low room with a fireplace and a heavy beam running across the ceiling, where a bright confusion of wooden toys and picture books are scattered across a blue Chinese rug. The room reminds her of a house she visited once as a child with her mother. A house as big as this one, light and cool, with a celery-colored carpet and a framed picture of ducks raising their wings in the living room. By the front door sat a wooden umbrella stand carved to look like a branching tree. You must be from HomeStyles, said the old lady who answered the door in slippers and a hair net. She'd stared at the two of them doubtfully, at Randi's mother standing on the door mat with her black mesh bag of brushes and steam rollers, Randi hanging on her skirt, nose running. Would your little girl like to wait in the kitchen? the old lady ventured at last. Remember, her mother had hissed, before she headed up the stairs, this is somebody else's house. In the downstairs bathroom of that house Randi had found three little pink soaps in the china soap dish. The soaps looked like rosebuds, so pretty that she put one in her mouth.

"CAN I GET YOU something to drink?" Howard is saying. "A cup of coffee? A glass of water?"

She licks her lips. "A glass of water would be great."

"Well, you've passed the first test." He picks up Jacob again. "When I asked the same question to someone who was here yesterday, she said, 'Why don't you surprise me?'" He laughs again, and an instant later Randi laughs, too. Pleased to have passed a test she hadn't realized she'd been given, she follows Howard and Jacob down the hallway to the kitchen, ready to admire the glass cabinets, the enormous stove, the bay window with a view of the back garden's azaleas and lopsided apple tree. The house has a smell she likes, old wooden boards and a trace of smoke.

On the kitchen table wait four yellow tulips in a glass vase that is too large for them. By the vase lies a small white card turned sideways, its scrawled message impossible for her to read.

"Would you like ice?"

"No thank you. Plain water is fine."

"That wasn't a test," he says, handing her a thick blue glass. And they laugh again, more quietly this time. Howard pours water for himself, then lifts his glass in salute. She raises hers as well.

Because it is almost celebratory, the feeling Randi senses between them, now that a joke has been established and shared, a joke that could come up again, a joke that has welcomed her into this house already as a person who belongs, someone who understands that ordinary questions require ordinary answers. It is a feeling not of intimacy but of shared accomplishment, like what climbers must feel in greeting each other on top of a mountain.

They both sip their water. "This is a really nice old house," she says again, looking at the tulips over the rim of her glass.

"Thanks," says Howard. "It's old anyway."

The little boy stands between them, staring from Randi to his father, then back at Randi. After a moment she puts down her glass and reaches out to him again. He drops his head and sidles away, and she thinks, as she watches him go, that she's never met a quieter child.

"Geographically," says Howard, steering the car with one hand, "this is an artless town, in spite of its history."

The way he says "history" makes Randi think hopefully of Indian massacres, public hangings, witches. She saw *The Scarlet Letter* on TNT and the town in it looked a lot like this one. But Howard doesn't mention anything more about history; instead he tells her that the village of New Aylesbury is laid out along a single main thoroughfare, with streets wishboning toward the harbor. The town rests on a granite shelf, which has created septic problems but also provided industry.

"What happened to the pond?" she says.

"Excuse me?"

"The pond of Lost Pond Road pond."

"Oh," says Howard, "I suppose the hydrology changed and the pond dried up. It's still a little swampy around here, though—you can tell by all the loosestrife in the ditches."

"Pretty," Randi says, not sure which plant she should be looking at.

"Yes, well, it's gotten to be a problem, growing all over the place. One of those alien species that colonizes everything."

It is just before noon, and Howard and Jacob are driving her back to the train station so that she won't have to pay for another cab. The houses they pass are mostly old, Randi notices, painted white or in shades of gray and brown, surrounded by privet and tall lilac bushes. "The Georgians, the Greek Revivals," says Howard familiarly, as if these are people he knows. Nailed beside many front doors are oval wooden plaques: EBENEZER HOWE, JOINER, 1782; FRANCIS BEEBE, SHIPBUILDER, 1759. In the village center the houses are smaller and even older, huddled together like people in the snow, their windows and old plank doors opening right onto the narrow twisting streets. "Cradle of the Republic," says Howard.

In the backseat, Jacob sits playing with a foil gum wrapper, folding it over and over on his knee. Every few minutes, Randi turns around to look at him and wave.

They circle the town green just as the sun comes out, passing art galleries, real estate offices, the Olde Candle Shoppe and Quaint Notions Gifts, an ice cream parlor and a coffee shop, Captain Albert's Bar and Grill, the Smiling Lightship toy store.

Briefly Randi wonders where people buy groceries, but she's pleased that no Stop & Shop hunkers in the middle of town, like a wide-screen TV in somebody's Ethan Allen living room. On the green itself looms a tall, dark granite monument shaped like an obelisk, which Howard tells her is dedicated to the Puritan settlers.

Howard seems to enjoy being a tour guide; he slows the car as they approach the harbor. Sunlight splashes against a pair of wooden docks, where a red fishing boat is just tying up and an old man in plaid pants and a captain's hat sits on a bench reading the newspaper. Across the street hovers a tall white church with a steeple; below the church lies a small graveyard, a thicket of slate wafers enclosed by a black wrought-iron fence.

"Were there any witch trials around here?" Randi asks at last, unable to help herself.

"That was mostly Salem," says Howard. "New Aylesbury had a big temperance movement, though."

"Oh," says Randi.

Soon they are driving by streets of little pastel-colored houses, some with plastic climbing toys in the front yard or a blue reflecting ball on a cement pedestal, scratchy grass, an occasional chained dog. They turn onto a broad commercial strip. "The hinterlands," announces Howard grandly. Auto World, Pet Express, hair salons, paint stores, Wal-Mart, Mattress King, Tune-Ups-While-U-Wait. To the left, blocking the shoreline, squats a power plant, surrounded by concertina wire and concrete lots, its gray stack gently puffing. A wide salt marsh once existed here. Half a mile of spartina grass and watery canals. Howard's elbow is angled out the window, his fingers tapping the hood of the car. The salt marsh had been filled a hundred years ago. Progress, he says regretfully. Not a nice business.

"We made it, buddy." Howard glances into the backseat at Jacob, as they reach the little train station. "Jacob loves trains," he informs Randi. "Steam engines, crocodile trains, freight trains. Switchers, monorails, high-speed electric trains."

Once again, she realizes she is witnessing a display, the naming of trains. Only this time, the display seems to be for Jacob's benefit.

"Right, buddy?" says Howard.

The train station itself is nothing more than an uncovered raised cement platform, as deserted as it was when Randi arrived there this morning, except for a fat herring gull peering down the tracks. Below the platform squats a square gray wooden building with a padlock on the door. There is a phone booth she used a couple of hours ago, decorated by graffiti and lovingly lettered obscenities.

Howard parks, then gets out of the car to come around and open her door, although Randi has already opened it. "You sit tight for a moment," he tells Jacob. The gull gives Randi a beady, malicious look as she climbs out of the car; then it struts away to peck at a cigarette butt. Howard walks over to the gray building to look at a train schedule nailed to the clapboards.

"About fifteen minutes," he says, returning. "It'll be the 12:25," he calls out to Jacob. "Amtrak."

"Don't worry about me," she says lightly, gripping her little knapsack. "I'll be fine."

Time for them to leave. She wants to close off this morning just as it is, friendly, calm, nothing gone wrong. The gull has moved on to a squiggle of pale plastic that looks like a used condom. Randi hopes Howard doesn't see it.

"Good-bye," she says to Jacob, leaning into his open window. He sits in his car seat holding the gum wrapper, staring at his knees with the unfocused absorption of someone doing equations in his head. "You're a good little guy," she says, "you know that?" And without planning to say anything more, she hears herself adding, "You're my kind of guy."

He looks up at her then, his dark eyes dilating, his face going pale. The red mark on his forehead bulges like a blood blister. Suddenly he begins to wail. It is a harsh, shocking noise, something like a car heading into a skid.

"Oh no," she says, backing away from Jacob's window. "I must have said something wrong."

Howard shakes his head. "He does that sometimes. He'll stop in a moment."

Sure enough, a few moments later Jacob does stop. He goes back to folding the silvery gum wrapper in half, then in fourths. Randi sighs and clasps her hands.

Still Howard lingers. "I could drive you to Boston, I suppose."

"Thanks, but I'm really okay. And I like trains, too. I'm kind of, you know, independent."

He has a funny quick way of moving, she thinks, watching Howard sprint up the platform steps to stare down the tracks, as if by looking for it he might make the train appear. Most rich people don't seem so jumpy, which is one of the things she's always admired about rich people, their way of gliding quietly along, unwrinkled and gleaming, contained in themselves like unopened packages. She watches Howard turn and jog down the platform steps again, his hands in his pockets.

"We'll let you know," he says. "One way or another." For a moment she imagines that Howard is promising to confide something to her, the way he confided Jacob's love of trains. "I'll talk to Mirella tonight," he continues. "She'll want to meet you, too, of course, and call some of your references." He frowns. "Did I ask for a list of your references?"

"They're in that envelope I gave you," she says smoothly, "with all my other background stuff."

Her first nanny job ended in February and she's been waiting over a month for another place. It was really too bad about the Lawlors. The Lawlors had been great at first, taking her along to Bermuda, giving her a green parka for Christmas and a jar of different-colored bath beads, until Mrs. Lawlor got so weird about the baby crying whenever Randi left the room, reaching out his little arms. Jealous Mommy Syndrome, another nanny had called it. The *Family Options Handbook* called it "attachment complications" and recommended "sensitivity and discretion."

Even though all Randi had ever done was love little Charles and make the house look nice and cook healthy dinners. Chicken à la king. Beef kebabs. A great mushroom-and-rice ring one night with parsley garnish. She'd read *The Joy of Cooking* the way some people read the Bible. And for a few months she'd been really happy, humming "Jingle Bells" in the kitchen, little Charles on her hip, taping paper snowflakes to the windows. *What would we do without you?* Mrs. Lawlor wrote in looping script inside the snowman Christmas card that went along with the parka. *A friend to our whole family.* One day Randi was baking apple crisp, the next day Mrs. Lawlor was calling her a cab. They'd leave it at "personal differences," Mr. Lawlor said.

More and more lately, Randi has been thinking how strange it is that you can be living a certain kind of life, a life that seems like it might go on forever, and the next minute that life could be over, like tearing off a daily calendar page, almost as if it had never been at all. One day, when she has her own home, life won't be so changeable. Because that's what a home is, a place where life can stay the same if you want it to, or be different, because you belong there, you made it, and you get to decide what happens.

FOR THE LAST MONTH, Randi has been staying with Alma Beatty, whom she met last year at St. Theresa of the Child Jesus. Alma is on disability because she is so fat. "It's my genes," Alma said. "The only ones I fit into, ha, ha." Alma has hair like a baby's, more scalp than hair, and her skin is a Swiss cheese color. Her neck looks like a handbag. All day she sits in her recliner smoking low-tar cigarettes and eating pink pistachio nuts. Alma is on a special protein diet, which she believes will help her lose weight without leaving her chair. The pistachios are for exercise, since you have to crack open the shells before eating the meats. "Ha, ha," said Alma, waving pink fingertips.

Not that Randi isn't grateful to Alma. Alma had taken her in when she arrived in Boston a year ago and showed up at a St. Theresa of the Child Jesus outreach potluck dinner in South Brookline. Randi isn't Catholic or anything, but the church door was open, with lights on inside and the sound of people's voices. Under a felt wall hanging depicting Christ turning loaves into fishes, Randi sat on a folding chair beside Alma with a paper plate of lasagna warm on her lap and told the story of her parents' automobile accident. She'd kept looking down as she told her story—mentioning the bent guardrail, the Jaws of Life brought in—noticing how grease from the lasagna was turning the white paper plate orange. "You poor kid," Alma said, her own lasagna long gone.

It's been nice, living with Alma. Randi has enjoyed cleaning up the apartment, as much as is possible, anyway, with its yellowed shades, always drawn, its greenish walls and smell of cats. She likes cooking Alma's fat-free meals and reading advice columns in the women's magazines Alma orders from Publishers' Clearinghouse ("You never know when your luck's about to change"). Especially she likes watching movies with Alma on television at night. They both look forward to eight o'clock, "movie time." Randi hurries a little in the kitchen, wiping the counter and rinsing the dishpan, calling out, "Is it starting yet?" even though she can see the TV set from the sink. Alma calls back from her recliner, "Still just commercials, kid." But Alma thinks Randi is too young to settle down with a fat old lady. That's what Alma calls herself. Alma is the one who told Randi to call Family Options in the first place, pointing out the number printed in a boxed classified ad: LOOKING FOR POISED, CARING, CREATIVE YOUNG WOMEN.

"That's you, kid," said Alma, tapping ashes all over the paper. "Caring and creative." When Randi pointed out the ad said "references required," Alma said, "Give me that." A few weeks later, the Family Options director spoke with Mrs. Norman Beatty, who couldn't say enough good things about Randi Gill. "Took *exquisite* care of my four little boys. But it's understandable, her not wanting to move to Houston. Please promise you'll find her a family that really deserves her."

Alma would do a great job of sounding smart and confident on the telephone as Mrs. Lawlor. Randi sincerely hopes the Lawlors' recommendation letter, written by Mr. Lawlor ("very conscientious," it said), will be enough for the Cook-Goldmans, but if Howard's wife insists on talking to Mrs. Lawlor herself, Randi has included Alma's number.

And from the way Howard had said "My wife will want to meet you, too," Randi figures this Mirella is going to be a worrier. Which Randi can understand; after all, mothers are supposed to worry. She'd be the same.

"A hard worker, certainly," Alma would say in a mincing voice. "*Ex*cellent people skills. We will be very sorry to lose her, but unfortunately my husband is being transferred to Chicago." She would cover the receiver with a puffy hand, wink at Randi. "Children just adore her. She's a real old-fashioned homebody."

"WELL," HOWARD SAYS, squinting in the sunlight. "I guess we'll push off." He puts out his hand for her to shake; Randi is surprised to find it slightly moist. "Good to meet you, and thanks again for coming all the way up here."

"You're welcome." She looks through the windshield of the car and smiles at the shadowy figure of Jacob, once more bent over his gum wrapper in the backseat.

"Oh," she says, just as Howard opens his door. "Can I ask you one last question?"

Howard pauses, smiling, one foot inside the car.

"How do you feel about fried cheese balls?"

"Fried cheese balls?"

She adds quickly, "It's just something I made the other day for the family I work for. I served it as an appetizer the night I fixed lemon chicken." Randi is pleased by Howard's look of respectful astonishment, as if she has just offered to reupholster his living-room couch or give the car an oil change.

"Sounds great," he says.

"I make up a lot of my own recipes. I've done stews, soup. I did this one soup with kale. I make up all kinds of things. I did a potato gratin last week that was really good."

Howard shakes his head, looking incredulous. "Fried cheese balls," he repeats.

"Grated cheese, egg whites, cracker crumbs. It's easier than you think," she says. "See you."

And she waves gaily good-bye, although Howard has yet to start the car and her train is still nowhere in sight.

4

THE COOK-GOLDMANS don't have a TV—
Mirella says Howard doesn't believe in TV. (How can you not
believe in TV? Randi wonders, with real interest.) They don't
have air-conditioning either. Howard works at home while
Mirella drives to an office in Boston. And in spite of being
named Mirella Cook, Mirella doesn't cook. If any cooking gets
done, Mirella tells her, laughing but looking embarrassed, it's by
Howard, and even then it's probably spaghetti because there's
never enough time for anything else.

Randi is trying to figure everything out, bedtime and nap-
time and where the park is, and of course what everybody eats.
She asks Mirella what the last girl used to make for the kids'
dinner. Mirella doesn't seem completely sure. Fish fingers, she
thinks. Peas.

"Pearl," says Mirella, "what did Grete usually feed you and
Jacob?"

"Rocks," says Pearl.

Pearl is sitting under the big kitchen table petting the dog and
chewing on the ends of her hair. From the minute she spotted

Pearl this afternoon, Randi has been itching to get a comb and fix Pearl's hair into a French braid or maybe pigtails. Maybe she could even trim those bangs. She'd spent half her time in school staring at girls in her class and imagining the makeovers she could do for them with scissors and some hair mousse. A makeover could make such a difference, even change your life.

"Cat poop," Pearl says from under the table.

"Well," Mirella smiles apologetically, "sometimes they'll eat eggs. There are tofu hot dogs in the freezer, and some turkey burgers. But you can add anything you want to the grocery list. I buy organic when I can. Jacob likes broccoli. And you like carrots, don't you, Pearlie?"

Pearl rubs her face against the dog's fur. The dog's name is Martha. "For Martha Stewart," Mirella had said a little while ago. "I wanted to order Martha Stewart to sit," she laughed. "Isn't that pathetic?" Randi didn't see what was pathetic about naming a dog after Martha Stewart, who after all had her own TV show and magazine and made millions of dollars; she just thought Trixie or Pepper would have been simpler, maybe Goldie.

"Noodles," Mirella is saying now, pushing back her hair, "are also a good bet. Really, if you can get them to eat anything besides popsicles, you're way ahead of us."

Every now and then, Randi notices, Mirella reaches up to slide her fingers through her thick, shiny hair, and the red color in it gleams like some kind of metal. She is forty or so, you can tell by her neck, and tall, the same height as Howard. She can raise one of her dark eyebrows all by itself. Randi once saw a movie about a queen who got her head chopped off but was brave to the end. Mirella has those exact same cheekbones.

RANDI MET MIRELLA for the first time last week at a downtown Au Bon Pain near Mirella's office. The sun had come out after a rainshower and the light was blinding, pouring in through Au Bon Pain's rain-streaked plate-glass windows and flashing against the chrome railings, hitting the dusty legs of the black metal café chairs. Randi had to squint when she first walked in. Then, out of that confusing, wet glimmer, rose a tall woman, calling Randi's name, as if she already knew who Randi must be.

"Right here," Randi cried out, not meaning to sound so relieved.

At Au Bon Pain, Randi repeated for Mirella what she'd told Howard during her interview, the part about wanting to move from Coralville to New England because she'd never seen the ocean and because *Little Women* was her favorite movie—she'd rented it probably eight times, she even read the book—and saving up to go to cooking school, plus really, really liking kids. She had no brothers or sisters; her grandmother had raised her alone. Her parents, she confided, shifting on her black metal café chair, were dead. A plane crash. On their way to Acapulco for their wedding anniversary.

Randi paused to accept Mirella's sharp intake of breath. Gazing at her napkin, she waited another moment before explaining that her mother had been a schoolteacher, her father a doctor. Gastroenterology was his specialty.

"Gastroenterology," she repeated, enjoying the word's somersault across her tongue. Quickly, she tried to think of what subject a schoolteacher mother would have taught, in case Mirella asked.

"You must miss them very much," Mirella said instead, the tips of her fingers pressed white against the edge of the marble tabletop. Randi nodded. She wished she hadn't ordered an apple croissant, which had crumbled past her napkin and drifted onto her short denim skirt, but instead settled for coffee, like Mirella. The tiny holes in her chair's metal seat were pocking the backs of her thighs; she'd have weird dots on her legs when she stood up. Mirella was wearing a silky dress the color of bran, with a chunky bead necklace and a brown velvet-patterned scarf. She was saying something about life's being unfair and taking comfort where you can that got mixed up in Randi's mind with Mirella's velvet-patterned scarf, so that it seemed as if her words themselves were soothing bits of brown velvet.

History, she decided for her mother.

When, after a long pause, Mirella had asked why she was interested in looking after children, Randi said truthfully, "Because they like me. It's kind of a thing I have, you know, kids getting attached to me? I really like taking care of people."

Her approach to problem behavior, she reported, was a firm voice and, if she had to do it, a time-out. "But I'm really into practicing positive discipline," she said dutifully, recalling a phrase from the *Family Options Handbook,* a thin Xeroxed booklet with boldface warnings: **Never shake a baby. Never contradict a parent. Never borrow household items without requesting permission.**

Did Randi have a child-rearing philosophy, Mirella wanted to know, stirring her coffee with the little red plastic straw supplied by Au Bon Pain.

"You know what I think?" Randi sat up straighter. She realized she would be taking a risk by saying what she thought instead of what the *Family Options Handbook* suggested in the "Your Interview" section—something about nurturing children's individuality —but the expression of anxious sympathy on Mirella's face since Randi mentioned her parents' plane crash gave her confidence. "I think," she said, taking a breath, "I think that children are just people and that's how you should treat them. Everybody acts like children are something special—I mean, they are, you know, special, but they're also not. You know what I mean? They're just people, and they should have to act that way."

Mirella nodded and said she did indeed know what Randi

meant, for which Randi felt grateful. That last part about children acting like people hadn't sounded quite right.

"I remember being a kid." Randi wiped flakes of croissant off her fingers onto her knees. "It's confusing, you know, figuring out what grown-ups want. Especially when grown-ups want kids to be something they can't."

Mirella suddenly looked nervous, so Randi smiled at her, excusing her from being one of those grown-ups. "But once the whole family understands the rules," she said quickly, "because there have to be rules, and they've got to be, like, pretty straightforward, it's a lot easier."

What sort of rules? Mirella had asked, smiling now, too.

"Well, nobody can hit or call names. And nobody should interrupt when somebody's talking." Randi paused to take a breath. "And people should be honest but respect each other's feelings."

For a moment the two of them sat looking out Au Bon Pain's wide window at the street, as if contemplating past failures walking by in tan raincoats and furled black umbrellas, and recognizing in the glitter of wet pavement the bright promise of future success.

The last question Mirella asked was whether Randi had experience with newborns. "Just curious."

"I love babies," Randi said.

ON FRIDAY FAMILY OPTIONS telephoned Randi to say she had a job with the Cook-Goldman family in New Aylesbury up on the North Shore and reminded her to fill out her W-4 form and sign her medical release forms, which indicated that she'd had a hepatitis shot and a TB test. "We assured Mrs. Cook that you would be an exceptional employee," the Family Options director said in a narrow voice. "We are hopeful this job will prove longer lasting than your previous one."

NOW IT IS MONDAY. Nice to have a whole new life start on a Monday.

In the Cook-Goldmans' sunny kitchen, Randi smiles at the re-frigerator and at the white ceramic canisters labeled coffee sugar tea flour, and at Mirella, who has just finished saying something about Jacob's special needs.

"He's an unusual little boy, but I think maybe what he needs most is encouragement. There's such a rush to diagnose every-thing these days. Don't you find?"

Randi nods, watching Jacob edge past the table in a striped Polo shirt, both hands stuck into the back of his blue dungaree pants. He is still wearing the Indian headdress he had on last week when she came for her interview.

"Each of us may shine at a different time," she hears herself say, "but that doesn't make our light any less bright.

"My grandmother made that up," she adds, blushing. "My grandmother wrote poems?" Randi gives Mirella a tentative look. "She used to publish them in the local paper. Sort of advice po-ems? Her name was Dolores Anne Spicer for the newspaper but just plain DeeDee for everybody else.

"Actually," Randi continues, "her name was originally Bertha Pitzer, but her last name changed when she got married to her first husband and she hated Bertha so she changed that, too. She always said a name should fit like a bra—snug but not pinching—and it should give you support."

Actually, her mother had said this about names. It was her mother who was DeeDee Spicer, who sometimes had limericks printed in the *Coralville Weekly* and once published a poem in an agricultural magazine called *North American Grain*. But Randi had never been able to resist the idea of a feisty, apron-wearing grandmother, sort of like the granny on reruns of a hillbilly TV show Randi watched with her dinner on the evenings when DeeDee was, as she put it, "going to be elsewhere." For a long time, Randi thought Elsewhere was what her mother called her-self on her nights out, the way she was Dolores Anne Spicer in *North American Grain,* or Miss DeeDee to the old ladies she vis-ited for HomeStyles to do their perms and rinses, or D. Spicer on her white name tag as weekend hostess at Huskee Prime Rib, or the way she had once been Bertha Pitzer.

You are who you want to be, her mother always said. She would be examining her own face in the mirror as she stroked on liquid foundation, or put bleach cream on her upper lip, taking this opportunity to deliver her favorite lecture. Reach for the stars. Be an astronaut if you want. Be a movie actress. And Randi listened, because it was nice having her mother give her advice just like mothers on TV.

Mirella laughs. "She sounds like an interesting woman."

"Yes," Randi says dryly. "I have very interesting relations. My great-great-great grandfather was scalped by Indians in North Dakota." This being a true documented event, and in fact men-tioned in an essay she'd written in sixth grade titled "The Affect of the Past," for which she had received an A–, despite spelling mistakes. Randi smiles. "Does he ever take those feathers off?" she asks, nodding toward Jacob.

Mirella holds her arms out as Jacob wanders by again, catches him, then releases him to continue on his way toward the refrig-erator. "Well, he's very attached to certain things. Usually he'll take it off at bedtime."

Randi nods again and waggles her fingers at Jacob. "No prob-lem. Indians have never bothered me. Boo," she says, aware that Mirella is watching her. "Boo," she says to Pearl under the table.

"I don't like your shirt," says Pearl.

"Pearl," says Mirella.

"Oh, that's all right." Randi shrugs. "I don't like it much either."

"It's a very nice shirt." Mirella clasps her hands together. After a moment she says, "I think you mentioned to Howard that the Lawlors had a daughter who couldn't—?"

"Couldn't read," Randi says. "She's nine. Annabelle. Kids used to tease her all the time. They called her Anna Dumbbell."

Although the Lawlors had not had a daughter, poor Annabelle leaps helpfully to life. Thin yellow hair scraped back with a white plastic hairband. Pale face, each temple branching with blue veins. Pink horn-rimmed glasses, exactly like the ones Randi herself had worn until she got contact lenses in ninth grade with baby-sitting money. Scabby stork legs.

"She's doing fine now," Randi goes on. "We did a lot of work using flash cards."

"Really." Mirella presses the heels of both hands against the sink behind her. "Flash cards?"

"Anna Dumb Bell," says Pearl from under the table as Jacob squats down to gaze at her. "Dumb bell, dumb bell," she sings. "Dummy dummy dumb bell."

"That's not a nice thing to be called, is it?" Mirella bends over to peer under the table. Pushing her hair off her forehead, she straightens up to smile again at Randi. "So, flash cards?"

"And word games. I Spy." Randi looks around the kitchen again, picturing herself stirring minestrone soup in the big copper pot hanging from the pot rack over the stove, chopping vegetables on the butcher block, calling Mirella and Howard in to taste the gravy before Thanksgiving dinner. "What do you think?" she'll ask, lifting a spoon. "More salt?" She will wear the striped chef's apron hanging from a brass hook near the back door. "Perfect," they'll say.

"Part of the job," Mirella is saying now, "does involve some light housekeeping. Emptying the dishwasher. Keeping the play areas neat. A cleaning service comes in once a week, but the laundry—"

Mirella is a really pretty name, Randi thinks. Different but not too different. And it makes her think of Marmee, the mother in *Little Women*.

"By the way," she says, "did you know my real name is Miranda?"

"I'm sorry?" says Mirella.

"Randi for short. Kind of close to Mirella, I know. So you can keep calling me Randi."

"Miranda is a beautiful name," Mirella says, after a moment's pause. "Your mother must have liked *The Tempest*."

Randi smiles, then glances at the floor.

When she looks up again, Mirella's eyebrows are gently furrowed. "I hope you'll be happy here, Randi," she says. She folds her hands again in a way that reminds Randi of the old nuns at St. Theresa of the Child Jesus, waiting to clean up after a potluck. "If there's any way I can help you feel at home—"

Miranda St. James her real name should be. Like a governess from a romance novel. Too bad she couldn't have told Howard her name was Miranda St. James at the interview. Hello, I'm Miranda St. James. I understand you require a nanny? Randi Gill has never felt like her real name, any more than living with her mother—and her father, what she could remember of him, and then disgusting Dale, and now disgusting Burton and their disgusting new baby—had ever felt like living in a real family.

Mirella is describing Pearl and Jacob's afternoon routine, which includes a visit to the park and sometimes, maybe once a week, if they are very cooperative, a stop on the way home for ice cream. "Though as a rule, we try not to allow sweets—"

"Excuse me for interrupting again." Randi drops her voice and leans toward Mirella. "But can I ask you something?"

"Yes, of course." Mirella also leans forward. She's wearing a lemony perfume. Randi hopes her breath doesn't smell like peanut-butter crackers, which is what she had on the train for lunch.

"I was wondering." Randi pauses to look at her fingernails. Mirella smiles at her encouragingly. "I've been thinking," Randi says, "you know, if you and Howard want to ask me anything personal? I mean, you read all the Family Options stuff. And—you know about my parents." She sighs. "But really, if you want to know anything about *me*? About who I am? I just wanted to say that it's okay to ask."

She leans back and looks at Mirella. "Thank you, Randi," Mirella says. "I appreciate that."

"I mean, I'm going to be taking care of your kids."

"Yes." Mirella reaches out to touch Jacob's hair as he trudges by, his hands once again jammed down the back of his pants. He continued on with his rocky, preoccupied gait, like a tiny porter on a ship in heavy seas. She clears her throat. "We did all agree—the agency's policy, I believe, is that the first two weeks would be—"

"A tryout."

"Yes." Mirella smiles again. "But you seem like someone who knows what she's doing."

Randi regards Mirella silently for a moment, attending for the first time to the simple gold band on her ring finger, hardly more than a circlet of gold wire. "I'll do my best, Mirella. I really will." Then she crouches down to peer under the table at Pearl, who has been listening all this time with her head pillowed against the dog. "Listen up, you guys," she says. "I think we're going to have fun. I think I'm going to like you guys a lot."

Jacob chooses that moment to wander back across the kitchen floor. He glances up at his mother, then leans against Randi's knees, the tops of his feathers tickling her elbow.

"Dumb bell," says Pearl, to no one in particular.

TONIGHT, RANDI'S FIRST night with the family, Mirella orders take-out Chinese food, which Randi, Mirella, and Howard eat at nine o'clock, after putting the kids to bed. Mirella carries the Chinese food into the dining room on a wooden tray. She tries to light candles, but can't find matches; they use napkins made out of yellow African cloth smudged with soot.

"They've been in the fireplace," Mirella explains. Raising a wine glass of club soda, she says, "Here's to Randi's becoming part of our family. You're a brave girl, Randi."

"Or crazy," says Howard, who has already started helping himself to Szechuan beef.

"Oh, that's helpful." Mirella makes a face. "Don't listen to him," she tells Randi. "He thinks we live like savages."

"Pass the carcass." Howard points a chopstick like a spear at the *kung pao* shrimp.

Passing Howard the black plastic tub of shrimp, Randi tries to smile. She is both disconcerted and enthralled by this conversation, which seems dangerously unpredictable and yet obscurely privileged, as though Howard and Mirella are used to telling each other whatever comes into their heads, no matter how bizarre. She imagines herself joining in, saying something like "Are there any entrails?" and Howard and Mirella gazing at her with appreciation. But then, for just an instant, Randi glances up and sees them looking at each other as if she isn't there. It makes her shiver, that look, the seclusion of it, the quiet shining little room that it makes between them, right there at the table, with the Chinese food and the musty napkins.

"Chicken?" offers Howard.

THE TWO WINDOWS, each set in a gable, are hung with rice paper blinds. At one end of the long room stands a rush-seated rocking chair with a lilac-colored wool shawl thrown over the back. The other end accommodates a cedar chest, which contains, when Randi lifts the lid, two pieced quilts and a small buckram sachet of dried balsam, with a green pine cone stamped on the front. It is a careful room, feminine without being girlish, almost prim. Against one wall sits an antique pine dresser topped by a mirror and a matching pine armoire, and beyond that a four-poster spool bed covered with a white chenille spread. An oval hooked rug, decorated with pink cabbage roses against a pale green background, lies on the floor.

Her old room at home wasn't a quarter this size, just enough space for a single bed and a laminated wood bureau with three sticky drawers; the wallpaper had water stains like the brown outlines of continents. She'd covered the worst spots with pictures from old *Family Circle*s, mothers holding pink babies or making Christmas cookies in big open kitchens, and pictures of gardens with stone benches and gazebos covered with vines, a tall white house in the background with someone opening a door. The upstairs tenant, Mr. Natoli, was always coughing up something. Randi's window had looked out at the garbage cans.

Everyone has an inner landscape, her mother once read out loud from a magazine article while she was waiting for her nails to dry. *It is essential to human happiness to match your inner and outer landscapes. If your inner landscape is a mountainous region, you will be unhappy living in a desert setting and vice versa.* "Well, that's fine," she'd said to Randi, looking up to blow on her nails, "but what if your inner landscape is a mansion on the Riviera and you're living in a dump next to a cornfield and a car repair in Indiana?" Randi had been thinking exactly the same thing, which was a rare enough occurrence that she'd never forgotten this conversation.

Her windows now overlook the Cook-Goldmans' yard; one window looks right into the branches of a budding dogwood tree. Next door, guitar music is playing and the low, strumming notes make her feel keyed up, like someone in a movie about to set off for some beautiful city. Someplace where people don't hang laundry outside and their porches don't sag and their cars don't rust, and the air doesn't stink of manure, and in the distance there's never nothing, stretching on and on, but always something.

It's all like a movie: the music, the green lawn, and the budding tree. Downstairs sit Mirella and Howard talking about their tax returns, so good-looking and smart and in love—she shivers again, remembering that look at the table—but a little pasty; they should stop eating take-out food, which is full of fat and salt. Downstairs sleep the children with their special needs. Jacob's hand rested on her shoulder tonight while she pulled off his socks at bedtime. Sock, she'd said. Can you say sock? And Pearl's mouth working when she couldn't manage all her buttons herself. Hey, Randi whispered to the children as they stood in the yellow lamplight. Hey, I know Rapunzel. I know Sleeping Beauty. I was Snow White in third grade. And they stared back at her with their big dark eyes.

Tonight, in her new room, in her new home, with her whole new life about to start up, she takes a deep breath and puts her hands over her face.

Then slowly she pulls her hands away and looks around the room once more, almost surprised to find it all still there, the rocking chair, the blanket chest, the bright cabbage roses on the green hooked rug.

5

"OF COURSE WE NEED to bring the children," Mirella told Howard on Wednesday evening. "I always spend Saturday with them. And this is only Randi's first week."

"They'll be fine," Howard said. "We'll leave Saturday morning and be back that night. Or we could stay over at Richard's after the bas mitzvah and leave first thing Sunday."

"I have to work this Sunday," said Mirella.

"Whatever you decide is okay with me," said Randi, who was chopping tomatoes on the butcher-block work island during this conversation. "It might be nice for you guys to have some time alone together." And she smiled at them in the Quakerish way she had adopted whenever she referred to their couplehood, arch and innocent.

"Bet you haven't had that in a while," she added.

"Well, no—" Mirella began.

"They'll be bored," Howard insisted. "And you know Richard, he wants everything to be perfect. What if one of them starts fussing?"

"It's so far away," said Mirella.

"Three hours," said Howard.

Mirella stood in the kitchen, fingering the collar of her blouse and watching Randi chop tomatoes. The knife flashed up and down, *tok, tok*. Randi was making something she called tomato-and-egg pie. The lemon chicken she'd made the night before had been a success, except for the peas she'd served on the side, which unaccountably she had tossed with vinegar. But it had been such a welcome sight, the dinner table set, candles lit, each dish of food separately radiant.

"Mirella," Howard said, "what's the big deal?"

She realized that he had scheduled this conversation to take place in front of Randi. He wanted to go without the children and Randi, steadfastly chopping, wearing a striped apron that Mirella had bought once as a joke for Howard, was inarguably there to look after them.

"I don't know." Mirella twisted her watchband. "We'd planned to take them."

"It would be so much easier not to," said Howard.

Jacob sat on the kitchen floor, driving a wooden mail truck through a scatter of blocks, one or two balanced on top of each other. Block building was something he'd just begun to do, after Howard and Mirella had for months tried to coax him with tunnels, bridges, castles. *Blocks are an essential tool in the development of fine-motor skills and logical reasoning,* said a magazine article Mirella had read. *Help your child by using blocks in constructive play.* But it was Randi who got him interested. She gave him a peanut M&M for each block he stacked on top of another.

Now and then Jacob looked up, but whenever Mirella caught his eye, he looked away. Upstairs Pearl was singing to the dog. "I love you, you love me," she sang, right on key.

"We won't stay overnight," Mirella decided at last. "We'll leave right after the ceremony."

"No we won't," sighed Howard.

"Really," Randi said, laying down her knife, "I know it's hard to leave them, but trust me, Mirella, they'll be fine."

A MOURNFUL-LOOKING PIANIST was playing ragtime in one corner of Temple Beth El's social hall, near the linen-draped buffet. Seventh-grade boys wearing jackets and ties, blue jeans and yarmulkes, plunged through the crowd, their mouths flashing with braces, ignoring huddles of seventh-grade girls in skimpy rayon dresses and thick-soled black shoes. In the center of the room, on a large round table swathed in blue drapery, billowed an enormous bouquet of yellow roses. Waiters were wading here and there in white jackets and black pants, carrying platters of hors d'oeuvres. On the buffet one could choose from salmon medallions, roast beef au jus, potatoes Delmonico or potatoes lyonnaise. Salad was to be served first, by waiters, as was the soup and the dessert. Floating island, Vivvy had said.

On the far wall, behind the buffet, hung a life-sized photograph of pouty Danielle Goldman, which, by some computer wizardry, had been insinuated into an enlarged photograph of a popular young movie star. The movie star was passionately embracing Danielle, who had her hair in her face and seemed to be sulking over something, Mirella thought, her math homework perhaps. At each of the twenty tables bobbed a cluster of blue balloons tied to a small replica of the *Titanic,* which foundered amid a centerpiece of plastic icebergs the size of teakettles.

The room felt very warm. Howard followed close enough behind that Mirella could feel his breath against her neck. As they passed by a mirrored panel, she could see that he was frowning in the fixed, ironic way peculiar to him; anyone who did not know him well might have imagined he was smiling.

On the drive to Greenwich that morning Howard and Mirella had argued in the car over whether Howard should buy a new

computer that could handle the latest architectural design software that was coming out—Howard said he didn't want a new
computer; he didn't work that way; Mirella said don't be a Lud-
dite, she was talking about a technology upgrade, not a spiritual
compromise, he hadn't wanted e-mail either, she reminded him,
and now look how much he used it—which slid into an argument
over whether or not Mirella minded that she made more money
than Howard did, an issue he raised because she mentioned their
federal tax refund was less than they'd planned on and then had
asked when was he getting paid for that kitchen. It all ended in an
argument over whether Howard was driving too close to a beige
Suburban in front of them, which led to Mirella's accusation that
lately he'd seemed unapproachable.

"You're so locked up," she said, standing on Temple Beth El's
white limestone steps, wincing at the unexpected shrillness in her
voice.

That was when Howard had turned to look at her, his hands in
the pockets of his gray flannel suit, and with a sudden throb of
dread, Mirella realized he meant right then to tell her something
important. Right in front of Temple Beth El, Howard was gathering himself for a revelation. Which must have been his reason
for wanting to leave the children at home.

She wished now that they'd turned around and gotten back in
the car, driven a few blocks, and looked for a quiet place to have
lunch before the service. It was true, as Randi said, they rarely
spent time alone anymore. In the anonymous afternoon clatter of
the restaurant, Howard could have told her what he wanted to
say—speaking curtly at first, as he always did when he was nervous, fidgeting with his silverware. Then she would try, as she always did, to solve whatever problem he presented to her, which
was not the same thing as listening to the problem.

Yet after all, there was really very little he could reveal about
himself that she hadn't already guessed at, worried about, made

peace with, even come secretly to value. They had been married almost thirteen years. Over glasses of red wine, because maybe she could allow herself just one, they would gaze at each other across the table. Howard's forehead would glisten. She would reach out and with her napkin pat where his black hair was thinning. As their meals arrived, fragrant and hot on white china, they would sit back and smile wryly, reflecting that soon enough it would be time to drive home, to the seductions and distractions of the children. But for the moment they had only each other; it was just the two of them. "I love you," she would say. "I have some news."

Mirella saw the scene so clearly she almost believed it had happened.

BY THE BOUQUET of yellow roses, Richard introduced Howard and Mirella to a couple of lawyers from his firm who were talking baseball. Affably the lawyers nodded moist faces, raising their glasses of beer. "She's a big shot," Richard told them, wagging his thumb at Mirella. "In the paper all the time. Had lunch with the first lady last year."

"Along with two hundred other people," Mirella said.

"Fifty," said Howard.

"Bosom buddies," Richard insisted to the lawyers. "Next she'll meet the president and start poking in affairs of state. Hah. Bosom buddy of the president. Poking in affairs of state."

"Richard." Mirella watched Howard gaze out over the crowd.

"Seriously," said Richard. "What's a smart woman like her doing with a schmuck like him?"

"Is this supposed to be political analysis?" said Mirella, annoyed that she was allowing herself to be provoked, especially by Richard, with whom she'd had this conversation twice in the past year already.

"Ha, ha," said the younger of the two lawyers.

Richard was wearing a tuxedo. He had put on weight since they'd seen him last in January; his neck folded pinkly over his white shirt collar. He was flushed and distracted, his eyes as luminous as a young girl's. All four men were wearing silken white yarmulkes held in place with bobby pins. Richard had provided both yarmulkes and bobby pins in two silver-plated bowls by the front entrance before the service. Only Howard's yarmulke seemed to sit naturally.

But then, whatever Howard undertook was done with a certain grace, Mirella decided, ignoring Richard, who had begun telling a joke about the similarities between the president's golf game and his appreciation of women. Even the way Howard pointed his toes to pull on his socks in the morning was graceful, or cradled a cup of coffee, or slept with an arm arced over his head. She loved to watch him draw. She'd fallen in love with him the first time she watched him take a sheet of paper and, in a few swift confident gestures, create a house out of nothing. His dexterity seemed deeply subtle to her, and the rigid standards he set for himself were something she always applauded, too enthusiastically perhaps. Long ago she'd realized that Howard's artistic principles were paired with an odd ineffectuality, a hesitation that seemed rooted in sorrow and loss, and had produced in him a kind of stillness.

Once, soon after they were married, they were walking on Newbury Street after buying bagels for breakfast, looking at the magnolias in bloom. Mirella had just finished fingering a magnolia petal, mentioning that it had the texture of human skin, when Howard began talking about the morning his mother died. His voice had been monotonous as he described the green curtains drawn around her hospital bed; a television laugh track roaring in the next room; the closed, aquatic feeling of the air. He was ten years old. His mother had not looked at him, but held his hand, forgetting or unable to let go, while his father and Richard stood weeping at the end of the bed. Against the white of her pillows, her face had been the color of clay, her nose sharp and pointed at the ceiling. Minutes ticked by, fraught, untenable, weirdly boring. Until finally, Howard had pulled his hand away.

"Do you understand what I did?" he said, confronting Mirella on that scented morning. "She was holding on to me."

"I understand what you did," she'd said gently, and tried to put her arms around him. But he marched off down the damp sidewalk, clutching the bag of bagels, and they'd never spoken at length about his mother's death again. He had been, Mirella gathered, her favorite.

His father died the year Mirella met Howard. From their single encounter, lunch at an Albany steak house, she had a recollection of a cigar, a dark face, a white short-sleeved shirt with buttons straining at the stomach. According to Howard, his father had preferred Richard. Richard played baseball; Richard was newspaper delivery boy of the year; Richard ate everything on his plate. Richard did not draw pencil sketches of the Chrysler building and Chartres on the kitchen baseboards, nor did Richard spend weeks shut up in his room, gluing strips of cardboard into a model of the Bank of England, then burning the imperfect results. Brute competence emanated from Richard's bluish jaws, along with the musky burlap smell of his aftershave. Which was, perhaps, simply the route sorrow had taken for him.

"Howard," Richard was saying now. "Howard. Hey, Howard. Listen, come over here, I've got some other people for you to meet. See that guy—"

"What guy?" said Howard uneasily.

"That fat guy in pinstripes. See him? He just bought three acres in Martha's Vineyard to build a summer place and I said, listen, I got this brother, a prize-winning architect—"

Howard sighed and glanced apologetically at the two lawyers. But he depended on Richard to be both a philistine and his champion. And Richard, Mirella thought, watching him grip Howard's shoulder, which made Howard spill the glass of champagne he'd just accepted from a waiter—for all his genuine brotherly affection and goodwill, for all his pride in Howard's graduate school prizes, Richard had always, in her opinion, required Howard to be something of a mess.

He's very green, her own father had said of Howard, after they first met. And once she got over her fear that he was somehow commenting on Howard's being Jewish, she understood that her father was trying to be insightful and was, in fact, succeeding. Green, her father said. He makes me think of green.

And there was a freshness about Howard, a sense of pliancy, even susceptibility. Howard believed himself to be cynical, but Mirella recognized his cynicism as another kind of youthfulness, a young person's pretense at accepting fate. When really there was nothing he loved so much as rearranging the future, imagining himself living in a log house in Oregon or in an adobe house in Arizona, always someplace rustic—a restlessness that she had never found threatening because it was paired with his almost obsessive devotion to their own house. In fact, Howard's yearning was one of the things she most loved about him. It struck her as poetic, essential, part of his maleness, this longing to be somewhere else. Only sometimes lately it seemed a little tiring. Where they were now, after all, seemed challenging enough.

It was very hot. A swell of nausea rocked through her, making her hands tremble. For a few minutes she continued to stand with the lawyers, who began asking her politely about Massachusetts's community property laws, while Richard made off with Howard, tugging him by the sleeve. Then she excused herself and staggered into the crowd to look for a rest room.

The drooping pianist launched into "Camptown Races." Mirella had just reached the rest room door when as a dark-haired boy jostled past her, then paused to apologize, giving her a surprisingly adult wink, and suddenly—in the nimble, veering way her moods could shift at a party—she decided that she must have imagined the moment on the temple steps, that Howard had not looked dark and agonized, that Richard was not going to patronize him, that her stomach had settled and it might be possible after all to enjoy the balloons, the roast beef, the plastic icebergs of Danielle's bas mitzvah. An elderly black man walked by wearing a red fez instead of a yarmulke. From their corner of the room, the yellow roses gave off a fresh and gracious scent, reminding Mirella of summer afternoons on a wide lawn.

When she emerged again from the rest room, she discovered Howard's sister-in-law, Vivvy, standing near the piano in a tourquoise batik dress, patting at her long, untidy ponytail of gray hair. Feeling cooler now, Mirella went over to kiss her cheek and say congratulations.

Vivvy did not immediately respond; a few years ago she had gone deaf in one ear and Mirella was on the wrong side of her. "Oh," she said, looking around in consternation. "I thought you were Danielle."

Danielle was the youngest of Richard and Vivvy's three daughters. The other two, Hannah and Eden, were in college, both dean's list, according to Richard.

"She did a great job," Mirella said. "It was a lovely service."

Vivvy peered at her. "You thought so? I was afraid it was a bit long."

Mirella began to repeat that the service was lovely, though it actually had been overly long—Danielle stumbled through her readings with peevish terror, hands fisted on the lectern—when they were interrupted by Danielle's flute teacher bobbing up in a damp-looking red kimono, her blond hair in a top knot pierced by a lacquered stick. "The darling," cried the flute teacher. Mirella took a step back to watch Vivvy dispatch the flute teacher, who had begun insisting that Danielle was a born performer. "Really?"

said Vivvy, sounding more English than usual, which was her habit when she wanted to be discouraging without being rude. "A natural," repeated the flute teacher, her high voice trembling.

"Ah, to be natural," murmured Vivvy, smiling at Mirella.

"So tell me, how are you?" Vivvy demanded when the flute teacher had floundered back into the crowd. She pinched Mirella's arm, and Mirella felt obliged, as she always did with Vivvy, to admit to something, and so she said she'd had a recent bout of flu.

"But it was over quickly."

"No vomiting?" asked Vivvy professionally. She had attended medical school before marrying Richard.

"Just a little queasiness."

"You look pale. Maybe you're still sick." Vivvy pretended to knock her knuckles against Mirella's midriff. "Anybody in there?"

"Oh please," laughed Mirella, shrinking backward.

"So where are the kiddies? Did you leave them with your mother?"

"They're with the nanny," admitted Mirella.

"I thought she vanished."

"Another one."

"Mary Poppins?" inquired Vivvy, once again summoning the clipped vowels of Epping Green, which she had left at seven and therefore must hardly remember. Yet she persisted in calling vacations "holidays," and referring to "fortnights," and asking Mirella if she wanted a coffee. Sometimes Howard and Mirella imitated her, crying "Wot?" at each other and declaring everything to be "brilliant." Still, Mirella reflected, of everyone in the family, Vivvy was the most sober in her way, her affectations being obvious, and never interfering with her astute assessment of her own situation, which was that Richard had the soul of a good-humored fishmonger, she had abandoned girlhood ambitions of doctoring coal miners to live amid tennis courts and security systems, and her beloved daughters were embarrassed by her gray ponytail, her refusal to get a nose job, and her tendency to bray into the telephone.

Mirella glanced over to where Howard was now talking with Richard and the man in pinstripes. At that instant Howard laughed, his lean face creasing in a way that made him look handsome and distant. "They're all Mary Poppins in the beginning," she said, turning back to face Vivvy. "Aren't they?"

Behind her, she could hear other people laughing as someone finished telling a story. The room had gotten stuffy again. An elderly lady sailed past in a black beaded dress, smiling furiously, rhinestones blazing across the prow of her chest, a petroleum-smelling perfume trailing in her wake.

"Ah, my charming mother," observed Vivvy. "Queen of the May."

Mirella laughed, trying to imagine herself thirty years from now, hoping that she might be similarly awful and glittering and that Pearl would say the same thing about her.

Because the attachment between Vivvy and her mother, though often storming, was one that Mirella had always admired. There was nothing mother and daughter did not perceive about each other or forbear to comment on. They were connoisseurs of each other's frailties, and their most censorious remarks struck any listener as equally tender and even somehow reverent. Their attachment privately shamed Mirella whenever she compared it to her relationship with her own mother, who demanded little besides small talk during their monthly lunch dates, but expected a stream of sentimental gestures—flowers on anniversaries, thank-you notes, holiday invitations to tea. If Mirella forgot one of these occasions, her mother's expression would be strenuously wistful the next time they saw each other; she would pick at her salad, sigh heavily, refuse to admit that anything was wrong, until Mirella deciphered what had happened and apologized.

For a moment she pictured her parents' narrow brick house on Mount Vernon Street, her mother's shade garden with its curving path of crushed shells, her father folded like a bat in his wheelchair.

"Can you believe this *Titanic* business?" Vivvy rolled her eyes. "That Danielle," she said, trying to sound disapproving. "She may not be a natural but she's certainly a force of nature."

"Danielle's a lovely girl," said Mirella.

"And how's Jacob doing?" Vivvy said, after a minute. "Everything all right with him?"

"He's fine," said Mirella.

"Talking yet?"

"He's getting there."

"Brilliant." Then Vivvy repeated what everyone repeated to Mirella and Howard, about Einstein not speaking until he was five.

The laughter behind them grew louder. People were beginning to find their place cards, preparing to sit down. Mirella shrugged, feeling hot again and disquieted the way she always felt whenever people began asking about Jacob. Inevitably their questions struck her as pointed, as if they had information about him that she did not. How's Jacob doing? the mothers at Pearl's school were forever murmuring, faces poised for sympathy. Why are you so interested? she always wanted to answer, and always stopped herself.

Jacob's face suddenly appeared before her, small, strained, his birthmark standing out like a tiny stop sign. She wiped her forehead with the back of her hand. Vivvy meant well, of course.

Vivvy was talking now about the caterer, about the floating island, which might not survive the heat. Perhaps, Mirella thought, she could slip outside for a breath of air, sit for a minute in the car. She would like to use her cell phone to call home, make sure Jacob was taking his nap and that Randi knew Pearl needed a bath tonight. Maybe Howard would come with her. But when Mirella glanced around again to find Howard, he was gone, swallowed up by the crowd as if he'd never been there at all.

6

"Vivvy was asking about Jacob," Howard heard Mirella say on the drive home. Warm, pinkish twilight seemed to sift into the car between them. They had stayed later than they'd intended and now Howard was driving fast.

Leaning toward him, Mirella made her voice flutey and confidential. "Is he talking yet?"

"What?" He hadn't meant to sound irritable, but he had been thinking about Richard's performance of the *Titanic* theme song for Danielle, the way he'd lounged on the piano, making torchy motions with the microphone, his tuxedo pant leg riding up to expose his black sock and a band of hairy white flesh. "What did she say?" he amended.

Mirella sat back and looked at him reproachfully. "She told me about Einstein."

"She's just trying to be encouraging."

"I thought we'd agreed not to talk to other people about Jacob. What have you been telling them?"

"Nothing. I may have mentioned to Richard a few weeks ago that we were having some testing done, that's all."

"Testing. You don't need to mention any testing."

"Look, I didn't say anything."

Mirella bit her lip, then sighed. "She also grilled me about Randi. She asked if she was Mary Poppins."

Howard glanced over at Mirella's flushed face. They had left Greenwich several miles back and were passing through a ruinous-looking neighborhood of chain-link fences and small, closed businesses. At a traffic light, they stopped beside an Electrolux vacuum supply storefront, which displayed gray coils of tubing looped beside an industrial-sized vacuum cleaner. Mirella turned and stared out the window.

A moment later she said, "So here we are. Three hours in the car together. What should we talk about?" Then, as she often did, she answered for him. "I apologize for calling you unapproachable this afternoon."

"It's all right."

"So where did you go before lunch? One minute you're right behind me, then you're gone. I looked for you everywhere."

"I was trying to talk to Richard."

She toyed with the catch on her gold charm bracelet. He realized that she was waiting for him to say something else, but he was thinking about Richard again, how puffed up he'd looked in that tuxedo, hurrying here and there embracing people, his yarmulke slipping sideways. Howard had hardly had a chance to speak to him, though he'd followed Richard around, while pretending not to, a grin stuck to his face. He wanted to mention Nadine's phone call, to ask Richard's advice in case she called again. He felt he needed to tell someone, and he'd confided in Richard when the affair was actually in progress. Richard called him a blockhead, told him Mirella was worth ten of him, accused him of irresponsibility, but in the end had seemed to understand. "Sometimes things have to happen," Richard said on the phone, "to make people realize how stupid they are. In your case, Howard, I'd say you got off easy."

Howard had finally managed to draw Richard into a corner behind the buffet, when Danielle came trotting up, eyes filled with tears; the strap on her dress had broken. "Oy vey," cried Richard, rolling his eyes, raising his hands in a hokey imitation of an old Jewish man. "Daddy," said Danielle in disgust. But Richard capered about beseechingly, lost in his own burlesque. "Now there's a good father," Howard overheard a woman say. Howard wandered off to sit down next to Mirella, who was talking about equitable distribution laws to a bristle-haired judge named Fiona. For most of lunch, everyone at the table was talking but him.

"Well, I guess that's taken care of," said Mirella. "On to the next subject."

Howard cleared his throat. "So what do you think of Randi?"

"So far she seems great."

"She's lasted a week. Practically a record for us."

Mirella laughed. As the light changed, she said offhandedly, "Do you like her?"

"She's very—I don't know what she is." He thought for a moment. "Domestic."

"The children really seem to like her." Mirella was staring out the window again at a black dog running along a sidewalk. "All that cooking. What a relief to come home and find the kitchen floor clean and the dishwasher empty. The kids' laundry done, everything folded. Did you notice how she got all those puzzle pieces back in the right boxes? She even found some of the lost ones."

Mirella found a dangling thread on her sleeve. She pulled the thread out and snapped it. "Poor thing. What she's been through—"

"Unbelievable."

"She's trying flash cards on Jacob."

"Flash cards," murmured Howard.

"Well, it's one more thing to try," said Mirella. And for some minutes neither of them spoke.

JACOB HAD BEEN to see several child specialists since he turned two, but the diagnosis remained inconclusive: significant speech delay, impaired reciprocal interaction, possible developmental disorder. On Wednesday afternoons an occupational therapist instructed Jacob on how to hold a pencil, hammer pegs, jump on one foot. On Thursday afternoons he visited a child psychologist, who wanted Jacob evaluated by a psychopharmacologist to see if he might be a candidate for Prozac. "Perhaps his serotonin levels are depressed," Dr. Michaels had said last week, and then, for the first time, he mentioned elective mutism.

"Elective mutism?" echoed Mirella.

"You think he's doing this on purpose?" Howard demanded, surprised by his sudden fury.

Dr. Michaels held up both palms. He was younger than Howard by at least five years, his oval face smooth-shaven above his blue Oxford shirt, unbuttoned at the neck. On his desk was a framed photograph of a laughing little red-haired girl about Jacob's age. "Not on purpose. It's an adaptive response."

"To what?" said Howard. Beside him on Dr. Michael's white sofa, Mirella touched his arm.

Dr. Michaels continued on, speaking of "internal pressures" and "environmental stress," concluding that it was too early to tell anything for sure. "Some kids," he said, as they all stood up, their hour over, "just need more time."

Jacob had been such an easy baby, so much easier than Pearl, fat and peaceful, sleeping through the night at six weeks. When he was awake he smiled an obliging, untroubled smile at everyone. Mr. Nirvana, Howard had called him then. Mr. Zen. Even now he looked utterly peaceful whenever he was allowed to sit on the floor by himself in his Indian headdress, lining up his wooden trucks, which lately occurred less and less often. Mirella stayed home with him on Tuesday mornings and every other Friday afternoon, playing classical music and trying to get him to make faces or paint pictures or touch pieces of ribbon, wool, leather. She read child-development books at night before she went to bed, poring over chapters with titles like "Ten Signs of the Securely Attached Child" and "The Emotional Life of Babies." Howard read these books, too, but found the writing ponderous and also, in the coded impersonal way of popular psychology, accusatory.

Still, he was willing to try the suggestions Mirella underlined. He and Jacob stacked blocks together, Howard doing most of the stacking. Every Thursday morning and on the weekends, he took Jacob to the park and practiced rolling him a ball, to improve his hand-eye coordination and gross motor skills. Although they had begun going grocery shopping on Thursdays instead, an activity they both enjoyed. In some ways it was their most intimate time together, trundling through the store's fluorescent-lit aisles, listening to piped-in music that always seemed to be "The Octopus's Garden," Howard choosing cereals and canned soups, Jacob perched in the cart, swinging his legs. Often they shared a muffin from the bakery section, trading it back and forth, then paying for a bag of crumbs.

The truth was, Howard had detected in Jacob actual panic whenever they attempted any of Mirella's child-development techniques. The ball rolling, for instance. Jacob would stand in the park, arms limp at his sides, watching Howard roll the ball to him. A kind of rigid attention would seize him as the ball came closer, as if the ball were much larger, enormous, something he could not possibly escape. Then the ball would bounce against his feet. Jacob would look down at it in surprise. Eventually Howard would retrieve the ball, talk about trying again, and the process would be repeated until they were both exhausted.

"It's all right, buddy," he heard himself saying, again and again.

Mirella claimed that Jacob enjoyed his sessions with her. He was making a lot of progress, she said. Recently they had been punching holes in clay with a straw.

"Something is wrong with him," Howard had said in the car after their consultation with Dr. Michaels. His throat was sore and he coughed several times; when he could speak again, his voice sounded scratchy and truculent. "Why are you pretending there isn't?"

"I am not pretending," she'd answered, motionless in her seat.

"You're scaring him by pushing him to do things he can't."

"We don't know what he can do. We have to help him find out."

"I'm just asking you to be realistic. He's probably never going to be a normal child."

Mirella had given him a fierce look. "He's two years old."

"He's almost three."

"No one ever knows what's going to happen to anybody," she'd said, wrapping her arms around herself. "The human brain is not a carburetor. Doctors can say what they want."

THEY WERE ON the highway now. Twilight had given way to true evening, always Howard's favorite time of day, when the last light turned blue just before it drained away. Headlights streamed past on the other side of the road, and he felt a familiar longing to be going somewhere, to a party up in the mountains or on the coast, a big gracious house lit up, music playing, cars parked on the lawn, couples silhouetted in the windows and doorways. Women with tanned, bare shoulders; men in loose-fitting shirts holding golden drinks. He had attended a few parties like this himself, mostly in college, although at the time they had seemed crowded and disorienting and he'd looked forward to leaving. And yet as he recalled them now, he saw these occasions as hallowed, full of young, striking, witty people, all of whom he might have known intimately, had he made the effort, but who had now disappeared into their exciting, far-flung lives without him.

Mirella was trying again to call on her cell phone, but the battery needed recharging. When they'd reached Randi earlier, she said the children were fine, they'd had a picnic in the yard, Pearl accidentally swallowed a gnat and was wondering if it was still alive in her stomach. Randi had told her about stomach acids.

"Do you think they've been having a good time?" Mirella said, tapping the little phone before putting it back in her purse.

"I'm sure they have."

"Of course Randi knows to stay in the bathroom with them during their bath."

"Why are you worrying?" said Howard.

"I'm sure she does," said Mirella, folding her hands.

A sudden tenderness came over him as he glanced at her, glimmering in her pale dress, dark hair falling around her face. She was such a determined person, despite her worries, or perhaps because of them. A kind of modern Valkyrie. Every morning she woke up, stretched her muscles, took a deep breath and decided that all of them would remain unharmed for another day. It was her responsibility, her job, to deny that disaster could happen to her family. How else could she manage? Into each brief day she bundled all her phone calls, her anxious clients, memos, court appearances, eighteen homemade valentines demanded by Pearl's preschool, play-date logistics, Jacob's appointments, the dry cleaning, something for dinner. And that long drive back and forth from Boston, which was his fault, though she hardly complained, which made it worse. He helped out; he did his share, more than most men, probably. Still, it was Mirella who packed everything in somehow, Mirella who kept them marching out the door.

And if it sometimes depressed him to be part of these uncompromising arrangements, he loved her for being so vigorous. Just as he loved the clear, aquiline planes of her face, which was beautiful to him still, with its lines and faint, moth-colored age spots, perhaps even more beautiful than when she was younger and her physical presence seemed both less defined and more distracting. Just as he loved the calm good nature with which she poured coffee for them both each morning, smiling gallantly over the children's crying, the dog's barking, Cheerios spilled on the floor. Though lately he sometimes wondered whether, beneath all her reassuring fortitude, she suspected that disaster could be small and dull and corrosive, and that it might already have come.

"FLASH CARDS," HE REPEATED on the Massachusetts Turnpike.

"At least she's energetic with them," Mirella roused herself to say; she had been lying back in her seat. "Which is more than I can say for myself these days. I could hardly get out of bed this morning."

Abruptly she fell silent. And always alert to her silences, he sensed something new unfurling between them in the car, some urgent opportunity, reserved until this minute, signaling like a white flag waving in the breeze. It was dark now, but he could feel Mirella watching him. So he was not surprised when a few moments later she said, "Howard?" in the bright, uncertain tone she reserved for beginning discussions in which they were destined to reach disagreement.

"I know we've talked about this before." She shifted in her seat to face him. "But I was thinking maybe we could—if you wouldn't mind—we could try again to talk about—"

"What?" he said briskly, hoping to forestall rather than

encourage whatever was coming next. He'd already guessed that sooner rather than later during this conversation he would be forced to defend himself.

But Mirella, once launched, was hard to deflect. "I suppose," she said. "I've been thinking about what it would be like if we had another baby."

"What it would be like?"

"Don't say it that way. I'm just asking you to consider how it might actually be, you know, if it happened."

He pretended to consider. "Catastrophic."

"Stop. I'm being serious."

He didn't say "So am I," because that was what she expected him to say. By now he understood that she had been preparing an argument for some time and that his only hope of winning it was to step over the lines she'd lain down for him. So he said, "All right. I'm sorry."

She paused and looked at him. "Go ahead," he said, to cement his brief advantage.

"Well," she said slowly, "I can't seem to stop thinking about it. Almost like it's haunting me. Another baby. Maybe because it's now or never. A last chance sort of thing."

He shifted his grip on the steering wheel, concentrating on the broken white lines in front of him. A truck roared past, making their car shudder.

"I know you've said you don't want more children," she went on. "But I've always imagined having a big family. You know, a car full of kids. Big table at Thanksgiving. It's just something I've always pictured." Her voice trailed off.

In spite of himself, he nodded. A big family was what Mirella had always pictured, probably because she came from such a small one—father always traveling, the mother going with him, Mirella home with a housekeeper. Just for a moment he stepped into her picture himself and was surrounded by a fluster of voices right before dinner, children running up and down the stairs, dogs barking, a grandparent dozing in a rocking chair, while music played from different radios in different rooms, shoes scattered everywhere, and coats of all sizes fell off the coat tree.

Carefully he shut off the radios, the voices. He knew there was something about Mirella and her desire for a large family that had nothing to do with this picture—a small, tenacious, unevolved part of her that two hundred years ago would have had her loading up a Conestoga and striking out for new territory, simply because she had enough energy to ignore all the reasons not to go.

Howard passed a truck hauling a tubular steel tank, which he first imagined must be for oil or a liquid chemical but then turned out to be carrying milk. Dairy-Glo. A cow with a flower behind one ear smiled down at him. It was both admirable and chilling, he thought, returning to his original calculations, this tendency of Mirella's to believe that doing a dangerous, demanding thing was somehow the more prudent choice. She was not the type to dwell on consequences or to fantasize about different futures than the one immediately facing her. And so it had surprised him, the last time they'd discussed having another child, when she said, "If something happened to one of them, there'd be only one left."

"You're not saying anything," said Mirella, sounding miserable.

"I'm thinking," he said.

Respectfully, hopefully, she stayed quiet.

He did not want more children. To be honest, he'd never wanted children in the first place, but he'd seen this as a coldness in himself, something deplorable, an infirmity, and was actually relieved when Mirella got pregnant. Parenthood, not amazingly, had proved difficult for him—though he loved them, he often found Pearl and Jacob overwhelming. Pearl, especially, always seemed to be crying. As soon as Jacob was born, she'd turned fractious, no longer willing to go on morning walks, screaming that she wanted Mommy, accusing Howard of choosing the wrong pants or socks whenever he dressed her. But then she was forever demanding to sit in his lap when he was trying to eat breakfast, dragging on his arm, demanding another banana, another story, one more bite of his toast; she fretted about the weather, had tantrums over broken crayons, misplaced shoes, the tangles in her hair. Hardest for him was the way she *infiltrated:* pressing her face into his, pushing her fingers down his shirt collar. Until past all patience, he heard himself bellowing, felt blood surge in his ears. "Don't be mad at me," she would shriek. More tears.

And Jacob. Howard sighed. With Jacob, something wholly unexpected was being required of him, an act, a feat, the mechanics of which he did not understand and therefore was afraid he could not perform. But that wasn't true either. Jacob by himself was one of the few people Howard could spend hours with and not feel suffocated. It was just that he wasn't prepared for the scenarios he found himself running in his head, of what might happen to Jacob, of what could become of him. Sometimes Howard lay in bed and imagined Jacob leaping through the house in a Superman cape, cheeks pink, socks falling down, shouting in a sandpapery little voice as he hurtled off the back of the sofa. And although he was not attracted to that sturdy, predictable little boy, he knew it was who Jacob should have been, what he should have hoped for.

A fast-food restaurant and a Mobil station rose up ahead of them. Howard had considered stopping for a Coke when he saw the sign for food and gas a mile back, but now he pressed the accelerator and the exit fled past in a blur of colored lights.

"So what are you thinking?" Mirella said at last. "Are you thinking about it?"

Her questions seemed to dangle from the rearview mirror, knocking together like a pair of felt dice. "I was just thinking," he said, "how a picture of a life is not the same thing as a life."

After a moment she said, "Of course it isn't."

"We can't do it," he said. "We're too old. Our lives are too crazy. Especially yours is."

"I'm just busy."

"You're not just busy. You can hardly find time to make a grocery list." His chest began to tighten. "When's the last time we went for a walk? When's the last time we spent more than fifteen minutes eating dinner?"

She said soothingly: "You're absolutely right, we do need more time for each other." And he knew he had lost ground, that she was interpreting his resistance as simply wounded male ego, the husband vying with the children for his wife's attention.

"That's not it," he said, unconvincingly.

For a few minutes they drove on, each planning what to say next.

Then Mirella sighed and said, "Howard. I just have to tell you, for whatever reason, it's something I really want." A moment later she added, "It might be good for all of us, you know, in some ways. Another one."

A last chance sort of thing.

"Mirella," he said, trying to be kind. Because he understood suddenly what she really wanted: another chance, another shot at getting it right—so that if something happened to one of them, there wasn't the chance that she'd be left with only Jacob—though he was almost positive that she herself did not understand what she wanted. For a moment he was horrified. Then as he listened to her breathing unevenly beside him, the sharpness of what he had realized wore away, and he felt only tired and sorry.

After a while he reached over and took her hand. She turned her face toward the window. For a long time they drove without saying anything.

"HERE WE ARE," he said, pulling into the driveway. The car's headlights swept across the side of the house, briefly illuminating a cluster of budding peonies, huddled like a crowd of miniature onlookers. The light over the front door was on, and the first, second, and third floors were all lit. The house looked awake and somehow alarmed, light blazing from every window.

Mirella got out of the car and began walking ahead of him up the drive, gravel crunching under her heels.

Inside, the house was silent, only the bubbling of the aquarium in the kitchen traveling down the hallway to greet them. They stood for a moment listening by the bottom of the stairs, as if they had intruded rather than returned.

"Hello?" called Mirella. "We're back."

There was no answer. Mirella looked at him. Then they heard it, a faint squeaking or sniffling from somewhere overhead. He searched for several seconds before identifying the sound of stifled laughter.

Together they climbed the stairs to the little landing before the doorway to Randi's attic. Mirella had that wide-eyed expectant expression she always wore when she was about to see the children, but Howard was conscious of a rising irritation, a feeling of being thwarted in some small but essential way. The door was closed. Hesitantly, Mirella pushed it open.

And there they found them, both children sitting in Randi's lap in their flannel pajamas, as she held open the oversized *Golden Book of Fairy Tales*. Their heads were tucked under her chin, their eyes shiny with delight at their trick, their moment of triumph, believing they had frightened their parents all the way up the stairs. Martha lay at their feet, amiably sweeping her tail.

"We fooled you," cried Pearl.

Lamplight glowed softly around them like firelight, gilding the tops of their three heads.

"Hi Mom and Dad," Randi said shyly. "Welcome home."

7

ANOTHER MILD, MISTY MORNING, green and humid. It is Randi's second Monday with the Cook-Goldmans. Dogwood blossoms are falling, littering the grass below with yellowed petals, like shreds of soiled tissues. A robin's nest, overtaken by starlings, is just visible in a cleft of uppermost branches. Across the street, in front of a big gray colonial, an Indian man drags a red recycling tub down his driveway.

From her window, Randi sees the Cook-Goldmans' garbage cans lined up on the curb and wonders if taking out the garbage is part of light housekeeping. But the thought of saying "garbage" to Mirella while Mirella stands there smiling in her pearl earrings and blue silk suit—maybe she could ask Howard. Or maybe she should wait for someone to say something about the garbage.

She loiters inside the door in her pink nylon bathrobe, scratching a spider bite on her arm, listening to make sure everyone is downstairs before she ventures out to the bathroom. Earlier she heard Pearl saying that she didn't want to sit on the toilet and Howard's murmuring voice.

Cautiously she opens her door and steps onto the landing.

Down in the kitchen, Jacob shouts something that sounds like "hat" and Mirella is asking Howard if he wants an English muffin. The growl of the coffee grinder starts up, and when it's done Howard offers Pearl a choice of Life or Chex. Haah, shouts Jacob. Pearl asks if she has to go to school. Then she says Life. Yes, says Howard to the English muffin. I don't want to, says Pearl. It's going to rain. With jelly, says Howard.

Randi pads down the narrow staircase, then crosses the hall to the bathroom and shuts the door, hoping no one in the kitchen can hear her, although there had certainly been a lot of toilet flushing earlier, even the sound of Howard peeing at about six o'clock. She herself is sensitive about things like bathroom noises, especially after staying with Alma Beatty, who was not, and living in the room underneath Mr. Natoli, with his stomach problems.

She turns on the shower. The Cook-Goldmans' shower has a shower head attachment with the options of massage pulse, jet or spray, so as usual she spends a few minutes trying out each one. She also samples Mirella's shampoo—spelled "champu" on the greenish bottle—and her conditioner, which costs, Randi notices, $9.95.

She soaps her body, thinking that today she will take Jacob on a walk through the village. Randi loves the village. She loves all those clean, flat-fronted old houses tucked together, tilting up and down the hills, flowers in the window boxes and the doors painted all colors. She especially loves walking at night, because then the houses are lit up and—if the people inside haven't yet closed their shutters—she can peer into the windows and see living rooms with their fat easy chairs and braided rugs, pictures of ships over the mantelpieces. Then there's those galleries and little shops selling pottery and wooden birds and massage oil, the windows heaped with pillows and calico cats, all of which Randi likes to think of as "goods." The pharmacy even sells peppermint sticks in an open glass jar. The whole place has a cozy, old-time feel, that makes it a more convincing place somehow, more *finished* than towns like Coralville, with its strip of superstores and the golden arches.

But what Randi loves even more is sitting on the pier by the harbor, breathing in the smell of fish and melting tar, watching the sailboats slide by, listening to the sound of ropes banging against metal masts. Where does it all go, she sometimes wonders, and enjoys the sense of herself wondering, watching water flow past the pier.

She finishes soaping. Then, worried that she is taking too long, she shuts off the water before she is quite finished rinsing her hair and grabs one of the thick white towels hanging on the rack. It's damp. She has forgotten her own towel upstairs. Today she will launder all the towels so that everyone can have a clean fresh one. Pressing her face into the towel, she breathes in deeply.

Everything in the bathroom is white or an oat color, which gives the bathroom a very sanitary appearance. Even the extras, like the glass jar of bleached pebbles on the windowsill, even the soap at the sink, which is as big as an ostrich egg and has speckles of some kind of grit in it. The bathroom looks right out of the copies of *House Beautiful* and *Country Living* that she and Alma used to look at together, sometimes trying to figure out who the people might be by their furniture. Wood was best and cost the most, especially if it was nicked up, the idea being to have your furniture look as old as possible, even if it was new. Most of the Cook-Goldmans' furniture looks like it has been around since the Pilgrims. Subtle touches, DeeDee Spicer would have said. Nicer than the Lawlors'.

Hurriedly Randi dries her hair with Mirella's blow-dryer—a long, shiny black thing holstered on the wall—worrying again that she should really be downstairs fixing somebody's breakfast, even though Mirella had said Howard liked to fix breakfast. Randi has noticed that the breakfasts Howard fixes—juice and cornflakes with milk—aren't the breakfasts of someone who likes food. At least she could get started on washing dishes. And maybe she could offer again to help pack Pearl's lunch.

Back in her room, Randi pulls on a pair of white cotton underpants and a bra, then goes to the armoire—she calls it the "armor," although she remembers how Mirella pronounced it—selecting, after a moment's consideration, a peach-colored blouse and her short denim skirt. Mirella's skirts come to calf length, which gives her a flowy look when she walks. Mirella wears silk scarves, loosely knotted, and she has a way of sighing at mishaps that makes whatever has gone wrong seem funny instead of stupid; even when she slings a dish towel over her shoulder it looks sporty, as if drying dishes is a game she's just taken up. Randi slides her feet into her clogs and clunks across the floor, deciding to buy some rubber-soled sandals along with a couple of new skirts.

Standing at her dresser, she puts on lip gloss and mascara, smearing one eye so that she has to dab mascara off with saliva and a tissue and try again. The face staring back at her from the beveled mirror is round and pale, the features unremarkable, except for being somewhat flat.

The longer she looks at herself, the less she sees her own face. Instead, Miranda St. James's face begins to surface, her high cheekbones rising up, her slim eyebrows two fine arcs.

HOWARD IS READING a Muppets book called *I Am a Monster* to Jacob and Pearl in the kitchen while Mirella butters a slice of toast. She looks tired this morning; the skin beneath her eyes has a purplish tint. "Good morning, Randi," she says, smiling as she looks up from the table. "Did you sleep well?"

Howard glances up and smiles also, then continues to read the Muppets book. He is wearing his usual blue work shirt and khaki pants. For a moment Randi considers his short, dark hair, his dark eyes. Something about his head seems unruly yet finicky, like a dog in a bonnet. He has missed a spot shaving this morning; a whiskery patch sprouts on his jaw.

Pearl and Jacob stop looking at the Muppets book to watch Randi over their cereal bowls. Under the table, Martha lies panting.

"Hi guys," Randi says. Pearl looks away but Jacob stares right at her, though not with an expression she can easily decipher. Somewhere between interest and resignation, which is how he has looked at her all week. "Need more cereal?" she asks him, but Mirella is already lifting the box, shaking cornflakes into his bowl.

"We sure had fun yesterday." Randi continues to stand by the table, feeling suddenly that her hands are too large, her feet are too big. Her stomach rumbles. Did she remember to put on deodorant? Mirella is only having toast for breakfast, which is not enough protein either. No wonder she's so tired-looking. Brewer's yeast, Randi has read in *Self* magazine, is good for working women like Mirella, coping with the stressful demands of job and family. She would put brewer's yeast on the grocery list.

"We had a great time," she says, looking at Jacob looking away from her.

Then surprisingly, Pearl says, "Yes we did. I forgot to tell you one thing. Randi showed us how to make cookies." Howard stops reading and glances up. "We had a really fun time," Pearl continues in a loud voice. "Randi put coconut in the cookies. And chocolate chips."

"Oh?" says Mirella, over her coffee cup. She smiles at Jacob, who is bobbing gently in his seat, holding a piece of toast with both hands. "That sounds good."

"Then we ate them all."

"Well." Randi blushes. "A lot of them got burnt on the bottom."

"We put green food coloring in some of the batter and made

frog cookies, too." Pearl looks deftly around the table. "We pretended we were starving on a desert island and had to eat frogs to stay alive."

Randi glances first at Mirella, then at Howard. "I hope making cookies is all right. I used less sugar than the recipe called for."

"It sounds like you had a very imaginative afternoon," says Mirella.

"I pretended that my frog was still alive," says Pearl, more loudly. "It was green and slimy and it was sitting on a china plate. It said, 'Buttercup, buttercup.' But it was all the food I had."

Mirella puts her toast down.

"Its guts were the color of strawberry jam."

"Hey, hey." Randi turns to Pearl. "We don't need to go into all that." She swings back around and shrugs helplessly at Mirella and Howard. But to her relief, they are laughing.

"Pearl is very suggestible," Mirella says. "By tomorrow she'll believe she actually did eat a frog."

"It was good," insists Pearl. "I liked it."

Mirella reaches over to smooth Pearl's hair, then tucks a lock behind her ear. "A few months ago," she says, "I had to cut Pearl's hair with poultry scissors because I couldn't find my regular scissors—"

"Oh no," says Randi, realizing too late that missing scissors are not the point of Mirella's story. Mirella smiles and continues, "Anyway, I said, 'Thank goodness I didn't have to use a butcher knife.' Two days later I got a call from Pearl's kindergarten teacher wanting to know if it was true I'd cut my daughter's hair with a butcher knife."

"Oh no," Randi says again. "What did you tell her?"

"Well, I explained what had happened, but her teacher's never looked at me the same way since."

Mirella takes a sip of her coffee, then makes a face and pushes the cup away.

Pearl says, "You *did* cut my hair with a butcher knife."

"Right." Howard leans sideways to bump her shoulder. "And I brush your teeth with the broom."

Pearl begins to rock back and forth on her chair. "And Mommy combs my hair with a rake."

"Next time I'll cut your hair with the hedge clippers. Sit down, Pearl, you're spilling your cereal."

A neighbor's cat begins meowing outside. Martha stands up from where she's been lying under the table and moves toward the bay window, toenails clicking lazily against the wooden floor.

"Anybody want me to read a story?" Randi says.

"That's okay," says Howard, reaching for another Muppets book. "I'm used to being the breakfast entertainment."

Mirella is now looking at the business section of the paper. Howard has gone back to reading to the children. In their aquarium on the counter, the two goldfish open and close their mouths. Randi squeezes past Jacob's chair toward the counter, where the coffeepot waits. Maybe she could start rinsing a few cups or dishes, or maybe she could find the sponge and wipe coffee grounds off the counter.

"Randi, I wonder if—" Mirella starts to say.

"Frog," says Jacob suddenly.

"JACOB?" SAYS MIRELLA.

Jacob faces her, his mouth open.

"He said 'frog,' " says Pearl.

Howard leans forward, his chest pressed against the table. "Jacob, did you say 'frog'?"

Jacob looks at Howard.

"Frog," he whispers.

"Oh my baby," says Mirella.

No one minds when Jacob won't repeat "frog" again, although Pearl tries to encourage him by croaking and hopping around on the floor. Mirella gets up and stands behind Jacob's chair, leaning over to kiss him again and again. It quickly becomes clear that a small miracle has taken place this Monday morning in the Cook-Goldmans' kitchen.

The family beams toward Jacob, who sits quietly in his booster seat, eating the rest of his cereal. "Way to go," Randi says, and picks up the milk carton to add a little milk to his cereal. Pearl reminds everyone several times that Jacob said "frog." Howard nods at Mirella, who blinks back at him, her mouth upside down, as if she might cry.

"Well," says Howard. He reaches out and cups the back of Jacob's head. "This is quite some guy we have here. This is certainly somebody."

"Frog," shouts Pearl. "Frog, frog."

8

"AND NOW A JELL-O concerto by Dvořák," intoned a radio announcer from the portable stereo behind Krystal Anne's desk. Krystal Anne, Howard's part-time secretary, usually preferred heavy metal music, although every now and then she was assailed by a pensive mood—Howard assumed it was premenstrual—and chose a classical station.

The Dvořák concerto began with a quiver of strings. Krystal Anne herself was outside smoking a cigarette and flicking the ashes into Mirella's azaleas. Recently Krystal Anne had struck up a friendship with Randi, who sometimes brought the children in to Xerox their hands at the copy machine and borrow paper clips for necklaces. Usually Howard quit working whenever the children came into his studio, grateful for the interruption. He liked to sit on the floor with them drawing boats and castles, making paper airplanes, letting them have cans of soda from his little refrigerator, but Randi always made a fuss about not bothering him, shooing the children back out almost as soon as they'd arrived. "Daddy's busy. He has to work."

Yesterday he'd overheard Krystal Anne on a cigarette break

talking to someone outside in the garden; he'd heard her mention his name questioningly, then lower her voice. Laughter followed. A few minutes later she shouted, "Howard, you've got a visitor." When he looked up it was Randi, coming in to ask if he had religious objections to shrimp *khorma*. Mrs. Gupta had given her the recipe. Mrs. Gupta was a super cook, Randi confided; she'd shown Randi how to make nan, as well. Unleavened bread. Kind of like matzoh.

Howard listened to the Dvořák concerto for a few moments, looking at a brochure from the North Shore Meditation Center, which Krystal Anne had dropped on his desk with the rest of the mail, unsorted as usual. He should have been adding French windows to his final plans for the Gourleys' kitchen, for which he had at last been paid, but this morning he was having trouble getting started. He'd just finished reading the first paragraph of the meditation center brochure when the phone buzzed.

"Howard," shouted Krystal Anne, who had returned from her cigarette break to answer the phone. "Pick up."

It was Randi, calling from town. Should she buy some eggs on her way home? She was thinking about making a cheese and asparagus omelet for dinner. Did Howard like cheese and asparagus omelets? Randi went in for a lot of egg dishes, he had noticed, thinking passingly of his cholesterol level, but he told her an omelet sounded great. How nice, he thought, as he hung up. Dinner at home.

Although by now Randi had cooked well over a dozen dinners at home, he continued to feel a mild euphoria at the thought of a plate of food on his place mat at the table. This same euphoria often overtook him whenever he glanced around and recalled that he had a home, rooms where he was expected, even awaited. Especially in the evening, if he happened to look out his studio window as neighborhood cars were returning from their day in a Boston parking garage or somewhere along Route 128. He would think of how in a little while he, too, would walk across the damp grass of his garden, open the back door, and step into his kitchen, where his children would be eating supper beneath windows steamy from pots boiling on the stove, and he would feel not simply relief at the existence of his own home, but the chill nearness of something else, a place he might equally belong, like the empty car lots his neighbors had just left.

The concerto ended. An announcement for Direct Tire Sales came on. He was still staring at the meditation center brochure a few minutes later when Krystal Anne shouted for him to pick up again.

"Hi, friend," said a bluff voice on the phone. It was the president of TownCommon, a beaming, orsine computer engineer named McConkey who, despite his name, and his red curly hair, and his predilection for neon-colored Polo shirts, reminded Howard of a Buddhist monk.

"Well," said McConkey, audibly smiling, "you got the job."

Howard said, "You're kidding."

"What we liked about your sketches," McConkey went on to say, after congratulating Howard and calling him "friend" again, "is that they're thrifty. Simple. Down to earth. Traditional but modern, without a lot of extra. Some of these guys think they're designing Monticello."

"Oh," said Howard, unsure whether to feel flattered. His heart had begun to pound. "Well, I tried to keep the site in mind. I've always been a contextualist, and my approach—"

"The thing about homes," McConkey broke in, "is that people have to live in them."

"Right," Howard said. "A house is a house."

"Exactly," said McConkey.

Howard spent the next forty-five minutes on the phone with McConkey figuring out an initial schedule for permit applications, site visits, the environmental impact report, another round of sketches. The TownCommon group proposed thirty thousand dollars up front, another thirty thousand dollars when all the permits were secured; the other half would come with the final plans. There would be meetings with the town planning board, which would have to consider land-use restrictions, and the board of health to discuss septic fields, then the conservation commission to examine wetlands issues. Not to mention the abutters, who would kick up dust about view lines and increased traffic and protest whatever road placement actually made sense, and the citizens groups, who would complain about everything else. McConkey kept calling him "friend" and laughing an excited barking laugh. Howard began to feel, as he always felt at the beginning of a job, overwrought and slightly sick.

Struggling in among all those meetings would also be Jacob's appointments, which he'd have to drive Jacob to, because Randi needed to be home for Pearl, and the plumber was going to start installing the new furnace next week, and he had to get someone out to look at the crack in the chimney fireback in the living room, plus no matter what Mirella said, he was always the one who wound up taking off time when one of the kids got sick, or it was a vacation day, or the sink backed up, because he was home, and visible.

After he hung up the phone he picked it up again to dial Mirella's cell phone, but then changed his mind, annoyed that he'd lost his initial exhilaration about the TownCommon contract and had instead made himself angry thinking about errands and vacation days. To calm down, he picked up the meditation brochure again. He'd been reading about a weekly chanting group. Chanting, the brochure claimed, helped develop powers of concentration. Chanting group participants would reflect on the Buddha's teachings and on the virtues of the Triple Gem. Beginners welcome.

Once more Howard picked up the phone to call Mirella, then

again changed his mind, this time in favor of straightening his desk. Outside, crows were squawking in the apple tree, punctuated every so often by a meow from the Pilkeys' cat. He shuffled bills and loose papers, including the meditation center brochure, into the old maple apothecary's chest he used as an organizer. He shifted a faded honeymoon shot of his parents, pudgy in dark overcoats, looking stunned at Niagara Falls, placing it behind the photograph of Mirella, Pearl, and Jacob perched on an enormous pumpkin at a county fair. Then he considered repositioning his desk altogether, perhaps setting it against the window. Or the drafting table could be moved to the window, the desk relocated to beside the door. He even got up, walked around his desk, and stood in the corner to visualize how he would appear to clients from this perspective.

This was Howard's favorite moment of his working life, the moment when a project was still new enough that it lay not just ahead but above him as well, when the countless small, effortful steps required to complete the project had yet to be taken, and he could still gaze in appreciation at the bright pinnacles of his own ideas. At this stage of design he might discover anything in his calculations, in the angles he devised, the circumferences he plotted. Careful geometry, every contingency anticipated, no detail superfluous—the Triple Gem: a simple, elegant, unassailable home. Howard got up and went to squint at his TownCommon sketches, which he'd tacked to the corkboard above his drafting table. Then he pulled a length of trace paper from the roll affixed to the table, sat down, stretched his arms, cracked his knuckles. He picked up a pencil.

The next instant he was imagining himself sitting behind a metal table in a wide, unventilated gymnasium facing ranks of gray folding chairs. The sound of shifting bodies, a muffled cough, the scrape of a chair leg. A down parka slides to the floor, is retrieved. Overhead looms a basketball hoop, its net dangling like

Spanish moss. Members of the local Audubon chapter are sitting together in their corduroy trousers and polar fleece vests, while behind them, wearing a bolo tie and hugging an old leather briefcase, hovers a gnomic emissary from the Sierra Club. Five selectmen occupy the front row, faces steak-colored and self-important, trench coats across their knees. And alone to one side, representing the Preservation of New Aylesbury Committee, is Alice Norcross Pratt in a cotton dress and clogs, nursing an infant and scrivening on a PalmPilot.

Pinned behind Howard would be his plans: TownCommon Co-Housing Development. General notes and requirements. Floor plans. North South East West elevations. Everything specified down to the basement subflooring, down to each joist system, down to the size of every lag screw. He taps the microphone, which emits a raspy boom, like a cannon shot into the fog, followed by a shriek of feedback. "My name is Howard Goldman," he begins, scanning the mostly middle-aged, Protestant faces in front of him, imagining—trying not to imagine, because it was self-defeating and absurd, but imagining anyway—that behind each still-polite expression lay the single thought: *Jew*.

"I'm here to give you some idea of—" And like an impresario, he would turn sideways to raise a hand to his plans, so diminished in the gymnasium, when they would have seemed so vast in the confines of his studio. Beautiful, tight, thrifty plans sailing across an ocean of blueprint. Twenty units of housing proposed for an abandoned swale of rocky old dairy farmland. Twenty little buildings, plus a little meetinghouse. A tiny settlement. That's all it was (it was everything, it was the effrontery of all creation), that's all it was.

∼

THE PHONE BUZZED again a few minutes later, and Krystal Anne shouted that it was for him. Howard was half convinced it would be McConkey, calling to apologize; he'd made a mistake, given Howard the wrong impression; the contract had actually gone to someone else. It would almost be a relief, Howard thought, reaching for the receiver.

But it was only Randi. "Should I also get butter? We only have half a stick and I was thinking I might bake something." He told her she was free to get whatever she wanted. "Okey-doke," she said, hanging up. He tapped his pencil against the drafting table, contemplated the designs in front of him.

"Howard," Krystal Anne called imperiously five minutes later. The voice that said hello this time was also not McConkey's.

"Howard?" she said.

He recognized who it was immediately but answered, "Yes?" Simply for an extra moment to steady the quake of dread and anticipation in his chest.

"It's me—it's Nadine. Hi."

"Oh," said Howard, shutting his eyes. "Hello."

She began to speak nervously, her voice going high. "I was just calling to see, I was just wondering if next week I could stop by? When we spoke a while back, we'd talked about, if I was ever in the area, my just stopping by, you know, to say hello?"

"Oh. Right," he said. "Right, right." He was conscious of repeating himself, of having lost, for an instant, all sense of where he was, only to discover that he was standing over his drafting table, pulling at his eyebrows.

"I mean, I hate to bother you if you're busy. I mean you probably are, busy. But it looks like I am going to be in the—area—for a few days, and I thought—."

"Yes. Sure."

"So maybe Wednesday? We could have lunch or—"

"Lunch," said Howard. "Lunch would be fine."

"Great. Well, should we meet somewhere, like—"

"My studio. We could meet here first." Howard looked down at the buttons on his blue work shirt. His studio was not near any restaurants. "Noon then?" He heard himself give Nadine detailed directions. He heard her say "great" again in a voice that was still perky, although the perkiness seemed counterweighted by something else, an understandable wariness, a lack of spontaneity, a hurry to get off the phone. She had probably practiced this conversation in front of a bathroom mirror.

Are you nuts? he thought. It wasn't too late, she was still on the line, he could tell her he'd just remembered an appointment, a meeting with a client, lunch next Wednesday would be impossible.

Howard stared at his loafers. "All right then," he said, exhaling. "See you next week."

Krystal Anne had left her worktable and come to press her hips against his desk, green bangs in her eyes, arms crossed over her Megadeth T-shirt, unashamedly listening. This was her habit whenever she felt like standing up from her chair for a bit of exercise. In a funny way, Howard found her intrusiveness restful—she seemed to view him with such absolute lack of curiosity.

"So." She cracked her gum. "You need me this afternoon?"

"No," said Howard, hanging up the phone too quickly. "Although next Wednesday I'd like you to stay late, if you wouldn't mind. Maybe just until two? And could you hold my calls for a while?" Krystal Anne sighed elaborately, flipping her ponytail back and forth, which was her way of acquiescing to most of Howard's requests.

"By the way," he added casually. "We're going to start to be busy around here. I just got that big development contract."

"Wow," said Krystal Anne. "Don't forget that you're supposed to go to Pearl's field day this afternoon. It's on your calendar."

She ambled back to her table. A moment later, Howard heard

her begin clattering at her laptop computer, continuing one of her spirited e-mail conversations with the agrarian cybergroup she belonged to called The Org. According to Krystal Anne, The Org planned to emigrate to New Zealand, where they would raise sheep and play heavy metal music. "We're into rejection," she once explained, giving him a pitying look. Part-time office help was hard to find these days, and he hoped that Krystal Anne would not be emigrating for several months.

The phone rang again. "Pick up, Howard," shouted Krystal Anne. "It's your wife."

9

EVE WAS FRAMED, read the bumpersticker on the green Ford Explorer stopped ahead of Mirella. Sunlight blazed off the car's rear window. On the sidewalk, a gray-haired woman in a lavender running suit and dark glasses was passing by with a baby carriage. Howard, Mirella thought, looking at the carriage. Today I'll tell Howard.

Mirella smiled at the Explorer's bumpersticker as the light changed. She was heading toward Route 1, having just said good-bye to Pearl at Happy Faces Preschool.

"So is the new nanny still working out?" said Ruth into her ear. Mirella and Ruth often called each other on their car phones during their morning commute. Without their car phones, they realized they might never get a chance to talk at all, though their offices were next to each other.

"She's great. Jacob especially seems to like her." Mirella watched the gray-haired woman turn a corner. Something was pricking the back of her leg; she reached beneath herself to feel around on the seat. "I'm sure Pearl likes her, too. But then again," she said, "when am I ever sure about Pearl?"

"That's what I admire about Pearl," said Ruth. "She knows no one should ever be sure about anybody."

Mirella paused, uncertain whether Ruth was complimenting or criticizing Pearl. Ruth excelled at ambiguously thorny remarks, which perhaps accounted for why clients often left her office looking frayed, and why she had been married three times, and also why Mirella liked Ruth so much, except when one of these comments was directed at her.

"Well anyway," Mirella said, after giving Ruth a moment to explain herself, which Ruth did not take, "Randi does everything. Cleans up the whole house. Cooks these great meals. We had spinach quiche last night. She even walks the dog." Mirella's voice dropped. "I think I told you, didn't I, about her parents."

"Awful," echoed Ruth. The light changed.

"So she's sort of adopted us. Or made us her cause, or whatever. It's amazing how she's gotten Jacob to start talking. He said 'tree' and 'moon' last week. I told you about 'frog.' She wants to get him using a computer." Mirella tightened her grip on the steering wheel as the Cherokee bucked over a salt heave in the road. "She finds these funny ways to encourage him. They play games where they imagine things together."

"Sounds wonderful."

"It is."

"But—?"

Mirella sighed. The complaint, of course, was what Ruth had been waiting for. "Well, I suppose she overdoes things a little. Washes the kitchen floor every day. Rearranges the coat closet. Vacuums out the car. She bought vitamins for me and Howard because she thinks we look stressed out. She's only supposed to be working forty hours a week, but she's always doing something. Helping, you know."

"She sounds like some sort of domestic missionary."

"Well, she sort of is. And I truly appreciate all her help, and I'm thrilled with what she's been able to accomplish with Jacob. It's incredible." She paused again. Ruth was breathing audibly on her end of the line. "Though I guess," Mirella continued, "sometimes when I talk to her I don't always feel quite—I don't know what it is—comprehended." She laughed ruefully as she passed a green minivan, stalled on the shoulder. A man in a white sweatshirt emblazoned with a black dog was standing beside the van, staring as traffic passed him by.

"Then again," she said, "I suppose comprehension isn't everything."

"It's almost everything," said Ruth.

"Well." Mirella stiffened. "I'm exaggerating of course." She had not told Ruth her news either.

Every weekday morning Ruth and Mirella drove into the city this way, Ruth from her house in Dedham and Mirella from New Aylesbury. Ruth had been a juvenile court judge for six years, after nine years as an assistant attorney general. She had trained Mirella when Mirella first arrived at the AG's office, right out of law school. When Mirella approached Ruth about starting their own practice, Ruth surprised everyone by saying yes. Her third husband had just left; her son was in college. Life, she said, was out of the way. She was a small, cricketlike woman, with neat, contained gestures and a round olive-skinned face that could look melancholy when she was happy and strangely exhilarated when she was not.

"By the way," Mirella said. "I've been wanting to ask you about this new client I've got, Jerry Vassbacher, whose wife—"

"That weird guy with the sandals who looks like Benjamin Franklin?"

"He's not weird. He's a writer. His wife runs a software start-up."

Ruth wanted to know who was suing for divorce. Mirella told her the wife. Vassbacher wasn't contesting the divorce, but he wanted custody of their two daughters.

"What kind of custody is the wife after?"

"Sole physical shared legal."

"What's her case?"

"He's irresponsible."

"Well, do you know he's not?" said Ruth. "What kind of writing does he do, anyway?"

"He's some sort of journalist. He works at home. According to him, the wife is never around. He's the one who does all the shopping, cooks dinner, takes the girls to the doctor, goes to Brownie meetings—"

"Hah."

"That's exactly what I'm up against," complained Mirella. "That's why I need your advice." For a moment static occupied the phone line; Mirella had driven out of a service area. Again something pricked her, just at the back of her thigh. Ruth's voice crackled on as the line cleared. "I'm a little worried about how we're going to look with a case like this," she was saying. "I mean, frankly, what if you win and he does get custody. Imagine the headlines: CEO LOSES KIDS TO HOUSEHUSBAND. Isn't it interesting that this guy came to us?"

"It makes perfect sense," said Mirella, frowning at the steering wheel.

She said good-bye to Ruth at the next light which, like all the traffic and streetlights in New Aylesbury, had been decorated with red, white, and blue bunting.

She'd reached the edge of New Aylesbury village, where the Marshes, the working-class section of town, began as a trickle of gas stations, pizza parlors, and video stores, interspersed with a few vacant lots of scrub oak, pine, and abandoned tires. Purple loosestrife choked the gullies beside the road. Separating this untidy zone from the rest of New Aylesbury was a stretch of weedy pastureland to her left, occupied by a collapsing farmhouse she'd always liked for its weary air of beseiged persistence. The house was set in a green depression with a red barn behind it. The barn had lost part of its roof; a lone black cow stood in the fenced field beside clumps of thistles and a gray boulder. Howard told her a group of high-tech Boston Unitarians had bought an option on the property for a co-housing development. A commune? she'd asked. A supportive community, he said. FRESH EGGS, read a faded hand-lettered sign taped to the mailbox.

Startled by a tap on her window, she looked up to see Alice Norcross Pratt, five months pregnant in running shorts, standing beside a double jogging stroller, in which sat two little boys eating raw carrots. Alice was damp-faced, flushed with exercise. Her blond hair was in its customary braid; besides running shorts, she was wearing sneakers and a T-shirt emblazoned with a picture of Emily Dickinson inside a box.

Alice gave a brief smile as Mirella lowered her window. "Hi there," said Mirella.

"Nice old place, isn't it." Alice nodded to the farmhouse. "I hate to think of patio furniture in that pasture."

"It would be a shame," said Mirella.

"Some sort of doomsday group wants to develop it." Alice peered at the mailbox.

"Unitarians, I thought," Mirella murmured.

Alice was the mother of one of Pearl's classmates. Mirella had always found her intimidating, perhaps because Alice was reminiscent of Mirella's Cook aunts, who had intimidated her own mother: hardy, practical women with receding gums who belonged to charitable organizations and horticultural clubs, always a piece of knitting or a trowel in their narrow, bluish hands. Mirella had recently visited Alice's eighteenth-century white farmhouse for a Happy Faces' fund-raising meeting. Pepperoni pizza was served on the family Wedgwood; paper daisy chains festooned an heirloom mirror in the front hall; crayons were scattered across a mahogany coffee table. Each Pratt family member, it seemed, owned a pair of rubber gardening clogs, lined up inside the front door.

Goody Pratt, Howard called her. Alice did not give her children fruit juice or let them play with plastic toys; she used cloth diapers, which she laundered herself. Alice once consulted Howard about building a solar-heated greenhouse for organic vegetables with an electronic sprinkler system that would mimic different types of rainfall. In the end she had not hired Howard but had designed the greenhouse on her PC. "The CyberPuritan," Howard said acidly. "Farming with her gourmet children." Alice had that effect, Mirella thought, inspiring in her acquaintances a desire to sneer that got confused with admiration.

Her children did seem remarkably attractive and well tended, Mirella thought, peering at the little boys, who were now kicking each other in their stroller. Blond, rosy, their arms like little fat loaves of bread.

And yet Alice's oldest son, Eliot, was a spitter. Twice this spring he'd spat at Pearl on the playground. Mirella found it so uncomfortable to be the recipient of Alice's stern apologies that she almost wished Pearl had spat at Eliot instead. "So how are you?" she said to Alice's belly.

"Fine," said Alice. "I wanted to remind you that you're in charge of publicity for the Happy Faces' bazaar."

"Oh yes." Mirella had forgotten completely.

"You should really be getting the flyers out."

"We'll get them printed up today."

"Don't forget the candle dipping and the spinning and weaving demonstrations."

Mirella waved to Alice's straw-haired boys, still chewing on their carrots. "Well," she said. "I should get going."

"By the way, I met your new nanny at the park." Alice smiled briefly again. "I think she was teaching your son how to do a Bronx cheer. How's he doing, by the way?"

"Great," said Mirella.

"She seems very conscientious."

"She's super." Mirella's own smile was beginning to feel thread-like. "I'll drop the flyers at your house tomorrow," she said.

"Off to the races," Alice called, backing away with her double stroller as the light changed. Mirella waved again, giving her car too much gas, so that it leapt forward with a screech. Alice Norcross Pratt and the double jogging stroller gradually diminished to a gray blot in the side-view mirror.

Conscientious, thought Mirella, catching sight of her own eyes squinting in the mirror. She looked back at the road, wondering where else Randi and Jacob went during the day, who else they encountered, who else was watching them. Where would they be right now? She glanced at the dashboard clock. Still at home, cleaning up from breakfast. Spinning and weaving.

She turned the radio on and listened for a few minutes to a report on allegations that President Clinton had had an affair with a White House intern. "Oh please," she said aloud. "Give the man a break." She switched off the radio. Alice, on the other hand, would never excuse an affair with an intern. During Happy Faces' winter solstice celebration, Alice had soberly announced that having children was her contribution to a better world.

Mirella shivered in the muggy warmth of the car, feeling again under her leg for whatever in her seat kept pricking through her stockings. Besides, if Alice was snippy, it was probably because Mirella had refused her invitation a few months ago to join a local mother's group that met for coffee on Tuesday mornings. "Oh I'd love to," she'd said, overly apologetic. "I just wish I had free time." They called themselves the Home Front. For weeks afterward, whenever she encountered Alice, or Blanche Pilkey, or her other neighbor, Vasanti Gupta, or any of the women in the group, Mirella thought they smiled at her abstractly, as if unused to considering her in person.

"Flyers," she reminded herself. Maybe Howard could do them.

Thinking again of Alice's melon stomach, she decided that she would call Howard right that minute. She couldn't wait any longer, she had waited too long already.

Just then her fingertips located whatever it was that had been scratching her under her skirt; a moment later she had pulled it out, running her stockings in the process: a small broken blue feather. Fortunately, she had another pair of stockings in the glove compartment; in fact, she had another pair in her briefcase as well. Shivering again, she tucked the feather into the gear shift, then signaled to pass another Cherokee.

As MIRELLA DROVE PAST an open arm of coastline, Boston's skyscrapers appeared suddenly across the water, like a collection of drab Lego towers, only to disappear again as she rounded a curve.

"Hello, Howard?"

"Mirella?"

"Hi. I was just calling to say hello."

"Well hello," he said. "I saw you less than an hour ago."

"I know, but I just thought I'd say hello." Mirella glanced at a farm stand stuck between a car wash and a U-Haul lot, flats of red and pink geraniums set near the road. She could hear Howard waiting and envisioned him sitting in his studio, rolls of blueprints neatly shelved behind him, many of them proposals for projects that had gone to other architects. He should really get that new computer. She admired his insistence on drafting by hand; she was certain it was more artistic, and he was a wonderful architect, but he was being left behind. Which used to be less of a problem than it was now that Jacob had started seeing so many specialists, plus the house was a sinkhole; yesterday the plumber said they would need a new furnace. Last fall it had been the gutters.

And yet Mirella worried that it wasn't just his antiquated computer that kept Howard from getting ahead. Perhaps his work was a little too pure for most people, too impeccable; his designs did not quite translate as comfortable. Most people liked odd little complexities: corners, alcoves, eaves, and attics. For Howard, everything had to be a straight line. But when she tried to tell Howard about his work being impeccable, he misunderstood and thought she was complimenting him.

"And there was something—" she said.

"Was it about Pearl's field day?"

"No. Oh, I forgot that was today." She stopped, no longer sure why she thought this would be a good time to talk to Howard. More and more often these days she had been experiencing moments like this one, moments that didn't used to feel so familiar, when she sensed herself losing an opportunity, feeling it slide away beneath her fingers, like wet glass.

"What, Mirella? Look, can we talk later? Things are crazy here." He paused, clearing his throat. "I've had a bit of a surprise."

Mirella waited, her heart beating clumsily.

"I got that co-housing contract."

"Oh Howard."

"Which means I'll be working late a lot for the next few months. It's a pretty big deal. Four firms submitted proposals."

"That's great, sweetheart," she said, understanding now the nervous hitch in his voice. The glare from the road was making it hard to see. "I'm really glad for you. How much is it going to pay?"

"A hundred and twenty grand," said Howard, sounding slightly offended. "Most of it contingent on permits, of course."

"I'm so glad for you," she repeated. And she was glad, and

relieved—because the money was coming in just in time, what with the furnace and Jacob's specialists and her garage fees going up. But also for the first time she was frightened. She pictured Howard at his drafting table, bending over his sketches with a protractor. She knew exactly how he would be sitting, angled forward, elbows on the table, one hand holding his head. And yet he seemed far away at that moment, and also oblivious of her, as if she were watching him from behind a one-way mirror.

"You don't sound glad."

"Yes I do. Howard. Of course I'm glad."

"A lot of people in town aren't going to be happy about this project."

With an effort, she said, "Well, I'm sure they'll come around."

"This project happens to be more than a real estate deal," he went on, as if she hadn't spoken. "This group just *happens* to have a vision for an alternative lifestyle." He paused. She could hear him grimacing at the piety of this last remark; it was unlike Howard to be pious about other people's visions, especially given his skepticism toward his own. "Not to mention," he added, "that if I don't design this thing, we'll get some monstrosity like that condo gulag on Box Point."

"Howard, I'm glad you got it."

"Listen," he said after a moment. "I'm not fooling myself." He paused again. Mirella pictured him tugging at his eyebrows, which he always did when he was upset. "I know what I'm in for. The permitting is going to give me migraines."

Mirella made a sympathetic noise into the gray mouthpiece of her cell phone.

"We'll talk later," he promised. "Okay? Maybe we'll even go out to dinner sometime this week." A moment later, good-byes complete, Mirella coughed and put the telephone in her briefcase, shutting the briefcase with an orderly click, pretending to herself, and to anyone glancing at her from a passing car, that she had accomplished a bit of business.

As she crossed the Tobin Bridge and headed toward Haymarket, Mirella tried to forget her phone conversation with Howard, and the conversation they still had not had, and tried to concentrate instead on Jerry Vassbacher's wife, who was demanding that Vassbacher move out of their house.

Yesterday Mirella had told Vassbacher they would work out an agreement allowing him and his wife to rotate through the house in Natick for a few weeks. When they went into court for temporary orders, she explained, it was important that Vassbacher be able to say he had not moved out, that he still lived in the house; this would have psychological significance for the judge. But she changed the locks on me, Vassbacher muttered over the phone. Now he was staying at a Ramada Inn off Route 9. He was a big sad-faced man who wore little round wire-rimmed glasses, Birkenstock sandals, and a scuffed leather vest. Mirella disliked the thought of him sitting on an orange hotel bedspread, staring at his reflection in a blank TV screen. She promised to procure a house key. The court had appointed a guardian ad litem, who would be visiting Vassbacher at home next week to evaluate his parenting skills. Get a haircut, Mirella told Vassbacher, picturing his long wispy gray hair. Buy a suit for the hearing, and a pair of wing tips.

"Shoes," she'd had to explain. "You can't wear sandals to court."

"Why not?" Vassbacher asked, mystified. "What do sandals have to do with getting my kids back?"

"Please," she'd said. "I know all of this is hard and confusing. You'll just have to trust me."

But as she tried to focus on Vassbacher's predicament, Mirella found herself instead thinking of Pearl's retreating back that morning, fading into the complicated snarl of playground equipment. She pictured Pearl's small, dark face, her faintly slanted

brown eyes that often now, whenever she and Mirella were together, seemed directed at a point just above Mirella's head. She
had acquired a way of shrugging whenever Mirella spoke to her.
"I know," she kept saying. "I *know*."

For a moment Mirella glimpsed Pearl as a teenager—tall, for-
bidding, a chemistry textbook clutched to her chest. Someone
who could vanish into another country, change her name. *Please
do not call me Pearl, my name is Bela Mahaya*. She was so em-
braceable still, so slight, almost ephemeral in the way she flitted
from one room to another, wearing a fire hat or pair of green
tights on her head. Mirella herself had been a hulking child,
forced into diets and exercise regimens by her mother by the time
she was six, her straight hair waved, permed, rigid with spray. Her
clearest memory of childhood was the echo of her own feet,
"clomping" (her mother said) through polished, hushed reaches
of the house. But miraculously here was Pearl, her own child, a
dark hummingbird, skimming up and down the stairs. As a baby
Pearl had worn pink overalls with balloons stitched on the front
pocket. She liked Mirella to make a fist and then Pearl would
slowly pull back Mirella's fingers, one at a time, always delighted
to find an empty hand. Somewhere in a box in the cellar those
overalls lay folded, waiting to be lifted out again.

As she reached her parking garage on Tremont, Mirella had a
sudden impulse to turn around and head back home. She would
like to take Pearl out for the day, go to the zoo, go shopping, buy
gardening clogs for the two of them. They never had enough time
together; especially lately Pearl always seemed involved with
some project Randi had set up for her—hooking pot holders,
sewing fabric squares. Pearl took these projects seriously, hanging
over them with an absorbed frown. "No Mommy," she would say
if Mirella sat down next to her or asked if she wanted to read a
book, "Mommy, I'm *busy*." She shouldn't worry, she knew it was
to be expected between mothers and daughters, this gradual

estrangement. And after all, how many times had she said the same thing to Pearl?

Mirella drove through the cement portals of the garage and found a parking space, then sat staring at the chipped wall opposite. She felt hot and a little faint; her throat hurt. Maybe she'd picked up something at Danielle's bas mitzvah; she hadn't felt quite right since, but then, nobody pregnant ever feels quite right. Her belly pressed against the waistband of her skirt and she began to massage it. It wasn't too late to do things differently. She could rearrange her schedule, especially now that Howard would be working late. Maybe leave the office by five every evening, be home around six; she could have three full work hours left after the children went to bed. It could be done, she thought, even as she realized that probably it would not be.

Sighing, she opened her car door. She had not failed to notice how often Pearl climbed the stairs to Randi's room in the last couple weeks, always to emerge with her hair in cornrows or ponytails, some of Randi's pewter-colored rubber bracelets around her wrist. "They're friendship bracelets," Pearl had explained. "You're supposed to give them to your friends. The more of them you give somebody, the more it proves you like them." And her eyes shone covetously.

10

"YOU SHOULD TAKE VITAMIN C," Randi
tells Mirella.

Mirella promises that she will, then carries her cup of tea into
the dining room, where she has spread papers all over the table.
Randi was planning to polish the table with lemon oil today,
which will now need to wait until tomorrow. It worries and
slightly irritates Randi that Mirella doesn't take better care of herself. Or rather, it bothers her when she gives Mirella perfectly
good advice—like taking vitamin C, which has been proven
in medical studies to prevent the common cold—and Mirella
doesn't follow it. Yesterday Mirella bought a bottle of Windex at
the grocery store when Randi has told her that plain vinegar
and old newspaper do just as well, and are so much cheaper. The
same is true for Play-Doh, which you can make yourself with
flour and water, salt and food coloring. Randi prides herself
on being able to make whatever is needed out of ordinary household supplies. "Resourceful" had been one of the adjectives next
to her senior class yearbook photo, along with "prompt" and

"considerate." But when she mentioned the Play-Doh recipe to Mirella, Mirella just laughed and said she was incredible. Today Randi has promised Pearl they will make a doll out of a white gym sock stuffed with lint from the dryer's lint trap, with buttons for eyes and orange yarn hair.

Though it's a Monday, Mirella is at home. She has a spring cold, and she says it's a good day for her to work at home; she can write her brief without all the calls she gets at the office. Some man keeps calling her anyway, a man with a soft, shaky voice that Randi finds offensive. The first time he called, she had thought —just for one black second—that it was Burton, that he and DeeDee had finally tracked her down. For some reason it has been weighing on Randi lately, the matter of the sapphire ring, which she took a year ago from her mother's underwear drawer, the ring having been promised to Randi someday, which actually made it hers.

But no, the man only wanted Mirella.

Mirella says she might try working at home one day a week. "I won't get in your way," she promised Randi this morning at breakfast. And even though Mirella smiled, there was something about her expression that made Randi feel as if she might have accused Mirella of getting in the way before, which she hadn't, of course.

Randi carries the laundry basket upstairs to Jacob's room. Jacob is asleep in his crib for his afternoon nap. His chest rises and falls, rises and falls. He looks sticky and worried, his eyebrows drawn down, one of his hands balled into a fist. She has noticed that when Jacob is asleep his face takes on a more alert expression than when he's awake. Several times she has meant to mention this fact to Mirella.

She puts Jacob's socks in his dresser, then puts away his ironed pants, folding each pair carefully. Downstairs Mirella is talking on the kitchen telephone again. "That judge is a dinosaur," she says. And a moment later laughs and asks, "What's a simple custody issue?"

Randi stops listening. Jacob's room reeks of A&D Ointment and a half-eaten cherry lollipop stuck to a paper towel near his crib. Carefully she wraps the paper towel around the lollipop and tucks it far down inside the trash can, inside an empty diaper bag. No use attracting ants. Ants have been crawling across the kitchen counters lately, probably because Howard and Mirella leave plates and cups around that still have food on them. The whole house was a wasteland when she arrived: mealy bugs in the breadbox, Howard's boxer shorts pale pink, the refrigerator grimed with dried milk and spilled apple juice. Clumps of dog hair blowing through the house like tumbleweeds, the dog herself with ticks swollen to gray jelly beans.

It took her a week to give the house a proper cleaning—that cleaning crew Mirella hired was hopeless; in fact Randi is thinking of telling Mirella that she saw one of those Puerto Rican ladies take something, a spoon maybe, so that Mirella will fire them, just a waste of money and besides she doesn't like the unfriendly, knowing looks the ladies give her when they come in with their rags and brushes, especially when she tries to remind them to scrub the tub well to get rid of the yellow. *No comprendo,* they always say, crossing their arms. *Puta,* one of them, the darker one, mumbled last week. Which Randi caught the meaning of exactly.

After she'd finished cleaning the house she'd started on the cellar. It took three days to clean the cellar. First she threw out old cardboard boxes, magazines, and dead leaves; then she organized all the recycling bins so that the right bottles were in the right bins and the newspapers were stacked and the cans were flattened. For the children, she put up shelves for paper and poster paints, crayons in a red coffee can. Then shelves for car wax and boots and gardening things. She even put up a shelf by the washer/dryer for laundry detergent, bleach, and fabric softener. This shelf is just for her, for her own convenience, and whenever she looks at it she imagines a tiny version of herself, curled up there asleep.

Mirella is still on the phone. "Jerry," she says, her voice rising. "The judge is the judge. She can decide whatever she wants to decide. In the meantime, you and Sylvia agreed to a four-way meeting—"

As Randi picks up the laundry basket, one of Pearl's socks leaps out onto the floor. Maybe she and Pearl should make two sock dolls, sock sisters, little friends. They could make a whole sock family. She bends down to retrieve the sock, and in doing so scratches her arm on a splintered edge of the laundry basket, where the wicker has come unwoven. A faint line of blood rises to the surface of her skin. "Look at that," she whispers, squeezing the scratch with her fingers. After a moment, she licks her arm, and squeezes again.

Randi has noticed that the Cook-Goldmans go in for a lot of things—like wicker laundry baskets—that may look attractive but are not practical. Like that teapot in the kitchen with the little bird on the spout that's supposed to sing when the water boils but burns your fingers when you try to pull it off. And that old clock in the dining room that Howard said was historic but never tells the right time. Plus that chain you have to pull to flush the upstairs toilet and all the gaps between the floorboards filled with beads, sand, and sticky pennies. Randi flushes, feeling a pleasant harassment at the responsibility of caring for so much impracticality, and also a nagging unease. No matter how she tries to understand the Cook-Goldmans, the closest she gets is teapots and laundry baskets.

"Of course," Mirella says downstairs. "Of course she can ask for child support." She stops to blow her nose. "So will you. In the meantime, we'll file a motion for early partial division of assets—" Randi stops listening. Whenever she hears Mirella use legal terms, Randi feels like she is listening to snow falling.

Before leaving the room, she takes another look at Jacob in his crib. He has rolled onto his side, one arm resting across his face. The other arm cradles the bottle he still likes to take to bed. Mirella has told her that she didn't get to nurse Jacob as long as she would have liked. Jacob loved nursing; he cried for days after she weaned him. Randi can tell Mirella worries about this. That's why she lets him have a bottle, even though Randi told her about a *Parenting* magazine article that says sleeping with a bottle promotes tooth decay.

"Night, night, sweet boy," Randi whispers. "Sleep well, my darling." She likes saying loving things to him; it feels like good practice for when she has her own babies.

And it also makes her feel, just for a moment, that he *is* her baby. There is something about him, maybe it's his sharp little chin or the bony nubs of his shoulder blades, that tells her it's all right to pretend he is her baby. He seems to need it, this pretending.

Mostly she pretends he's her baby when they take walks, Jacob in his stroller in his little Red Sox cap she bought him; he liked it so much he even took off his Indian headdress. Randi plans to have five children. She's already picked out their names: Sam, Tyler, Julia, Sophie, and little Emma. Her husband, she hopes, will be named Matthew or Dave. He will have light brown hair and a shy smile. They will live in a big brick house with carpeting and flocked wallpaper. A secretary will answer the phone when Randi calls him at work. *Oh hello, Mrs. (Andrews? Carter?). Your husband's been waiting for your call. How are those darling children?*

People in the village smile at her whenever she takes Jacob out, thinking what a good young mother she is already, stopping to rub sunblock on Jacob's face, adjusting the cap so the sun stays out of his eyes. "You first?" said a Chinese woman in the park the other day, and, without exactly meaning to, Randi had nodded. Most of the neighbors are gone during the day, the children all in camp or day care. Sometimes the neighborhood feels like a ghost town, just Randi with Jacob riding down the burning gray sidewalk in the stroller. At those times, he is her baby—her practice baby. She's the one he says words to. Juice. Ball. Cookie. He doesn't talk to anybody else. *Rannee,* he called her just this morning, while they were sitting on the floor in the living room, looking at a book. He put his hand on her arm. *Rannee.* "Mirella," she had called out. "Jacob just said my *name.*" And it was true, he had, although he wouldn't say it again when Mirella came running. He hadn't said "Mommy" yet. They'll have to work on that.

Her scratch has stopped bleeding, although her arm still stings. Smiling to herself, she shuts Jacob's door and steps into the hallway.

THE LILACS BEHIND the Cook-Goldman house have long finished blooming; now it's fat red roses and honeysuckle. Jacob and Randi are lying on their stomachs in the grass near the lopsided apple tree, staring up at its knobby branches.

They have just finished sitting in Mirella's Jeep, bouncing up and down on the seats, Martha the dog in the back, pretending they are driving to California. Jacob held the steering wheel and Randi said vroom-vroom. They love driving to California; sometimes Randi packs them a picnic of raisins and ginger ale, which they eat "on the road."

Now Martha is sleeping under the Jeep, drooling onto the driveway gravel, and they are resting from their trip. Randi has been imagining picking apples from the apple tree in the fall and baking apple pies, making apple sauce. All organic. But it will be months before the apples are ripe. Maybe she could try baking bread.

All day it's been hot and cold, hot when the sun is out, then right away it's cool if a cloud passes overhead. Randi feels everything. Every breeze, every blade of grass under her elbows. She feels her own body against the bumpy ground, the softness of her breast through her T-shirt, pressing against her arm. She sighs, stretches, then rolls over and stares at the sky. The breeze is picking up. A storm might be blowing in. She pictures boats in the harbor with waves breaking over them, people in yellow slickers being thrown into the sea. It always makes her feel safe, even cozy, to think about other people in distress. She remembers reading a book in eighth grade about a pioneer family starving on a prairie during a terrible winter; she ate a whole bag of potato chips while she read, even after she stopped being hungry.

Reaching over, she tickles Jacob beside her. "Eeek," he says, opening his mouth wide.

She peers into his mouth at his perfect little white teeth. Then very lightly she presses her thumb to the raised round mark on his forehead. "Beep," she says. "I'm turning you on."

Randi has drawn up a whole schedule for the two of them—playing with blocks, reading for an hour every day, and doing what she calls word drills, which are funny games they play where she gets him to pretend to eat different animals and objects. Jacob likes pretending, she's found.

"Rat," Randi whispers into his ear. "R-r-rat." She waits for a moment to see if Jacob will say "rat" after her. "You are a c-c-cat. Chewing up a rat. Squeak squeak."

"Eeek," he says again, as she tickles him under the arm.

Jacob rolls over and gets on his hands and knees to look at something in the grass. His face goes blank, which it often does when he's concentrating. Now he raises his hand closer to his face; a black ant is crawling along his thumb and he blinks at it, keeping his hand absolutely still, letting the ant travel across the tips of his fingers, up and down, like a miniature mountain range.

Randi shudders, but Jacob doesn't mind at all, not even when the ant starts crawling up his forearm and disappears inside the sleeve of his T-shirt.

"Ant," says Randi.

"Ahn," says Jacob.

He doesn't cry hardly ever. And he really is sweet, the way he puts his head on her shoulder when he's tired and sometimes fingers her hair. Jacob has gone back to inspecting the grass, frowning a little, the ant gone who knows where inside his shirt. Much sweeter than Pearl, who acts like a spoiled brat half the time, although she's gotten much nicer. Last night Pearl was lying all over Randi's bed, wanting to try on her makeup and paw through her necklaces. "Don't tangle those up," Randi told her. And Pearl drew her hand back neat as a kitten. Randi never has to lose her temper with Pearl the way Mirella sometimes does. The way she's doing now.

Inside the house, Mirella and Pearl are arguing over whether Pearl can have a popsicle before dinner. Howard is out all day walking around some property with clients, or he would have come in by now to yell at them for making noise. Ever since Mirella picked Pearl up at school and brought her home this afternoon, they've been at it. First it was about Pearl's sandals— they're dirty, take them off in the house. No, I want to wear them. Honey, I said take them off. NO. Screaming, crying. Then it's a sweater. Pearl wants to find her winter clothes. I'm cold. I'm afraid it's going to snow. Honey, it is almost eighty degrees outside. I'm COLD.

Randi pulls up a small handful of grass and trickles it over Jacob's head. He sits back on his heels while she does it again. Soon she's created a little bald patch in the lawn. "R-rat," she says again.

"Raaa," says Jacob. Across the street, the two little Indian neighbor girls and their little tan mother have trotted one, two, three single file out of their front door and onto their brick front stoop. Both little girls have their own computers. Randi can see into their bedroom windows from hers and has glimpsed them sitting up straight, peering at blue screens. The father is in computers; he probably got them for free.

Today the girls are wearing matching purple culotte dresses with purple ribbons in their hair. Parvati and Aparna. When Randi asked their names they answered Parvati and Aparna, like children reciting world capitols. Their shiny pigtails are the color of motor oil.

Inside the Cook-Goldman house Pearl has begun to howl, her voice high and ropy. Randi sees the Indians halt, mother bumping into her daughters, who bump into each other. For a moment they stand very still, their faces tilted up as if they are checking for signs of rain. Then they turn in unison, the mother's hand on the youngest child's back, and one, two, three they slip back inside. Their front door closes.

"I hate you," screams Pearl.

A door slams. And suddenly everything is quiet, save for the watery sound of wind through the maple leaves.

"Can you say Mommy?" says Randi. "Mom-mee."

Jacob looks at the little bare place she has made in the grass.

The ant has emerged from the collar of his shirt and is crawling up his neck. Gently, Randi brushes it away. Together they watch the ant struggle tinily away through the grass.

"Come on, kitty. Eat this rat. Dee-licious rat." She wants Jacob to have a computer like the one in the library; he could do those maze games and solve cartoon problems. He should have those things, she thinks, feeling her face heat up. He should have whatever those little girls have.

"Raa-aa," Jacob says, sounding so forlorn that Randi sits up and gathers him into her lap. So sweet, his head against her chest, the way he reaches up to cup her chin. She likes how he smells like a new package of bread; even his pee smells clean when he forgets at bathtime and pees on the mat while she's running the water. They linger together for another minute on the cooling grass, long, green shadows falling around them.

HOW IS IT THAT Mirella tells Randi, this very afternoon, that she is pregnant, when she has not yet told Howard? She is over three months' pregnant and Howard does not know.

Upstairs Pearl is in her room, wailing. Downstairs Mirella sits at the kitchen table, her face in her hands, a cup of chamomile tea beside her.

Randi sits next to Mirella, patting her shoulder and looking at the vase of white snapdragons she picked that morning for the table. Jacob is in her lap eating a pear. It is deeply exciting to be in on a crisis, to be in the middle of such warm confusion, like a bird in a nest. Randi has to force herself not to smile at the snapdragons. Her heart is beating fast. She has never been in such a position, where she gets to pat the shoulder of someone she admires as much as she admires Mirella, fix chamomile tea, put pear slices on a china plate, and make consoling noises. To know a secret that has not been shared with anyone else.

Jacob slides off her lap and does his funny, dipping walk across the room to sit down by the aquarium with his wooden trucks. Mirella confides how much she loves her family, how much she wants to do for each one of them. She would do anything for them. But sometimes it is all too much. Next month, she whispers, is Jacob's third birthday. When will she have time to buy him presents, or plan his birthday party? She has two depositions this week; she has a hearing and a pretrial memo to draft. New clients are coming in. Then there is the Happy Faces' bazaar, for which she has forgotten to make flyers. She has an appointment at the dentist's to be fitted for a crown. And now a baby.

Randi says she understands. "You are a Capricorn," she tells

Mirella sagely. Randi has looked up the zodiac signs of each Cook-Goldman family member so that she can follow their horoscopes for them in the newspaper. Howard is an Aquarius —creative but a dreamer—while Pearl is, of course, a Taurus. Jacob is a Cancer; she herself is a Virgo. Randi explains that Krystal Anne is into astrology and has been telling her about rising planets and moons during her cigarette breaks, and what they do in different houses. She is still patting Mirella's shoulder, trembling a little, wishing this moment could go on and on, yet worrying that she still has not thought of the right thing to say, the thing that will convince Mirella that Randi really does understand.

Mirella wipes her eyes, takes a sip of tea. Encouraged by this show of interest, Randi eats a pear slice herself and reveals that once she had her horoscope read in Boston. You will be significant in the lives of many people, she says the astrologer told her. You have a gift for nurturing.

The astrologer had looked disappointingly ordinary: bouffant red hair, blouse with gold horseshoes on it, pink nail polish, like a secretary in an insurance office. When Randi told Krystal Anne this story, the astrologer's prediction was that Randi was going to be loved by a good man and own a vacation home. What the astrologer really said, as best as Randi can recall, was that the past never leaves you and that she should watch her step.

Mirella starts to cry again. Randi offers to make more tea. She offers to take care of Jacob's birthday. She quotes the poem Dolores Anne Spicer published in *North American Grain:*

> Do what you can,
> Do what you must.
> If you do anything else
> Your life might just—
> BUST.

"He's not going to want it," says Mirella, putting her hands over her face again. "He doesn't want it."

"Well I do," says Randi, softly indignant, gazing at Mirella over the top of Jacob's head. Although she is already wondering about where the baby will sleep. Right now Jacob is in the nursery, still sleeping in the crib under a mobile of stars and teddy bears. All that's left is a little room at the end of the second-floor hall where Mirella and Howard throw everything they don't know what to do with, tubes of wrapping paper, broken toys, a gym bag full of yellowish sneakers. Maybe tomorrow, while Jacob is napping, she'll take a little time and see what she can do.

11

Wednesday was a bright, hot, breathless day, the sort of tranquil day that seems unlikely to hold any surprises, even by the sea, where people should expect them, and Howard's lunch date with Nadine at first promised to be similarly uneventful.

Howard spent the morning hunched over his TownCommon sketches. His meeting on Monday with the planning board agent had gone well. The agent, Joy Fiorella, a fat, sour-faced woman from Danvers with dyed-black hair, actually became animated as he described the project, pointing out all on her own the innovative way he'd looped the access road, so that most of the houses would be invisible from main thoroughfares. She liked the group's idea of donating part of the land as a bird sanctuary and was particularly impressed with the state-of-the-art sewerage system they were proposing, which would treat all their waste water before discharging it into the ground.

"This is a great proposal," she said, shaking her head, looking both startled and slightly dejected. "Can't recall a better one, especially given the scale of the project."

But now Howard was having problems with scale. McConkey wanted each house to look small but feel big. The group kept insisting that they liked the idea of unpretentious little colonials clustered together, but they didn't want to feel cramped. "We want the sense of historicity without the limitations of history," McConkey said on the phone, only half joking.

Howard said, "You want a colonial house, you inherit the box."

"Isn't it our job to think outside the box?" McConkey asked mildly.

Some of the TownCommoners wanted basement recreation rooms; they all wanted big kitchens; lately they were requesting cathedral ceilings. "There's only so much you can do," Howard kept saying, "with two thousand square feet and three bedrooms." There was also only so much he could do with a $300,000 budget per house. On the other hand, he wanted to specify custom moldings instead of prefabricated colonial casing, which would be much cheaper, and he wanted six-over-six double-hung windows instead of standard single panes. Last weekend a TownCommon delegation had visited his studio. They nodded as he described the practical limitations of their future homes, as well as his aesthetic aspirations, smiling gravely in their khaki shorts and T-shirts. Two of them clutched recent issues of *Architectural Digest*, like hikers with trail maps. Then they asked again about cathedral ceilings.

And yet he found himself dreaming every night of the plans he was drawing, dreaming in architectural terminology, something he hadn't done since graduate school. Pediment, lintel, coping stone. One night he dreamed of the green oval of the little common, surrounded by a rosary of quiet houses. In his dream, the common became a reflecting pool of green water, swimming with golden carp.

Howard was lost in calculating the precise angle of each house foundation around the common when Krystal Anne shouted, "Howard, you have a visitor."

Nadine was wearing red sandals and a white sundress patterned with tiny red lariats and cowboy hats. She was smiling, but looked blonder than he remembered, and thinner, less muscular, even a little bit withered; maybe she no longer rode her bicycle. There was a blemish on her chin that she'd tried to cover with makeup. "How*erd*," she cried.

He gave her a quick, fraternal embrace and stepped back to usher her inside. Then hovering in front of Krystal Anne, who the day before had pierced her eyebrow to go along with her nose rings, making her look both ornate and persecuted, Howard introduced Nadine: "Here's an old pal from my days as an indentured servant." Interrupted from refilling a stapler, Krystal Anne peered across her empty table with a lack of interest so profound that for once Howard felt irked.

"If my wife calls," he said, "tell her I'll be out most of the afternoon."

Then he took Nadine on a tour of his studio, where his preliminary sketches of four different house styles for TownCommon were tacked onto corkboard. "Oh, these are wonderful," she'd said, hesitating over "wonderful," as if she might have been about to say "beautiful" instead. She pointed to the Palladian window in one house sketch; she praised his refinement of a classical entablature on another. "I'm glad Old Quigles didn't get his paws on this project," she said. She held a finger to her chin, tipping her head first one way then another.

It had been months since he'd talked with another architect, Howard realized. And the only people who had commented on his designs so far had been Krystal Anne, who said they were "cool," and Mirella, who had wondered if his clients would mind not having attics. Attics are wasted space, he told her. "Not psychologically," she'd said.

As he watched Nadine look at his sketches, Howard remembered how likable she was, how intelligently she'd always studied his designs, how irreverent she could be about other architects, how enjoyable it had been to sit with her by Salem harbor the day they had lunch, watching the water shimmer, while gulls wailed and flapped around tourists trying to eat sandwiches on the rocks, and he drank his lemonade and tried not to imagine the color of her nipples (burnt siena, cameo pink) beneath her thin blouse.

He found himself telling her about the town's opposition to the project and the rumors being circulated about the Town-Common group: shared wives, antitax, into home schooling. The home-schooling rumor was actually correct. "People have called them high-tech mafia, cultists, communists, computer nerds. I got an e-mail last week," Howard went on hotly, "accusing us of stockpiling guns for Armageddon. This town goes beyond narrow-minded. They're a bunch of bigoted rich isolationists. I'm looking forward to cramming this project down their throats."

He hadn't meant to speak so violently and felt blood rushing to his head. To steady himself he began describing the co-housing group's eccentricities: the solemn group meetings in McConkey's Cambridge living room, with its lacquer tables and framed Chinese scrolls, where everyone sat on paisley floor cushions and drank ginseng tea; the disproportionate number of TownCommoners who wore round gold-rimmed glasses; the group's insistence on reaching total consensus before approving any part of his plans. "You can imagine what a nightmare that is," Howard said. "They seem remarkably harmonious, though. Maybe they do share wives."

He worried, then, that he'd been inappropriate. But Nadine did not seem to be paying attention.

"What a great studio," she said, slowly taking in his drafting table, the bookshelves of pattern books, his old mission desk, the oak rocking chair he'd designed in graduate school and built him-self, the arched windows and exposed beams. Randi had brought Jacob and Pearl in for a visit the day before and taped up pencil drawings they'd done on sheets of letterhead. Jacob's picture was a line and two dots; Pearl's was of a girl being eaten by a witch during a blizzard. Nadine picked up the photograph of Mirella and the children on the pumpkin, examining it with the same ex-pression she'd worn while examining his sketches.

"Lucky guy," she said at last, looking up to meet his eyes. Her gaze was level, even challenging, and yet there was something else as well which Howard could not read but imagined to be regret. Her mouth twisted slightly. He blushed again, temples dampen-ing, heart lunging in his chest.

Nadine put the photograph back in its place and regained her chipper smile; she was looking almost indulgently at him, as if she might reach up and chuck him under the chin. "Congratulations," she said. "Really."

"I guess things have worked out pretty well," he said quietly, feeling that it would be disingenuous and somehow disrespectful to pretend otherwise. He cleared his throat and made a pretext of considering the foyer on one of his sketches. "So tell me what you think. I've been fooling around with tectonics with this interior pediment. So that when you head out of the house, you also get a sense of heading toward it. To illustrate, you know, that you never really *leave* your house, especially if you've got a family, that it's always—"

Maybe, he thought, watching Nadine bend close to the sketch, brushing back her hair and cocking her head again to the side, maybe he could do something for her. Refer a client, find her a freelance job. He would like to offer something to compensate, however belatedly, for any pain he might have caused her, and also because she looked to be in some sort of need; but really he wanted to appease her because she envied his good luck. He had what she did not, and their silent acknowledgment of this in-equality made him humble and lighthearted, almost giddy. His hands began to shake.

"No pediment," Nadine said, straightening up and giving him a comradely look. "People get tired of little deceptions."

"Oh," he said. "Right."

And yet the lunch itself was stilted and embarrassing. Reluctant to take Nadine into town, he drove her to a Mexican restaurant off Route 128 that was dark and noisome. Their pock-marked waiter had grease stains on his red shirt; the beer tasted sour; a nearby potted ficus smelled like urine. The trembling largesse Howard had felt in his studio soon dwindled to petulance. Nadine spent half an hour describing a duplex she'd helped a younger architect design in Montpelier. "I mean, these baby architects don't know how to *draw*," she said, which was a sentiment he usually shared; but it sounded grating and boastful coming from Nadine, who herself was hardly thirty. She described her part-time job at a health food store and related an involved anecdote about mislabeling a box of cayenne pepper.

There was supposed to have been a job for her at Quigley & Morrow, but it hadn't worked out. Howard recalled supplying a reference about a year ago. Enthusiastic, he thought he'd said. She talked about her therapy. "It's been pretty intense," she revealed over her cheese enchiladas, which she kept prodding with her fork. "I've had to confront a lot of things." A recent romance with a carpenter had turned ugly, she confided, hinting at worse.

"I've got some issues," she said.

Howard slouched against the red Naugahyde banquette, wishing he were outside in the hot, glittering afternoon with its bracing scent of tar, listening to trucks hurtle down the highway. Everyone, every moving thing in the universe was outside this restaurant. He thought of Pearl running through her school playground, and Jacob and Randi taking a walk to the harbor. Mirella was probably on her way to a meeting downtown, stepping onto a curb, sunlight glinting off her sunglasses, people surging around her.

He watched Nadine nudge her enchiladas again. Behind him, someone dropped a tray of silverware. And suddenly he couldn't wait to get home. Couldn't wait to run up the front steps, stand in the hallway and gather the children in his arms, call Mirella's name, see her face appear at the top of the landing, although he knew she wouldn't be back for hours. "You're *home*," he imagined her singing out. He thought of the first time he saw her, sitting by himself at Souper Salad in Kenmore Square while she waited on the next table. She'd looked about nineteen, her hair in a ponytail, thin gold hoops in her ears, although he found out later she was in law school. He watched her listen to a small, red-faced man with a blond goatee complain about his fish chowder. He watched her apologize, clear away the man's chowder bowl, return with a bowl of vegetable soup, set it down with a clean spoon and a new package of crackers—all performed with serene direction, as if she could solve this problem and any other that came to her with equal skill—and this calm authority had struck him as almost unbearably erotic.

He'd take her out to dinner tonight. They would have wine. He would explain how much he loved her. And he would confess everything, the Naugahyde banquette, the sour beer, the trucks on the highway. His desire to rush home and unburden himself was so strong that he pictured jumping to his feet, overturning the table, fleeing his half-eaten chili relleno and this sad, droning woman with her awful dress and chaff-colored hair.

He said, "Everybody's got issues," then winced at himself.

But Nadine appeared heartened by what she must have perceived as a confession. "Yeah?" She looked up from where she had been drawing circles with a fingernail in the condensation on her glass of ice water. Then, with a tentative aggression that Howard found wounding, she asked, "So how's family life?"

"Good," he said brusquely. "Great."

Wilting back behind her enchiladas, Nadine seemed to realize that she had bored him, that he was only waiting for her to eat a few more mouthfuls so he could politely declare that it was time for him to return to work. He saw her understand that there would not be another lunch. Whatever balance might still have been due between them was settled. He would pay the check; they would get into his car and drive back to his studio, making strained and unsurprising comments about the monolithic office complexes crowding like loosestrife along Route 128. He would say good-bye to her in the driveway.

And that would be that. What else could she expect? This once valiant, warm-skinned girl, who had cycled across France, who had daisies on her bedsheets, who had accepted his ashamed apologies quietly, with humanity and grace, would hobble back to her health food store and her malevolent carpenter, whatever hopes she had carried to this lunch extinguished, the whole encounter (who knows how long she'd been planning it) made to seem pathetic.

"Sorry," he almost said. But just then, as if to prevent him from an even worse infraction—reaching across the table to pat her hand, for instance—just then something bright and artificial flew past, something actually impossible. It was a pink and yellow bird piñata, hanging from a pole by a string, being hustled by their waiter over to a table of businessmen who were celebrating a birthday.

"Great," Howard repeated stupidly.

"I'm really glad," Nadine said to her water glass. "Really glad for you."

She had started talking again about Quigley & Morrow and the job she'd wanted but mysteriously been denied, when one of the businessmen, a big, wide-chested man in a tight gray suit, laboriously stood up to accept the plastic yellow bat the little waiter was holding out to him. The piñata wobbled.

Go Dolan, shouted someone. The man took a stance, waggled the bat. Once, twice, he swung. Each time the waiter twitched the pole and the piñata flew away. The businessmen roared. The big man swung again and again, and again and again the waiter twitched his pole. Until finally, with a look of such bland hatred that it took Howard's breath away, the little waiter allowed the piñata to hover motionless, and the fat man swung hard and smashed it. Foil-wrapped candy burst into the air, landing with a derisive patter on the floor and across the businessmen's table.

Immediately the men resumed talking. The waiter smiled, displaying a gold front tooth, his face ravaged and formal. And in the instant between the waiter's smiling and the man's awkward answering salute as he returned the bat, Howard felt something cold hit just below his eye and slide down his cheek.

He turned back to his own table to find Nadine staring at him. She flicked another ice chip across the table, this time hitting him on the jaw.

"Hands-on experience," she said.

12

THAT SAME WEDNESDAY morning Mirella went to see Dr. Kaitz, her ob-gyn, who had delivered both Pearl and Jacob. Lying on the examining table in her white paper sheath, awaiting Dr. Kaitz, who was always late, she stared at three new postcards pinned to the ceiling. Like other postcards in the past, they pictured Caribbean beaches and had been pinned up by the nurse, who understood better than Dr. Kaitz the special discomforts of that table.

While she waited for Dr. Kaitz, Mirella considered her situation. She was forty-one years old. She was pregnant for the third time with a baby that her husband did not want, and would be furious to hear about, because she had waited too long to tell him. Her accountant had called yesterday to say the firm owed fifteen thousand dollars more in taxes than Ruth and Mirella had planned for. Dr. Michaels wanted to begin seeing Jacob twice a week, at $130 a session, and the dentist now thought that in addition to a crown, Mirella needed a root canal, without dental insurance. The last time he visited to check the new furnace, the plumber said the upstairs sink would leak till they replaced it.

Howard's contract would help, but Mirella would have to start billing more hours. She'd donated her maternity clothes to Goodwill last year. She couldn't remember who'd borrowed her breast pump. Pearl had discovered the box of baby clothes in the cellar and before Randi could stop her had cut them up to make doll quilts.

Night feedings and wakings, the diapers, the crying, the holding and tending and rocking. So much crying. And then those terrible moments when the baby was absolutely quiet, had been quiet for too long, when Mirella's heart froze and she would rush upstairs to find it breathing peacefully, in out, in out, while her own heart thundered back to life like their old furnace every time they relit the pilot light.

So much so much.

"Hello, hello," said Dr. Kaitz, striding in and rubbing his hands together as if he were about to sit down to dinner instead of a pelvic exam. "How are we today?"

Mirella started to say that she was fine but found she was weeping and could not speak. Tears ran down the sides of her face, which reminded her of a song her father used to sing: *I've got tears in my ears 'cause I'm lying on my back crying over you.* She began to laugh in the middle of weeping, which made her weeping appear more hysterical than it actually was. "What's this?" said Dr. Kaitz gently. He was a kindly older man with daughters of his own; one of them, he had told Mirella, wanted to go to law school. After a moment he handed her a box of tissues and helped her sit up. The nurse arrived, a small woman with a commiserative expression; her name, Mirella recalled from previous visits, was Diane. Diane held Mirella's hand between her two hard little dry ones while Dr. Kaitz took up his clipboard. "Now then," he said, sitting down. "Try to tell us what's the matter." Mirella drew a deep breath.

What could she tell them? That Howard had always pictured a

family as compact, contained, presentable—like the architectural models he built, with their heartbreaking toothpick trees and exact cardboard steps? I hate mess, he'd told her on their first date. If I ever have children, I'll keep them in the basement. He'd been joking, as he always did about anything he took seriously, which was one of the reasons she fell in love with him, that unexpected way he could have of looking at things from upside down. Howard, she would tell Dr. Kaitz and Diane, was the one who kept up the photo albums, selecting and arranging photographs of their vacations, discarding any that were out of focus or poorly composed. Howard was the one who bought most of the children's toys, choosing expensive wooden trains, wooden dollhouses, even a wooden stove, to prevent Mirella from buying plastic versions in bright, bellicose colors. He did hate mess. His happiest family moments, she sometimes thought, occurred when he was the only one at home.

How can I have another baby? she would ask them.

Dr. Kaitz and Diane were peering at her with concern; from a distance she heard them murmur like pigeons in their white laboratory coats.

Then again, she could also point out that Randi, their new nanny, no longer even so new, had already proven to be someone of surprising ability; she was kind, imaginative, and she possessed also a curious, an unexpected, what was the word? Mirella wrinkled her forehead and blew her nose into another tissue. *Potency*. Like something let out of a bottle. All that housework, done with such energy, even zeal, and her way with the children, which went beyond energetic, as if they were not relative strangers but more like little cousins with whom she had been reunited. She had lost her entire family, such attachments must make sense.

Although, Mirella realized, she would have to be careful not to rely too much on Randi's affections, which might be based on needs that should be understood and condoled with, but not encouraged. Her mother pointed this out at their last lunch. She is an employee, she'd said crisply, then gone on to complain about a visiting nurse who had used up all the mayonnaise while making herself a ham sandwich. Watch out for the treasures, she said. They cost the most. But to Mirella, sitting up straighter in Dr. Kaitz's examining room and wiping her eyes—feeling limpid and qualmy from so much weeping and from having her hand held by someone she hardly knew—it seemed clear that Randi was simply a young woman who needed a home, who had found one, and who would do whatever was required to keep it.

"This wasn't planned," she said to Dr. Kaitz.

He nodded, arms folded over his lab coat.

"My husband doesn't know."

"Well, all right," he said quietly, as she began once more to cry. "You're not the first." After a moment he wrote something on his clipboard. Diane squeezed her hand.

13

"HELLO," CALLED HOWARD, opening the front door. He listened to his own voice echo down the hall. "Hello? Anybody home?"

Deep within the branches of the dogwood tree, an invisible bird cried out three high, sundering notes. Howard cleared his throat and hesitated in the doorway, gazing down at the welcome mat under his feet, its faded pattern of twining green leaves. "Hello?" he called again. As he stood waiting for a reply, he had a sudden panicked feeling that he had somehow entered the wrong house, that at any moment he would be discovered, with screams, accusations, a call to the police.

Quickly he glanced over his shoulder at the lush entreaty of the Guptas' blue-green lawn across the street. *Fall into me,* it seemed to cry. Next door old Mr. Applewhite, home at last from Florida, was watering his hydrangeas. The sky was a seductive pink; the air felt balmy and enveloping, with the slight carnival breeze that kicks up on summer evenings. From the Pilkeys' backyard wafted the enlivening scent of lighter fluid. There was the sound of a motorcycle backfiring in the distance.

Martha barked at him.

"Hi," said Randi, materializing in the dim front hall, holding Jacob in his headdress. "How was your day?"

"Okay. Thanks." Howard shut the front door behind him and set his canvas satchel on the floor by the coat tree. Someone had recently pruned all the coats from the coat tree, he noticed; today it held only his favorite old green windbreaker, which he hadn't seen in months. "Get down," he told the dog, who had jumped up and put her paws on his chest. He pushed her off with both hands. Martha barked, almost snarled, and jumped at him again. "Will you cut it out?" he said, fending her off with his elbow. "What's wrong with you?"

"Martha," said Randi chidingly, holding out her hand; the dog subsided, padding over to lick her fingers.

As if frightened by this display, Jacob clung to Randi's neck, eyes averted, his bony little knees pressing into her sides, like a tiny jockey astride a horse.

"Hey buddy," Howard said. Leaning over to kiss Jacob's forehead, and mostly getting feathers, Howard accidentally brushed against Randi's bare arm with his chest. Both Randi and Jacob had bits of grass in their hair.

"So how's he doing?" he asked Randi.

"Just great," she said, tickling Jacob, who was still wrapped around her neck. She bounced him on her hip until his headdress jiggled; still he refused to look at Howard. "He's doing great, aren't you Mr. Mystery Man?" She had appropriated Mirella's nickname for Jacob, Howard realized. "We went for a walk to the harbor to watch the boats and feed the seagulls," she continued. "Then we went to the library. There was this whole display? Costumes hung up and clay pipes and old dishes and pots. I got this book out called *The Story of New Aylesbury*. It's got stuff about Indians who lived here and the Pilgrims and how they used to dry fish on wooden racks. Then we played in the backyard. We're making a fort," she said, widening her eyes and pushing out her lips as she looked at Howard.

"A fort?" Howard touched Jacob's hair. Jacob gave him a wary sidelong glance, then buried his face again in Randi's shoulder.

From upstairs came the clogged sound of Pearl's weeping. "We're being Pilgrims and Indians," explained Randi. "Did you know wolves used to live around here?"

Howard smiled in spite of himself, aware that Randi was offering this anecdote of her day with Jacob the way wives on fifties television shows used to greet their husbands at the door with slippers or a cold beer. And suddenly it was exactly what he wanted, this instant of banter in the cool hallway, the simplicity of it, the cheering glint of benign flirtation. He smiled with relief. "Who are you going to be?" he asked. "Pocahontas?"

"Oh," laughed Randi, crinkling her nose.

Howard tilted his head toward the staircase. "So what's with up there?"

Randi grew instantly serious. "Well, Mirella came home early today because she wasn't feeling well and needed to lie down. But then she got up and I think she was hoping to spend like some quality time with Pearl? Only I had already promised Pearl she could make another sock doll with me, and I think Pearl wanted to do that instead. We've got a whole family going." Lightly, apologetically, she shrugged, then kissed Jacob's forehead herself.

"Mirella couldn't figure out how to distract her?"

"Mirella tried everything." Randi smiled.

Watching her, Howard thought she seemed a person of exceptional tolerance just then, as wailing erupted once more above her and she stood calmly by the coat tree, holding his son, sharing with him a moment's complicity. He liked her for that bit of sympathy for him, as much as he had liked her hostessy offering of Pilgrims and Indians. He also liked the roundness of her shoulders under her white T-shirt, the generous spread of her hips, not yet matronly, only full. Not that she was his type—he found her homely, in fact, with her wide face and round eyes, snub nose, like something a child might draw. But he liked looking at her tonight in the warm evening light, her hair lit up red and glowing. He noticed for the first time that her hands were unusually large, almost masculine; they looked shapely and beautiful, one spread against Jacob's belly where his shirt had rucked up, one clasping the flesh of his bare leg. She smiled at him demurely, blinking a little, and he was reminded of his mother.

Pearl squealed out something overhead. "Stop it," he heard Mirella demand in a brittle voice. "Stop it right now."

"All right," he said, holding out his arms for Jacob, beckoning with his fingers.

Jacob at first refused to let go of Randi. To Howard's surprise, he hung on to her neck as she tried to disengage his fingers; she had to peel his fingers back one at a time, and then he kicked at Howard with his foot. Finally he allowed himself to be lifted onto Howard's shoulder.

"You two have a nice thing going." He pretended to cuff Jacob's ear. Always Jacob had come quietly into his arms, more quietly than he went to Mirella, who sometimes had to coax him. He and Jacob had at least had that, a kind of physical affinity. Now Jacob stared over his shoulder, his arms limp, his face mutinously blank so that it seemed to Howard that he was not holding Jacob so much as retaining him. "Hey," he said. "Buddy, what's this?"

Jacob suddenly lunged forward, and if Howard had not just as suddenly tightened his hold, the little boy would have fallen to the floor.

"Whoops," said Randi. "What do you think you're doing?" she

said scoldingly to Jacob. "Going sky diving?" She reached up to pat his head. "He has a mind of his own, doesn't he."

She smiled again at Howard, and with a beat of gratitude Howard realized that her affection for Jacob was at least partly for his benefit. Not that she didn't care for Jacob, which she clearly did, but she also wanted Howard to know that she was doing a good a job for *him*. Asking what he wanted for dinner, reporting on her doings with the children, resurrecting his old coat. All the nannies fell a little in love with him. He'd come to expect it—not in a fatuous way, but realistically—and so, in one way or another, did the nannies. Falling in love with Howard made their job more interesting, lending novelistic possibilities to diaper changing and formula mixing and loading the dishwasher. He and Mirella had discussed all this with good-natured sarcasm before hiring Pilar, their first nanny. "Occupational hazard," he said. "Part of our benefits package," she said.

But these crushes did sometimes make things a little harder for Mirella. A moodiness could result on the nanny's part, a lethargy, even a sullenness—Grete had been the worst in this way—which dissipated when he arrived home, transforming into helpfulness, a showy exuberance with the children. So far Randi seemed to be holding an admirably even keel. In fact, until this moment she had seemed more in love with Mirella than with him.

"I've had enough," Mirella shouted from upstairs. "No," shrieked Pearl. At the same moment, Jacob gave a grunting little wail and lunged again at the floor.

Howard sighed and handed him back to Randi, who held out her arms like a child who has tried to be good about sharing her doll. "I guess I'd better go up there before one of them gets scalped."

"By the way," Randi said, hugging Jacob, "somebody called for you a little while ago. She said her name was Nadine."

Howard forced himself to continue smiling, his hand resting on the newel post at the bottom of the stairs. "Did she leave a message?"

"She just said to tell you she called. She said she'd call back." Randi's expression held the faintest note of inquiry, he thought.

"Thanks." Howard gave a brisk nod, the sort of nod someone would give whose clients insisted on calling his home, a nod that said: what a nuisance these people are, always intruding, but what can you do? "Was Mirella the one who spoke to her?"

"No, I did. Hey," Randi called after him as he headed up the stairs, "turkey loaf for dinner."

14

"LET'S EAT OUT TONIGHT." Howard touched Mirella's lip where Pearl had banged it with the top of her head. "We could both use a break."

Mirella could feel her lip already swelling. She felt drained and unwell, sitting there on Pearl's rainbow-colored comforter, wishing she could pull the comforter back and crawl in underneath it. It had taken ten minutes to quiet Pearl's latest tantrum, caused by her request to sleep in a sleeping bag in Randi's room from now on, with the sock family, for whom Randi had made shoebox beds. When Mirella said no, Pearl opened her dresser drawers and threw her clothes onto the floor. Now Pearl was downstairs confiding everything in low tones to the dog.

"She's too old for this," said Mirella, staring gloomily at the heaped clothing. "We were having a nice time, too, playing with those sock things, until Randi walked in and mentioned shoeboxes. I don't know why she got so mad."

"Let's go out," Howard said, leaning over to kiss her cheek.

"What about Randi's dinner?"

"We'll eat it tomorrow night."

Watching him as he sat down across from her on Pearl's bed, looking rumpled but composed, even elegant in his blue work shirt—with which, for some reason today, he was wearing a tie— Mirella found herself remembering how once upon a time, in the early days, before Pearl was born, before they bought the house, even before they were married, she and Howard had lived as closely as a pair of mittens on a string. They'd occupied a third-floor Somerville studio as if it were a pocket, one long, over-heated room with three wooden kitchen chairs and a folding card table, a mattress on the floor, milk crates for their books. The apartment's entrance was hidden at a dim turn of a dusty staircase that smelled of kitty litter and mildew. She envisioned the apart-ment's peeling wooden porch, the two plastic chairs they'd sat in on summer nights with bottles of beer, and the funny pink-tiled bathroom with the shower curtain that always fell down. Every morning before he left for class, Howard brought her orange juice in a wineglass, while she was still in bed. She'd hung a lace tablecloth over their bedroom window. It had seemed like good fortune itself to be young then, to own almost nothing, to want almost nothing, yet sure that there would be a house for them someday, and children, and all the suitable, practical, immoderate things that go with life if you are certain people and have a certain future.

"Do you want some ice?" he said, touching her lip again.

And so it was decided, despite the surprisingly agreeable scent of turkey loaf baking in the oven and the green beans Randi was preparing, along with a salad of spinach leaves and cucumber slices. They would go out. Mirella followed Howard into their room as if her legs were filled with sand and watched him change his shirt, then let him lead her into the bathroom, where she washed her face and brushed her hair while he went downstairs to tell Randi their plans. It was kind of him to want to humor her, she thought bleakly as she put on lipstick, to see that she was unhappy and to want to help. She only wished that she could be unhappy about something else.

When he came back upstairs, she was sitting on the edge of their bed feeling that at any moment she could fall backward and be instantly asleep, but she had managed to pull on a skirt and a loose jade-colored silk blouse. Downstairs once more, Howard ushered her into the kitchen to kiss the children good night, then escorted her back past Jacob on the floor with his trucks, past a crestfallen Randi—who was trying to interest Pearl in snapping beans into a colander—past the old dining room clock, out the front door, and into the car.

Across the street, Vasanti Gupta was standing on her lawn in a purple linen pantsuit, watching her little girls turn neat cartwheels. "Very nice," she kept calling out. "Very nice." She waved to the Cook-Goldmans and Mirella waved back as she climbed into the passenger seat of Howard's old green Saab, which he refused to trade in, even though the chassis was rusting and the windshield wipers didn't work.

"Where are we going?" She turned away from him to watch the Applewhites' shubbery blur as they slid backward down the driveway, gravel popping under their tires.

"Captain Albert's, I guess. I can't think of anywhere else."

Mirella groaned and leaned her head against the seat. Howard reached over and squeezed her arm, then left his hand there, periodically tightening his grip, then relaxing it, only to tighten his hold on her again. They drove through the muted streets of New Aylesbury, where in every house dinners were being prepared, or at least heated, children flickering through doorways, cars parked for the night, here and there a silver fan of water waving back and forth in a green front yard.

But she and Howard were not at home. They were going out into this mellow evening, the air scented with honeysuckle and low tide, the sky flung wide above them and turning lavender. She began to feel the mild hopefulness that accompanies almost any excursion in fine weather, no matter how brief or circumscribed, or what the forecast ahead. A warm brackish breeze blew against her face. She pictured sitting at a window table inside Captain Albert's, where the ceiling and plank walls were hung with fishing nets and old glass floats, looking out at the harbor over their paper place mats, eating swordfish, and coleslaw from plastic cups. Tonight she would tell Howard.

But once they were seated at their wooden table, with its little brass hurricane lamp and humid salt and pepper shakers, her brave mood evaporated. She sat staring out at the empty lobster traps and an old bilge pump piled on the docks.

Howard did not notice her preoccupation. He seemed nervous and excitable, first straightening the tablecloth, then rearranging the salt and pepper shakers. Briefly he drummed his fork on the table, then picked up his spoon. He had been talking for some time about Alice Norcross Pratt, who was circulating a petition against the TownCommon development. "She's like a cross between Betsy Ross and the NRA. The worst kind of idealist. One of those people who'd shoot her grandmother if she thought it was for a good cause, then go back to sewing flags. Or in Alice's case, one hundred percent cotton diapers."

"Howard," said Mirella, looking around the restaurant. She noticed that everyone save the two of them seemed to be wearing shorts.

But Howard had wound himself up. "I told McConkey, 'We're dealing with the Puritans.' I told him, 'Alice just climbed off the *Mayflower,* waving her blunderbuss.'"

"The *Mayflower* never made it this far north," Mirella said. "It landed in Plymouth."

"What?" Howard stopped fidgeting. For a moment neither of them spoke, but instead looked out at the harbor where a regatta was just ending as the sun began to set. The sky was an unlikely pink and orange. White sails cut back and forth across the water like fins.

"So what do you feel like?" Howard snatched up his claw-shaped menu and began examining it as if it were a guidebook. "I'm thinking crab."

"Maybe something poached," she said.

"Not here."

"Why not?" She looked up, puzzled at his abrupt tone. Their blond waitress was bearing down on them in her blue skirt and white sailor blouse, smiling with that bright, solicitous misanthropy perfected by waitresses at seaside restaurants.

"Go for something simple," he said.

"Well, all right."

"Flounder."

"I don't *feel* like flounder. I want something less fishy."

"Less fishy?" he said. "This is a seafood restaurant. We'll need a few more minutes," he told the waitress, and Mirella was struck by the desperation in his voice.

"Take your time," the waitress said, inspecting them indifferently. Then she pointed to the candle in their hurricane lamp. "Want your fuse lit?"

LATER THAT NIGHT, as she and Howard were getting ready for bed, after their dinner during which both of them paid too much attention to the harbor view, neither had eaten hardly anything, and Howard had seemed put off when Mirella wanted ginger ale instead of a bottle of wine, she coughed and said, "It seems like Randi's been good for Jacob."

"What do you mean by 'been good'?" he said.

Ever since they'd gotten home and found Randi's message about a phone call for Howard scribbled on the back of an old grocery receipt, he'd had a drawn, white look.

"Just what I said. Good. He likes her, she likes him. She says he's been doing computer games at the library."

"Which was what was missing for Jacob before, someone liking him, is that what you mean?"

"No." Mirella stared at him. "You know that wasn't what I meant." She sat down on their bed and pressed a tissue to her nose.

"He's getting a little overattached, if you ask me," Howard said. "And I don't want him playing computer games. I want him outside, playing with other kids."

"I feel terrible," Mirella said, choosing to leave the subject of computer games for another time. "My cold is worse."

"Have you taken anything for it?" Howard suddenly sounded concerned, as he always did when something was physically wrong with her. All during her past pregnancies he'd bustled around with crackers and club soda, reminding her to lie down, taking bags of groceries away from her, looking almost disappointed when she said she felt fine. This time she did not feel fine; in fact, she'd felt sicker with this one than with the other two combined.

"I could get you something," he said.

"No, I'm just going to go to bed." She turned her back to him to blow her nose again, then began unbuttoning her blouse, fumbling with the little pearl-like buttons as soon as she felt him watching her.

"What?" she said, looking halfway over her shoulder. "Why are you staring at me like that?"

"Sorry." He took off his shirt and began hanging it up. Slowly he took off his shoes, then his trousers, which he folded and hung up as well. He closed his closet door. Mirella had left her own closet door open—she always left doors open, she didn't know why, even the car door she sometimes left open—so he closed that as well. When at last he turned around again, naked except for his boxer shorts, she had gotten herself safely in bed and was reaching for a stack of deposition transcripts on her bedside table.

He came to stand over her, then put his hand on her hair.

"I've got some work to finish," she said, not looking at him. "By the way, I gave Randi my credit card. She's going to order some things for Jacob's birthday." She could see Howard thinking about protesting this decision for a moment, envisioning an onslaught of plastic action heroes and grinning stuffed animals, but then he evidently decided to let it go. He let his hand slide down her head, trailing his knuckles along the side of her face.

Mirella forced herself to read, frowning unseeingly at the pages in her lap. She lifted one hand to tuck a lock of hair behind her ear. A fly had gotten into the room and was blundering against the walls and the window panes. Howard went back across the room to his closet and opened the door again to reach for his bathrobe.

But before he had finished tying the belt, she pressed her hands to her cheeks and said, "We need to talk."

White sheets of paper spilled across her knees, sliding across the blue floral comforter like playing cards from an oversized deck.

He said, "I know."

PART II

1

"THEY SAY WE'RE IN for some rain," said Mirella, coming into the living room. "As if we haven't had enough already."

It was the first time she had spoken directly to Howard in nearly two days.

Howard was sitting on the floor with his back against the sofa, bare feet crossed, reading the Sunday *Times*. Jacob sat beside him on the carpet with his wooden tracks and train, which he had set up so that the train could climb a pile of blocks, then go hurtling down the tracks to break up by the coffee table. "Click clack," he whispered, each time this happened.

Mirella could hear Pearl on the second-floor landing, playing with her collection of tiny china dogs, who kept barking and baying and having to be sent to their rooms. Last night she had been up three times with nightmares, coming sobbing to the doorway—"I want *Mama*"—settling down only to wake up again, until finally Mirella climbed into Pearl's bed to calm her and to get back to sleep herself. But she had not gone back to sleep; hour after hour she lay with Pearl in her arms, stroking Pearl's hair, breathing in her uncomplicated smell of scalp and skin and the strawberry yogurt she'd had before bed.

Now Pearl's voice was tender and strict, periodically comprehensible, transmitting down from upstairs like bulletins from a radio broadcast. "No more whining," she was saying, "or you will be thrown into the garbage can."

Randi, Mirella knew, had gone out to take a morning walk around the village to see if she could buy some live yeast. She was planning, she'd said, to bake bread today.

At the sound of Mirella's voice, Howard had looked up and lowered the paper. Now he said: "Rain, rain."

She sat down in the gray velvet armchair that matched the sofa opposite. "Jacob," she said evenly. "I want you to go upstairs and play with Pearl. Mommy needs to talk to Daddy."

Howard folded the paper in half and put it beside him on the floor. He gave a questioning look at Jacob, but Jacob had become absorbed in stacking blocks into a shaky tower. For a minute they both watched him build his tower, then regard it tensely. He tilted his head first one way then another. Then slowly he took hold of the bottom block and pulled it out. When the tower fell, blocks cascading onto the carpet, he looked grateful.

"Jacob, Mommy asked you to go upstairs."

"Now, Jacob," Mirella said sharply, watching herself make a strict chopping motion with one hand; she could have been dicing an onion.

Jacob looked up and stared at her with polite disbelief, which grew into bewilderment. On his forehead the little red thumbprint seemed to darken. Slowly he stood up and wandered out of the room, pulling at his little khaki shorts.

Mirella watched him go, digging her fingernails into her palms.

"That was a little harsh," said Howard when Jacob was gone.

"We have to talk."

"I've been waiting to talk. You're the one who didn't want to talk." He crossed his arms over his chest, then uncrossed them again. "So go ahead. Talk. Say whatever you want to say."

But instead she looked out the window at the enormous dark green rhododendron in the side yard. The rhododendron needed pruning. It looked like a mastodon out there, butting against the house.

"Mirella, I've told you how I feel," she heard him begin after a long minute. "You made me say that I didn't want another child when I didn't know you were pregnant. What do you expect me to tell you now?"

The striped hostas were wider this year than last. The grass was too high; the borders were overgrown. All that rain.

"What a mess," she said roughly.

Howard said nothing.

"Look." She turned away from the window, her whole body starting to tremble. "This isn't about me or the baby. This is about you. What *you* did."

Howard looked at his bare ankles. "I've apologized. I'll apologize again, if you want. As I told you, it wasn't that meaningful to me—"

"All right," she said, grimly interrupting. "I won't try to be reasonable. I've spent the last two days"—she heard her voice begin to get high and tremulous, and she took a breath to steady it—"trying to figure out what to do. Well, I've figured it out. I want you to leave. I want you out. I want you gone. *Now,*" she said, not meaning to speak exactly as she had just spoken to Jacob.

Howard was watching her, his arms crossed now over his stomach.

"The fact is"—she lowered her voice—"I don't care why you did what you did. I don't care what it meant to you. I don't even care if you're sorry."

After another moment she said harshly, "The fact is, you"—her voice tripped—"you *fucked* someone else while I was pregnant."

She was never fluent with profanities, and she could tell Howard noticed this tiny awkwardness. The shadow of a smirk she either saw or imagined on his face infuriated her further.

"I want you out," she repeated, feeling the back of her head vibrate. "Out. Out of my house."

"Whoa," said Howard, looking suddenly absent, as if this was not a moment he had imagined possible and therefore could not possibly inhabit. She was shocked by the ugly pleasure it gave her, to see how completely she had surprised him.

"Whoa," he said again. "You're being irrational." He sounded almost amazed.

"Am I?" she said. "Am I? Is it irrational to want to get rid of someone who lied to you, cheated on you." She paused. "All while *living* off you?"

"Wait," said Howard. "Wait a minute."

"I paid for this house. I own it."

"There's more to owning a house than paying for it."

"As for the baby," she went on bitterly, looking at the red half-moons her nails had left on her palms, "I couldn't do it. I went in and I tried to say I didn't want it, but I couldn't."

This was not, strictly speaking, true. She had told Dr. Kaitz that she wanted the baby but was afraid to have it. Dr. Kaitz had said that was certainly a problem, and not one he could solve for her.

"I want the baby," she said to Howard. "And that's all there is to it."

"Why?"

"Why? Why what?"

"Why do you want another baby?"

"Why do I want another baby?"

She wanted to scream that it was none of his business why she wanted another baby, but that was a ridiculous response—he had a right to know why she wanted another baby. Yet she couldn't think of an answer. Always before when she and Howard argued, she was the one who stayed calm, the one who asked questions that eventually unsettled and disoriented Howard, until he was reduced to furiously repeating her questions, finally estranged even from the source of the argument itself.

Howard's eyes had strayed back to the newspaper beside him on the floor. Her fingers stiffened. But then she looked also, to see what he was looking at. An advertisement for designer underwear displayed a very young man and a young woman entwined, almost naked save for the panties on her, briefs on him. It was hard at first to tell which was the young man and which the young woman.

Mirella took a deep breath and sat forward in the chair, raking her hair away from her forehead. "Look. I was wrong not to tell you before about the—about another baby. I put you in a bad position. But what you did is so much worse, especially not telling me until this person, this woman starts calling you, calling the *house*.

"Why did you do it?" she said. "Howard? And why did you want to see her again?

"Is she pretty?" she whispered.

Howard continued to look at the newspaper beside him, which, in addition to the underwear advertisement, featured a photograph of what was supposed to resemble a stony mountain, but was actually a confusion of leather briefcases and handbags.

She waited for him to get up off the floor and come to her, kneel beside her, try to put his arms around her. But he stayed where he was.

"Why did you, Howard?" she repeated at last, wiping her face with her arm.

"I don't really know," he said distantly. "Curiosity. Guilt."

"*Guilt?* Guilt about *her?*"

"Maybe," said Howard, meeting her eyes.

Mirella stared back at him. Howard no longer looked stunned, but instead seemed defiant.

"Did you sleep with her again? Is this why you've been working late?" She jabbed her nails once more into her hands. "Don't answer, because even if you say no, I won't be able to believe you."

"Mirella," said Howard. "Nothing happened."

Outside a car drove past the house, tires swishing over the wet pavement, a catcall of music snatched from its open windows.

When the car had passed, she said, "Get out," with less energy than before. Her head ached. "I want you to go away."

"And what are you planning to do?" he said, frowning. "Have the baby by yourself and then hand it over to Randi along with the other two? She's not going to stay here forever, you know. You can't count on her. You hardly even know her. She could leave at any minute."

"Hand over?"

For a moment Mirella sat quite still.

"You know," she said, when she could speak again, "if you don't want this baby, then maybe you don't want the rest of us very much either."

She was conscious of a rising theatricality in her voice. "Howard," she said, then stopped again to control herself. "Howard, this is a family. Not some plan for a family."

"For Christ's sake, Mirella."

"No, I really mean it." But even as she struggled to think clearly, to tell Howard whatever it was she really meant, an opacity seemed to settle between her and the moment itself, a yellowish scrim, so that she saw the two of them sitting opposite each other as if they were part of a silent movie, the celluloid scratchy and thin, their movements jerky, an unreliable light flickering behind them.

Howard watched her over his crossed arms, his mouth pursed. Finally he said, "Okay." He gave an exaggerated sigh. "Okay. All right. Say whatever you want to say."

But the longer she stared at him, sitting on the floor staring back at her, so intact in his black T-shirt and olive-drab sweatpants, the more convinced she was of something unrepentant in his face, something obstinate, swaggering, almost impudent. And at this precise instant, as she was thinking that Howard looked almost impudent, she had the abrupt, unwelcome image of his erect penis. Right in front of her: its purplish, veiny shaft, its tipped tender swollen bald head. Which, of course, the other woman must have seen, too. And appreciated, probably more than she ever had. Before she could stop herself, Mirella had imagined a pair of glossy pink lips, parting in front of Howard's penis.

"Please," she groaned. "Please go away."

"Is that really what you want, Mirella?" Howard was staring at her tightly, one eyebrow raised. "Is it? Because I'd say right now you need to be careful about what you ask for."

"Shut up," she shouted suddenly. Reaching down, she picked up two of Jacob's blocks and hurled them across the room. "Shut up, shut up. Shut up right this minute. How dare you lecture me about wanting things. How dare you speak to me about what I need. How dare you," she continued.

She paused to take a breath, then turned on him, literally baring her teeth. "And now," she said, without hesitation, "get the *fuck* out of my house."

2

IN THE LITTLE WORKROOM attached to his studio, Howard finished planing a piece of plywood with his table saw. He was not wearing gloves or protective goggles or even a long-sleeved shirt. He hoped he would hurt himself. Slice a finger, maybe, gouge his arm. Not maim himself, he wasn't that stupid or hapless. But he hoped for the clean, clear, demanding problem of blood.

He would need gauze, perhaps stitches. Mirella would have to drive him to the hospital, steering through the motley Sunday traffic herded around the town green—townsfolk outfitted in pastel linen church dresses, slacks and madras sport coats, mixing with the blue jeans and backpacks of tourists. Near the Puritan memorial, two elderly women in tennis hats and sunglasses would be selling congo bars, lemonade, and NO NEW DEVELOPMENT bumperstickers at a folding table, their customers stooping to sign Alice Norcross Pratt's petition. He was hurt. He was bleeding. Mirella would glance over to see how he was holding up.

But he was finished with the table saw, and he had not hurt

himself. On his worktable sat the hollow half-constructed house that he had spent the last hour building. It would be a martin house, one of those expensive white birdhouses he'd seen in gardening catalogs and which Mirella had once expressed an interest in ordering: a rectangular box with a pitched roof stuck atop a long white pole, studded with holes and perches like tiny balconies. "Think how happy the birds would be," she said, "to have such a nice house."

Setting his jaw, he decided to paint the roof green. Then he considered adding a piazza, an overhang, imagining that it might protect the birds if they wanted to peer out of their holes on a rainy day.

It was an idiotic project. He understood how idiotic it was even before he'd gotten started. He should be working on the TownCommon foundation plans to present to the planning board in two weeks, which he needed to get going on before he left tonight for Greenwich. "Come right now," Richard had said on the phone an hour ago. Howard said, "I can't." Then he tried to explain about his foundation plans. Richard paused to let Howard get ahold of himself, before saying softly, "Howie? Do you want me to come get you?"

Howard kept working on the birdhouse, now picking up the piece of roof and fitting it into place, now nailing the roof together—missing his thumb with the hammer, he noticed—now taking his drill and drilling out a pyramid of eight holes, one, three, four—again missing his fingers entirely—now giving himself another chance by drilling eight more holes the size of pencil erasers for the dowels he'd cut for perches. (It was always when you were careless, he decided, that nothing happened to you.) Now taking a square of sandpaper to rub along the edges.

Mirella didn't really want to kick him out. He pictured her face, the way she had stuttered over "Fuck you," in her fury and mortification, looking so lost in her armchair that he'd had to force himself not to go to her. But he thought he should let her finish berating him first. He'd even expected her to tell him to get out, which is what women did when they found out about their husbands' affairs. She *wanted* to want him out of the house; that was what he'd meant to make her see. He just hadn't quite been prepared for her ferocity. But she was pregnant. Women got emotional when they were pregnant. They had two children. They had a house. She didn't want him out. She just wanted him to leave.

He nailed the bottom rectangle of wood to the rest of the house. Then he fitted the dowels into their appointed holes, first dabbing them with glue. While he shook up a can of primer, he imagined a scene in which he went up to the bedroom to talk to Mirella. He watched himself walk purposefully up the stairs, even hearing the treads creak. She was lying across the bed, face pale and tear-blotched, hair stuck to her forehead. He fetched her a tissue and stroked her hair. *Let's forget about what just happened. It didn't happen. Nothing really happened.* Looking up at last, she gave him a watery smile.

He opened the can of primer with a screwdriver. Mirella and his bedroom vanished, replaced by Nadine's small square face, squinting at him with contempt in the Mexican restaurant. "You told Quigley I needed more experience," she hissed, haggard and childish. "I got my personnel file. I couldn't believe it. I couldn't *believe* you would screw me over."

He hadn't told Mirella that part. Nor that Nadine had imitated him, saying in a mocking voice: "I guess things have worked out pretty well." Then she added menacingly, "Well, How*erd,* enjoy your lunch," throwing down her napkin and stalking out of the restaurant like the villain in some spaghetti western, sombreros and serapes trembling on the wall behind her.

Nor had he shown Mirella the message Randi had written

down for him: "Thanks for everything. Looking forward to seeing you again soon."

Choosing a thick paintbrush from a bouquet of brushes in a coffee can, he dipped the brush into the primer and applied a coat of white paint to the birdhouse; the paint flowed like heavy cream across the wood. With an effort, he returned to the scene in the bedroom, Mirella clinging to his hand as he talked, his voice firm but gentle. *Nothing's really happened. I'm the same person as I was two days ago. You're the same person.*

Except, of course, for the baby.

"Baby," he said aloud.

The word hung in the air for a moment, a blur, a fast-beating heart, a bird considering one of the holes in the birdhouse.

He stroked on a last stroke of white paint. Now the birdhouse would need to dry before he could give it another coat. While the paint dried he could work on those foundation plans, which were flawed he'd noticed yesterday; he needed to redraw the boundary lines. But instead he sat down on the workroom floor near his table saw and a stack of plywood sheets, leaned his elbows on his knees, and put his arms around his head.

As he sat there, he was visited by a memory of himself at about Jacob's age, sitting on the wooden floor of his father's grocery in Albany, playing with orange boxes of soap powder while he listened to his father joke with Mr. Berg, the pharmacist from across the street. Fluorescent light buzzed and glowed from overhead tubes. Outside it was snowing. Howard stacked soap boxes, snow whirling past the windows, while the enormous, dismissive voices of the two men volleyed above him, rolling past canned pineapple and jars of mayonnaise to bounce against the glass dairy case. Cigar smoke yellowed the air, a dense stink that made Howard imagine seaweed. Gradually the men's voices became the thunder of the sea, muscular, persistent, while he was a boy on a raft, like the castaway boy in one of his picture books, floating toward a mysterious brown island. *These are men,* he thought—his first remembered conscious thought. Then a box fell, broke open, spilling white soap powder over his pant legs and shoes.

He understood that he was full of self-pity, that he was unseemly and clownish, a forty-two-year-old man sitting on a sawdust-covered floor, wishing that his wife would come looking for him. He understood that he should fall upon his knees and beg her forgiveness. He understood and did not care. In fact, he felt a reckless surge of glory, as if he were a soldier in a bunker taking part in a conflict that everyone already realized would be historic. Mirella, he wanted to bellow. You lied to me, too. You're not so pure. He would grab her wrist, twist it behind her back, say to her: Listen. I had an affair. I'm a man. Men and women have different needs.

And with this thought came a brute throb of desire for her as well, he could imagine climbing on top of her, yanking at her dress, her long bare legs sprawling on the wooden floor.

But Mirella was upstairs in their room, lying on the chenille bedspread with a damp washcloth over her eyes, pregnant, inviolable, with a headache.

His own headache was beginning to drum at the base of his skull. He staggered to his feet to check if the primer was dry, knees cracking, both legs stiff. The paint was still tacky to the touch, but it was a birdhouse, he reminded himself. He picked up the paintbrush and quickly painted the five lower sides of the box, not caring where his fingerprints embossed the paint, then took out a can of forest green semigloss from under his workbench, shook it up, and painted the roof. Stepping back, he wondered if he had made the holes too small.

It was then he noticed that he'd forgotten to cut a trapdoor in the floor, with hinges and a latch, so that every now and then the birdhouse could be cleaned out.

Too late. Too bad. So the birds, purple martins, whatever the hell they were, might not fit into the birdhouse. So they might drown in their own crap. The birdhouse looked more or less the way he'd wanted it to look. From a distance anyway, it looked like the birdhouse Mirella had wanted in the catalogs. Stuck up on a pole in the garden near the lilac bushes, it would hint at marshland, open swaths of wet grass, a white flaunting sky.

If she wanted him to go, he'd go. In fact, he'd get in the car and leave right now.

But as he was handling this decision in his mind, gingerly, as though it were one of Mirella's glass vases, or as though it were a bird itself, a little purple martin, trapped, shocked and warm and bony in the cage of his fingers, all claws and pinions—as he held on to this decision, he walked around his work room pushing tools onto the floor, his anger cooling, until he was feeling almost idle. Then he switched on his table saw and picked up the birdhouse, smiling at the geyser of sawdust that lit the air as he cut through the roof.

RANDI IS WATCHING Pearl pull apart the peanut-butter-and-jelly sandwich Randi has just made for her lunch, and then drop the peanut butter half onto the kitchen floor, which Randi washed just this morning. Jacob sits at the table eating peas and rice, shooting the peas crazily off his plate.

"Sorry," says Pearl tonelessly.

Randi looks up to see a pool of Pearl's grape juice spreading across the table, already dripping onto the floor and onto Jacob's new khaki shorts.

"It's going to rain," whimpers Pearl, twisting in her seat. Pearl is always fretting about the weather. She frets about hurricanes and tornadoes and avalanches. She frets about earthquakes. When it rains, she frets about floods.

"If it rains we will make gingerbread," says Randi. "Or we'll make a volcano out of baking soda and a paper-towel tube. Now clean that up."

Howard has told her that Mirella is upstairs lying down with a bad headache and must not be disturbed. He would be in his workroom, he said, looking tight-lipped and pale. From across the back garden, Randi has heard hammering intermittently for the last half hour, and the sound of a power saw.

"Jacob did it," says Pearl.

Randi returns to reading aloud from *Peter Cottontail,* a book she enjoys because of the pictures of Mrs. Cottontail's house with its little wooden hutch and checked curtains, her basket of currant buns. "One of the bunnies is named Cottontail Cottontail," Randi observes to Pearl and Jacob. "What do you make of that?"

The children stare back at her worriedly.

There has been trouble between Mirella and Howard. For a couple of days now, something gray and hard has been shouldering through the house, even when one of them is gone, and one of them has usually been gone—Mirella working late Friday, Howard in his studio all day Saturday. Whatever it is, it's been there ever since the night when they decided to go out to dinner so all of a sudden, just like she hadn't already made dinner, and not even a real apology.

Today, however, there is a difference, a shift of some kind that seems almost chemical, like gas leaking from a stove. Randi sensed it the moment she got back from her walk, a packet of yeast (dried) rattling in the brown paper sack in her hand. She felt it in the thickened air of the front hall, the unnatural quiet, like the forced hush in a game of hide-and-go-seek: Mirella vanished; Pearl and Jacob crouched behind a pile of blocks in the living room; Howard outside in the garden, jabbing at a bush with pruning shears. Had Mirella told Howard her news? Had something else happened? Randi closed the door quietly, reminded of the air that used to follow the disappearance of one of DeeDee Spicer's boyfriends. Spongy with wrath.

But now bread is baking in the oven. Preparing the dough had soothed her; the yeast looked lively enough bubbling in its dish of warm water, even if it was dry; the dough rose in its bowl. A nice loaf of oatmeal bread. She found the recipe yesterday on an old piece of newspaper when she was cleaning out the brass coal hod by the living room fireplace: "Light but nourishing, a wholesome addition to any meal." And as usual, she had improved on the ingredients. Some bran would add fiber, she thought, which was always a good idea. Especially because Pearl has been having a little trouble in that department lately.

Perhaps she will take a slice of oatmeal bread to Howard when it's ready. He must be hungry out there in his studio. She worries about Howard: he often seems sad and distracted; he needs a haircut; probably he also needs fiber. She worries that Mirella doesn't worry about him. A wife should worry about her husband, Randi thinks, straightening a little in her chair. In *Little Women,* Mrs. March was always worrying about Mr. March, even though he was never home, which was maybe the reason she worried. She herself intends to worry about Dave, or Matthew. Men like to be fussed over. Men are children, her mother used to say.

Then again, her mother was no authority on men. And if anybody acted like a child, it was her, climbing into Burton's lap, using baby talk. "Does dis boy want a kiss-kiss?" She certainly had picked enough rotten boyfriends, always fawning on them like some kind of dog. Burton was the worst, with his big stomach and hair coming out of his nose and the way he used to pat Randi's behind when she passed by his chair. Her mother didn't believe her when Randi said Burton grabbed at her. "He's just physical, honey. He just wants you to love him like a daddy." And now that screamy, disgusting little Ryan, who looked exactly like Burton.

The telephone rings by the stove and Randi gets up to answer it. "Clean that up," she says again over her shoulder to Pearl, nodding at the bread on the floor. "Hello?" she says into the phone. A female voice asks for Mrs. Goldman. A credit card company, or somebody offering newspaper subscriptions. "I'm afraid Mrs. *Cook*-Goldman isn't in," says Randi, in her phone voice, which is low-pitched and slightly nasal. "May I take a message?"

The caller says it's very important that Mrs. Goldman get her message.

"I'll let her know." Randi looks at Pearl and points toward the paper towels, snapping her fingers. Obligingly, Martha heaves herself up from her post under the table and lumbers over to eat the slice of bread, licking the peanut butter off the floor with her pink tongue.

"Who is this?" raps out the voice at the other end of the line. "Is this the baby-sitter?"

"Excuse me?" says Randi, turning around in surprise. She feels a pang of dread and rapidly begins to consider why she might be the target of that sharp voice on the telephone. It has been her fear for months and months that sooner or later her mother will succeed in tracking her down. Because in addition to taking the sapphire ring when she left Coralville, Randi also took all the HomeStyles tips DeeDee had been saving, six hundred dollars in tens and twenties inside the china cat on the top shelf of the kitchen cabinets—her mother's "disaster fund," hidden even from Burton—again, in a way, really Randi's, because the china cat had been given to her in fourth grade by Mrs. Petersen next door at Christmas, and her mother took it without asking, just as she had so often "borrowed" Randi's baby-sitting money to buy cigarettes.

Besides, mothers were supposed to help their daughters, not the other way around. DeeDee should see it as buying Randi her bus ticket, like paying for college. Mothers were not supposed to

marry men like Burton, who lumbered around with his fly un-
zipped half the time. Mothers were not supposed to moo like
cows and whine "Come on, come on, come on" in the middle of
the night when their daughters were sleeping next door. Mothers
were not supposed to have babies when they were practically old
women.

Randi reflects that her mother and Mirella are actually the
same age and that Mirella is having a baby even later in life
than DeeDee. But it's different, she decides, picturing DeeDee's
kitchen with its dirty windows and fake brick linoleum, countertops buried under open baby-food jars, doughnut boxes, empty
Diet Coke cans. The high-chair tray upended in the sink, crusted
with dried oatmeal and milk. Worlds different.

For an instant Randi pictures Howard and Mirella and
DeeDee Spicer sitting companionably on the living room sofa,
DeeDee in her Huskee hostess uniform, smoking a Virginia Slim.
I just love this old house, DeeDee would say. *Did George Washington
ever sleep here?*

"Excuse me?" she says again into the telephone.

She hears the sound of quick breathing, as if the caller has
climbed a flight of steps. Then: "With whom am I speaking?"

Randi answers, "Mr. Goldman's niece."

The caller seems to consider this response for a moment. "I'll
call back," the voice says at last, in a tone that is both suspicious
and trying hard to sound convinced. "Thank you very much."

When Randi hangs up the telephone, she is surprised to see
Howard hunched in the kitchen doorway, wild-eyed, sawdust in
his hair. At the sight of him, Jacob puts his hands over his ears.

"Daddy," shrieks Pearl.

Howard holds up his hand, fingers spread. A gash near the
thumb is dripping blood. Blood twines down his forearm.

"You cut yourself," Randi exclaims, noticing that blood is spat-
tering the kitchen floor. "Let me get you a Band-Aid."

"Who was that?" he asks whitely.

"Just somebody wanting to sell something. Oh Howard, your poor thumb." And Randi bustles around to open a drawer by the sink, which she has designated the first-aid drawer, going so far as to tape a little red cross below the handle so that in case of an emergency even a child would know what to do.

3

HOWARD HAD BEEN GONE three days when Vasanti Gupta appeared at the front door to bring Mirella some syrupy-looking orange pastries on a blue-flowered china plate.

It was Thursday morning, just before Mirella left for work. Vasanti was wearing a nectarine-colored silk print dress that made her dark skin look lustrous. In the hand not holding the plate of pastry, she was carrying a leather briefcase identical to Mirella's, but newer, and without the place where Pearl had written her name in pink Magic Marker.

"We made these last night," Vasanti said, in her low breathless voice. "We thought you and the children might enjoy them. These are Indian pastries," she added, with a slight cough, as if Mirella might not otherwise have been able to identify what was on the plate.

"How nice of you," said Mirella automatically accepting the pastries. "Thanks so much."

Vasanti smiled. "Maybe sometime soon, we have been thinking, our families can have dinner?" She paused to cough again. "You and your children. Would you like to come to dinner at our house sometime?" She did not mention Howard.

"Thanks so much," repeated Mirella. "How nice. We would love to."

But as soon as she closed the door, she began thinking of excuses for why they couldn't possibly have dinner with the Guptas. A fever for Pearl. Jacob exposed to chicken pox. Don't you dare feel sorry me, she thought, picturing Vasanti's kind, round face.

Howard was in Greenwich with Richard and Vivvy. He left Sunday afternoon, taking only a small suitcase, the little green L.L. Bean bag he'd had since college. Twice he'd called to speak to the children; each time Randi answered the phone. "Daddy sounded weird," said Pearl after the second call. But when Mirella questioned her she was vague and evasive. "He sounded like his teeth hurt," she finally allowed. Then she said, "He told me they rented a movie. He said it was called *Howard's End*."

Pearl was staying home today. Happy Faces had metamorphosed for the summer into Happy Faces Camp, which meant the addition of a plastic wading pool, but part of the preschool floor had been scorched the day before during a candle-dipping project. Camp was closed until tomorrow. Fortunately none of the children were injured, although a teacher had a burn on one foot.

"Don't go, Mommy," wailed Pearl, running across the front lawn as Mirella was getting into the jeep. "Don't leave me."

"Stop crying, Pearl," said Mirella, aware of Mahesh Gupta across the street, leading his little girls into the garage.

As she was driving to work, Mirella thought about the call she'd had from Vivvy last night, after the children were in bed. "He's still here," Vivvy said, too loudly as usual.

"Is he all right?" Mirella asked.

"What?"

"Is he all right?"

"He's all right. He spent the whole day out by the pool."

"The pool?" It had never occurred to Mirella that Howard might be in any way enjoying himself in Greenwich. "What did he tell you?" She hesitated. "Did he tell you about the baby?"

"Yes," said Vivvy crisply. "I think he's being an ass. Though of course I can see why he's pissed at not finding out until now."

After a moment, during which she could hear background noise at Vivvy's, the sound of water running, dishes clinking, Mirella said, "This affair business has been a shock. I don't know what to do. I'm not sure I'll get over it."

She was unreasonably depressed to think of Vivvy doing the dishes while they discussed Mirella and Howard's marriage. All day Mirella had been watching people drive their cars, cross streets, sip from plastic cups of beige frozen coffee drinks. It continued to astonish her, although it no longer should, that one person's life could be cracking apart while everyone else's went on as normal.

The sounds of dishwashing stopped. "It's supposed to be a shock," Vivvy said. "If it's not a shock, then you should really worry. That's when things are really bad."

"Did he—" Mirella paused to moisten her lips. "Did he say anything about her?"

"Not really. He thinks she might be sort of stalking him."

"Stalking him." Despite herself, Mirella laughed. "After three years?"

Vivvy turned the water on again. "Three days, three years. Don't forgive him," she'd advised, "until you understand what you're forgiving."

Now Mirella sat in her office on Boylston Street staring at the draft of a motion she needed to file before five o'clock. A clerk called to say that Betsy Hayman's divorce settlement had been approved by the judge. A lawyer called to change a deposition date because her client wanted to go to Disney World. A few minutes ago she herself had tried to telephone her mother. Let's have lunch, she wanted to suggest. How about this afternoon? But the visiting nurse, whose name she couldn't recall, answered the phone and said with a faintly hostile lisp that Mrs. Cook was out walking. Mr. Cook was at home. Did Mirella want to speak to her father?

Hauugh, said her father, when he came on the line. *Harrgh.* Mirella's eyes filled with tears. "It's all right, Dad. I'm fine. Everyone's fine. Just calling to say hello." *Haawgg.*

The morning went on. Her throat felt sore. This afternoon she had a court appearance in a second-parent adoption case with lesbian partners, for which she was unprepared. Her client was the child's birth mother; the partner, a dentist, was the financial support, but the judge seemed to be balking. One of the ironies of this case was that the two women had such similar last names. Coners and Kahners. Oh life's little ironies, thought Mirella grimly. She ate an orange.

Ruth was in court until one o'clock. Mirella had called Ruth on Sunday, right after Howard left, and Ruth drove straight over, arriving at three with two bottles of Chianti and a bag of candy corn. "Comfort food," she announced, folding herself onto the sofa. "Okay, tell me everything," she said, after Mirella sent Randi and the children out to get ice cream in town. At first it had been consoling to talk to Ruth, but it became less so as Ruth revealed the ways in which she had always distrusted Howard. "Frankly, he's too good-looking," she said at one point. At another, she said thoughtfully, "His fingers always seemed too short for an architect's."

And somehow, as the conversation wound on, Mirella kept forgetting to tell Ruth that she was pregnant, which she had meant to confess from the moment she refused a glass of wine, but opened the bag of candy corn. Then the children returned, faces smeared with chocolate, the phone rang, and Ruth had to get home to walk her schnauzer. The opportunity was lost.

"Like so many opportunities," Mirella found herself typing onto the computer screen. She let the words remain for a moment, before backspacing over them and returning to the motion she was drafting. "Plaintiff alleges," she typed.

Calls were buzzed through. Randi telephoned to remind Mirella that Pearl needed a costume for the historical play Happy Faces planned to perform on the Fourth of July, in honor of New Aylesbury's 350th anniversary celebration. A wainwright Pearl was supposed to be. Could Mirella buy leather breeches anywhere? One of Ruth's clients, a thin, red-haired woman wearing stained denim pants, began sobbing in the waiting room. Laura, the new paralegal, who seemed hardly older than Danielle, tapped at Mirella's door with a question about the Vassbacher case: "What is the precise legal definition of primary caretaker?"

Vassbacher himself sent Mirella an e-mail: "Any news from that lady the court sent over? Not sure how well the evaluation went. The girls didn't say much. The toaster caught on fire while she was here." A jackhammer pounded below on Boylston; her computer hummed like a refrigerator; the smell of orange peel rose from the wastebasket.

She was pregnant. Howard had slept three years ago with a woman named Nadine. Possibly he'd slept with her again. Three days ago he left to go stay with his brother in Connecticut, after nearly slicing his thumb off with his table saw. During the commotion, the dog stole an entire loaf of oatmeal bread from the kitchen counter, ate it, then shat all over the blue Chinese rug.

All of this had happened and here was Mirella at her desk.

It seemed like some sort of strange algorithm, these separate occurrences; she had an urge to sketch them out on a clean sheet of paper, to add them up, subtract what she could, multiply the consequences of each, already accepting that no equation would work. Sunlight from the plate-glass window behind her fell squarely against her back, heating her skin through her putty-colored linen dress. She felt a thick lurch of nausea. Time to focus, she instructed herself. Time to concentrate on the motion in front of you. Instead, she kept picturing Vassbacher's toaster on fire.

Swiveling in her chair so the sun sluiced along her arm, she understood that she would continue to compute it all, no matter how pointless the exercise became. She would continue to search for a common denominator that would explain Howard's affair and another baby and the possibly ruined rug and why she'd felt so distraught at the sight of Vasanti Gupta's plate of orange pastries. She would try to comprehend all of this because she was a rational person, who put her faith in solving problems, which she was beginning to believe was one of the best facets of her character, and also one of the worst.

Oh Howard, she thought.

An oily weariness seeped through her. She lay back in her chair, bones swimming, and closed her eyes. In the hallway the woman's weeping faded away, then ended entirely. Cheryl, the receptionist, was answering the phone rapidly in her South Boston accent each time it rang: Cook & Zeigler. CookaZeigler. CookaSeagull.

Mirella opened her eyes and picked up the phone. She dialed Richard and Vivvy's number, then hung up and snatched her hand off the receiver when she heard a knock on her door.

"Am I interrupting?" Ruth stood at the half-opened door, her short gray hair looking greenish in the hallway's fluorescence. "Hey, are you okay?" Coming a few steps into Mirella's office, Ruth gave her a quizzical glance and balanced the sheaf of documents she was carrying on the end of the desk. "You're the same color as your dress."

Mirella fanned herself with a court order. "Is the one who was crying in the hall all right?"

"She'll survive," Ruth said dispassionately. "She's just got to get her priorities straight."

"Don't we all," sighed Mirella.

"No," said Ruth. "Not like that."

About a third of Ruth's clients were battered women and sometimes also drug addicts, referred by the women's shelter where Ruth volunteered on Monday nights. They slumped in the waiting room chairs in baggy jeans and nylon jackets, eyes bloodshot, radiating a strange languid belligerent despair. Later they sent religious greeting cards with shakily written statements of gratitude penned at the bottom. "You saved my life," most of them said, in one form or another. "I thank God for you." Ruth occasionally read these notes aloud to Mirella in the conference room at lunchtime, adjusting the reading glasses she wore on a long, clear-beaded chain.

The rest of her clients were corporate wives going after their husbands' assets. The high-tech boom had been excellent for business. Getting rich quickly had a deleterious effect on marriage, Ruth claimed. Particularly for middle-aged male executives, who had been comfortable in the shade of modest success, but were finding it difficult to remain modest and middle-aged in the brilliance of their own new prospects.

"So how are you surviving?" Ruth gave her the same clinical look she'd probably given her weeping client.

"All right, I guess."

"You know, you could take the day off."

"I need to finish this motion, and I've got a court appearance in an hour. Plus Jerry Vassbacher just blew his GAL evaluation." Mirella began plucking at the front of her dress. Ruth had a perspicacious way of smiling and frowning at the same time that seemed especially disconcerting today. "This was his chance to show off his great parenting skills. Then his kids sat like mummies while he practically burned down the house."

"Who's the opposing counsel?"

"A piranha from Rabb, Lowell & Goodfriend who was the

wife's roommate in boarding school, which means she'll probably write off half her hours. Plus we've got that rhinoceros Foley for a probate judge."

"Life in the jungle," murmured Ruth.

"My guess is we'll lose everything but visitation." Mirella stared at her hands, feeling her stomach lurch again. "Even though his wife couldn't remember the pediatrician's name in her deposition."

"My advice," Ruth said, sitting down comfortably on the edge of Mirella's desk, "is to get a bunch of women to testify. You have to persuade Foley that your guy is the kids' mother, so get some women to say so. Teachers, friends, Girl Scout leader. If there's a bias in favor of mothers, which, in this rare situation, there is, then go with the bias, show how it fits. Honor the rule you're breaking. What you *could* do—"

Gazing at Ruth across her desk, only half listening, because this strategy had already occurred to her, Mirella found herself thinking of the shower curtain she had still neglected to buy at Filene's, and of Pearl's rest blanket at school, which had not been brought home to be washed since Christmas, and also of the nutritionist appointment she still meant to schedule for Jacob.

If she lost her children, she would never recover. This was not a hysterical or melodramatic idea; if she lost her children she knew she would come close to dying. Or simply become somebody better off dead.

You have to get to work, she told herself. You have so much work, don't think about anything but work. But just at that moment, Mirella had a distinct image of Jerry Vassbacher in his bathrobe. He was standing in his daughters' room, watching them sleep. She saw it all quite clearly, just as if she were with him in the room. He was wearing a blue terry-cloth bathrobe. Light glowed from a mushroom-shaped nightlight, for a moment illuminating the peaceful attentiveness on his face as he bent to retrieve a hairband, a plastic bracelet tossed to the floor. She watched him straighten up to brush a strand of hair away from the mouth of one child and cover the thin legs of the other, his bulky body unobtrusive, almost graceful in performing these tasks, his eyeglasses shining here, there as he moved through the darkened room.

"You aren't listening to me," Ruth was saying sharply. "Mirella. What is it? Can I get you some water?"

As she heard this question, and even tried to respond to it, Mirella had the feeling that once again she was forgetting something essential, something that shrank and wobbled as she tried to catch it, rolling down the incline of the tilting room.

"Mirella," she heard Ruth say, as if she were calling from under the desk. "Mirella?"

"I'm sorry." Mirella opened her eyes. "I'm pregnant."

"I'm sorry?"

"That's what I just said." She tried to laugh, hot and breathless, trapped in her square of sunlight, with Ruth bending over the desk, smelling of coffee, her thin face close enough that Mirella could see the pores in her nose. No one, she thought irritably, should get that close. Up from her wastebasket floated the stinging scent of orange peel. "Although I'm not really," she managed to say, "sorry about being pregnant."

An instant later, she said, "Oh God, Ruth."

Quietly, Ruth closed Mirella's door and came around the desk. She bent over, gathering back Mirella's hair with one hand, giving it a twist. "It's all right," she said. "Go on ahead," and with her other hand, she picked up the wastebasket to hold until Mirella was done.

4

ALL MORNING RANDI occupies the children with raking up a little plot of ground in the back garden. She has bought packets of seeds: carrots, lettuce, zucchini. The children use plastic rakes. Jacob uses his rake mostly as a cane, hobbling around on the grass looking for ants and caterpillars. He finds a worm in the dirt and wraps it around one finger. "Yuck," squeals Pearl. "You're sick."

Jacob looks up at Randi, the hand with the worm in midair.

"Hush," Randi tells Pearl. Bending down close to Jacob, she whispers, "You're my sweet boy," and gives him a kiss.

After lunch that afternoon, Randi leads Pearl and Jacob into the front yard to check on their nest of starlings in the dogwood tree. A month ago Randi had glanced out her window while folding laundry and spotted four pale blue eggs swaddled under the oily-looking mother bird. Since then the nest has lured all three of them like a polestar. Randi had even looked up starlings in the Audubon bird guide at the library. "Conditioned by centuries of living in settled areas in Europe, the starling easily adapted to American cities when one hundred birds were liberated in

Central Park in 1890," Randi read aloud to Jacob, while he punched keys on the keyboard of the library computer. "Since then the starling has spread over most of the continent."

Then last Thursday, there they were, a pair of egg-damp chicks. Randi, Pearl, and Jacob took turns watching them from the front steps through Howard's binoculars. The chicks' unopened eyes were filmed by membrane, hideous and miraculous as they shuddered toward each other, mouths gaping upward like tulips.

All week the starlings have been busy, ferrying grubs and insects to their babies. Randi is almost embarrassed of how proud she feels at having discovered this nest, of how much she enjoys showing the children nature and the world. She is giving them lessons on life, even without television. Some days when Pearl is in preschool, Randi and Jacob sit under the dogwood tree and she explains anatomy to him, and evolution, and gravity. "We all have bones," she says softly, holding up her hand. "We all started as nothing. What goes up must come down." Jacob lies rapt in the grass, watching her.

But this afternoon something awful has happened.

Just as Randi reaches the front steps she can see, even without binoculars, that the nest has been disturbed. Bits of twig and fluff have fallen onto the grass below. Up in the tree sits an enormous blue jay, choking down a smash of pin feathers.

"Hey," screams Randi, as Pearl and Jacob freeze beside her. "Hey, get out of there." She runs toward the dogwood tree, waving her arms, but the chicks have mostly been eaten. The blue jay plunges away. The starling parents have vanished.

Pearl and Jacob drift toward her and stand at the bottom of the tree. The three of them examine the feathers and a slimy bit of something like black cartilage lying in the grass. Pearl squats down to pick up a feather as Martha the dog ambles toward them across the lawn. Martha bumps against their legs and pushes her nose into their hands, tail swishing. Then she sniffs at the black thing in the grass. Randi drags at her collar. "Leave it," she says.

Across the street, Mrs. Gupta waves at them as she helps Aparna and Parvati out of the car. Sunlight flashes off the car windows. The Guptas all wave again as they walk up their front steps. Pearl and Randi wave back; Jacob is still gazing at the grass.

When they look up again, they see that one of the adult starlings has come back. For a minute or two the bird hops from branch to branch. Finally it perches on the edge of the nest, pointing its yellow beak up, down, sideways in questioning, robotic fractions. Its wings have a dull purplish cast that reminds Randi of sweat stains inside a coat lining. The bird lingers for a minute longer. Randi and the children watch, holding hands.

Then the bird flies off.

"Is it sad?" Pearl asks.

"No," says Randi, looking away. "It's just a bird."

RANDI LEADS THE CHILDREN back inside. Although it is a beautiful day and the whole world beckons—the blue sky and the shorn green grass and the gray squirrels leaping along telephone wires and the shouts of the two little Guptas playing hopscotch on the sidewalk and down at the harbor the waves shushing and sighing and nudging black garlands of seaweed onto the sand—and although fresh air would do them all good, Randi assigns Pearl and Jacob a project.

They sit at the kitchen table armed with glue sticks, colored construction paper, pipe cleaners, and Magic Markers. Jacob's birthday present, which Randi ordered from a catalog, arrived this morning and is lying bulkily in the garage, wrapped in a plastic sheet, hidden behind the snowblower. His birthday isn't for three weeks, but Randi has already been making plans. She intends to give him the best birthday ever, a party he'll always remember, a party that will make everyone forget that Howard is gone. Better even than the party Pearl went to last week where all the little girls got magic wands and fairy wings and threw gold glitter at each other.

She'd gotten her idea for Jacob's present from *The Story of New Aylesbury,* which is due back at the library tomorrow. According to the book, the local Indians were at first friendly to the English settlers but then began killing them after a settler shot an Indian who stole an iron toasting fork. Randi makes a mental note to renew *The Story of New Aylesbury* while she stitches together two lengths of fawn-colored suede. She has set the children to making decorations and favors, which otherwise Mirella will buy for too much money downtown at PartyLine.

Ever since Howard left, Randi has been making things. More sock dolls for Pearl's family. A scrap pillow for Jacob's nest in the fireplace and a shoebox signal tower for his trains. Raisin scones for Mirella. She has answered the phone each time it rings, both to save Mirella the trouble and because she's half hoping, half fearing to hear the voice that demanded to know if she was the baby-sitter. If whoever it was called again, Randi planned to say that there was no baby-sitter. She was Howard's niece, helping with the children until college started in the fall. "I attend Boston University," she would say. "Majoring in economics."

Along with making things, Randi has been cleaning house. Last night she polished each pane of the glass-fronted kitchen cabinets using white vinegar and newspaper; she also took a knife and pried all the bread crumbs, crushed Cheerios, and dried peanut butter out of the crack where the table leaves join. She swept the floor and threw out all the old folded grocery sacks wedged under the sink. She even scoured out the aquarium, scum-green with algae, which she figured the fish would be happy about, although they seem sluggish this morning; they haven't eaten their fish food.

She doesn't know why Howard left. Mirella hasn't told her anything except that Howard is visiting his brother, and Randi hasn't figured out a polite way to ask if he's coming back. But she's not stupid. Whenever one of DeeDee's boyfriends left, it was always because he was sleeping with somebody else. Randi's eyes narrow as she recalls the phone message she took for Howard from someone named Nadine. "Tell Howard that I look forward to seeing him again real soon."

Cheat. Liar. Dirtbag. Scum. He is not worthy of his beautiful home and his darling children. He is ruining everything. Randi pricks her thumb with the needle and watches a bright red dot well on her skin. Last week there was a message written in the dust on the back window of his car: "Land-Rapist," it said.

Pig. Dog. I would like to see him hung up by his balls.

This last thought makes Randi get up from her chair. She goes to the sink to wash her thumb, then sits back down again and very carefully pictures a blackboard and an eraser and then erases what she has been thinking.

The kitchen is clean and welcoming. The children are busy and quiet. By her feet, the dog snores and twitches. Tucked inside the refrigerator are all the ingredients Randi needs for strawberry shortcake, which she intends to make this afternoon to cheer up Mirella. Maybe she will also make strawberry shortcake for the Guptas, in return for those orange pastries, which tasted a little like cough medicine but otherwise were pretty good. She imagines bearing her strawberry shortcake across the street, carrying a glass bowl of strawberries and a platter of little golden cakes on the tea tray, also a carton of whipping cream for preparing on the spot. Mirella and the children follow behind. Pearl's hair would be in a French braid; Jacob would have on his new striped shirt and the khaki shorts she'd just washed. Mirella would wear one of her silk dresses, maybe the one with little pink flowers on a yellow background.

Scowling gently, Randi returns to her sewing.

To be perfectly honest, she is angry at Mirella, too, even

though Mirella is having a difficult time. But she minds that Mirella has begun to look so unattractive these last couple weeks, neglecting to comb her hair, wearing the same blouse two days in a row, wandering through the house since Howard left as if she's at a hotel and has forgotten her room number. She doesn't drink her milk or remember to take her prenatal vitamins. Yesterday Randi found an open bottle of wine in the refrigerator. Worse, Mirella didn't even seem worried last night when Randi told her about the candle-dipping accident at Pearl's school; she hardly said more than "thank you" when Randi described how she had raced to Happy Faces with Jacob in his stroller to collect Pearl, how she had comforted Pearl and bought her an ice cream on the way home. Even though Mirella is pregnant with her third baby, she hardly looks like a mother at all. In fact, she is beginning to look a little bit like DeeDee Spicer after one of her big nights out—baggy-eyed, clumsy, a flat set to her mouth.

Randi gets up again and walks over to the aquarium. She raps on the glass with her knuckles. "Wake up," she says to the fish.

When she returns to her chair, Randi notices that Pearl has cut off a few small locks of her hair with the scissors and is using a glue stick to glue hair to the table. Jacob is watching her, his own glue stick suspended midair.

"Pearl," says Randi. "What are you doing?"

"Nothing," says Pearl.

The table looks as if it has sprouted a thin beard. Jacob begins to pick his nose.

"Is it going to rain?" Pearl's lip is trembling.

"The radio said sun." Randi gives her a severe look. "Besides if you're ever in a flood, all you have to do is climb onto your roof and the National Guard will come and get you in a helicopter."

Jacob stops picking his nose to stare at her in wonder.

"It's true." Randi nods. "It happened to my grandmother. They even saved her cat."

For a moment she pictures an apple-faced grandmother sitting on a rooftop, a tabby cat in her lap, quietly crocheting an afghan while a helicopter hovers above her like a gigantic dragonfly. It is a heartening picture; it is another thing that should have happened in her life and didn't but now, in a way, has. "So stop worrying," she tells Pearl.

"Could a helicopter save baby chicks?" says Pearl.

"Nature is nature," says Randi. "Leave it alone."

Obediently, Pearl bends over her sheet of construction paper, cutting out small yellow triangles. Jacob watches her, then turns to Randi. "Daa?" he says, pointing to the window.

"That what?" says Randi.

It's then that she hears the sound of car tires in the driveway.

The dog scrambles up from the floor, toenails skittering, and begins barking. Turning in her chair, Randi peers out the window. She turns quickly around again. "Stay back from the window," she tells Pearl and Jacob, and she reaches for the phone to call Mirella.

5

"Goldman Associates, Howard speaking."

"Too bad it isn't three hundred years ago," rasped a voice on the other end of the line. "We could have put you in the stocks."

Howard heard a click, then a few moments later a dial tone. Setting the receiver back in its cradle he wondered briefly if the caller had been Nadine, then decided the voice was male. He'd had several calls along these lines in the last few weeks and attributed them to local cranks who were irate over the Town-Common development. It was almost a relief to get this call, reminding him that he was back right where he had been.

He continued to stand by his desk for a few moments, gazing out the window at the house. When he arrived an hour ago no one appeared to be home. He'd sat in the car for a minute or two in the driveway, absurdly certain that the front door would fly open and the children would come tumbling out, crying his name. But nothing stirred save a fat blue jay, which flew down from a tree making rude shrieking noises. Feeling that he was trespassing, and also that he was being melodramatic, he got out of the car and went through the garden. The whole neighborhood seemed deserted, but then it usually was on hot days in late June, when everyone who wasn't at work was probably at the beach.

He looked at the phone, waiting to see if it would buzz again. A greenhead fly buzzed instead, looping around the studio, lighting first on a bookshelf, then on the coffee cup on Howard's desk, still half full of three-day-old coffee, speckled with tiny islands of mold. Heading back to his drafting table, he decided that he should have called Mirella before coming home. This thought had tormented him all during his drive back, and yet he hadn't allowed himself to stop along the way. He'd left Richard and Vivvy's house before they were up, leaving a note for them propped on the coffee grinder. *Thanks for everything. I'm going home to seek my fortune.*

This last bit was probably too cute, Howard realized, sitting down and rapping his wrist with a mechanical pencil. He pictured Vivvy grimacing as she read the note, handing it to Richard while she went to get the bag of espresso beans out of the freezer. *"Puer aeternus,"* she'd say.

But he couldn't have stayed another ten minutes in Richard's house. He felt almost allergic to its ugliness, particularly to the sunken living room with its unyielding lozenge-shaped furniture in primary colors and to the icy marble tiles in the foyer, the enormous frosted-glass chandelier hanging overhead like a massive stalactite. The house echoed with doleful plashing from the five-foot "water feature" Vivvy had installed in the dining room, a noise that was supposed to be calming but which reminded him of the leaky upstairs sink at home. Especially he couldn't spend another night sleeping in his niece Eden's bedroom, which had been preserved as she'd left it the last time she was home, complete with tiger-striped panties on the floor, an open bottle of crimson nail polish, and posters of snarling female rock stars wearing black leather pants and what looked to be armor breast-plates.

He missed the children. He was surprised at how much he missed them, the sharpness of their elbows and knees as they clambered onto his legs, the solid weight of them in his lap, the hard roundness of their heads under his chin. Without them he felt lethargic and superfluous. There was nothing for him to do at Richard's except read the newspaper and Vivvy's gourmet food magazines by the swimming pool, waiting for lunch or dinner, like being on a cruise ship that landed nowhere. He had forgotten the sheer occupation of being in a household of small children, the practical, necessary ways they made you their property.

And he missed Mirella. As he walked around Richard's house, he missed joking about it to her, pointing out that the custom-made butcher-block work island in the kitchen was shaped like testicles, or that Richard had recently installed phones in the bathrooms. Most of all he missed the pressure of her bare skin against his at night, the way she sought him out when she slept, like a heat-seeking missile, sometimes pressing him all the way to the edge of the bed. He missed waking beside her, hearing Pearl call out for a glass of water or Jacob mutter in his sleep, listening to the odd shifting and groaning of timbers in the house.

His hand throbbed from where he'd cut it on the table saw. Carefully Howard pried up a bandage edge to peer at the wound, which was not very deep or very wide, but still a raw purple color.

Besides, he had his first meeting with the planning board in two weeks, and he still hadn't finished the foundation plans. Work was work, no matter what else was going on. He intended to abide by Mirella's request; he would stay completely out of the house, at least until they settled their differences, or she had settled hers.

In the meantime, he would live in his studio. On the way

home this morning, he had stopped in Danvers for an early lunch at Friendly's, then went to the army-navy store and bought a thin mattress and a folding cot. Afterward he walked across the parking lot to Wal-Mart and bought a hot plate to go above the little fridge next to Krystal Anne's desk. He bought a box of cereal, a carton of milk, crackers, a few cans of soup. Maybe tomorrow he would buy a microwave. It occurred to him that he might even buy a small TV set.

He still hadn't decided how he would explain this new arrangement to Krystal Anne. She'd taken the week off, but was due back right after the Fourth of July. Maybe he would simply fire her, which would probably suit Krystal Anne anyway. Last week he'd found an open *Boston Globe* on her desk, circled classified ads rising like air bubbles from the bottom of the page.

It was almost pleasant contemplating this spartan strategy, the possible bareness of life. He was reminded of stories about his father's youth in a Lower East Side tenement, eight immigrants in a one-bedroom apartment. His father had slept on three kitchen chairs pushed together.

Unable to concentrate on the plans he was drawing, Howard got up and went back to his desk to look at his mail, then turned on his computer. The screen appeared, accompanied by the brief orchestral bounce that always greeted him, as if the computer were overjoyed to be switched on. He checked his e-mail, discovering three messages waiting for him from members of the Preservation of New Aylesbury Committee. One message read: "You and your capitalist-imperialist co-conspirators are responsible for the rapine of all nature. When the children weep for their lost vistas, know you are to blame."

He should junk this thing altogether. Donate it to Krystal Anne and The Org. Simplify, simplify.

Maybe he would reread *Walden*. Maybe this weekend he would take Pearl and Jacob swimming at Walden Pond and describe how Thoreau had built himself a cabin and lived there with a molasses jug and one chair, watching ants for entertainment.

The phone buzzed again as he was shutting down the computer.

"Howard?" said Richard's voice, irritated and placating. "You could have at least waited for breakfast. And you left your shaving cream. Are you all right? Vivvy and I are very worried about you. Howard, are you okay?"

"I'm fine," said Howard, starting to sweat. "I just needed to get back."

"We're coming up," announced Richard. "We want to visit you both. We're coming for the Fourth of July weekend."

"I'm not sure that's such a great idea."

"We're coming up. Vivvy's calling Mirella."

"Richard."

"We're coming. Don't worry. We'll work everything out."

"Richard, please," said Howard, intending to explain that he was a grown man, who needed to solve his own problems and control his own life. I am a man, he thought, suddenly picturing his father standing in his grocery store, huge in a white apron.

But as he listened to Richard ignore him and go on to outline a campaign for the Fourth of July, it occurred to Howard that no matter what was solved, or wasn't solved with Mirella, somehow in the end everything in his life would still happen to him.

"Keep your chin up," said Richard. He took a noisy breath and let it out. And then in the curious way Richard had of occasionally reading Howard's mind, he added, "Listen to me, Howard. You and Mirella are adults. The lives of adults are complicated and generally somehow bad."

"Thanks," said Howard, surprised to find this observation reassuring. "I'll try to keep that in mind."

6

ACCORDING TO ALL FORECASTS, Mirella told Pearl at breakfast the next morning, the weather should be beautiful all week. For some reason, Pearl was worrying about the roof being too pitched for a helicopter to land on in case of a flood. She was also convinced that Happy Faces had burned down and refused to believe that Mirella was taking her to camp this morning. Mirella tried to be sympathetic to Pearl's troubles, but they continued to increase. Yesterday Pearl and Jacob had apparently found a dead bird—Mirella couldn't quite understand the story, something about the dog trying to eat it—then this morning the goldfish, Lucky and Snowbell, had been discovered floating belly up in their aquarium.

"We'll get some new fish, sweetheart," Mirella said.

"I don't want new fish," Pearl wailed.

And now, all of a sudden, Howard was home.

The maples in the Pilkeys' yard next door were heavy with wide green leaves. Their daylilies had opened overnight, reflecting pumpkin orange in the still blue water of the swimming pool.

The roses in the Applewhites' garden seemed to bloom more profusely than ever before, hybrid teas, species roses, floribunda, ramblers and climbing roses, roses the Applewhites referred to by gaudy provocative names: Gipsy Carnival, Party Girl, Double Delight. "Look, honey." Mirella pointed out the window, trying to distract Pearl, who was still crying. Near the fence, roses bloomed as big as softballs, cream and pink, their fringed yellow hearts bursting.

Mirella had not yet spoken to Howard. Yesterday afternoon Randi called her at work to say he was back, so at least Mirella had a little time to prepare herself. According to Randi, he'd spent a few hours in the backyard with Pearl and Jacob, helping to stack a pile of sticks that was supposed to be a fort. But when Mirella drove up yesterday evening, he was gone again. At around eleven, she saw the studio lights go on, but she was in bed by then and also too angry to get up and go downstairs, cross the garden, and knock at his door. There was no sign of him this morning, except for his car next to hers in the driveway.

"Let's go, sweetie," Mirella told Pearl.

"Can we dry them?" sniffed Pearl.

"Dry what?" said Mirella desperately. She felt if she stayed in the house one more minute, she would lose her mind.

"The fish. Can we dry them?"

"We have this book," explained Randi, who was holding Jacob by the sink and wiping his face with a paper towel, "that tells how the early settlers lived, and they did a lot of fish drying, you know. To eat."

As soon as Randi set him down, Jacob ran to the fireplace to sit in his nest. Ever since Howard had left, Jacob had wanted to spend nearly all his time in there.

"You want to eat Lucky and Snowbell?" said Mirella, watching Jacob pull his headdress over his ears.

"No," yelled Pearl. "You never understand anything. I just want to keep them forever."

At last they were safely in the Jeep, Pearl strapped in her car seat, clutching the bodies of Lucky and Snowbell, shrouded in a paper napkin. Mirella adjusted the rearview mirror and put her seat back, wondering briefly if Randi had been using her car. The emergency brake wasn't all the way up; it sometimes got stuck in a half-released position. She'd warned Randi before to check the brake, but then possibly Howard had moved the Jeep last night, although why would he? She glanced up, relieved and furious that Howard was not this minute hurrying out to the driveway, trying to catch her before she left for work. She had been ready, almost ready, to forgive him yesterday. Or if not forgive him, then at least to try to forbear what he had done. Now she was convinced she'd been spared a terrible mistake.

She turned on the radio and found a news channel to distract herself, half hearing something about the Clinton administration and new allegations from the independent counsel of sexual misconduct, at the same time backing out of the driveway, thinking about Howard and how he had betrayed her.

"Who is Fellatio?" said Pearl after a moment.

"Someone in a play," said Mirella, quickly turning off the radio.

As they drove toward Pearl's school, Mirella looked out the window, appalled once again at how normal, even absurdly healthy everything looked outside. Purple loosestrife bloomed rampantly along the side of the road; honeysuckle drowned every other stone wall. Passing Alice Norcross Pratt's wide front yard, Mirella noticed red and orange marigolds parading around the edge of a vegetable plot, crowding against the chicken wire. Enormous moss baskets of pink and white petunias swung from the porch. The grass was spangled with dew.

Twenty minutes later—after extracting the napkin of dead

goldfish from Pearl, and assuring her once again that it would not rain—Mirella emerged back into daylight from Happy Faces' subterranean hallway to discover Alice herself standing in the parking lot in running shoes and blue maternity overalls. In the jogging stroller sat Alice's two little boys, this time eating cucumber spears. Alice was telling a tired-looking Vasanti Gupta that she had recently ordered praying mantis eggs, an all-natural pesticide, for her vegetable garden. "Very nice," said Vasanti, with her palm to her head.

Mirella wiggled her fingers, hoping to slip past unnoticed. But just as she was edging by, Alice looked up and said, "Hello there, Mirella," and pulled a clipboard and a ballpoint pen from the quilted diaper bag slung over her shoulder. "Do you have a moment?" she said. "I'm collecting signatures for an antisprawl initiative."

"Good-bye," called Vasanti Gupta, suddenly looking less tired. She gripped her handbag, glancing with furtive sympathy at Mirella. "So sorry. I must be off."

"Thanks again for the pastries," Mirella said. "They were delicious."

"Oh yes, you're very welcome." And Vasanti Gupta was gone, darting into a hedgerow of station wagons and minivans.

"What's this initiative?" Mirella asked Alice, conscious of trying too hard to sound like an ordinary person on an ordinary morning. "Have I heard of it?" An engine kicked over, coughing into a roar.

Alice shrugged, smiling. "By the way," she said, handing her the clipboard. "Please tell Randi I appreciated her help on those flyers for the bazaar. Fuschia was a great color choice."

"I'm sorry—?" Mirella gazed in confusion at Alice's long, incurious, lightly freckled face.

"I called your house last week to remind you again and Randi said you've been busy and she'd take care of it. She was going around town the other day, posting them for me. What a worker," Alice added.

"Oh," said Mirella, scanning the petition in front of her without reading the words. "Great. I'm glad it got done."

"We've collected almost five hundred signatures." Alice patted one of her little boys on the head.

But just as Mirella was about to add her own name, on the line right below Vasanti's signature, Mirella saw the phrase "another new development" and realized what Alice had handed her. For a long moment she hung over the clipboard, pen poised, her hand trembling.

"Thanks for your support," said Alice.

"Oh, I'm sorry." Mirella dropped Alice's pen. "I just realized—" She bent to pick up the pen. "This is about Howard."

"Beg pardon?" said Alice coldly.

"This is a petition about subdividing the dairy farm, isn't it? I guess you didn't realize. Howard is the architect for the project." Mirella felt her face go scarlet. "That would have been awkward, wouldn't it?" She handed the clipboard back to Alice.

"And I apologize about the flyers," she went on, attempting to read Alice's expression without actually looking at her. "I've been under the weather lately. Plus," she added, "Howard's been out of town and our goldfish decided to expire this morning. Exhibit A." She opened the napkin she was still holding to display the tiny grayish corpses nestled there. One of the goldfish rolled off onto the pavement; Mirella had to squat once more to retrieve it, almost brushing against Alice's big belly on her way back up.

"Don't worry about it," said Alice, blinking at Mirella for a moment before taking hold of the handle on her double stroller and wheeling it around. "Done is done."

Off to the races, thought Mirella, watching Alice trundle away toward the street. Alice paused to stoop down and pick up a squashed paper cup lying on the sidewalk. She pushed the cup into a plastic bag hanging from the stroller handle, brushed her hand against her thigh, then continued on toward the corner.

Standing alone in the hot diffractive sunshine of the parking lot, Mirella was startled at how desolate she felt. Of course Alice had known about Howard. Alice would do anything for a good cause, Howard was right. And yet Mirella found herself wishing that she could have signed below Vasanti's name, just one more concerned mother.

Maybe she should have signed. Howard certainly deserved it. She imagined his mouth falling open as Alice stood up at the next town meeting. *I have here a petition signed by over five hundred New Aylesbury residents who oppose this project, including, you may be interested to hear, the wife of the architect.*

"Hold on to your hat," Mirella muttered aloud, looking for her keys in her briefcase. It was something her mother used to say whenever Mirella got upset as a child. *Hold on to your hat, Miss.* Lose your head, but keep your hat. She could almost see it, that valuable hat: pink straw, trimmed with a black grosgrain ribbon and little plastic red cherries. Spinning like a pink space ship into the blue-blue sky.

Something was dissolving in her, something vertebrate about herself. It was only hormones, of course. Just a mood swing, this peculiar, awful disintegration. She should have eaten more at breakfast; she should have taken Randi's suggestion to have some yogurt.

Randi, who was such a worker. Randi, who had remembered to wash Pearl's rest blanket and was making Pearl's costume for the Happy Faces' historical play, who was ordering Jacob's birthday presents, who was conscientious and good with children and who loved babies.

For a moment Mirella pictured Randi holding Jacob, how she had wiped his face with a paper towel this morning, dabbing gently, while he wrapped his arms around her neck, an intent, collusive look passing between them that seemed, suddenly, to shut out everyone else in the world. Dr. Michaels said last week that it wasn't unusual for a child like Jacob to choose one adult to begin to speak to. The important thing was to get him talking.

A child like Jacob.

Mirella pulled a hand across her eyes. It wasn't Randi's fault that Jacob had gotten so attached. In fact, according to Dr. Michaels, attachment was a developmental leap. "Think of attachment as a muscle," he said, sitting back in his leather swivel chair, which gave an arthritic creak. "Jacob is getting exercise." Mirella had wanted to slap his face.

It was just another morning, she told herself, and tomorrow would be another morning as well. And that was how a person lived her life.

Alice had now crossed the street with her jogging stroller and was starting toward the village. Two other mothers passed by, chatting on their way to their cars.

"My husband—"

"I said—"

"Then he goes—"

Mirella looked down at her hand. Yesterday she had taken off her wedding ring. Her hands were getting swollen. Around her finger ran a pale groove where the ring had been, a warp of flesh.

She closed her eyes and leaned against her car, realizing that she was late for work, but unable to move. Ruth wanted to meet with her at nine. There was a cash flow problem and the accountant had some bad news about their quarterly filing. Coners thought she might be changing her mind about staying with Kahners; the adoption proceedings had made them both edgy and accusing. And now Vassbacher's wife was reneging on her agreement to share the house. Vassbacher was still in the Ramada Inn. His wife's lawyer had called yesterday to say, in an inauspiciously

pleasant voice, that she had something Mirella would be surprised to hear about her client, something the GAL would find
very informative. But somehow, with the keys in her hand and
the sun burning her face, Mirella could not quite manage to open
her car door.

Instead, she thought of Alice Norcross Pratt rolling through
New Aylesbury with her little boys in their cloth diapers, feeding
them organic cucumbers. How obdurately Alice's blond braid
shone, how indefatigably she stepped forward in her white running shoes despite that enormous belly. How startling what
Mirella had heard the other day from Randi, who had overheard
Blanche Pilkey talking to another mother in the park, who had
heard from her lactation consultant that Alice was pregnant by
artificial insemination. Alice was so determined to have a girl this
time (Randi said Blanche's friend said) that she'd convinced her
husband to have his semen sorted and scrutinized and selected,
then the winning sperm injected into Alice's uterus, to race like
greyhounds at the Wonderland track.

Such a frantic way for life to begin. Mirella took a deep breath,
leaning one hand on the warm hood of her Cherokee. Planned,
unplanned, always such risks. Always, no matter who you were or
when you were born, the same perverse, mysterious, inexorable
division of cells. Then a subdivision, then another, then singular
coils of DNA sprawling irretrievably, the blessings and the damage done. And before you knew it, there was Alice. Or Vasanti
Gupta, or herself, for that matter, or Pearl. Or Jacob.

On and on and on.

Hold on to your hat.

Mirella opened the car door and climbed heavily into the front
seat, then turned on the ignition. Something was wrong with
her; her joints felt loose and there was a kind of burning in her
groin. She picked up the car phone and dialed her voice mail.
"Call Dr. Kaitz," she said into the phone. "Call Vassbacher. Get

extension on hearing. Make another appointment with Dr. Michaels. Return Vivvy's call."

She paused, gripping the phone, then added, "Call Howard."

Carefully, looking out for stray children running away from their mothers, Mirella backed into the parking lot and then turned onto Ware Road. Something rolled out from under her seat and ran into her foot, one of Jacob's wooden trucks. It was early, so early, just after eight-thirty, and already she was late for work. And already her head ached, and she had no time to stop for Tylenol. And what made it so much worse was the smell of roses, roses everywhere. Roses smearing past her window as she drove toward the highway. Roses in the ditch. Roses in the traffic islands. Roses spilling over new chain-link fences and old stone walls.

RANDI IS SITTING on the steps of the New Aylesbury Library, watching a rehearsal of the Happy Faces' play, which is being performed on the town green. Beside her sits Jacob, half hidden under his Red Sox cap, rhythmically swaying from side to side as he eats a granola bar. On the green stands Pearl holding a cardboard wagon wheel. She is wearing a white blouse of Mirella's, tied with one of Howard's ties, black ballet tights, black party shoes, and a tricorn hat made out of newspaper. This is not the costume specified in the Happy Faces' note to parents, sent out last month, but it was the best Randi could do, given that Mirella had forgotten about Pearl's costume altogether until Randi reminded her yesterday.

The breeze is warm and salty with the scent of french fries from Captain Albert's across the green. Directly ahead is the Puritan monument, which has been defaced over the weekend by graffiti. Puffy red *Z*s and *X*s ending in arrows, curving defiantly around each other, spelling some kind of demand or warning that no one can read.

Overhead a gull screams on its way to the harbor. Squinting into the sun, Randi stares at the costumed children capering on the green. There is a cooper, a joiner, a miller, a mason. Aparna Gupta is a cobbler. There is the minister and his wife. There are fishermen and blacksmiths. Everyone needed for the new settlement. In among them strides Pearl's teacher, dressed in a white cap and a long, gray gown, waving a wooden spoon. In the afternoon heat the scene keeps dissolving and reconstituting as Randi watches, until she can almost imagine that it is 350 years ago, that the figures on the town green are in the right place and she and Jacob are the ones wearing costumes.

This morning had been very upsetting for Randi. She was just trying to be helpful when she suggested to Mirella that Mirella eat some protein with her breakfast—an egg, maybe, or even bacon, or at least some nice yogurt—instead of only dry toast and tea (think of the baby, she wanted to say, but didn't), and for no reason at all, Mirella said, "Will you please stop pushing food at me?"

Afterward Mirella apologized, said she hadn't slept well, that Randi should just ignore her, but how could you ignore something like that? Especially with Pearl and Jacob sitting right there eating cereal, and then for a long minute no one saying anything so you could hear the dog licking her paws under the table. It was Mirella's tone of voice that hurt. Icy, as if Randi wasn't anybody she knew, wasn't the person who had patted her shoulder while Mirella cried in the kitchen, wasn't the person who made chamomile tea and said she wanted the baby, even if Howard didn't. That tiny, pretty baby, whom Randi can already imagine holding, rocking to sleep, feeding with one of those bottles that has a hole in the middle, which DeeDee would never have thought of buying, using of course only disposable. Randi has been reading a copy of *What to Expect When You're Expecting* that she found buried under some old cookbooks on a shelf in the broom closet.

It isn't right that Mirella forgets her protein and dairy products. Even DeeDee drank skim milk. Randi does not consider herself a pushing person, no matter what Mirella thinks. She is just taking care.

She also does not consider herself the sort of person who opens other people's mail. But this same morning when she saw the lavender cardstock envelope on the front hall floor under the letter slot, she picked it up to look at the return address and recognized her mother's small spiky handwriting. "The Goldmans" was written across the front, sent in care of Family Options and forwarded on. The envelope had slightly dirty corners, one of which was bent.

Inside was a card with a picture of a big flabby-looking white flower on the front against a background of pale violet. "Dear Mr. & Mrs. Goldman," the card began, "I regret the necessity of writing to you, but as I have learned that you have my daughter under your employ, you will be wanting to know a few things about her that probably she has not made clear . . ."

When Randi finished reading, she shuddered. Then she put the card back in its envelope and carried it over to the kitchen trash can, where she buried it under a brown cone of wet coffee grounds.

On the library steps Jacob has finished his granola bar and is making tuneful, grinding noises beside her. It is something he's started to do lately, sing little songs in a way that is not quite singing and not quite not singing either. Leaning toward him, Randi thinks she catches a few bars of "Michael Row Your Boat Ashore" through his hums and hiccups, which could also be "Kumbayah," or even "Swing Low, Sweet Chariot." She sings these songs to him regularly, believing them to be soothing and motivational, although often she isn't sure he is listening.

Watching his small face as he croaks arduously through whatever it is he's singing, she realizes that she feels differently about

Jacob than she does about other people. She feels related to him somehow.

On the town green a dark-haired woman is approaching the children, who stand now in a circle singing a song about corn and freedom in the land of promise. Jacob raises his voice a little, as if to sing along with them. For an instant Randi thinks the woman might be Mirella, looking for her to apologize. But the woman is just another teacher, coming to hand the children little flags to wave as their finale. All the stores have decorated their windows with red, white, and blue. Swags of bunting hang from the telephone poles. Tomorrow afternoon there will be a parade, everyone dressed up in old-time outfits and a real cannon shot off on the green.

Jacob stops singing.

"Hey little guy," Randi says, lifting Jacob's chin with her thumb.

He looks at her briefly, then gazes back down at his fingers, which have been plucking at his pants leg. His fingers begin to pluck faster. Something seems to have unspooled in him; Randi wonders if he feels what she is feeling. She takes his hands and holds them still between both of hers. "Hey," she murmurs into his face. "Hey baby boy. Hey, calm down."

He stops then, and looks up at the sky, neck stretching, his mouth open. He looks damp and helpless and a little bit blind.

"Close your mouth," she tells him.

Yesterday, right after Mirella came home to find that Howard was back but still not there, she told Randi she was going to put Jacob in a special school in the fall. "A place for children with his sort of challenges," she'd said, hair drifting into her face, looking as wrung as a mop. But Jacob's been doing so well, Randi said, they'd been doing so well, with his words and not having to wear that headdress all the time, or sit in the fireplace, and pulling on his own pants in the morning. Mirella just blinked at her. "You'll have to trust me," she said, "to know what's best for him."

You should trust *me*, Randi says to herself on the library steps. I'm the one who's helping him. I'm the one who cares about him. He just needs somebody to think about what he thinks about, the way he thinks about it. That's made all the difference. Though for a while, after all the shouting and crying last weekend, then Howard leaving and now showing up again, Jacob seemed headed back to where he was when she first saw him.

If only there were someplace she and Jacob could live together, maybe someplace in California, a little pink house with palm trees and oranges, where they'd never have to deal with anybody else.

Just the other day at the playground, for instance, a heavy blond lady who Randi first thought would be nice—she and her little blond girl had on matching pink T-shirts appliquéd with shells and starfish, and the lady kept on chatting to Randi about the weather and how expensive sunblock had gotten and a new kind of fabric that can screen out UV rays, which not all mothers did once they figured out she was a nanny—this lady looked at Jacob sitting near her daughter in the sandbox, then leaned over to Randi and said in a satisfied voice, "He's one of those special needs kids, isn't he."

Jacob was spooning sand onto his head with a blue plastic shovel. His nose needed wiping. And he was staring straight ahead with the little empty look that he used when he was with people he didn't know. Randi could see what the lady saw, but she felt such a stab of hatred that it made her flinch right there on the sandbox ledge.

"Excuse me," she said, and she picked up Jacob, sandy hair, shovel, and all, and carried him right out of the park, bumping the stroller ahead of her.

Special needs don't have a thing to do with it, Randi thinks now, massaging Jacob's tiny cool fingers.

Above them two gulls swoop and circle, shrieking out their lonely, ratcheting cry: *naah-naah-naah.*

"Let's go home," she whispers, her own hands trembling. "Let's go home and play in the Jeep. We'll drive to California."

Jacob lowers his head to look at her. It's a funny, long, considering look, his head tipping to one side, his eyelids wrinkling.

Pearl and her classmates are taking off their caps and cloaks and sitting down on the grass. Pearl waves to Randi. A pregnant woman is pushing a stroller toward the town green, heading past one of the little church graveyards. It's not a very nice picture, Randi notes as she begins gathering up the books and Jacob's granola-bar wrapper, that baby in the stroller and its pregnant mother and then those thin gray tombstones behind the shiny iron fence. Just then a silver tour bus passes between her and the green, bumping slowly over the cobbles, sending up a bright white blaze that is sunlight reflecting off the metal side of the bus, but also something else:

A terrible fact that Randi has never guessed was coming at her.

Because it is here, sitting on the granite steps of the New Aylesbury library, holding Jacob's hand, the sun in her eyes, gulls crying overhead, that Randi experiences for the first time in her life the true, hot blossoming of grief, as fierce and pulsing as love, a grief that has as much to do with the child at her side as it does with the sudden, transient, unbearable recognition that the world will care as little for him as it does for her.

7

MIRELLA COULD TELL BY the density of the morning air drifting through her window, lush with the pickled smell of low tide, that it would be another hot day. Though it was just past six o'clock, already the heat was settling on her like a humid quilt, even with the fan whirling a few feet away. Already it seemed she had never been anywhere in her life but in this bed, hot, swollen, her bare belly rising above a pool of damp sheets.

Mourning doves were giving their soft wooing call in the trees outside her window. A dog began barking. She recognized the stentorian tones of Martha announcing her first neighborhood foray of the day. Someone must have gotten up to let her out.

Closing her eyes again, she breathed carefully in through her nose, out through her mouth, hoping to quell the cold sliding feeling in her chest, which had begun with the bleeding yesterday, then worsened when Dr. Kaitz told her it might be a miscarriage.

Let's get a sonogram, he said, helping her up from the examining table. Let's see what's going on. It might be that everything is just fine.

Mirella opened her eyes. Bars of yellow sunlight fell across her bed. On her night table clustered a jug of spring water and a glass smudgy with thumbprints, a vial of Tylenol, a roll of Tums, a stack of depositions, a historical novel she did not like but was reading anyway, an apple. Her laptop computer lay next to the cordless phone beside her on the bed, where it had rested all night, closed for now.

A kind of roaring filled her ears and despite the morning's heat, she began to shiver. If only it were six months from now, and she could be in bed remembering how she had once lain here covered in sweat, knowing that in the end everything, everyone, really had turned out just fine. Because when she peered past the cheerful radiologist in her white trousers and white clogs—who kept humming "You Can't Always Get What You Want," as if to remind patients in case they demanded a different picture—and gazed into the snowy gray murk of the sonogram screen, Mirella had beheld the beating of not one but two four-chambered hearts.

Placenta previa. The placenta was down low in her uterus, Dr. Kaitz said when she met him back in his office. That explained the bleeding. He must have missed the second heartbeat earlier because the two were beating together. Dr. Kaitz looked embarrassed. He kept folding and unfolding his hands while she sat in the chair opposite him, watching him do this. Bed rest, he said finally, pushing a glass jar of jelly beans around on his desk. At least until the bleeding stops. Let's hope the placenta moves up as the pregnancy progresses. He reached into the glass jar and took a handful of jelly beans, then forgot to eat them. There was a good chance the babies would be premature, he said, holding the jelly beans in his cupped hand; it often happened with twins. How premature he could not predict. Mirella kept waiting for him to eat the jelly beans. It began to drive her slightly crazy, Dr. Kaitz talking to her with jelly beans in his hand. Boys. Identical boys.

Downstairs someone was moving around in the kitchen.

Mirella heard the clang of pot lids and rattle of silverware, the kitchen faucet turned on, then off. The rattling increased, followed by a scraping sound. It was Randi, of course, probably baking muffins. Getting ready for the Fourth of July picnic she seemed to have begun planning in April. Yesterday, she asked Mirella if they had a big wicker hamper. "No," Mirella said, then felt ashamed at the satisfaction she'd taken in Randi's disappointment.

Pearl and Jacob must be still asleep, at least they weren't making any noise in their bedrooms. Mirella twisted her shoulders, trying to settle into a more restful position. It was ironic, she thought distractedly, how uncomfortable lying in bed could be. After years of wishing she could sleep late, here she was, dying to get up.

Last night she and Howard had discussed Dr. Kaitz and the sonogram; she called him right from Dr. Kaitz's office with the news, then told him they needed to talk. Howard seemed shy when he appeared in her bedroom doorway. He kept his hands in his pockets and he stood in one corner during the entire conversation. She saw him glance at her wedding ring sitting in a little yellow cloisonné dish on her dresser. Once, briefly, he rested his forehead against the wall. Mirella did most of the talking. Finally, looking drawn and tired but also, with part of his shirttail coming untucked from his pants, somehow boyish, Howard said: "I guess we need to circle the wagons."

Mirella shifted her shoulders again, looking for a cooler place on her pillow, not finding it. She turned over, then turned back, rolling onto what felt like a rock, but turned out to be her cordless phone, buried in the bedclothes. Richard and Vivvy were driving up this afternoon; she'd told Howard she still wanted them to come. Howard would have to remember to change the guest room sheets. Danielle would be sleeping in with Pearl. Pearl was looking forward to seeing Danielle, who would paint Pearl's fingernails green, give her temporary tattoos and let her try on flavored lip gloss, and urge her along the reliable path of ignoring her parents.

Mirella flattened her hands against her stomach. It was the partly untucked shirttail that had convinced her to try to forgive Howard. That and the way he'd reached down and touched her foot as he said good night. Although for now, he should stay in his studio. She needed some time and her bed to herself. And she wanted to talk to Vivvy about Howard. She and Vivvy had never had much in common, aside from being married to brothers, but Vivvy was no fool when it came to family matters, deafness included.

AT TEN-THIRTY that morning, Randi brought Jacob upstairs to see Mirella for a few minutes before she took him and Pearl into the village to see the parade. He sat on the bed by Mirella's knees, looking at her. Together they examined the little plastic bow-and-arrow set he was holding, with suction-cup arrows, which Randi had bought for him at the five-and-ten. Jacob held up an arrow, to show Mirella. This was not the sort of present Mirella normally would have wanted him to have, but she smiled at the arrows and pretended to test the sharpness of a suction cup.

"Ouch," she said, wringing her hand.

Then Randi left the room for a few minutes to find Jacob's sneakers and Mirella and Jacob were alone together. There was a smudge of dirt on his nose. He gazed at her in an interested, cockeyed way that seemed oddly sophisticated.

"Hello baby," she said. "Are you hunting something?"

He picked up the bow and put an arrow to it, aiming at her.

"Oh no. I'm a goner." Mirella was aware her voice was too enthusiastic and that she was trembling; she should be careful to speak slowly and not upset this moment with Jacob. Lately he refused to let her hold him, even on her lap at bedtime. But she was so glad to have him to herself that she couldn't help reaching out one hand to cradle his chin. "My sweet boy," she whispered. And with her fingertip she began tracing the silken skin just below his ear.

Jacob's eyes flew open. As if she had bitten him, he reared back and began to thrash away across the bed, clutching his arrows to his chest. "Mah-mah, Mah-mah," he shrieked.

"Jacob," she said, reaching for his arm, "sweetheart."

As she tried to hold on to him he began one of his harsh, skidding wails, wailing louder and louder, his eyes wide and unfocused, until Randi rushed in and grabbed him up.

He clung to her, shoulders heaving, growing gradually quieter, his face buried in her neck.

"Sorry," Randi said. She was panting a little, her own face red. "Sorry, I shouldn't have left him like that." She pressed Jacob against her, smoothing his hair, and kissed his forehead. "I don't know what it is," she told Mirella. "He's been like this all day. Sort of jumpy. Maybe it's with your being—" she hesitated. "You know, and everything."

She gave a funny little laugh. Then clasping him under the armpits, Randi held Jacob away from her to peer concernedly into his face. He dangled, hunched like a little mole, before he reached for her again. "But did you hear that?" she added, smiling in a way that Mirella took to be triumphant. "He said, 'Mama.' That's another word. He's getting so big. Aren't you? Such a big, big, smarty boy."

Mirella kept herself very still. She watched as Jacob burrowed into Randi's neck once more, whimpering and twitching, thin arms wound around Randi's shoulders, knees squashed against her full breasts. Ten-thirty-nine A.M. read the white numbers on her clock radio. And at that instant, at exactly 10:39 A.M., as she looked from the clock back to Jacob in Randi's arms, Mirella felt a quiet, violent unmooring, as if she had taken leave not of her senses, but of a vast intricate vessel, all hidden thwarts and rigging, which she had until then assumed was firm ground.

Outside her window a host of crows rose up out of a maple tree, squawking murderously, then flew in a black cloud toward the harbor.

"Time to say bye-bye," Randi told Jacob, glancing at Mirella. "Do you need anything? Can I get you anything?"

"No," said Mirella.

When they were gone, Mirella lay back against the pillows, trying to understand what she had seen, pressing her hand against her rib cage.

"I can't bear it," she said to the ceiling.

"I cannot bear it," she said again.

A few minutes later she picked up the cell phone to call her mother.

Almost as soon as her mother answered, Mirella wished she could hang up. It was only because she could not lie in bed alone for another instant that she had called; she and her mother never talked well on the phone, wandering from the weather to vaguely contrarian political pronouncements, always resorting to listing for each other the number of things each had to do. But when her mother said, "How are you, darling?" Mirella began reporting what Dr. Kaitz had said, what the sonogram had revealed, all in a high-pitched rush, her tone falsely chatty, forgetting that she hadn't yet told her mother that she was pregnant.

Her mother listened calmly, not even interjecting "Heavens" or "Goodness gracious," which was what she usually said when Mirella told her anything important. Mirella found herself saying much more than she had intended to say, telling her mother also for the first time that Howard had left, but returned, and then she told her about Jacob and Randi. "They are too attached," Mirella said finally. "It doesn't feel right."

To her surprise, her mother was philosophical. "You can't organize everything," she said. "Are you scared?"

"Yes," said Mirella.

"You can't organize that either."

Mirella could hear her mother wheezing gently on the other end of the line and that tiny sound, that delicate susurration, part age, part emotion, made Mirella's eyes fill with tears. "Look at me," her mother went on after a moment. "I spent years chasing your father around the world on export trips, waiting for him to retire so I could settle down. Then he has a stroke. Did I really ask for that?"

Once more her mother paused, this time rhetorically. Mirella had the unhappy feeling she was enjoying this conversation. But when her mother spoke again, her voice had become deliberate. "Here's my advice. Let your little nanny do everything for the moment. Let her do her job. She's not hurting Jacob. And leave Howard to his own devices. He came home. He wants to be home." Her mother gave another faint wheeze before adding, "You just stay in bed and think about Queen Victoria."

When Mirella asked what on earth Queen Victoria had to do with anything, her mother said, "She had eleven children and ran a kingdom. Don't you think she had help?"

After Mirella said good-bye and hung up she felt a little better, at least she felt more collected. Her mother had promised to visit soon. She closed her eyes and tried to do a deep-breathing exercise.

But in a few minutes there it was back again, that ugly jagged ache beneath her rib cage.

"Looks nice around here, Howard. Very homey."

Richard thrust his neck out to peer at the gleaming kitchen cabinets, the blue glass vase of roses on the table, the crayoned sign Randi and the children had made and taped to the refrigerator:

WELCOME TO UNCLE RICHARD, AUNT VIVVY, AND COUSIN DANIELLE. The sign struck Howard as oddly disingenuous, with its crude colorful hearts and balloons, like something engineered to look childlike. On an old gate-legged table in the corner sat Jacob's computer, on loan from the Guptas. "Nice," repeated Richard to the computer.

"How's Mirella feeling?" said Vivvy. Howard had told Richard and Vivvy only that Mirella was having a little bleeding and that the doctor had ordered her to stay in bed.

"All right," said Howard. "Considering."

"What?" Vivvy cupped her ear.

Danielle said, "Uncle Howard, do you mind if I use your phone?"

"Use your cell phone," grunted Richard. "This isn't the Ozarks. They've got service. So where are the kiddies?" he asked Howard.

"Randi, our nanny, took them to the parade and to watch some sort of battle reenactment on the green. We thought we'd let you settle in before subjecting you to any festivities. Pearl's in a patriotic play this afternoon," Howard added, "which we have to attend. Mirella's feeling okay," he said to Vivvy.

"Who's been baking?" Vivvy was sniffing and looking around the kitchen, drifting here and there as if she wasn't sure of her bearings. "I need a glass of water," she muttered, finding a glass for herself.

"My cell phone isn't working. I have to make a call," insisted Danielle, raising her dark eyebrows in a way that reminded Howard exactly of her father. "Please."

"Oh, sure," said Howard. "You can use the phone in here. Or," he added, watching her eyebrows swoop, "if you need privacy there's an extension upstairs."

"That one," said Richard, watching Danielle disappear. "Destined to be a prosecutor." He lowered himself into a chair and leaned forward, putting his elbows on the table. He looked sleek as always, his springy black hair combed back, his face so closely shaven it looked almost babyish. A gold chain glinted in the V of graying chest hair where his shirt collar was unbuttoned.

"So." Richard cracked his knuckles. "The Red Sox are having a pretty good season. Of course they'll end up croaking as usual."

"As usual," said Howard, leaning against the sink.

"The Yankees are doing great. Have you been watching Cone pitch?"

Howard nodded, although of course he had not.

"The Yankees are always great. They are a great team." Richard knocked on the table for emphasis. "A great team," he said musingly. "No matter what anyone says, the Yankees are the best."

"Not if you like the Red Sox," said Howard.

"I can't stand the Red Sox," said Richard. "Bunch of superstitious losers. Get over it already. Get therapy or something." For a moment he stared abstractly at the children's crayoned sign. He sighed. "And so now Mirella's home in bed."

Howard nodded again, feeling dazed and, as he watched Vivvy drinking a glass of water, suddenly thirsty. "She's in bed," he repeated.

"Has that made things better or worse?"

"What?" said Vivvy from beside the refrigerator. She finished her glass of water and put the glass on the table. Her mother had not been well, Howard remembered. Kidney stones. Unlike Richard, Vivvy looked blurred and faded today in her blue sundress, hair hanging untidily around her thin face.

"I'm asking about him and Mirella," Richard told her.

"Mirella's upstairs," said Howard, leaning toward her good ear. "She'd love to see you."

But instead of going upstairs Vivvy began moving around the kitchen, picking up a fork, a pot lid, putting them down again, picking up a cookbook, displacing everything she touched until the kitchen looked as if someone had lightly shaken it.

"There," she said at last, resting her hands on her hips. "Now I'm going up to visit Mirella."

When she was gone, Howard sat down at the table opposite his brother. They looked at each other over the vase of roses. "To answer your question, things are worse," Howard said. "And also better. Can I get you something, a beer?"

"No," said Richard. "Worse how?"

"Well, not exactly worse," Howard said. "Intensified."

"Is that girl still calling you?" Richard began drumming his fingers on the table, a nervous habit that used to make their father snap, What are you, the cavalry?

"No, she gave up. I haven't heard from her."

"So it's the baby?"

"Babies," said Howard, pleased in spite of himself to have such dramatic news to impart, and to have imparted it so casually.

Richard's fingers stopped galloping. As he waited for them to begin again, Howard considered for the first time the possibility that Mirella might not have any baby at all—she had been bleeding again that morning—and he was shocked at the dejection that swept over him. In the last week he'd grown used to the idea of not wanting another baby, of feeling it forced upon him, an unlucky slip of fate; he'd forgotten that he was also getting used to the idea of having one. A baby had, in fact, already taken up residence in the house.

Just for an instant, Mirella's big family surrounded him. He saw himself sitting at the head of a large table that was bright with dishes and silver candlesticks. Ranged down either side of the table were beautiful, tall, intelligent-looking adult children in somber shades of woollen grays and reds, all humorously waiting for him to speak.

So bring them both on, he thought. With two babies, every other problem between him and Mirella would vanish, sucked into a tornado of exhaustion. He knew this was a foolish and dangerous way to think, and yet it was true that simple exigency had united many families. In a year or two he and Mirella would not look much different from any other couple, who had manipulated, ignored, and transgressed against each other as married people inevitably must, if they are to accommodate a houseful of children and survive their life together.

"Twins?" Richard frowned, looking dyspeptic and rabbinical. He began drumming his fingers again.

From upstairs came a bump, then the rattle of something falling to the floor. Someone gave a sharp laugh.

"Listen." Richard clasped his hands in his lap. He leaned forward, pressing his big chest against the table, prepared to say something. He was always, Howard thought, prepared to say something. And for a moment the dependable nature of Richard, who was bossy and coarse and loyal and wise, made Howard almost drunk with gratitude.

But then Richard changed his mind and sat back, looking dissatisfied. "Maybe that's not helpful. All right, all right. We'll think of something. We'll figure it out."

"Figure what out?" said Howard, anxious again.

Richard gave a magisterial wave. "I said I was thinking. Now I'd like a beer."

WHEN RANDI RETURNS from the park with Pearl and Jacob and Martha the dog, she is momentarily dismayed by the sight of suitcases in the living room. Three suitcases, made of sleek, gray nylonlike material. They look like small boulders by the coffee table.

"Hello?" she calls softly.

She spent an hour tidying up this morning, putting away all of Pearl's and Jacob's toys, giving a last dusting to the end tables and the mantelpiece, then hurrying out to the garden to pick flowers for the kitchen and the guest bedroom. She has been drilling

Jacob all morning on how to say hello to his aunt and uncle. It is Randi's plan to impress them with her hard work so that they will see what a good home she has made for Jacob and that he doesn't need a special school. Frog, moon, juice, rat.

Everything looks so nice, except for those suitcases. The warm fragrance of baking still hangs in the air from the chocolate hazelnut lace cookies she baked early this morning for the Happy Faces' bazaar. Mrs. Pratt had asked for something for the baked goods table and she had been proud to say yes. Delicately crispy, like eating sweet dreams, the recipe said.

She got the recipe from a cooking chat room on America Online; Krystal Anne had showed her how to get into chatrooms one day on Howard's computer when Howard was out at lunch. On the Gourmet Challenge website, Randi had posted one of her own recipes: Randi's Chewy Nut Rolls. When Krystal Anne checked the website again, kitchinqueen from PA had called the nut rolls "unreal."

Now her hazelnut cookies are resting in the pantry, hidden between sheets of wax paper; she thinks they could sell for a dollar apiece. Her picnic is all planned. Last night she roasted a chicken, then put it in the refrigerator to be cold for today. All she has left to do this afternoon is make the potato salad and some deviled eggs, plus pack up paper plates, napkins, cups, and two bottles of lemonade. The blanket is already folded on the backseat of the car.

It really was too bad about the picnic hamper. Fleetingly she considers the wicker laundry basket, draped with a red-and-white checked cloth. She reminds herself to bring a plate up to Mirella before they leave for the picnic, with a glass of milk and maybe some carrots. Mirella's being in bed has made more work for Randi, but she doesn't care; in fact she feels vindicated. Twins. All along Randi has told Mirella that she needed more rest and she was right. She understands better than Mirella what Mirella needs. She also understands that with twins coming, Mirella will not mind so much about Jacob's preferring Randi as she seemed to mind this morning.

"Hello," she calls again, as Martha trots into the kitchen. She wonders if she has time to run upstairs and comb her hair. "Go," she says to Pearl, giving her a little push. "Remember to give each grown-up a hug." Pearl runs to the kitchen without looking back.

Randi takes Jacob's hand and kneels in front of him. "Hel-lo," she says. "That's all you have to say. Hel-lo."

He rocks from side to side, staring at the floor. "Hel-lo," she prompts. He butts his head into her shoulder.

She sighs. "Okay. Say 'how' instead. That's shorter. Put your hand up like this." She demonstrates raising her arm, her hand held up like a crossing guard. "How."

Jacob lifts his head and stares at her. She watches him move his lips.

"How," says Randi. "You're an Indian. Indians say 'How.' Or if you want, just say 'Hi.'"

Tentatively, Jacob holds out his hand, but at that instant a girl comes stamping down the stairs, a chubby girl with a mane of long dark hair like Pearl's, but who has big red lips and a harness of gold necklaces. She is wearing a tight pink T-shirt and baggy blue jeans that don't cover her bellybutton.

"Jacob," she squeals. And without saying hello to Randi, or even looking at her, the girl picks Jacob up and whirls him around the hallway. Jacob's eyes go wide in alarm. "Look who's here. You cutie," the girl cries. "You're not a baby anymore." The next moment they are whirling away into the kitchen, Jacob clinging to the girl's shoulder, his face pale and frozen above her pink T-shirt.

Randi stands by the front door, still holding the mesh bag of sand toys she carried to the park for Jacob. In a moment he will come running back to her, as soon as the girl puts him down.

A trail of sand has dribbled onto the floorboards; she tries to whisk it away with her foot. From the kitchen comes the exclusive clamor of reunion, mirthfully quarrelsome.

"Hey," shouts someone. "Look what I found. I found them, you pig. Don't eat them all."

And Randi knows her chocolate hazelnut lace cookies are under attack.

8

"FOR GOD'S SAKE," said Richard.

They had found a spot to spread their blanket on Old Harbor Beach, crowded already with people waiting for the fireworks. But Howard had forgotten to warn anybody about the bugs or to bring insect repellent. Now a cloud of midges haloed each of their heads.

"Ugh," said Danielle, making battling motions with both hands. Pearl was watching her with absorption.

In the distance floated strains of "Yankee Doodle Dandy," played on the town green with senescent verve by elderly members of the New Aylesbury Band, all in red jackets resplendent with gold braid.

"This is awful," said Vivvy placidly. She was staring out at the harbor, her hands folded in her lap. That afternoon she had spent over an hour in the bedroom with Mirella, the door shut. Once Howard went upstairs, to see if they wanted any tea. When he knocked at the door their voices went silent; it was several moments before Mirella called out, "Who is it?"

"Anyone like some roast chicken?" said Randi in a brave voice.

Howard had apologized earlier about the cookies, explaining that Danielle didn't realize they were meant to be saved.

"They were meant to be eaten," Randi had answered. "Eventually anyway."

But she'd continued to look stricken, drifting around the house with a bottle of furniture polish and a cloth, then retreating to the kitchen to wash the floor again. Randi seemed to have taken a dislike to Danielle. The phone rang soon after she and the children returned from the parade and Danielle had answered it. Some old woman, Danielle reported airily a few moments later. "She asked who I was and I said I was Howard's niece and then she hung up." Randi stood in the kitchen listening to Danielle, her lips going white; then she disappeared up to her room. "I guess Randi usually answers the phone around here," Howard said, when Danielle looked at him questioningly.

"We've got potato salad," Randi offered now, with a bruised expression.

"Bug salad," said Richard, producing a fifth of scotch.

"I hate this," complained Danielle. "I'm getting bites on my face."

Vivvy smiled out at the water. "Oh look," she said. "See the boats."

Howard looked up as two tall-masted schooners, sober as swans, sailed across the wide mouth of the harbor.

Behind him he heard children playing on the beach, calling to each other like birds. Marco, they cried. Polo. The sound of their voices was high and sweet, spiraling through the salt-scented air, which felt so soft, so laden, and the sky was such a deep blue. Far away, the band struck up "Moon River." Howard took a breath. All of life seemed suddenly present, breathing, sighing, right around him, close as the insects flying around his face, dignified as those old ships, and it was such an aching, inspiring sensation that he wanted to go home and tell Mirella about it.

"Did you bring napkins?" said Richard.

"What did you say?" said Vivvy.

"Napkins," yelled Danielle.

"Here," said Randi, rousing herself, reaching into a paper bag. "I packed wet wipes, too. And extra forks."

Maybe, thought Howard, watching them unpack Randi's picnic, maybe here was a way to settle this ruined feeling, this banishment that lay between them. All he wanted was to talk to her, just talk. Talk about anything, talk about something besides babies or what he had done and she had done. *We're not so different. If only you would let me explain.* Because as he sat holding the paper plate Randi had just handed him, with his cold chicken leg and lump of potato salad, Howard saw that all of the world's problems really came down to this: Human beings believed they were different. When, in fact (and this idea sprang into his mind as Richard poured him a second paper cup of scotch with Jacob bumping against his knee), human beings were like fingers on a hand.

"Daddy," said Pearl. "I have a bug in my ear."

He drew her to him and peered into her ear; seeing nothing, he blew into it gently. "How's that?"

"I also have a bug up my nose," she said proudly.

"You were a lovely wainwright today," he told her.

After leaving the car in the public lot beside Captain Albert's at four o'clock, they had walked to the green to watch Pearl in her play, standing with the Guptas and other Happy Faces' parents. "There's a cartload of opportunity in the New World," was Pearl's single line, which she delivered almost inaudibly but with conviction, rolling her cardboard wheel along the grass. Howard and Richard clapped.

"Very good performance," said Mahesh Gupta, as the play ended with the children marching in a circle, waving flags. He was smiling broadly, his teeth very white, wearing crisp khakis and a pink Polo shirt. Then Aparna came running and threw herself into his arms. Mahesh reached down and set her tricorn hat on his own head.

"What propaganda," sniffed Vivvy.

The town green had become a village of canvas booths, each housing a demonstration of some historical activity. A serious young woman in a T-shirt, denim skirt, and little gold-rimmed glasses, who reminded Howard of the TownCommoners, was making natural dyes out of pokeweed berries, oak bark, and goldenrod. Soapmaking was under way beside the monument, next to a display of butter churns. Bleating piteously, a sheep was being sheared across from the ice cream parlor. Two weavers had set up looms near the bank.

"Quite a business," Richard remarked, swabbing his forehead with a handkerchief.

"Hurrah for the industrial revolution," said Vivvy, as she watched a bearded man grind corn.

They toured the tables of the Happy Faces' bazaar, presided over by Vasanti Gupta and another mother, who looked hot but sanguine as they waited for people to buy baked goods and poke through a jumble of used clothing, old storybooks and faded-looking toys. Before heading the few blocks down to the beach for their picnic, Randi led everyone into the library to view five *tableaux vivants* prepared by the New Aylesbury Historical Society. In the first, two Wampanoag Indians had been imported to sit cross-legged beside a wigwam in deerskin robes and stare dourly at a bark basket of blueberries. Jacob stood transfixed before them, refusing to let even Randi coax him away, until at last one of the Indians gave him a faint nod. Another *tableau* featured Myles Standish with his harquebus, portrayed by the chairman of the planning board, standing over a seven months' pregnant Alice Norcross Pratt as his sweetheart, Priscilla Mullins, who was threading a spindle. Howard had given them what he hoped was an appreciative smile, but beside him, Danielle yawned and said, "Weird."

Now at Old Harbor Beach, the sun was beginning to set. Howard sipped his scotch and ate a bite of potato salad. He thought the rose-colored water looked like pink glass, as if you could step across the sand and skate right across it. Then, as the color intensified, he found himself thinking of the settlers who had lived here 350 years ago, how lonely they must have been, and cold, how estranged and tired, and how in winter the sunset was probably the brightest color they would see for months, save for the color of their own blood. Across the ocean glowed the home fires of England, orderly, preoccupied, lost to them.

"This chicken is delicious," Vivvy said to Randi.

"Thank you," said Randi. She put her arm around Jacob.

"So what's for dessert?" said Danielle.

"Faugh," said Richard, spitting. "Bugs."

"Bugs for dessert," crowed Pearl, waving her fork.

Howard continued to stare at the harbor, trying to imagine the strange and frightening world in which the settlers must have found themselves. Nothing to guide them. All alone, clinging to the rocky edge of a continent that had no maps, no roads, that was filled with vine-choked forests, Indian camps, blizzards, wolves. Chop wood. Light the fire. Fetch water. Each day they must have despaired, grown determined, despaired again. No one to tell them where to build their villages, how to predict their future, whether anything would ever get easier. Make candles. Make soap. Chop wood.

And stretching out past each back door, each little box-shaped house, nowhere, anywhere. Cartloads of opportunity.

"Faughh," said Richard, spitting again.

～

THE FIREWORKS BEGAN at nine o'clock. Out in the harbor, past the moorings and channel buoys, two men on a barge set them off, one at a time. Howard could just make out the tiny black figures whenever they lit a fuse. Whump, went each explosion, followed a moment later by a reverberative tympanic crack he felt in his chest. Chysanthymums of green, yellow, red, blue. Screaming silver eels. Showers of gold that evaporated with a sound like hard rain. "Take cover," yelled a man jokingly. All around them sat other families on their blankets, afloat on the dark sand, faces upturned, contentedly astonished.

All except Jacob. Jacob was crying.

Actually, Jacob was doing more than crying. He was howling, keening, legs jerking, his small face a knot of fear. "Buddy," said Howard, trying to pull Jacob into his lap. "Don't be scared."

But Jacob fought free of him, kicking over a bottle of lemonade, soaking the blanket and Richard's shorts.

"Oh shit," said Richard forgivingly.

Jacob kicked and moaned, covering his head with his arms. People began turning to stare at them. Howard caught sight of Alice Norcross Pratt several yards away, still in colonial costume, her face lit up by the fireworks, seated amid a battalion of rapt children. "Come on, buddy," he pleaded, trying once more to hold Jacob in his lap. Jacob flung around and hit him on the nose.

"Hiii," Jacob cried. "Hiii."

The entire fireworks display began to seem eerily like the artillery attacks it commemorated. Rockets red glare, bombs bursting in air. What were they all doing out here, Howard thought, trying not to duck. Pearl stuck her fingers in her ears. Only Vivvy, sitting with her back to them, seemed to be enjoying herself. She clapped several times, calling out, "Look, look," and held up Pearl's little flag, waving it gaily.

Now Jacob was frankly screaming. He bucked against Howard,

thin legs and arms flailing. Richard and Danielle were gathering together plates, napkins, cups, stuffing them into bags; Randi was standing up, dragging at the blanket. As he wrestled with his son, Howard felt like screaming himself. He wanted to dig a hole right there in the damp sand, scramble in, and pull seaweed over himself.

Then there was Randi, kneeling before him, pulling Jacob away. Pulling Jacob backward into her own arms.

Boom, boom. Another rocket burst into streaming red spangles overhead.

Randi pinned both of Jacob's thrashing legs with one of hers and wrapped an arm around his chest. Then, as Howard helplessly watched, she laid her free hand across Jacob's forehead and bent his head backward, onto her shoulder, so that Howard was looking at his child's naked jumping throat.

"Stop," she said powerfully, lowering her head so that she was speaking into Jacob's mouth. "Stop it."

Jacob made a glottal, strangling noise. His small body arched once, twice, then collapsed against her chest. Almost instantly, he seemed to fall asleep. Randi hoisted him onto her shoulder and prepared to stand up.

"Is he all right?" said Howard. He moved toward her, thinking to take Jacob himself, but she held up a hand, fingers spread.

"He's okay, I've got him," she said coolly.

In another moment she was on her feet, moving with surprising swiftness through the huddle of blankets and spectators toward a black bank of rocks, Jacob draped across her like a stole.

Then they were gone.

HOWARD TURNED BACK to find Richard and Vivvy staring at him. Danielle was now holding Pearl in her lap. Pearl was sucking her thumb, which Howard had never before seen her do. Above them exploded a waterfall of green and blue stars.

"Howard," said Vivvy, clutching at a paper cup, "where is she going with him?"

Before Howard could answer, Pearl took her thumb out of her mouth and said, "They're going to California."

"What?" shouted Richard.

"Randi says she's taking him to California. They're going to take Mommy's Jeep."

"No they're not," Howard said to Richard. "She's just taking him to the car to calm him down."

"They are, too," yelled Pearl, sitting up. "They've been packing food. They're taking raisins and ginger ale."

"Howard," said Vivvy, who had crawled forward to hear better until she was inches from his face. She was breathing hard and Howard could see a few grains of sand stuck to her eyebrow. "Howard, listen, we have to go after them."

"This is ridiculous." Howard reached out to detain her. But Vivvy had gotten to her feet and was pulling at Richard's arm. "Sit down," said Howard. "Pearl knows that going to California is just a game they play."

"No it's not," insisted Pearl.

"Get up," gasped Vivvy, succeeding in pulling Richard upright.

"I can't believe this," said Howard. "Richard, what are you doing?"

"Come on, Howard. Let's go." Richard bent to yank at the blanket.

"Sit down," called someone from behind them. "We can't see."

"Will you *stop* it," hissed Howard.

"I think we should go find them," said Danielle, helping Pearl stand up. "Okay, Uncle Howard?"

"Sit down," shouted the people behind them.

The schooners were out in the middle of the harbor again. Each time a rocket flared up and detonated, the schooners leapt into ghostly relief, their masts and spars black and skeletal.

Richard, Vivvy, Danielle, and Pearl stood ringed above Howard, staring down, faces dark, as orange flames spun in the sky behind them.

"Ridiculous," he said at last. His tongue felt thick and awkward in his mouth; he found he'd been drooling slightly and he reached up to wipe his lips with the back of his hand. "You'll see how ridiculous you're being. They're in the car, they're in the parking lot, they're listening to the radio. But all right," he said unsteadily, getting to his feet, "by all means, let's go."

WITH A CUP OF TEA chilling on the nightstand, Mirella had spent the last several hours in bed, picking at Randi's cold chicken, looking over a Supreme Court decision on the rights of minors to sue parents, and finally, when her head began to hurt, leafing through *The Story of New Aylesbury*. She had meant to read an article Jacob's speech therapist had sent her on amino acids and frontal cortex development. But Pearl had left this library book on her bed after using it as a stage for a sock doll performance of "Here We Go Loop-dee-Loo." Sick of briefs and court decisions, sick of articles on child development, sick of checking the pad in her underpants every few minutes, and sick of wishing they had a television set, Mirella had opened Pearl's book and begun reading.

An Ephraim Norcross ("there are Norcrosses still living in New Aylesbury today") had served as the town's first minister. In 1648 Pastor Norcross arrived from Suffolk, England, with a flock of sixty-two followers, his wife, four children, a cowhide trunk, an iron bedstead, and four pewter candlesticks. He preached his earliest sermons under a big pine tree on the present town green. At night wolves howled; Pastor Norcross and his fellow colonists fired muskets to scare them away. Fires burned in nearby Indian encampments, flickering in the black woods. Hurricanes blew; snow fell in drifts eight feet high. Pastor Norcross spent three winters in a low wooden hut with a chimney made of logs daubed with clay. He lived on fish, clams, and pumpkins. His wife died in childbirth. Pastor Norcross worried about covenants, colonial charters, the theological fine points of infant baptism. His house burned down; smallpox killed two of his children. Pastor Norcross fined people for wearing buttons. He recited Genesis to the Indians. His flock used pine knots for candles and lent each other live coals. They buried their dead with feet pointing east, and piled the graves with rocks so wolves would not eat the corpses.

"Colonial life can be read as a grim record of sacrifice," intoned one chapter. "Puritan idealism often vanished when confronted with the sheer expedience of survival." Mirella skipped ahead to a section listing colonial remedies for common ailments: *For trembling: bathe in liquor mixed with hot human urine. For swollen glands: sip syrup made of sow bugs in white wine. To ease childbirth pain: drink cow's milk with ant eggs and the hair of a young girl.*

"Child mortality rates remained high into the eighteenth century," the chapter concluded. "Disaster, disease, and death were common visitors in every family."

Mirella closed the book and lay back against her pillows, imagining a low wooden hut, hollow-faced people eating dried fish beside a smoky fire. Babies coughing in the shadows. Pigs running under a rough-hewn bench. She imagined Pastor Norcross's wife, groaning in childbirth, retching and rolling in delirium on a bloody straw pallet while her husband attempted to give her teaspoons of milk floating with hair and ant eggs.

The front door banged open. Flushing guiltily, Mirella dropped the book and picked up the article from Jacob's speech therapist. A few moments later Pearl came hurtling into the room.

"Randi ran off with Jacob," she cried.

"She did not," said Howard angrily, following behind her. "Jacob got a little scared by the fireworks."

Mirella sat up and looked around the room. "Where is he?"

"With Randi," Howard answered, shooing Pearl out of the way. "She's putting him to bed. He was pretty done in," he added. "How are you feeling? Are you okay? Can I get you anything?"

Richard and Vivvy appeared in the doorway, looking subdued and wrinkled. Both of them had sand on their legs. Mirella looked up at Howard standing beside the bed and noticed that his hands were trembling. "I'm okay," she said. "What happened with Jacob?"

Pearl said, "Can I drink your tea? Can I sit in your lap?"

"Leave Mommy alone," said Howard, turning over Mirella's pillow and patting it. Gently he pushed her shoulders back until she was lying down again.

"If Jacob is still awake," Mirella said, "I'd like to see him."

"Well, he's not. He fell asleep during the fireworks."

"He was scared so he fell asleep?"

"Being scared is tiring," observed Richard from the doorway.

Howard looked down at her and smiled thinly. "He fell asleep in the car. He got frightened during the fireworks and Randi took him to sit in the parking lot. By the time we got there, he was asleep."

"We all got a little frightened during the fireworks," Vivvy said, looking at Howard. Then she said loudly: "If you ask me, Randi was a bit out of line tonight."

"Vivvy," said Richard, peering over his shoulder into the hallway.

"No, I mean it. I didn't like what I saw."

"She was great with him," Howard said stiffly.

"What's going on?" Mirella's throat tightened. "What happened?"

Vivvy glanced at Richard. "She took charge of Jacob in a way that I—we, Richard and I—thought was inappropriate."

"Inappropriate how?"

Pearl was climbing over Mirella's knees to sit beside her on the bed. "See my fingernails," she said. "Danielle glued these little flowers on them. Then she put clear stuff on over. Danielle wants to get her nose pierced like Krystal Anne. Can I get my nose pierced?"

"No," said Mirella.

"Why not?" Pearl looked relieved. "I want to. I want to have my eyebrow pierced. Danielle has little marks on her arm, she says they're burns. She says Randi looks like a cow."

"Hush, sweetie," said Mirella. "Can you go find Danielle and let us talk for a few minutes?"

"No," said Pearl, but she slid off the bed and in a moment was gone. Mirella listened to her hop down the stairs on one foot. Richard and Vivvy were talking now in the hallway. She heard them pause; then Howard reached over and started to shut the door just as they appeared again, shoulder to shoulder in the doorway.

"I'd like Richard and Vivvy to stay," Mirella said. She looked squarely at Vivvy. "Inappropriate how?"

"Too possessive, I'd say."

Mirella closed her eyes, picturing Jacob in Randi's arms, his knees pressed against her breasts. Randi stroking his hair, kissing his forehead. *He said "Mama."*

"Howard," she said, opening her eyes. "This is what I've been worried about. Please hear me out before you say anything."

"ARE YOU CRAZY?" Howard asked seriously a few minutes later, when she was done. "You must have lost your mind. Nothing happened."

Mirella reached for a tissue from the box on her night table. "I don't want her here."

"If you had been with us tonight," Howard said, "you wouldn't feel this way. She was *heroic* with him. I don't know what I would have done."

"That's just it," said Mirella. "You would have calmed him down somehow. You would have. He would know that *you* could."

Howard shook his head. "I can't believe this."

"I agree with Mirella," said Vivvy, leaning forward, her hand cupped around her good ear.

"You don't have to live here."

Vivvy shrank back. "Watch it, Howard," said Richard.

"Listen," Mirella said, speaking carefully. "I'm not saying I'm not grateful for what she's done with him. Of course I am. But it's too much. It's time for us to take over."

"Take over what? I have a huge public hearing coming up on this project. I have twenty houses to get built. Who do you think is going to watch the kids?"

"We'll find somebody. We have before."

"I know what you're thinking," said Howard savagely. "This is all about you. It's your goddamn picture again."

"Howard."

"You're not telling her to go. He loves her. She's the one person who's made a place for him."

"I don't think—" Vivvy started to say.

"I'm not going to be here picking up the pieces this time," Howard shouted over her. "I won't be home, Mirella. If you go ahead with this, it's all up to you."

Mirella realized that Howard was panting. She stared up at his damp forehead and unshaven chin, the dark smudges under his eyes. An enormous indifference began to settle into her mind. It was almost like the exhaustion to which she'd become so accustomed, but more penetrating. Again she saw the low smoky hut and the rough bench, the windows covered with greased paper, a log falling in the hearth, sending a shower of sparks into the gloom, and it seemed to her that more than anything in the world, she would like to live all alone in such a place.

After a moment, Richard said quietly, "Nothing has to be decided now. You've both said what you needed to say. I think that's enough for tonight."

Outside, the Pilkeys' cocker spaniel began barking, high-pitched, hysterical. A man's voice spoke harshly, and the barking stopped.

"Jacob will be fine," Mirella said, hearing her own voice as if she were standing outside listening to it, with the dog. "We'll get him the proper help, from people who are trained, who know what they're doing. He has his mother and father and sister, who love him. Soon he'll have more siblings. He is part of a big, loving family. He will be fine."

"No he won't," Howard said.

Richard said, "Howie, stop it."

"He will be fine." Mirella spoke evenly to let Howard and the others know that she believed what she was saying.

There was a moment, just a moment, when Mirella thought Howard would hit her. In fact, she closed her eyes and put up one hand. It would, in a way, be a relief. But no blow came.

"She's not going anywhere," he said.

"EVERYTHING IS A MESS," writes Randi in her diary, on the page following a recipe for baked Alaska.

But she does not have the energy to write down anything else. Instead she fingers a few things she keeps in a cardboard box with her diary: the sapphire ring, a cornhusk doll she found behind the merry-go-round at a county fair, a red ribbon she won in fifth grade for perfect attendance. Ashley Duby had actually won the ribbon, but Randi *should* have won it; she was always ready for school by eight o'clock, except that DeeDee was sick so many mornings, throwing up all over the bathroom, asking for someone to bring her aspirin and a Coke with ice. There is an un-opened package of plastic barrettes and a bag of cotton balls taken from the Coralville drugstore. There is a photograph of herself and her mother when Randi was three. In the photo Randi is in a pink bathing suit, wrapped in her mother's arms. Her mother wears blue slacks and a print blouse, unbuttoned at the neck so that the dark hollow between her big breasts is just visible. Her bronze hair is neatly curled and she has on lipstick and black sunglasses; she is laughing as she holds Randi's face pressed close to her own.

Randi picks up her diary again and leafs back to some earlier entries—descriptions of her word drills with Jacob, the knitting project she has started with Pearl, a recipe for beef stew. She thinks of Alma, recalling her months in Alma's apartment as remarkably peaceful, the two of them in that dark little living room watching TV movies, Alma in her recliner like a toad in a teacup, eating pink pistachios. Crickets have started up outside the window. A breeze bumps the rice paper blinds against the window sills, bringing with it the sound of voices and laughter from the Pilkeys' pool party next door. The Pilkeys are always having parties but never seem to invite Howard and Mirella. There is the smell of burning meat. Suddenly a woman's voice calls out, high and full of excitement, "Can you believe who's here? All the way from sunny Seattle?"

Downstairs Mirella and Howard are talking about her with Uncle Richard and Aunt Vivvy. Twice she has slipped past their closed bedroom door and heard her name.

It occurs to Randi that she has done her very best, that all she has ever done was her best. She wraps her arms around her stomach, rocking on the bed. And if no one else can appreciate how hard she has worked, at least she knows it herself. At least she knows what she has done. Maybe she'll get on the next bus to sunny Seattle and they'll find out what goes with her.

Someone does appreciate her, though. Jacob appreciates her.

At the thought of Jacob, his peaky white face and dark eyes, her mind suddenly goes blank.

A little while later Randi reads over the recipe pasted in her diary, a Fannie Farmer recipe, which just a few days ago she snipped out of the newspaper:

The wonder of a baked Alaska: its cold, frozen filling comes right from the hot oven where its topping has just been browned. In this true American dessert, invented by a physicist around 1800, ice cream rests on sponge cake and is covered by meringue which is browned in the oven so quickly that the ice cream doesn't have time to melt. Any kind of ice cream that appeals to you can be used.

There follows a list of ingredients: sponge cake; egg whites; sugar; cream of tartar; quart of ice cream, frozen hard. *Put the egg whites and cream of tartar in a bowl and beat until foamy. Slowly add the sugar and continue to beat until stiff but not dry . . .*

Nice to be Fannie Farmer, Randi thinks, putting her face into her pillow. Nice to spend your life figuring out ingredients and instructions, writing recipes down in plain English that anyone can understand, even if it's for something invented by a physicist, even if it's something that no one else on earth would have thought of because it should be impossible, like baking ice cream in an oven.

9

"OH COME ON," SAID RUTH. "You're just over-wrought. I'm sure Howard's right, and the nanny, what'sher-name, is just trying to help out. I mean, what did you expect anyway?"

"What do you mean, what did I expect?"

Ruth said, "Don't underestimate how difficult it is to be in your position."

"My position?" Mirella lowered her voice. "I'm lying here in bed, trying not to lose these babies, and I feel like I'm losing everything else."

"I understand," Ruth murmured. In the background Mirella could hear the phone ringing and a voice calling out something about federal regulations. "Try not to fret. We've got you covered here at work. It's not easy, of course, but we're getting by. Let's see: Coners and Kahners are going ahead with the adoption. The governor's office called about that parental leave commission you're on and they said it's okay to miss a few meetings. That state custody case with the grandmother—Walmsley?—is on hold for the moment. I got a two-week continuance in the Vassbacher case; I'll go to court for you for the temporary orders—although to be honest, I don't have much truck with your client after that business about smoking dope in the basement."

"That's what his *wife* says he did," Mirella said. "Vassbacher swears he only smoked once or twice in the garage, and never when the kids were home. He says his wife exaggerated for the GAL. And that GAL is a wretch anyway, I've dealt with her before. He's scared," she said, fighting to keep her voice level. "He raised those kids. When you go for temporary orders, will you remember to tell the judge about his wife never making dinner? And point out the place in the deposition where she admits missing the older girl's ballet recital to have drinks with clients."

"How about the part where she doesn't bake cookies."

"Ruth." Mirella flinched. "That's not what I meant."

"Well that's how it sounds," snapped Ruth. "As you should know better than anyone."

Mirella held the phone away from her ear for a moment. Then she brought it back and said lightly, "You're right. I'm getting too worked up. Maybe I'm identifying with this case a little too much."

"Maybe you shouldn't be the one litigating it."

"Of course I should be the one," said Mirella. "Ruth. Why are you jumping on me like this?"

Ruth sighed. "I guess I'm just feeling overwhelmed. Look, it'll be fine. It'll all work out. Anyway, Cheryl's FedExing you the research you wanted for Walmsley; a lot of the discovery you can do from home, thank *God* for e-mail; I'll do that Women in Law panel thing for you—"

"Ruth, listen, it's not work," said Mirella. "Or it is work, too. It's all of it. It's my—"

"I'm sorry," said Ruth. "Can you hold on a minute?"

Mirella lay looking out the window at the white sunlight glaring off the Pilkeys' slate roof, wondering how long she would be on hold. Ruth was famous for leaving people on hold. Once she'd left her second husband, Adam, on hold for forty-five minutes; when she remembered to check the line and discovered he was still there waiting for her, she called him a *putz* and said she wanted a divorce.

And it was just possible that, unintentionally, or perhaps intentionally, Ruth was punishing her for being in bed when the office was so jammed up and for having been less confiding, less daughterly, and even—though not by choice certainly, but to the pressed person circumstance can look like choice when it requires staying in bed—for being somehow less feminist. But Ruth also said she understood. "I wish this could all be different," Mirella tried to tell her, a few days after Richard and Vivvy left. Ruth had come for lunch and sat by the bed in a straight-backed chair Howard brought in, balancing a tuna sandwich on her knee. "I know, I know. Don't worry about it," she kept saying, in a tone that was not unlike the one Alice had used about the flyers. Then she said, "So what are you going to name them, Cain and Abel?"

When Ruth came back on the line, she apologized again, but she had another call that she really had to take. "Can I call you tonight? Do you need a visitor?"

"I'm okay," Mirella said. "I guess I'm just feeling—not paranoid, exactly, but—"

"I'll call you tonight," said Ruth.

THAT AFTERNOON MIRELLA's mother came to visit. For the third time in the last week she had driven all the way from Beacon Hill in her ancient white Cadillac, bringing flowers and novels by women writers that she checked out of the Boston Public Library. Mirella was not much of a novel reader; especially she did not read women's novels, which always seemed to be about families and people having affairs and waiting around in train stations. She preferred detective stories, where the plots focused on solutions to problems rather than on the problems themselves.

Today her mother had also brought along a pink silk bed jacket from Filene's, which Mirella refused to wear, feeling like Pearl when her mother exclaimed that the bed jacket was lovely and just her size. "Mom," she said, "it's ninety degrees in here. I would take off my skin if I could."

"What a horrible thought," said her mother imperturbably.

She sat on the bed and gave a regal, disappointed look at the screen on Mirella's laptop computer. In her purple St. John knit, she did appear momentarily majestic, her face massive and official above her seed pearl choker. "Why can't you simply *rest*," she said, pushing the computer across the bed. "You are supposed to be resting."

She reached up to touch her cap of hair, dyed auburn and cut shorter than usual on the sides, which made her head look slightly like an acorn. Mirella noticed that she was now grayer than her mother.

"Are things any better for you and Howard?"

"Up and down. He's still sleeping in the studio."

Her mother nodded understandingly. "And how are you?"

"I hate lying in bed. I lie here and dream all day of going for a walk."

"You sound just like your father."

"I hate it," said Mirella after a moment. "I'm not a bed person."

"Your father wants to visit, you know."

"Oh really, I don't think—" Mirella began.

Her mother eyed her impassively. "He wants to. I've been telling him about your—" Here she paused and glanced around the room. "He wants to give you a vote of confidence. And he wants to get a look at *her*."

"Don't call her *her*," said Mirella irritably.

"She." Her mother stood up and began moving about the

room, gathering pages from the fax machine that had fallen to the floor, rearranging things on Mirella's dresser. "Although, for what it's worth, she seems fine to me. A little eager-beaver, maybe—"

"What's this," she interrupted herself, "why aren't you wearing your ring?" She held up the gold band, dark eyes moistening. When she was younger, Mirella's mother had often been compared with Hedy Lamarr, a comparison she pretended to deprecate. To look more like Hedy Lamarr, she developed the habit of pursing her lips to accentuate her cheekbones. She was doing this now.

"It doesn't fit anymore," Mirella said.

"You listen to me—" her mother began.

While her mother talked about the importance of working through marital disappointments for the sake of the children, Mirella thought how surprising it was that she and her mother were spending so much time together. She had been dodging her mother for more than twenty years, outside of lunch, where there was always a tablecloth between them, and yet now she could hardly bear it when her mother's visits were over.

"You and Howard have a sacred trust—"

As Mirella watched her mother talk, she thought about her origins as Miss Helen Essel of Milwaukee, born into a family of gaunt German confectioners who brooded over imaginary bouts of food poisoning and criticized each other's hygiene in their dark kitchen. "Ach," they cried in real alarm if one of them sneezed. Then Miss Essel became Mrs. Cook. The Cooks were positive thinkers who ate raw oysters and believed any indisposition could be cured by playing tennis or swimming in cold seawater. They had muscular limbs, prominent blue eyes and a good-natured way of dismissing anyone who did not play tennis or eat oysters as "oddball." It had always seemed to Mirella that her parents were completely mismatched, and yet she found herself wondering if her parents' marriage had lasted—in fact prospered—because each had perceived the other as a mild lunatic, which allowed them to forgive all sorts of habits and tendencies that should have driven them both crazy.

"How long can you stay today?" she asked, interrupting her mother's views on family as the last bastion, an outpost, a clearing in the wilderness.

"Oh, well." And her mother launched instead into a catalog of errands that included stopping at the bank and buying butterscotch pudding at the grocery store. Most of the time, Mirella knew, her mother's afternoons were spent wandering through the house, inquiring where she had left her reading glasses. Even with an invalid husband to manage, she was often haunted by an unfocused disquietude. If she did have an errand—a trip to the dry cleaner or pharmacy—the day was immediately cluttered with demands. If she did not have an errand, she thought of all the things she needed to do, but had put off doing, and then felt unjustly burdened and would stand pensively at the window, watching leaves blow down the street.

Mirella used to feel judgmental about the way her mother lived; now she regarded her almost enviously.

"Could you stay for dinner?" she asked her mother. "Please."

"Darling, I have to get back to your father." Her mother pointed to the laptop computer with a small grimace of distaste. "And I thought you were working."

"I'm just writing a memo. Actually, it's kind of an interesting case, I think I've mentioned this client, Jerry Vassbacher, whose wife—"

Her mother interrupted with a sigh. "Don't tell me. Tell me something about people being happy."

"That's not really in my line of business," said Mirella, meaning to be funny. But her mother reached over to take her hand.

∾

MIRELLA'S MOTHER LEFT in the late afternoon. Howard did not come upstairs to sit with her as he usually did before dinner; he had his public hearing, she recalled. Last night he'd bent over her, smelling of fresh air and plywood, to ask if she'd mind listening while he rehearsed the speech he intended to give at the hearing's opening. As the twilight faded and, one by one, the mourning doves quit calling, he stood by the window and played with the blind, pretending to work an overhead projector, explaining how the TownCommon development would minimize their use of open space and that most of the land would be made into a wildlife preserve. He outlined the common sewerage system they'd planned, the voluntary two-hundred-foot buffer zone from all wetlands. Most of the building materials would be recycled wood. His eyes shone and his Adam's apple dunked up and down. He kept wiping his hands on his shirt.

"Very impressive," she told him sincerely when he was done. When he sat down on the bed to go over the fine points of the septic system, she reached out and patted his hand. "Good luck."

Howard was continuing to be solicitous. In the mornings he strode in with her breakfast tray. He asked if he could bring her anything else, then straightened up the bedroom, later carrying away her breakfast dishes. He was polite and scrupulous in his khaki pants and blue work shirts; recently he'd begun wearing a tie. Ever since the night of Richard and Vivvy's visit, he had avoided mentioning Randi. He was also, Mirella decided, doing what he could to prevent her having to see much of Randi at all. Usually he brought up her trays. Most questions about the house or children were relayed through him. Not that there were many questions. Almost ten days had passed. Mirella thought he looked coolly satisfied about something.

She picked up the novel her mother had brought and left on the nightstand with a bouquet of sweet william. *Sheltering Love*, it was called. She looked at the cover, which pictured a woman in

Victorian dress standing in front of a train station, then dropped the book back on the nightstand.

Randi brought up her dinner on the painted tea tray: broiled fish, steamed broccoli, brown rice with bits of raisins in it, milk. For dessert, a plum. Mirella ate some of everything, even taking a bite of the plum, which was unripe, so that Randi would not make the dire clucking noise she made whenever Mirella said she wasn't hungry. At seven, she heard the children clatter up the stairs for their bath. Just before bed, they filed down the hall and into her room to allow her to exclaim at how clean they looked and to kiss their foreheads. "Sleep well," she told them, and was rewarded with opaque looks.

The sky began turning mauve outside her windows. She could feel the babies kicking now, little taps, like internal Morse code. Three days ago she'd insisted on going downstairs to make herself some coffee, then went into the garden to pull a few weeds and had started to bleed again. Now she was allowed to walk to the bathroom and to have a daily five-minute shower and that was all. Everyone, everything else had to come to her.

Except they did not. Which was the most unexpected thing she'd found about being at home. Hour after hour she spent alone. She'd thought, for instance, that Pearl would come and sit on her bed and they would talk. But she wasn't sure what to talk to Pearl about lately; often a shyness overtook her when they were together—she felt inarticulate, strangely disqualified. In the mornings Pearl came in to say good-bye before Howard drove her to camp. Hugging the doorjamb, her hair tamed into a French braid, Pearl emanated a kind of restrained longing and re- vulsion at the sight of Mirella in bed, which, along with the French braid, made her seem darkly mature. "Hello Mother," she said from the doorway. Before she disappeared, she would add, "Have a nice day."

Randi usually brought Jacob up around then as well, to receive a kiss before Randi took him downstairs to play on the computer or out for a walk or a visit to the playground or down to the harbor, or wherever it was they went together. They were always headed somewhere. Each time Mirella tried to get Jacob to stay with her, even to sit on her bed, he shrieked or went rigid. Randi tried also, saying, "Hey mister, don't give Mommy such a hard time. All she wants is five minutes. Who do you think you are, a movie star?" But he slid away as she placed him back on the bed and ran into the hall.

That was the worst thing. Mirella had expected at last to have enough time for Jacob, to have him curl up against her in bed, to read to him, practice words, tell him what a good sweet boy he was, smooth his hair, let him be her baby a little bit longer. He'd grown so tall, legs skinny in his plaid shorts. Lately he looked almost aged; his small face had taken on a pinched sallow fixedness that reminded her of her father's face after his stroke.

So often these past years with Pearl and Jacob had seemed endless, hours passing like winter months, too much confinement, too much weariness, too many quarrels with Pearl over getting dressed, over the weather; the hours coaxing Jacob out of the fireplace or away from his wooden trucks. And now there seemed so little time left.

"Tap, tap, tap," reported the babies inside her. "Tap, tap, tap."

She wished she could have all those years back, the years since the children were born. She would do everything differently if she could do it again, although she was not sure how this different life would look, except that somehow it would be more joyful. She had a hazy image of herself running with the children through fields of daisies, or maybe it was poppies.

From down the hall, she heard a child's voice call out. "Mama," she thought she heard, and unthinkingly swung her legs over the side of the bed to stand up. The cry came again, from which child she couldn't tell. It was a long, thin cry, frightened and disoriented.

As she reached her door and opened it, she saw Randi hurry into Jacob's room.

"I've got him," Randi said, glancing down the hall at Mirella. She gave an impatient flicker with her hand. "Really, I've got him. Go back to bed."

10

WHEN HOWARD WALKED into the second-floor auditorium of town hall, he was stunned and alarmed and also slightly gratified to find the room overflowing with people. Every seat was taken; people lined the walls and stood two deep at the back of the room. Howard paused for a moment to rub his neck. He'd never liked speaking in front of large groups. Even small groups made his mouth dry. Here and there he recognized a face, but it struck him painfully that he should know more of them. ("Know your neighbors," he recalled his father saying. "They'll know you.") Usually planning board meetings attracted four or five citizens at best, one of whom usually stretched out on chairs in the back row and fell asleep. But tonight the long paneled room, hung with gilt-framed paintings of eighteenth-century New Aylesbury merchants and a clumsily executed frieze of the town seal, was filled with a tumult of voices that sounded neither hostile nor welcoming to Howard, as he pushed his way through, only loud.

On the dais at the front of the hall sat the five members of the planning board, arranged decorously around a conference table.

Four men in their forties and fifties, sunburned, barbered, three of them wearing chinos and blue Oxford shirts, leaning comfortably back in their chairs; in spite of the age difference, they all reminded Howard of Dr. Michaels. The one woman on the board turned out to be the silver-haired realtor from whom Howard and Mirella had bought their house, who wore a blue pin-striped dress and enormous red-framed bifocals. He wished he could remember her name, also regretting for the first time the brief but heated dispute they'd had at the closing over a brass light fixture.

Joy Fiorella, the planning board agent, hunched at the end of the table. She was clad in pigeon-colored stretch pants and a flowered blouse; gray roots were showing at the part in her black hair as she scowled at something being said by the chair. But she looked up to give Howard a friendly smile as he sat down beside McConkey in a reserved front-row seat. In the aisle next to him stood a microphone stand. Beyond that waited a podium and an overhead projector.

McConkey looked nervous. Four or five other TownCommoners had come with him and leaned forward to wave. Howard waved back and shook McConkey's hand, disconcerted when McConkey held on. "Howard," he said hoarsely. "There are a lot of people here."

"I know," said Howard, discreetly trying to pull his hand away. But McConkey hung on, squeezing harder.

"Is that good or bad?" McConkey's face was damp above the collar of his turquoise Polo shirt.

"We'll find out," said Howard, conscious that the planning board was watching him hold hands with McConkey. Gently he freed himself, then opened his portfolio case to check again that he had all his drawings and maps, everything neatly numbered and covered in acetate.

Hubbub from the crowd receded as the planning board secretary read out the minutes from the last meeting. Then the chair, dressed in a seersucker suit, stood up and came to the podium. He was a slight-featured man named Emerson with thin, fair hair, pale blue eyes, and a high forehead. In a nasal, Brahmin accent that might or might not be genuine, he thanked everyone for coming tonight, noting that he hadn't seen so many people in this room since the night they'd voted on whether to replace the post office roof. No one laughed.

The chair cleared his throat and put on a pair of reading glasses. "Let's get started. This is a public hearing to review plans for a subdivision proposed on a fifteen-acre property on Old Prence Farm Road. We'll hear from the applicants first, who will give their presentation and answer questions." He looked down at Howard and beckoned.

Howard gathered his folders and portfolio and stepped over to the podium, wishing that he'd asked Krystal Anne to come along as his assistant. He could have used her help in laying out his materials, and also her sedative air of impervious disinterest—but who could predict how all her body piercings might have affected the board? He rested his portfolio on the conference table and spent a few minutes arranging an overview map on the projector, then trying to find the light switch. When at last he managed to turn on the projector, he found himself staring at an unfamiliar topography. It took him an instant to realize the map was backward. Hastily he reversed it.

"My name is Howard Goldman," he said into the podium microphone. "I am the architect for the TownCommon development, and what I'd like to try to explain tonight is what our project will look like, the community benefits we think it will bring to New Aylesbury, and how we intend to minimize any visual and environmental impacts on the town."

In spite of his trepidation at confronting a muttering sea of faces, as Howard began pointing out features on the overview map, his confidence returned. He'd drawn everything so carefully, it was all laid out. "Here's a bird's-eye look at the property itself." He tapped the map with a pencil. "Here's the water, a wetland area, pastureland, existing forest." He heard his voice grow steady, persuasive, even deeper. "We intend to cluster twenty houses toward the northwest corner of the property. Here." Howard pointed his pencil to a circled area. "We've planned a small common, around which houses and a small meetinghouse will be situated on quarter-acre lots, amounting to a total of five and a quarter acres."

He pulled off the overview map, replacing it with an architectural drawing. "The houses are all colonial style, three or four bedrooms, with four slightly different models to give a sense of variety amid continuity. A typical house will look like this."

It was a beautiful drawing. Even Howard, preoccupied with getting the drawing straight on the overhead projector, could see how elegant and austere and perfectly proportioned this house would be. He pointed out the simple cornice and the classic architrave; he pointed out the two long sidelights beside the door, each shaped like a traditional pilaster. "Because," he said, embarrassed by his own enthusiasm, "a front door should be a contemplative object, a moment of projecting outward or inward, not a means for shutting everything out."

Howard glanced up and saw McConkey smiling in the front row. He gave Howard a thumbs-up sign.

Switching to a side-view drawing, Howard showed how he had planned a two-story wall of small windows alternating with larger ones so that the house would stay protected from northeast gales, yet fill with light even on winter afternoons. "A house of many viewpoints," he declared, beginning to enjoy himself, "held in common." The rear-view sketch demonstrated a back door as respectable as the front, though without sidelights, opening onto a small circular deck with built-in benches to encourage informal gatherings.

He could feel the crowd listening as he spoke and he imagined them comparing this graceful house with their own. He displayed a drawing of a typical lot, remembering to mention the group's intention to put in only indigenous plantings. With mounting enthusiasm, he described the common sewerage system with its advanced water-treatment technology.

When he glanced over at the planning board he saw that several of them were nodding; the chair caught his eye and smiled, canted forward in his seat. To the left of him, the realtor had taken off her glasses and was cleaning the lenses with a tissue.

It was when Howard introduced the project's open-space plan that the audience, which had begun rustling and whispering, began to grow more restive.

"What we're proposing," his voice ratcheted up an octave, "is to use one and three-quarters acres for the common, which is designed to mirror the New Aylesbury green and tie TownCommon thematically into the larger community. Down to the placement of our meetinghouse at one end." He slid another sketch onto the overhead projector's lit square to illustrate the common and the dimensions of the meetinghouse.

"The remaining eight acres," he said, as he removed the meeting house and replaced it with another copy of the overview map. "The remaining eight acres," he repeated, "four of which are waterfront and wetlands, we propose to deed permanently to the town as an environmental preserve, to be kept in a natural state."

With his pencil, he indicated the dotted line demarcating the sanctuary, then stepped back from the projector, smiling. "When you consider that this land has been a privately owned farm, overgrazed and almost completely deforested, I think you'll see that our development would be a significant land-use improvement."

The chair shifted in his seat on the dais. "Quite a proposal, Mr. Goldman."

As Howard turned to thank him, a patrician voice from the audience called out, "Environmental preserve, my eye."

Howard swung back around, squinting to see who it was. "Excuse me," said the chair wearily behind him. "We have not begun the period for public input."

"It's a scam," cried a voice. "If you believe this guy, you're an idiot."

"Hold on, hold on," said the chair.

A short man with a bulldog face and square-cut chinchilla hair stood up. "These developers always say they're going to do nature stuff. Then they just build all over the goddamn place until there's nothing left. Look at what happened to Box Point."

"Hear, hear," said the patrician voice behind him. Squinting into the audience, Howard spied a tiny, white-haired lady in a mossy-looking sweatshirt.

"We don't want to be another Danvers," puffed the bulldog man.

On the dais, Joy Fiorella bristled visibly. Howard said quickly, "Box Point is a good example of a bad project. In this case, the land will be legally deeded over. Your town counsel can draw up the transfer. What we propose—"

"You propose putting a bunch of houses on open land, that's what you propose," shouted a husky-voiced woman toward the back of the room. The crowd's muttering began to billow into a din.

"Please," said Howard tightly.

"Let Mr. Goldman finish," demanded the chair.

Howard slid another sheet onto the projector, this one of typed text. "If you'll hear me out, these four points outline our intentions—"

"My intention," said the bulldog man, "is to stand here until this project is voted down."

Two other people stood up. "We don't want eight acres," called out the husky-voiced woman. "We want the whole fifteen."

"Are you prepared to *buy* the whole fifteen?" Howard flung back, his face growing hot. "This parcel is appraised at two point seven million dollars. Considerably more," he added sharply, "than it cost to replace the post office roof. And as I seem to recall, the funding for that was almost voted down."

As soon as he had spoken, he realized that he had made a mistake. The chair frowned at him; Joy Fiorella was tugging at her dyed hair, her mouth a moue of distress.

"It's always about money," shrieked someone.

Then suddenly there was Alice Norcross Pratt, standing at the microphone. Howard was actually glad to see her; she was familiar, at least, almost soothingly so, with her neat braided hair, her pink cotton smock dress and swollen belly. She faced him composedly, a sheaf of papers in her hands, and after a moment gave him a small nod.

"Hi, Howard," she said into the microphone.

Immediately the crowd settled. The three people who had been standing glanced around and after a moment sat down.

"State your name and address," sighed the chair.

"My name is Alice Norcross Pratt," she said evenly. "I live at two twenty Briggs Road. I'm here tonight as a representative of the Preservation of New Aylesbury Committee to present to the board a petition signed by seven hundred town residents who oppose this project. No matter how worthy it is."

To Howard's amazement, she looked at him with something like sympathy. "We firmly believe that developing Prence Farm will destroy a historic landmark and further erode attempts to preserve our town's heritage."

"Have you considered—" Howard began.

"Plus," Alice went on, consulting a notepad. "We are concerned about possible ground water contamination, increased auto traffic, and the endangered habitat of several threatened species, including the marbled salamander."

"Marbled what?" asked the chair waspishly, plucking at the lapels of his seersucker suit.

"Salamander," said Alice. "We have discovered a breeding pool near the site where the applicants propose their meetinghouse."

"We've sited the meetinghouse basically on top of where a barn exists right now," said Howard.

"Which is another point we'd like to raise," Alice continued. "The farmhouse and the barn date back to the late nineteenth century. They are excellent examples of Edwardian agricultural architecture and should be restored."

"With all due respect, Alice, there's no such thing as Edwardian agricultural architecture. The barn is falling apart." Howard tried to control his voice, which was getting reedy. "And most of the house burned down fifty years ago and had to be rebuilt. It has aluminum siding, for God's sake," he said, appealing to the board.

My house has aluminum siding," shouted the husky woman at the back. "You want to tear it down, too?"

"Our petition has been duly notarized," said Alice briskly. "I would like to submit it to the board and ask that it be placed on permanent record."

She stepped up to the table on the dais and placed her petition in front of the chair. On her way back to her seat she gave Howard a prim smile, then stepped aside as a woman with stringy hair pulled back in a tight bun, wearing a purple T-shirt, wooden beads, and khaki pants, pushed up to the microphone.

"My name is Kristina Fisher," the woman said in a trembling voice. "I'm the mother of three girls and I live at seventy-four Catbird Lane. I would just like to say that in the last five years, two women on my street have come down with cancer and there's a little boy with a peptic ulcer."

The crowd grew reverently silent.

"I have been doing a lot of research on the Internet," she said, "and I've read a lot of studies linking auto exhaust and cancer."

She drew a shaky breath. "I think it's completely irresponsible of the town even to *consider* a project that would bring more cars into our community. My children deserve a chance to grow up strong and healthy."

People began to clap and whistle. Howard tried to think of something to say besides, "This is bullshit," but he couldn't think of anything. As the woman sat down, another woman embraced her; several people reached out to pat her shoulder.

"Look," said Howard, attempting to sound forthright. "I appreciate hearing your reservations, and of course the Town-Common group wants to work with you on any environmental concerns, but I wonder if we're getting a little off point. This is a modest development of twenty clustered buildings. Twenty families."

He paused to swallow and glanced at the four points of the summary he'd planned. "We do respect New Aylesbury's heritage, and, in fact, you could view this development as an expression of the principles our town was founded on. A safe, tolerant, cooperative society. That's exactly what TownCommon Co-Housing is after—a place to live responsibly within a larger community, in accordance with their beliefs and ideals—"

"Like Waco," yelled someone near the door.

People began to laugh caustically, calling out "Jonestown," "Ruby Ridge." Someone shouted, "Silicon Valley."

"What I've always admired about this town," Howard said, hanging on to the podium as if it were a raft, "is its commitment to sharing its wealth." Gazing around, he focused on the town seal hanging over the dais, which depicted a reluctant-looking Indian carrying a staff in one hand and a codfish in the other. The Indian was presenting the codfish to a bearded Puritan, who had come ashore carrying a plate-sized biscuit. In the foreground was a rowboat; in the background, a skinny pair of wigwams.

"Look at that," Howard said, pointing upward. To his surprise, the audience quieted as everyone turned to look at the town seal. "This was the town's first moment as a town." He continued to point at the seal. "The convergence of two different elements into a new kind of community." A few nights ago, he'd discovered a library book about New Aylesbury on top of the toaster oven and read the first chapter. Lucky coincidence, he realized now, although the chapter went on to explain that the Pilgrims who participated in this historic exchange weren't allowed to settle in New Aylesbury, not being members of the Massachusetts Bay Company, and had sailed off to live in Dorchester. The Indians were soon obliged to move their wigwams as well.

"That seal is a reminder of what kind of town we really are," Howard cried out, suddenly passionate and convinced. "We are a dynamic community, willing to grow and evolve. We're not a museum."

For several seconds the room was almost still. People continued to peer thoughtfully at the town seal and the woman in the back put a hand to her mouth. But as Howard paused to catch his breath and consider what to say next, he became aware of another figure, dressed in white, coming up the aisle toward the microphone. It was a long moment before he recognized who it was. So unlikely did this presence seem, so completely out of context, that he literally shook his head as if to clear his vision.

"Hello. My name is Nadine Fouch," she said hesitantly into the microphone. "Excuse me, I live in Vermont, but I'd like to add my comment. I am an architect who has worked with Mr. Goldman. Several weeks ago I had the opportunity to review plans for this project at his studio." She was careful not to look at Howard, but paused to give a diagnostic glance at the planning board. In her belted white linen dress she reminded him of a nurse, coming to take everyone's blood pressure.

"This isn't," he said confusedly, turning toward the planning board. "This is not—we were having lunch, and I happened to mention—" Bifocals neatly transecting her eyes, the realtor stared back at him.

"In the course of our discussion," interrupted Nadine, "Mr. Goldman confided that he knew he'd meet opposition to this development. He knew it would be unpopular. But he said, and I quote—" She produced a small, crumpled piece of foolscap. "Mr. Goldman said, 'This town is full of bigoted rich isolationists. They are stupid and narrow-minded. I can't wait to cram this project down their throats.'"

There were several audible gasps.

Putting his mouth too close to the microphone, Howard said, "That is completely implausible," hearing his breath boom on each plosive. He caught sight of McConkey's wide face, which looked waterlogged. "That is a complete lie. This woman—"

"This woman," said Nadine, radiant above her spotless white dress, "is a licensed architect who does not believe communities should have housing projects forced on them."

All over the room, people began clapping. A low hectic sound was rising from among them, almost like the hum of massing insects, and although he had never heard it before, Howard recognized the perilous noise of collective outrage.

And yet, for the first time since entering the auditorium, he felt calm. As he stared out at the excited crowd, he found himself recalling advice from a wilderness survival course he took in college: Before responding to the scene of a disaster, take enough time to smoke a cigarette and assess the situation. Thus one is more likely to administer appropriate rather than hasty care to the injured, avoiding additional injury, perhaps even saving lives. It seemed sound advice at the time, delivered by the course instructor, a soft-spoken man with a graying ponytail and a frayed red bandanna, who had actually saved people in mountain rescues.

But since Howard did not smoke, and since the injured person was himself, he realized this old advice, like so much old advice, would not serve.

"Excuse me," he called out in a voice that sounded tinny to his ears. "Please. Just a moment."

"You may also like to know," Nadine's voice drowned out his. "That despite everything Mr. Goldman just said about his clients' wanting to live responsibly in your community, he told me that dealing with them was 'a nightmare.'" She was folding away her piece of paper, but leaned forward to add, "He also gave me the impression that your new neighbors were into wife swapping."

"I never said that," shouted Howard, remembering at the same instant that he had indeed made a wisecrack about wife swapping. "This is ludicrous." He turned once more to appeal to the planning board chair. "This woman was fired from an architectural firm and she thinks it's because I gave her a poor reference. It's absurd," he said, almost choking.

"Would you like me to tell the real reason behind that poor reference?" Nadine drew herself up and shook back her pale hair, looking athletic and incorruptible, much as she had when she'd described for Howard her bicycle trip through France. "Would you like me to add sexual harassment to—"

"Someone should flog that guy," called a man near the door.

"Fortunately, his wife is a lawyer," Howard heard the realtor say.

"All right, all right," called the chair, springing up and striding around the table. He motioned Howard to step away from the podium and took the microphone himself. "Thank you, Mr. Goldman. This concludes the applicants' presentation. I would like to invite further comment from the audience, but, folks, I insist on courtesy here. No more outbursts. Now we'll hear from one person at a time—"

Blindly, Howard gathered together his drawings and maps, shoved them into his portfolio and swung into his seat next to McConkey. Nadine shot him a final glance, her expression managing to combine scorn, triumph, and something indefinable that might have been remorse, or even fear, or perhaps it was only pity. Then she slid once more into the throng.

He put a hand over his eyes, aware of McConkey immobile beside him. Unable to look up, Howard whispered, "Sorry about this." Then he pressed his eyes shut, hearing someone else begin speaking into the microphone, saying something about unwelcome elements.

Another voice followed, and another. Perhaps half an hour passed, perhaps more. As he sat on with his eyes shut, Howard tried to envision the bedroom he no longer shared with Mirella, the way the white lace curtains stirred at the windows in the morning breeze, the rectangle of peach-colored sun that fell on the floor by his side of the bed.

At last he felt the pressure of a heavy arm settle across his shoulders. Warm breath wreathed his ear, and he heard McConkey murmur, "Wife swapping. How seventies. Even we Unitarians have *evolved* past that."

Howard opened his eyes to find McConkey frowning at him.

"I'm sorry," Howard repeated. "I didn't—"

McConkey inclined his head. "Friend," he said, "I know you're sorry. Believe me, I know." He nodded to himself, then sat pondering for a long moment. Finally, with an air of profundity, which made Howard think of ancient philosophers and seers, struggling to share the burden of human knowledge, McConkey sighed and removed his arm from Howard's shoulders. "You're a sorry-ass bastard, friend," he said softly, "that's what you are. A good architect. But a sorry-ass bastard."

11

FORTY-TWO YEARS AGO TODAY, intones a radio announcer, the *Andrea Doria* sank off the coast of Nantucket. Over fifty people died. The announcer perks up as he notes that today is also the birthday of a child actor from movies about a boy left home alone and a woman who once ran for vice president.

And now it is Jacob's birthday. Randi switches off the radio after the weather report. Showers likely in the afternoon. Humid, high of eighty-five. Happy birthday, Jacob.

Randi is busier than she has ever been in her life. Jacob's lemon cake is baking in the oven, but there's still the vanilla icing to make and, of course, breakfast to fix. Spoons, bowls, put on water to boil Mirella's egg. Milk, orange juice. For three weeks now, ever since Mirella's been in bed, Randi has gotten her to eat an egg at breakfast. There is also the dog to feed. Fresh water. Then she has all the little sandwiches she is planning to make for the birthday party this afternoon, the raspberry punch, too, and the decorations to hang, the balloons to blow up. Chairs, table to place outside in the garden. Jacob's present to haul out of the garage and assemble. And the costumes. Howard said he would get the children ready this morning to give her a little extra time, but she is going to have to hurry.

No matter what the weather report predicted, today is a beautiful day for a party. The Pilkeys are having a party, too, but not until tonight. Yesterday she heard Mrs. Pilkey on her cordless phone, walking around her patio and ordering a case of champagne. Randi realizes that she hasn't thought about having champagne at Jacob's party. Maybe it would be nice for the adults to have champagne, but then again Mirella should not have alcohol, plus it is a child's party. Mrs. Cook is coming from Boston; she is even bringing her husband. Jacob should have his grandparents, his whole family there for his third birthday—a big party, or anyway as big as possible. The Guptas are coming, Mrs. Gupta and Parvati and Aparna. Mrs. Gupta said she would pick up Pearl at Happy Faces when she picked up Aparna and bring all the girls together. Randi has also invited Mrs. Norcross Pratt, who became sort of a friend of hers during the Happy Faces' bazaar preparations, and her three little boys. Fifteen people, counting the Cook-Goldmans and, of course, Randi herself.

She wonders if she should have asked Mirella before inviting so many people, then waves the thought away. Mirella said she could have a party for Jacob and a party must have people. Mrs. Gupta said she would make vegetable *pakoras*. The Guptas are giving Jacob a screen saver for his birthday, planets and stars.

As soon as Howard leaves with Pearl, Randi can start on the sandwiches and the punch. Ice the cake. Then she will bring out Jacob's present and set it up outside. She will tell Mirella not to look. A surprise for everyone. Randi hears the children running back and forth in the upstairs hallway, followed by Howard's voice calling them into the bathroom. She has her own costume to try on. Right after breakfast, when Howard has gone, she will dress herself and Jacob in their costumes, just to see how they look. Just to see Jacob's face.

Quickly she sets the kitchen table and puts on the timer for Mirella's soft-boiled egg, then slips two pieces of whole wheat bread into the toaster oven. At least Mirella is taking better care of herself nowadays, at least she is eating protein and taking her vitamins. Although she was out of bed again yesterday, walking down the stairs to get the newspaper, standing for a few minutes to watch Jacob on the computer.

Randi narrows her eyes as she works, reaching up to push her hair off her face with the back of her hand. If anything happens, Mirella will have only herself to blame.

Today is Jacob's birthday. The best birthday he has ever had. The perfect birthday. She will give him just what he's been wanting. Her darling little boy. He will be so happy.

Ding, goes the toaster oven. The water is boiling; drop in Mirella's egg, hope it doesn't crack. Three cereal boxes on the table—Randi lines them up. Here is the milk, here is the juice. Here is a knife for Howard's bagel. She even remembers to sprinkle fish food into the aquarium for the new goldfish.

WHEN MIRELLA GLANCED out of her window on the morning of Jacob's birthday, Randi was dragging a strangely shaped object across the back lawn. She was wearing something unusual as well—a leather dress of some sort and leather slippers. In her arms was a long, lumpy, plastic bundle, heavy enough that Randi's mouth hung ajar as she pulled her burden across the grass and she appeared to be perspiring.

"Don't look," Randi called out, gesturing dramatically. "It's supposed to be a surprise. Pull down your blind."

Which Mirella did, unwillingly. Sitting back against her pillows, she concentrated on the wavering screen of her laptop but found it impossible to read the paragraph she'd just written. Two days ago, the planning board had voted to deny subdivision approval for the TownCommon development, effectively killing the project, although Howard mumbled something about an appeal. For the last week and a half he'd looked like a beaten dog, skulking around the house, drinking beer and reading *Walden,* staring morosely at her whenever he came up to the bedroom to visit, refusing to go to the grocery store or even, until this morning, to drive Pearl to preschool. All of which, naturally, made more work for Randi, although she hadn't complained.

Mirella tapped a key. Something seemed to be wrong with the computer's battery, which she had recharged once already this morning. Words on the gray screen creased and straightened, then creased again, flickering ominously. "Plaintiff demands," she typed. And then, with a silent pop, like the snap of unseen fingers, the screen went dark.

A gentle hum persisted, as though the machine continued to perform its task without her, as informed and efficient as she was, presently, helpless.

"Damn," she said aloud. Although, to be honest, she was relieved. Her back hurt. She felt huge and torpid and hot. And she wasn't thinking well these days: her brain seemed sticky, caught up in muffled apprehensions and recollected practicalities that she forgot as soon as she remembered them. Was Jacob's bassinet still in the attic? Had anyone given Martha her heartworm pill? Where was that green raincoat with the hood she'd taken last winter to be dry-cleaned—had she ever gone to pick it up?

She fell asleep for a little while, then woke with the startled feeling that once again she should be remembering something, that there was something important she had meant to do. Within her belly she detected a tiny drubbing, as if the fetuses were struggling, trying to elbow each other out of the way.

Earlier that morning, she'd woken to the sounds of Randi making Jacob's birthday cake. Randi had said something yesterday about trying to find time to make it, and when Mirella suggested she order a cake from the bakery, Randi said, "Oh I'd never do *that*," as if Mirella had suggested that Randi serve Jacob a frosted hatbox. Mirella's parents were both coming for the little party Randi had planned. Howard's idea was to carry Mirella downstairs—stairs were forbidden by Dr. Kaitz—and set her up on a chaise in the garden.

"I'm too big for you," Mirella had said.

"We'll see," said Howard grimly.

Martha began barking downstairs. An instant later the doorbell rang, and before she could stop herself, Mirella had thrown back the sheet and started to stand up. But then she lay back, listening for the sound of Randi's footsteps in the hallway. The doorbell rang again. "Randi?" she called. "Someone's at the door."

"*Coming.*" Randi's voice floated up from outside, sounding harried. Mirella could hear her murmuring urgently to Jacob, who must be accompanying her around the side of the house, past the unpruned rhododendron and the striped hostas, to see who was at the door. Mirella resisted the impulse to lift her blind and peer out at whatever Randi had done to the garden. Instead she picked up the phone and dialed her office number.

"Hello, Cheryl? It's me calling in for my messages. It's Mirella. That's all right, I have a bit of a cold. No, I'm fine. Is Ruth there? Well, when she gets in, please tell her I called. Any idea how yesterday's hearing went for Vassbacher?"

While she waited for Cheryl to look through her messages, Mirella listened for Randi and Jacob to come in with whomever was at the front door. Randi had been so secretive about Jacob's birthday; maybe she'd hired a magic act, someone who made balloon hats or discovered rabbits behind people's ears. She reminded herself how grateful she was to Randi for all the trouble she was taking over Jacob's birthday.

"Mirella?" Cheryl was saying into her ear. "Do you want me to fax you that letter or not?"

"I'm sorry," said Mirella. "Something's wrong with my connection. Can you give me all that again?"

AFTER DROPPING OFF Pearl at Happy Faces, and remembering to put her lunch box in her cubby—where he discovered several drawings that looked like black Magic Marker clouds blotting out a small white house, but had been given titles like "A Colorful Duck" or "My Rainbow"—Howard drove back home, parked, and went to his studio. He glanced at his unmade cot, then started the coffeemaker and looked for his favorite ceramic mug with the blue glaze, which he could not find. He was embarrassed at himself for wondering if Krystal Anne might have stolen it when she quit last week.

Settling for the plastic red mug usually reserved for holding sugar packets, he turned on his computer and checked his e-mail, which he had not been able to bring himself to look through for over a week. There were eight or nine messages concerning the co-housing development. One read: "Take flight, Urban Blight." A two-day old message from McConkey informed Howard that the TownCommon group was meeting to consider their options. There was also a message from Krystal Anne for Randi about a clambake she was hosting for New England members of The Org. And there was one message, dated six days back, from someone named Mrs. Burt Tibbetts. "Dear Mr. Goldman," he read, "I am trying to track down a person named Randi Gill and understand that she may be working as a nanny for your family. If I have located the correct party, would you please contact me at dtibbetts@homestyles.com."

After reading through his messages, Howard deleted them all including, by accident, the one from Mrs. Tibbetts. He could have retrieved it, but he had forgotten the mechanism for doing so, and anyway he figured he was probably doing Randi a favor, probably she was being hunted by her high school alumni association.

Brooding on the relentlessness of associations, he picked up the North Shore Meditation Center brochure, which lay where he'd tossed it weeks ago into one of his plastic organizer trays. He leafed past descriptions of practice groups for working with fear and directions for how to obtain refunds for canceled registrations. But he couldn't find the description he'd read before, the weekly chanting group that focused on the virtues of the Triple Gem. At last he dropped the brochure into his wire trash can. "I should get out of here," he said aloud.

But he continued to sit at his big mission desk, gazing at his stack of business cards in their little pine box.

12

THE SPARE WOMAN standing on the front steps has one hand hovering toward the doorbell, the other knuckled on her hip. She has a wide-brimmed white straw hat pulled low over her forehead, obscuring her face.

Snatching up Jacob before they are seen, Randi shrinks back behind an overgrown rhododendron bush that shields one corner of the house. "Excuse me," she calls out with a sharp lilt, disguising her voice by seizing onto Vivvy's accent. "May I help you with something?"

"I'm looking for the Goldman residence." Filtered through the rhododendron, the woman's voice sounds uncertain and tired and almost shrill.

Martha is barking inside the house. Jacob stares at Randi, his mouth going round. He still has a yellowish grain of sleep in one eye and there is a purple ring around his lips from the popsicle she allowed him to have right after breakfast. She can feel his little heart beating through his shirt where he's pressed up against her arm. Her own heart is knocking so hard she can barely hear, although in a funny way she doesn't feel nervous. Instead she feels precisely prepared, as if she has been expecting this moment, has rehearsed for it, her agitation now simply supplying an extra push, the way a parachutist might feel listening for the order to jump.

Rhododendron leaves tickle her neck. A few feet away a bumblebee fumbles around a blue hydrangea flower. Sunlight coats her arms, hot and heavy. Far off she can hear the fan in Jacob's room upstairs, its blades whipping fruitlessly at the muggy air.

Holding Jacob closer, she says, "Yes?"

"You're Mrs. Goldman?"

Randi squeezes deeper into the bush and looks at Jacob. With one finger she brushes the sleep out of his eye, then she draws a deep breath. "I'm sorry. Mrs. Goldman recently passed away."

After several moments of silence, the woman comes slowly down the steps, leaning on the railing with one hand and holding onto her broad-brimmed hat with the other. A tiny black patent-leather purse dangles from her shoulder by a skinny strap. She pauses a few feet away from where Jacob and Randi are hidden, hesitating on the brick path.

She looks older than Randi remembers. Lines track from the corners of her small blue eyes and her skin has a new slackness. She is wearing a blue sailor dress with a white collar and flat brass buttons and cork platform sandals that look too big for her. When she came down the steps she sounded like someone with a wooden leg.

"I'm Mrs. Tibbetts," she says, faltering over the *T,* as if she'd been about to supply a different name. "And I apologize for troubling you, but I've called and left messages. I wrote a letter. I'm trying to find my daughter."

"Yes?" says Randi. Jacob is clutching at her neck, scratching her a little with his fingernails. He does not like strangers. Soon he may begin to whimper, even cry, and she will have the perfect excuse to tell her mother that she must go away and leave them all alone.

"Does she work here?" her mother asks humbly.

"Your daughter?" says Randi. "I'm afraid not."

Her mother is trying now to see between the branches of the rhododendron, head tilted to the side. Peering back, Randi realizes that her mother's outfit is brand new, still stiff with sizing. Bought from Yolanda's Fashion Salon in Coralville especially for this occasion, because her mother had figured that if she was going to a seaside town, she should look nautical. You never look right, Randi wants to scream, gripping Jacob so tightly that he cries out. You have never looked right.

It is at this moment that Randi glances down and realizes that she and Jacob are wearing their birthday costumes. They are standing half inside a rhododendron bush in front of the house clad in moccasins from Wal-Mart and fawn suede outfits decorated with plastic beads and fringe. Jacob is wearing his headdress. She herself has a construction-paper band around her forehead, to which she has taped a single blue-jay feather.

"Hello?" her mother calls, teetering on cork soles. "Could I trouble you to come out of there for a few minutes?"

Randi glances across the street at the Guptas' house, where just half an hour before Parvati and Aparna had been sitting cross-legged on the lawn stringing necklaces. But they have vanished and now Lost Pond Road stretches away, empty and quiet in both directions.

"I'm sorry but you'll have to leave," says Randi. "The family cannot be disturbed at this time."

Her mother is running a hand up and down her purse strap. "I came out here alone," she says softly. "My husband and the baby are back at home. It's just me."

Randi kisses Jacob again. "I'm afraid this little boy can't handle strangers right now. They're hard on him," she adds. "Strangers."

Her mother continues to stand on the brick walkway in her sailor dress, sunlight glinting off the brass buttons. Her legs look skinny and bruised against the green of the lawn, and somehow unstable. "Listen," she says finally in a croaking voice that reminds Randi, just a little, of Jacob's. "Listen, I didn't want to come out here like this. I'm glad you found a nice place for yourself, but I need to say a few things and it didn't seem like there was any other way to get through to you. You've got to know what you did to us by running off like that. All the scare we've had. Not knowing what might of happened. We about died from worry." For a moment she stares down at the walkway, as if watching some upheaval under her feet. "You can't treat family this way," she says.

"What family," says Randi.

Still clinging to her purse strap, her mother steps backward and stares once more through the rhododendron branches. Her face twitches. Randi has an urge to apologize for everything she's just said, the way she used to apologize after swearing and throwing things around the kitchen, not as if she was sorry, more like she had just awakened from starring in a bad dream.

But just then her mother wrinkles her lips as though she's bitten down on a piece of gristle. "I haven't been perfect. But you weren't the world's easiest kid to raise either." She stops, chewing on her lipstick. "At least," she says finally, "I think I deserve an apology."

Martha has gotten out through the back door and is now bounding around the corner of the house, past Randi and Jacob, barking excitedly, her shaggy rear end waggling. She leaps and wriggles, her tongue hanging out of the side of her mouth. Randi watches her mother reach out to pat Martha's head, then draw back her hand. After prancing around hopefully for a few more moments, Martha wanders over to the driveway and lies down under the Jeep, metal tags clanking against the gravel.

"An apology at least."

Jacob begins to squirm in Randi's arms, wanting to get down. "No," she tells him, shifting him onto her other hip. "We'll go inside in a minute."

At any moment she chooses, she can walk right past her mother, up the front steps, open the front door, and close it behind her.

"Don't make me sorry I came all the way out here," says her mother in that sad, croaky voice. "At least get out of that bush and talk to me for a little while."

"How long," says Randi at last.

Her mother pushes back her big hat and looks toward her steadily. "Why don't you surprise me?"

Although she cannot remember where she has heard this phrase before, Randi nods at it. The conversation has suddenly become exhausting. In her arms, Jacob is making a low, grizzling noise; his diaper needs changing. And there is still so much to be done. The cake. The little sandwiches. "How long?" she says again, her heart beating like a tom-tom.

Which is when she realizes that something is missing, a steady light rush of background sound she has been relying on without realizing it—the fan in Jacob's room has stopped. And now from above, at his window, comes Mirella's voice, calling out querulously like an old woman or a child: "Randi? Who is that? Randi? Is there someone down there who wants to see me?"

Randi sees her mother's face tip upward; she is holding on to her white hat with one hand and her purse strap with the other.

"Who is that?" cries Mirella. She is standing in the window in her white nightgown, like a ghost behind the screen. "Where's Jacob? What's going on down there? Randi, *who is that?*"

"Nothing, nobody," shouts Randi, at the same time her mother says dryly, "Mrs. Goldman? Aren't you passed on?"

Jacob wraps his arms around Randi's neck, his face pressed

into her hair. And in a moment it begins as she's sensed, from the tautness of his body, that it would: his high, frenzied, one-note wail, the wail that blots out everything else once it starts, because it sounds like harm, and because it seems irrevocable, like a siren, like an accident, like hearing from somebody in a sailor dress that you are dead.

"THIS IS VERY STRANGE," said Mirella, when she got downstairs and was standing in the kitchen. "I am very upset. I need to understand what this is all about."

But because she was not yet prepared to understand whatever she was about to hear from Randi and the thin woman standing by the refrigerator, Mirella walked around the kitchen until she found the painted tea tray. She began loading it with the coffeepot, still half full of lukewarm coffee left from breakfast, mugs, spoons, a carton of milk, the sugar bowl.

"You should be in bed," said Randi in a dull voice.

"I will decide," said Mirella crisply, "where I should be."

"My name is Dolores Tibbetts," announced the woman in the white hat. "I'm Randi's mother."

"Randi's mother," repeated Mirella, carrying the tray to the table. "She told me her parents were dead."

"Well, I guess we have something in common then," said Dolores, taking off her hat. She had short, rough-looking red hair, Mirella saw, and a broad face like Randi's.

Randi was still holding Jacob. He had stopped wailing and was picking at his shirt, staring around the room in bewilderment. When Randi sat down at one end of the table, he pulled away from her and darted off to the dining room. Mirella watched him go, less surprised than she felt she should have been to see Randi and Jacob dressed as Indians.

"What *is* all this?" she said.

"Jacob's birthday." Randi looked away with an ambushed

expression. On the counter near the stove sat Jacob's lemon cake, still needing to be iced.

By then Mirella had caught sight of what was in the backyard and everything began to make sense.

"Please sit down," she said to Dolores. Then she sat down herself and began pouring coffee, though her hands were not steady and she spilled a quantity of coffee on the tray. She was aware of being within one of those dangerous moments in life that require extreme attention, and yet she could not concentrate. She forced herself to look at Randi. "What have you been doing?" she said, almost pleasantly. "What are you doing here?"

Dolores seemed to decide this question must be for her. She laid her hat on the table and said quietly, "I have been looking for this girl for the better part of a year. She ran off in September, about eight months after my little boy was born. I contacted the police. I put ads in the papers in Terre Haute and Indianapolis, even Chicago, papers. Then I hired a detective, this woman who finds runaway kids? And finally she started calling nanny agencies all over the entire country until she hit the right one."

Dolores nodded at Randi. "Though the lady that owned the agency wouldn't tell us hardly a thing except that Randi worked for her. 'My girls,' she kept saying. 'I got to protect my clients and my girls.'" Dolores gave a snort and pushed her coffee cup back and forth between her hands. "Finally I said, 'Lady, what kind of agency are you running?' But they said I could write a letter to her family and they'd send it on. So that's what I did. But I never heard anything back."

"I hate Chicago," said Randi to no one in particular. "I'd never go there."

"She takes things," Dolores continued soberly, looking at Mirella. "It's a problem she has. She's not a bad girl, but she'll never tell you the truth. Or if she does tell you the truth, it's not going to be in any way you can recognize. Sometimes she doesn't know it herself."

"Well, she hasn't taken anything from us," Mirella felt obliged to say, glancing at where Randi huddled in her chair. "At least not that I know of."

"Well, I'm glad," said Dolores. "As I say, she's not a bad girl, but she took off from home with about everything I'd saved from doing hair, plus my mother's engagement ring. That's not why I'm here, though," she added, leaning toward Randi. "I want you to know that."

Again, Mirella found she was having difficulty paying attention to what was being said. She kept focusing instead on how Dolores's jaw muscles twitched every so often above the wide white collar of her dress, and the appreciative way she occupied her chair, as if all her life she'd been on her feet too long. She had a smoker's yellow complexion, and a weary but determined face. A weathered face. The face of someone who had long ago stopped being disillusioned, because it required too much effort.

"She wants money," said Randi coldly.

"I do not," said Dolores with dignity. "I want you to come home with me."

Mirella realized her hands had levitated of their own accord and were hovering in the air. Carefully she folded her hands in her lap and turned to Dolores. "You want to take her home? Today?"

"I would, yes. I have a rental car out front."

"Wait a minute," Randi broke in furiously. "This isn't right—she has no right to come here like this. She isn't part of this." She stared wildly at Mirella. Then she said, "It's Jacob's birthday."

Mirella twisted her hands in her lap. "Oh Randi," she said. "I'm not sure he even realizes." She sat back in her chair, looking at Randi in her feathers and beads. A branch scraped against the side of the house.

"Please," said Randi. And then she did a curious thing. She

began pulling beads off her costume, one by one, and lining them up on the table.

"I think," Mirella said quietly at last, watching the rows of beads march toward her, "that in light of the circumstances, today would be best. I think it would be better for everyone. I'm sorry," she said to Randi. "I know this must be hard."

"We kept your room for you," Dolores told her daughter softly. "Looks just the same."

Randi stopped pulling beads from her dress and sat staring at the floor.

Mirella glanced away from Randi to give Dolores a business-like nod. "We're prepared to give her severance pay of a month's wages. We'll settle things up right now, and then Randi can leave with you."

For a moment no one said anything.

Outside, the light shifted and the kitchen glowed with a clear brightness. Mirella thought she heard a small sound from the dining room, just a small sound, like a sigh or a cough. Perhaps the screen door had blown open. Or maybe it wasn't even a sound at all, just the foundation of the house shifting another infinitesimal degree. She waited one moment, two, waiting to hear the sound again. She could hear Randi breathing unsteadily from across the table; she heard a creak from Dolores's cork-soled shoes.

Slowly she stood up from her chair, her legs leaden and unde-pendable from so much unaccustomed movement. "I'll be right back," she told Dolores.

But by the time she'd made her way past the table and into the dining room to look for Jacob, there was nobody there.

13

HOWARD STOOD IN the kitchen doorway, stunned to find himself where he was: in his own house, which seemed in this instant to have transformed not simply into someone else's house, but into a house from another world.

A glass pot of coffee sat on a tray between two women at the table, sending up a curl of steam. One woman, whom he did not recognize, wore some sort of maritime uniform. The other sat with her back to him, clad in moccasins and a suede sheath decorated with pink and green beads, which made a rattling sound when she turned to face him, like wind through dry reeds.

Beyond the two women, framed by the kitchen's bay window, and set naturally against the garden's dense tangle of green, as if it had always been there, stood a large canvas tepee.

"Howard," said Mirella from the dining room.

But before he could ask her why she was out of bed, or why there was a tepee in the garden, or even who was sitting with Randi at his kitchen table, Mirella said, "Howard, have you seen Jacob?"

"Jacob?" Mirella said again, looking at Randi.

Whenever Howard was to recall this particular day, it was the rush of searching he would remember most clearly, how the search had grown almost instantly frantic. Frantic, surreal, and at the same time familiar, and even, in a dreadful way, expected. Everyone knows the story of the missing child; every parent has rehearsed it.

"Jacob, Jacob," he called.

"He was here just a minute ago," Mirella kept saying.

Jacob was nowhere in the house, nowhere in the garden. Not even inside that tepee pitched under the apple tree, Randi's long-awaited birthday surprise. Howard rushed back inside to run up the stairs two at a time, while Randi ran to the cellar. Even Dolores, to whom he had been hastily introduced, joined in the hunt, peering into the living room, patting at the drapes.

Howard had to remind Mirella to go back to bed. "Right now, Mirella," he said when he got downstairs again and discovered her in the hallway. He seized her arm as she pushed past him toward the front door. She turned and blinked at him and started to say something. Then she pulled her arm away and went silently up the stairs.

How much time had passed? Five minutes? Half an hour? Had anyone checked the Pilkeys' pool?

Jacob Jacob Jacob.

Run back out to the garden, leap the fence, stand for a moment gaping at the tranquil, chlorine-blue emptiness of the Pilkeys' pool, where no small body floated, where only a maple leaf drifted on the surface and a beer bottle by a lounge chair attracted flies.

Crawl back over the fence, look under the lilacs, look again in the tepee, look behind the garage. Back into the house, open the closets, check the bathrooms, under the beds.

No one there. Howard hurried to Mirella's room. "What happened," he gasped. "Why would he disappear like this?"

"Randi," she said, staring up at him, her hands on either side of her head. "He knows Randi is leaving."

"Leaving?" shouted Howard.

"Her mother," said Mirella, taking her hands away from her head, "has come to get her."

Up the stairs to Randi's room. Under the bed, open the armoire, open the blanket chest. Downstairs again, look in the fireplace, pull apart the coil of towels and dishrags.

From outside came the sound of Randi's voice, crying, "Jacob, Jacob." The sky darkened as clouds moved over the sun.

In the midst of the search, the phone rang. Howard picked up the receiver, heart walloping. It was Mirella's mother calling to say that Mirella's father had fallen in the bathtub that morning while the nurse was giving him his bath; he had cracked a rib. Nothing too serious, not to worry. But they would not be coming to Jacob's birthday party; she'd put his gift in the mail; he'd probably get it day after tomorrow. A little something for Pearl, too, no one likes to be forgotten—

Howard hung up. More minutes passed. Dolores was still in the living room, now down on all fours, looking under the sofa. Howard could see the top of Randi's head bobbing as she ran past the rhododendrons in the front yard.

JACOB WAS ROLLING across the street in the Cherokee. Somehow he had managed not only to open the door and climb into the driver's seat, but also to release the emergency brake and back down the driveway's short, steep incline and into the road.

He just missed running into Aparna Gupta, who was right that moment walking across the street with Pearl.

Howard got to the front door in time to see Randi run into the street as the Jeep hit the opposite curb with its back tires, then rocked forward. Both little girls began screaming, clutching at their white dresses. Vasanti Gupta, rushing out from her driveway in an aqua sari, screamed, too.

The girls continued to stand in the road, the shadow of the Cherokee falling over them.

But nothing had happened, Howard reminded himself, running into the road along with Vasanti Gupta. Each swept up a child and carried her to the curb. Randi was reaching into the driver's seat for Jacob. He was not crying. His face was white and somehow deserted-looking. "Daddy," sobbed Pearl, grabbing at his shirt.

"I'm so sorry," Howard heard himself say, as the sun came out again. He felt the back of his neck burning. Through the leaves of the Pilkeys' maples, the sunlight winked and whirled.

SUCH A BRILLIANT DAY. Mirella had not been outside in three weeks. The air brushed her skin like warm silk as she tried to run barefoot across the grass. But her body felt suffocatingly slow, enormous and confining.

"What happened, what happened?"

Ahead of her Howard and Vasanti Gupta crouched over Pearl and Aparna, who were sobbing loudly, heads thrown back. Vasanti seemed to be having trouble breathing; one hand was splayed against her chest. Howard was urging her to sit down. "Were they hit?" Mirella cried, kneeling down beside Pearl. "Did someone hit them?"

"Jacob," said Howard tensely.

"Where is Jacob?"

"Hooo," gasped Vasanti Gupta, slapping at her chest.

"Please sit down," Howard said. He stood up and led Vasanti to the curb. Aparna clung to her mother's arm, moaning unintelligibly. Pearl collapsed against Mirella and sobbed with increased volume.

"We almost got killed," she shrieked.

Mirella looked up to see the other little Gupta running across the street, waving a broom. The girl leapt onto the sidewalk, thrusting the broom into the air, until her mother called to her sharply. Aparna had begun crying louder in competition with Pearl, and now her sister joined in, with Vasanti still gasping on the curb and Howard leaning over her. Across the street sat the Cherokee.

"Howard, what's going on?" Mirella tried to stand up, but found she could not. Pearl was hanging from her neck. "Have you found Jacob?"

"Everyone is all right," shouted Howard. "He's with Randi."

At this Mirella's heart rose and sank and rose again. "Stop, Pearl," she said, detaching Pearl's arms. "You're not hurt."

Pearl ceased crying and looked at her with hostility. "I was almost ran over," she said. "Jacob did it."

Mirella looked back over her shoulder to see that Dolores had followed her out onto the lawn. She was standing a few feet away, brass buttons blazing, looking self-conscious but persevering in her ungainly dress, shielding her eyes with one hand.

Howard left Vasanti Gupta and came to stand over them. "Mirella, what do you think you're doing? You have to go back to bed."

"Where is Jacob? I need to see him."

"I'll find Jacob. Go back to bed."

"Please, Howard. You don't understand." Mirella got to her feet, and then looked down at herself. "Howard," she said. A tiny spray of roses had blossomed on her nightgown. She covered it with her hands.

"He's fine." Howard was looking over her shoulder. "Randi's got him. I saw her carry him toward the house."

"But I didn't—" Mirella began.

Howard was staring down the street, his face turning red, and

Mirella turned to see what he was looking at. There on the sidewalk, like a mirage above the heat shimmering off the pavement, pushing her jogging stroller with one hand, and carrying a splendid bouquet of sea lavender, Queen Anne's lace, sweet pea, and black-eyed Susans in the other, was Alice Norcross Pratt.

"*Now* for God's sake." Howard touched Mirella's arm. "Please go back to bed." He gave her a little push.

"Daddy," Mirella heard Pearl say, just as she reached the front door. "Look at Martha."

IT WAS NOT SURPRISING that no one had noticed Martha in all the excitement. She must have been asleep in the cool shade under the Jeep, Howard decided, when Jacob climbed into it.

Afterward she dragged herself to the Applewhites' yard next door, where they found her lying half under a syringa bush, still warm, her back legs sticking into the lawn, her golden fur bloody and matted with dirt.

"Oh dear," said Vasanti Gupta to Howard. "This is very horrible."

"The poor thing," said Dolores, standing behind them.

"Here," said Alice, handing Howard the bouquet of wildflowers.

Cradling her big stomach with both arms, she knelt down beside the dog. The children pressed behind her, gaping and excited, as she placed her hand on its chest for a few moments, then its neck. She frowned and bent as far forward as she could to put her ear near the dog's mouth. A fly danced around the muzzle, which was drawn back, exposing long yellow teeth. Finally Alice sat back. She passed her hand over the eyes to close them and, with Vasanti reaching down to hold her elbow, got heavily once more to her feet.

"I wouldn't bother with the vet," she said kindly to Howard, taking back her flowers.

Howard picked up Martha and groaned. Not knowing what else to do, he carried her to the Cherokee, still sitting in the middle of the street, and laid her across the backseat, tucking her tail under her, as if that might make her more comfortable. Then he went inside to find the keys.

"COME WITH ME," whispers Randi, leading the little boy around the side of the house. He will not let her hold him. Clear mucus runs from his nose; one hand is fisted at his eyes. She knows where he was driving. What she doesn't understand is why he didn't wait for her.

They are behind the house now, their feet buried in thick grass, which needs to be mown. The wind is picking up; the sky is the color of an old cake pan. Above sway the branches of the apple tree. A squirrel leaps away, then chitters angrily from a mound of cedar bark mulch. Everyone else is still out in the front yard, shouting and explaining, their voices thin and insubstantial, like voices on a boat overheard from shore. It will be a little while, Randi guesses, before anyone comes to look for them.

Quietly she pushes Jacob into the tepee, lifting the flap for him. Then she follows him inside, looking once over her shoulder as she closes the flap behind them. Inside the tepee is warm and dark. Splinters of light shift in from the top where six pine poles with white plastic connectors meet, securing the canvas in place. The canvas is fire resistant; it said so on the packaging. The tepee came with three tubes of paint and ten different Native American stencil designs, plus a paintbrush. Randi had meant to decorate Jacob's tepee before his birthday party; she had selected a geometric design that looked like dots and deer antlers and one that was a series of triangles of different sizes with a notched border. Then everything happened and now it is too late.

She and Jacob settle onto the grass, breathing in the raw scent of new cotton and damp earth. They sit without making any noise. Randi closes her eyes and feels him there beside her, breathing, breathing. She matches her breathing to his so that they breathe together.

Gradually the voices quiet. There is the sound of a car starting up. Maybe, Randi thinks dreamily, everyone has gone off and left them alone.

Now the rain has started, blowing gently against the canvas sides of the tepee, bringing with it the smell of damp pavement. Jacob leans against her; after a few minutes, he seems to fall asleep. His face is sticky. Wetting two fingers with her tongue, she does her best to clean him up, wiping also at his cheeks with a handful of grass. A bit of mud smears across his cheek.

Time passes, Randi cannot say how long. She took off her watch when she put on her costume.

Jacob's chest rises and falls, soft puffs of air coming from his mouth. His headdress is pulled down over one eye and the collar of the little suede jerkin she made for him has rimpled up around his chin. One arm rests across her lap.

It is very peaceful inside the tepee with the rain falling. Sounds from outside come to her muted and faraway. An ice-cream truck bell is ringing on another street, *deedle-deedle-dee*. Someone's dog is barking. Away on the beach, little waves are foaming onto the sand, hissing over pebbles and strands of seaweed. "Shhh," she says to Jacob, although he is quiet. "Shhh." She leans down to kiss his cheek, then the mark above his eyebrow. All her life she has been waiting for someone to care about her more than anything else in the world. There's nothing wrong with that, everybody wants that, maybe it is the one thing people keep wanting right from the beginning of their lives. But even better, she realizes now, is to be the person who cares more than anything in the world about somebody else.

She strokes Jacob's hair; she touches the white skin of his

forehead, imagining him as a newborn baby, imagining him even as an egg.

At last Jacob opens his eyes. His stomach is rumbling. It has been hours since he had breakfast. He must be starving. No one has come looking for them; no one cares where they are.

She bends over him, parting his hair with her fingernails. "My little love," she whispers.

He looks up at her and then lifts his arms.

They cannot go inside just yet. She cannot imagine facing Howard and Mirella in the house, hearing what they will say, what they will tell her. She sees blade-faced Mrs. Lawlor in her flat black shoes. She sees DeeDee Spicer in her hostess uniform, smoke pouring from her nose. She sees an old woman with singed hair and nicotine-stained teeth sitting in the Cook-Goldman's kitchen, leaving lipstick prints on her coffee cup. Who are these people? She cannot listen to them.

But Jacob is hungry. His eyes are dark, beseeching. "Maaa," he whispers, although they have not done word drills for days. He buries his face in her lap.

"Yes," she says. "Yes," she says again. "All right."

Whimpering, Jacob pulls at her dress. He nudges her with his head, butting into her belly. He is her hungry baby. No baby should be hungry. A baby must be fed. Any mother knows that.

AT FIRST IT SEEMED to be one of those incomplete summer storms: a purple shock of thunder, a lightning flash, and just enough warm rain to dampen the sidewalks. The scent of wet grass blew in past the lace curtains, which filled like twin sails. As Mirella stared into the darkened garden from her bedroom window, she saw the flap on the tepee below suddenly part, then open. A face looked out. It was a wide face, flat and contented. An oddly ageless face; it could have been any face, but of course it was not. In her arms was a child.

For the third time that day, Mirella heaved herself out of bed. Once again she walked barefoot down the hall and down the stairs. The old floorboards were cool under her feet, slightly gritty. There were handprints on the walls. In the distance, a bell was ringing as rain flung against the windowpanes. She walked through the house with all it contained as if she did not notice any of it, or, if she did, none of it impressed itself upon her, but instead seemed to flow past, as a brook parts to flow past stepping stones, and in this way she walked out of the back door and into the garden.

In a moment she had bent down to pull back the flap to the tepee. She saw the child and the woman who were sitting inside. The woman's bare breast. The child's open mouth.

"GET OUT OF THERE," said Mirella, standing in front of the tepee.

The rain began to fall harder, streaming down her face.

"Get out," she said again.

The sides of the tepee shook. There was the impress of an arm, a knee against the wet canvas.

"I said get out."

The tepee trembled. Then the flap parted again and Randi looked out at her.

No one had ever looked at Mirella in that way. It was a look of complete, annihilating disbelief. She might have been a talking bear, or a cartoon come to life.

Once more the flap fell closed. In the silence that followed Mirella felt a vital rending and twisting within her, worse than burning, worse than flaying, a vivid mortal ache. With a cry, she reached into the tepee and took hold of Randi's hair.

She grabbed Randi's hair close to the scalp and yanked. It felt enormously satisfying to do this. She yanked again. The next moment she was dragging Randi by her hair out of the tepee. Randi was heavy, heavy as a sack of stones, bare legs bending, kicking. Her hands flew up, dancing around her head, slapping at Mirella's arm. Mirella could feel the fleshiness of Randi's body, the thick resistance of it as she hauled her onto the grass by the hair.

How could this be happening? she thought, with one part of her mind. This cannot be happening. At the same instant she observed herself lift her fist and bring it down hard on Randi's head. A child was crying. And there was blood. Children were crying, and on the grass a woman lay weeping. Wind tore the branches of the Pilkeys' maple trees and the rain poured down.

When Mirella next looked up she saw the Guptas and Howard appear at the far end of the garden, near the bed of striped hostas. Randi was lying face down in the wet grass under the apple tree, an arm thrown over her head. One of her moccasins had fallen off, Mirella noted, and her bare pink toes were wet and curled tight. Mirella herself was kneeling in front of the tepee. And in the same detached way that she had watched herself drag Randi by the hair, she saw that her hands were almost as white as her sodden nightgown, wherever the gown was not stained red.

14

SHE LOOKED SO SMALL in the bed. Howard reflected that this was a common perception of people in hospital beds, even he'd had it before; they looked pale and cruelly diminished, out of context, like fish laid out on a pier. But Mirella seemed smaller even than he had expected. Her hands moved restlessly on the starched hospital sheets, pausing for an instant, then moving again. A metal IV pole hung over her, suspending a bag of clear fluid; a tube attached to the bag led to her arm, where it was fixed by a length of gauze and strips of white tape. Here she was, his wife, who had been someone different only a few hours ago. Her eyes opened, then closed. Watching Mirella come slowly awake, Howard had the strangest sense of understanding what the rest of their lives would be like: eventful, claustrophobic, at moments opening up so completely that everything they'd ever asked for would seem within their grasp, the next moment folding shut, but always complicated, always moving on.

Especially Mirella would always move on, because she was that sort of person. Never fully in one place, forever planning where to be next, wanting whatever she thought she could have. He himself was more like Jacob, attempting for the most part to want simple, durable things. A few wooden trucks, an old house.

He got up from the chair and came to stand by the bed. After a moment he reached out and stroked Mirella's hair. She gave a tiny, convulsive jerk.

"How are the children?" she whispered eventually, her voice thickened from anesthesia.

He stroked her hair again. "I talked to Vasanti half an hour ago. She says they're all watching television and eating carrot sticks. Even Jacob is watching."

She turned her face toward the wall.

"You were trying to take care of him," he said, trying to sound reasonable, afraid that instead he sounded vague. But surely such a thing could be possible, to harm someone you loved and also protect him. Surely this was what people did all the time.

"Do you understand what I saw?" she whispered.

She had turned her head to stare at him.

He sat down on the edge of the bed. She had asked him this question over and over in the car on the way to the hospital. Out in the hall nurses discussed a malfunctioning ice machine. Doctors were paged. A short bald man walked past, repeating in a low combative tone, "Is this the entrance or the exit?" Beeping began from the IV machine beside Mirella's bed and after a few minutes a young nurse with a long, brown ponytail came in to reset it and to change Mirella's pad. "Can I get you anything?" she asked, then gave a sympathetic smile when Howard said no. She said she would be back to check on Mirella soon.

"No, no," said Mirella, when the nurse had left. "No, no, no."

"What?" said Howard softly. "No what?"

"It can't be like this. I don't want it to be like this. I want them back."

He took Mirella's hand. "It wasn't your fault."

"Yes, it was," she cried out.

"Please, please," she begged.

"Hush."

"Please, please."

"Hush now," he murmured. "I know. I'm sorry." He reached up to put his free hand over her eyes. Then he took it away again and for a few minutes she lay quietly.

Sitting on the bed beside her reminded him of long ago, when his mother would come in to read to him at night. Except that he did not really remember her doing this; instead he remembered Richard reading to him, cross-legged on his bed, hunched over a book about King Arthur. He recalled the pleasure he had felt at having Richard there, solid and predictable in his baseball jersey, night after night reading aloud in his dogged voice, narrating the astonishing moment when Arthur pulled his sword from the stone, then all the feats and tragedies that followed. As he pictured Richard's baseball shirt in the dim room of his childhood, Howard saw that although he had not grown up with parents the way he thought he should have grown up, and that this deficiency had caused him bitterness all his life, he'd had his parents, like everyone else.

Beside him Mirella was staring at the ceiling.

"Is the dog dead, too?" she asked suddenly.

He thought of the way Martha's bones had slid around in her body when he pulled her off the backseat of the car.

"Ah, sweetheart," he said.

Mirella was crying in a way that sounded as if she were being sick. He leaned over so that he was almost lying on the bed and put his arms around her. She shook against him, shaking the hospital bed. But after a little while her crying became more normal, and Howard felt himself relax. He was glad to be holding her under the fluorescent light of the ceiling panels, glad that his holding her seemed to be having a calming effect, glad to feel the warm pressure of her in his arms, and yet he could not quite attend to the moment the way he felt he ought to.

She said, "I let this happen." Howard kissed her forehead.

When she seemed to have finished crying, he took a tissue from the box beside her bed and wiped her face.

"How badly does it hurt?" he whispered.

Mirella rocked her head from side to side on the pillow.

Afraid that she would begin to cry again, and feeling that he needed some time to recover himself before this happened, he asked, "Do you want me to get the nurse to give you something to help you sleep?"

She said that she was afraid to fall asleep.

After a while longer, he said, "Vasanti told me that Randi's gone. She packed and left with her mother." When Mirella continued to stare at him, he stood up and said gently, "I need to go home and see about the children."

"Please," she said. "Stay with me."

He let a moment drift by, then said, trying to sound humorous, "Apparently Alice called Vasanti and offered to take them for a night."

Mirella fingered the gauze and tape over the IV needle in her arm. "All right, go home."

"Decent of her, though."

He sat back down on the bed, a dull pain starting over his left eye.

"What are we going to do?" she said.

Howard was quiet for several minutes as he contemplated all the ways to answer this question. At last he said, "It seems to me we have a choice. We can let all this be who we are. Or we can decide not to."

Mirella stared at him. "Not to what?"

"Be just what's happened."

"I don't understand," said Mirella fretfully.

He took her hand again and saw that it was true, that she didn't understand, perhaps because, unlike him, she had never been in danger of reducing their past to a history of mischance.

The young nurse returned with a little paper cup holding three white tablets. She poured some water into another paper cup from a plastic jug beside the bed and then shook the tablets into Mirella's free hand. After Mirella put the tablets in her mouth, the nurse gave her the cup of water and watched her drink it. "There," she said, before she left. "This should help."

Howard sat holding Mirella's hand, waiting for her to fall asleep. It didn't seem to take very long, although when he looked at the clock he saw that almost an hour had passed.

Out in the hallway, a nurse called out in a bell-like voice, anxious and merry, You're here, you're here, like a hostess welcoming her first guests.

AT EIGHT O'CLOCK Howard rang the Guptas' doorbell. Vasanti let him in, smiling gravely as she led him down the carpeted hall to the dining room where Aparna, Parvati, Pearl, and Jacob were eating Good Humor bars. A cardboard pizza box sat in the center of the table, surrounded by dirty paper plates and empty lemonade bottles. On the dining room's rose-colored walls hung two cloth tapestries set with tiny mirrors and a large, painted papier-mâché elephant mask. Mahesh was in the kitchen, a striped dish towel over his shoulder. The house smelled intricately of spices Howard did not recognize.

He had never been inside the Guptas' house before and was surprised to find how similarly it was laid out to his own. Staircase, hallway, living room, dining room. A center-hall colonial just like his, yet the Guptas' rooms looked more comfortable somehow. Perhaps it was the sand-colored carpeting, or the fact that they had painted all the interior moldings and trim a temperate cream.

"Hello," he said to Pearl, who had turned in her chair to look at him. Jacob was still wearing his little leather costume, although his headdress was missing. He was not looking at Howard. He did not, in fact, appear to be looking anywhere, although he faced everyone across the table.

Pearl stared at Howard obliquely. "I want to stay here."

"I don't blame you," he said.

From the kitchen came a clatter and the sound of a gas jet turning on. A radio was tuned low to a news station; Howard could hear voices debating something interminable about domestic policy. "Take the House Ways and Means Committee," one voice demanded. Outside a car sped past, honking its horn.

With a glance at Howard, Vasanti moved to the table and touched Jacob's head. "Yes," she said softly. "It is your bedtime. You need to go home to bed."

Jacob slid from his chair without protest and stood looking at the table with the same unoccupied expression. "Come on, Pearl," said Howard. "I don't want to argue."

Pearl seemed to be considering this statement, its various possibilities; abruptly she climbed off her chair and joined Howard in the doorway. "Say thank you to the Guptas," he said.

"Thank you," she said, turning dutifully to wave.

Aparna and Parvati waved back from the table. "Good-bye," said Vasanti. Crouching down she gave Pearl a kiss. When she tried to kiss Jacob, he flinched away.

"Good-bye," called Mahesh, coming out of the kitchen. He bobbed his dark head.

"Thank you for everything," said Howard.

"Bring them back tomorrow," Vasanti called as he turned and hurried Pearl and Jacob out the door.

When the front door had closed behind him, he paused on the Guptas' brick walkway, looking up at the dull pink evening sky. Across the street waited his own house. No lights had been left on for them and the house seemed to recede into the shadows, vanishing behind the rhododendrons. Next door the Pilkeys' party was getting started. He heard women's laughter and the notes of a jazz guitar; cars lined the curb.

A young couple was walking across the Pilkeys' front yard, heading around the house to the pool, where Howard glimpsed little white lights strung across some privet bushes to blink like fireflies. Between them, the couple carried a baby in a car seat, swinging the car seat festively, as though it were a basket of fruit.

"I don't want to go home," said Pearl by his elbow.

"We need to," said Howard.

"Why?" Pearl lifted her face to look up at him.

"Because," Howard said, "that's where we have to live."

He took her hand, then Jacob's. Together the three of them crossed the street and unlocked their own front door, opened it and went inside.

PART III

Late August brought with it a longing for fall. By the end of the month the grass was brown, singed by days of heat and no rain. Mirella's impatiens, usually a bright pink and red mound on either side of the back doorstep, were small and lackluster. The air smelled strangely of basalt and car exhaust, and of marine life flung up on the beaches by the tide and cooked by the sun.

The only one made happy by these endless clear days was Pearl.

"Mama," she said, when they had arrived at the first week of September. "Mama, will you hire me to take care of Jacob?"

"Oh honey," said Mirella. "If only I could."

"I don't want anyone else," said Pearl crossly.

Mirella reached up from where she was pulling weeds in a flower bed to touch Pearl's cheek, but Pearl moved away. A honeysuckle vine was strangling the azaleas, twining all over the fence and into the Applewhites' rosebushes next door. Mirella began tearing it away, stuffing the vine into the cardboard box of weeds beside her.

Already she was finding it hard to remember that Randi had

ever been with them, that she had ever slept in the antique spool bed in the attic, had ever roasted chickens in the oven, hooked pot holders, organized the closets, had ever held Jacob. She was gone, her room swept, vacuumed, and dusted by the Puerto Rican cleaning service.

They had heard from her once. A postcard arrived three weeks ago, picturing a red race car and a shot of the Indianapolis Motor Speedway. "Greetings from the Crossroads of America" was written in black letters across the top. The postcard was addressed to Jacob and read simply: "It's been sunny every day. The neighbors have a cute kitten. My little brother loves trucks. You would like it here." Howard had insisted on reading the card to Jacob. Mirella would have thrown it away.

She sat back on her heels and watched Pearl drift around the garden, peering into the windows of Howard's studio, tearing leaves off the lilac bushes, snapping twigs. Tomorrow Pearl would start kindergarten at New Aylesbury Elementary School. Yesterday she and Mirella had gone to Wal-Mart to purchase a purple plastic lunch box and a red umbrella with a handle shaped like a duck's head.

In a week Jacob would begin at the Rainbow Center in Salem, which Dr. Michaels had recommended.

Howard said it looked like a nice place, friendly staff, lots of blocks, a computer for the children with enough coordination to use it. Whenever Mirella thought about the Rainbow Center, she pictured Jacob sitting in the fireplace inside one of his nests.

Upstairs in their bedroom, Howard was lying down, watching a show about renovating old houses. All morning he had been in the garden with her, working silently but companionably, trimming hedges, mowing the grass. Now he deserved a little rest. Howard had bought a color TV set, which he placed on the dresser. Every evening the four of them gathered in the bedroom to watch television shows, even Jacob, although he would not sit on the bed. They watched almost anything, but everyone seemed to like nature shows best. Howard said they should consider getting cable.

Pearl finished touring the garden. She lay down on the newly cut grass a few yards from Mirella, then sat up, bouncing her feet up and down. Bits of grass clung to the soles of her feet. Mirella smiled at her, then together, mother and daughter gazed up at the small hard green apples in the apple tree and at the tepee underneath, breathing in the curiously congested air. The tepee was partly collapsed. Jacob had been caught one day throwing rocks at it.

When Mirella last checked on him, Jacob was lying inside on the kitchen floor with his wooden trucks and cars. He was there most of the time these days, sitting under the table, lining up his vehicles. Howard had bought him more trucks for his birthday, and also a fleet of fifty shiny metal Matchbox cars in bright colors. Jacob liked to arrange the cars chromatically. Then he would lie down on the floor with his eyes close to the lines of cars. Perhaps he was imagining them in motion, rushing down the highway. Sometimes he would lie there for hours.

"Let him be," Howard told Mirella.

Mirella's mother had been coming up every other day, driving herself back and forth from Beacon Hill, although she complained that she wasn't seeing as well as she used to. Twice she'd brought Mirella's father along, whom she parked in the living room. Pearl liked to sit on his lap and roll the wheelchair into the hall. Last week, Mrs. Applewhite had told Howard that she and Mr. Applewhite were thinking of selling their house and living year-round in Florida. "Aha," said Mirella's mother at this news.

"Can I at least *have* something?" demanded Pearl now, flopping across the grass to lie beside Mirella at the flower bed. Then she jumped up and headed for the fence to gaze at the Pilkeys' glittering blue pool.

Mirella reached out to pull a clump of dandelions. Shaking the dirt from the roots, she thought of her mother's wedding admonition about not expecting too much, which she felt she at last fully understood. It had been a solid piece of advice, unromantic but shrewd. She tossed the dandelions into the box beside her. With so much wanting came all the promise and damage of the world.

Soon it would be time for lunch. She would go into the kitchen and say Jacob's name. She would tell him that they were having soup for lunch, crackers, sliced cucumbers. While she opened a can of soup and got out the crackers, she would hear him breathing under the table, encircled by his gleaming automobiles. If she were lucky, if this was a good day, his face might appear above the table edge, a raw-looking patch under his nostrils.

He didn't look unhappy. He looked to be waiting, his expression withheld. At certain moments she would stare at him and remember kneeling in the rainy garden in her wet nightgown, the grass slick under her knees. Then she would stop before she pictured the rest. Perhaps today he would sit on a chair at the table for lunch and let her sit down with him. Or maybe not. Maybe not today.

She reached through the Applewhites' picket fence and picked a rose to give to Pearl, who had returned from envious contemplation of the Pilkeys' pool. Pearl stuck the rose behind her ear, then leaped barefoot around the garden in her shorts and T-shirt, doing arabesques. In a clear, unmelodious voice, she sang: "Shall we dance? Te-dum-dum-dum. On a bright cloud of music, shall we fly?" Mirella stood up slowly, aware of the ache low in her abdomen and how it pressed all the way into her back. Cautiously she put her hands on her hips and arched her spine, hearing her joints crack.

At two o'clock this afternoon, Vassbacher was coming to see her to discuss his appeal. He seemed to prefer visiting her at home to meeting at the office. Ruth said she was being unprofessional, but Mirella decided that his visits were productive and perhaps even therapeutic. She made him tea; last week she put some cookies on a plate. Not only had Vassbacher's wife received custody of their daughters last month, she had convinced the judge to order Vassbacher to undergo parental counseling. At present, he was not allowed to see his daughters except in the presence of his counselor. The odds weren't in his favor, but Mirella knew he had no choice but to appeal. "We'll take it one step at a time," she told him. Vassbacher would sit at her dining room table, smelling of unwashed flannel and motel soap, heavy and defeated and yet reassuring, in the way that people whose luck is worse than your own are always reassuring. Or if not exactly reassuring—because luck, of course, can change—then fortifying. After all, he hadn't subsided; he was still there. Together they would fashion his argument.

Then at three-thirty, an applicant from the Homelife Agency would be arriving for an interview. The agency, recommended by a friend of Blanche Pilkey's, specialized in what it referred to as "mature women." Old bags, Mirella's mother said approvingly.

Richard and Vivvy's oldest daughter, Hannah, was another possibility; she wanted to take a year off from college ("Identity crisis," Richard had said on the phone) and might be interested in being an au pair. Lately Mirella and Howard had also been talking about moving back to Boston, to end Mirella's commute. Yesterday Howard mentioned that his co-housing clients were looking into converting an old paper mill on the river in Watertown. "The idea has merit," he said speculatively; whether he was talking about co-housing in general or the old mill in Watertown, she wasn't sure.

She looked up at the house to see the curtains in her bedroom window belling in and out. Above the roof, a few leaves on the maple trees had already turned red.

"I could do it," said Pearl, who had finished her dance and come to lean against the apple tree. She kicked at the bark with her bare heel. "I could take care of Jacob."

"You could," Mirella agreed.

"Then why won't you let me?"

Mirella closed her eyes, then opened them again to find Pearl standing close beside her. Pearl's hair was in her face; she was wearing a yellow T-shirt that had several reddish-colored stains. It could be spaghetti sauce. Recently Pearl had started helping Howard cook dinner. But she did not seem unkempt; she looked instead preoccupied, like a person who has given herself over to a day of household tasks—unpacking after a long trip, or rearranging furniture. Mirella studied her daughter carefully, noting that her nose might be just on the point of declaring itself, and that it might be declaring itself to be Howard's long nose, and that in the last few months Pearl's mouth had acquired a determined set that reminded Mirella strongly of her mother's mouth. There was even a hint of Richard in the slant of her dark brown eyes. How strange, she thought, to gaze into the face of your child and see other faces, other histories, beginnings that were not yours. And above all, to see the face of a person who was herself, unto herself. A person who would not be with you for very much longer, because she had plans of her own.

Indeed an instant later Pearl seemed to forget about being hired to care for her brother and instead wanted to know if she and Aparna could make jelly sandwiches for lunch. They would drink milk, Pearl promised. They would make Jacob drink milk, too. Maybe after lunch they could pop popcorn in the microwave. Daddy had rented a movie, *Little Women*. Aparna had seen it twice.

Looking into Pearl's intent face as Pearl discussed lunch and *Little Women,* eyes bright, strands of dark hair sticking to her cheek, Mirella wondered if what she herself had been forgetting all this time, for years and years, was that none of this would last very long, that all of this, the terrible, desirable, exhausting plenitude of her life—the children, Howard, this house, her job—all of her worries and failures and abilities and cares, all of it mattered so dearly, but so briefly, and that it was all in a way nearly over, even the parts of her life that were still to come.

It was at that moment, as she stood bending over Pearl, that Mirella for the first time felt the rough stuff of existence pass under her fingertips like a bolt of sand. Bargains, mistakes, gambles —the life she had made, guided by hurry, guided by hope, counting on other chances for every chance she took.

"I will cut off the crusts," swore Pearl, grumpily pushing her away. "I'll even cut the corners off. I can do it myself. I'll do even more than you."

"Yes," said Mirella, straightening. "But maybe I can still help."

As Pearl skipped off toward the house, Mirella closed her eyes once more, letting the hot, grass-scented breeze brush against her face. Then she laid her hands on her belly, spreading her fingers wide. And after a little while it seemed that the warmth of her spread hands calmed the precariousness within her, at least for the moment. At least for a moment, everything felt bearable.

ACKNOWLEDGMENTS

Thank you to the following people for their invaluable suggestions, advice, and insights: Renee Hausmann Shea (for literally decades of encouragement), Eileen Pollack, Marcie Hershman, Laura Zimmerman, Madeline Drexler, Phil Press, Susan Elsen, Cathy Scott, and Julie Harrison. I am forever indebted to E. J. Graff and, once again, Maxine Rodburg. Thanks also to my agent, Colleen Mohyde, and my editor, Shannon Ravenel. My gratitude for the generosity of Eve Berne and Ken Kimmell goes beyond words.

Grateful acknowledgment is made for the colonial remedies as listed in Dennis B. Fradin's *Massachusetts Colony,* published by Children's Press, 1987.